02 JUN

EVERY TIME YOU SAY GOODBYE

June Tate

headline

Copyright © 2004 June Tate

The right of June Tate to be identified as the Author of
the Work has been asserted by her in accordance with the
Copyright, Designs and Patents Act 1988.

First published in 2004
by HEADLINE BOOK PUBLISHING

10 9 8 7 6 5 4 3 2 1

Cataloguing in Publication Data is available
from the British Library

ISBN 0 7553 2108 1

Typeset in Times New Roman by
Letterpart Limited, Reigate, Surrey

Printed and bound in Great Britain by
Mackays of Chatham plc, Chatham, Kent

HEADLINE BOOK PUBLISHING
A division of Hodder Headline
338 Euston Road
LONDON NW1 3BH

www.headline.co.uk
www.hodderheadline.com

With much love and gratitude to Ron Phillips, my future son-in-law, for his affection, support and good humour. And not forgetting his generosity; in particular, the annual treat at 'Glorious Goodwood'!

Acknowledgements

With heartfelt thanks to Peter Flawn-Thomas, whose intimate knowledge of army life was like manna from heaven. Any errors in this area are mine.

My love, as always, to my daughters, Beverley and Maxine: two fine young women of whom I am so very proud.

Chapter One

'Come on, Kitty. It's a lovely evening, let's go for a walk,' Gerry Stubbs urged the young lady beside him.

'Only if you promise to behave,' she said. 'I know you – your hands are like the tentacles of an octopus!'

He laughed at her and, with twinkling eyes, said, 'How can I help it? You look good enough to eat.'

'Flattery will get you nowhere,' she warned, but she hid a smile nevertheless.

Gerry was a good-looking chap who, even during their school days, had interested her, although he used to tease her unmercifully in the playground. He was three years older than she and now, at twenty-two, was very much a confident young man, so sure of himself. She knew she was the envy of other girls of her age, but she also knew that Gerry had a passionate nature, which at times was hard to control. There was an element of danger about him, but this only added to his attraction.

'What if there's a raid and the sirens go?' she asked. 'Mum will be worried.'

'I'll look after you, she knows that. Come on, Kitty, live a little, you're a long time dead!'

Southampton had been devastated by constant bombing during the autumn of 1940. It had been so bad that King George VI himself had come to see the damage. Now, in 1941, the raids had ceased, but nevertheless, the population was always on constant alert.

They made their way to the Common, a vast expanse of woodlands, walks and lakes, much of which had been taken over by the military, though the edge was still approachable. It was a warm spring evening and they sat on a grassy path surrounded by shrubs.

Gerry lay back with his arms behind his head, looking up at the sky. 'Have you ever studied the way the clouds move?' he asked.

'No, I haven't.'

'Lie beside me and watch,' he invited.

They lay side by side, making objects of the shapes of the puffs of white as they moved overhead.

Soon bored with this, Gerry put his arm around Kitty and pulled her to him. Gazing into her blue eyes he said, 'You really have grown into a beauty. When I think of you with pigtails at school, I can't believe you are the same girl.' And he bent over her and kissed her. His mouth moved seductively, his hands stroking her long dark lustrous hair, then her elegant neck, moving slowly to her slim waist.

'You are like a ripe peach,' he whispered as he reached for her breast.

She caught hold of his hand. 'Now you stop this,' she said. 'I told you to behave!'

'But you didn't really mean it, Kitty darling. Why don't you let me love you properly? You know you want to.'

Deep down she knew that he was right. Gerry had such a way with him that his kisses and caresses excited her, awakening her sexuality, her needs as a woman, but the thought that she might give way and her mother discover the fact was the one thing that preserved her virginity.

'I'm waiting until I get married,' she told him.

He stroked her cheek. 'Then what are you doing here with me?' He gazed into her eyes and gently caressed her hip, then smothered her with kisses that became more insistent as he pushed up the edge of her skirt and caressed her thigh.

Pushing him off her, Kitty sat up. 'That's enough, Gerry. It's time we went home.'

He suddenly pulled her backwards and sat astride her, catching both her hands by the wrist, pinning her down. He grinned wickedly at her. 'Now what can you do? I could take you right now if I wanted to.' With his other hand he pushed up her skirt and ran his thumb over her womanhood.

Kitty was really scared. 'Don't you dare touch me like that.'

He just smiled and continued to do so. 'Now tell me, doesn't that make you feel good?' He spread her legs just a little and carried on with his teasing, his fingers slipping inside the leg of her knickers, feeling the soft matt of hair. 'Oh, Kitty, Kitty, if you only knew what this was doing to me.'

For one moment she gave way to the feelings seeping through her, spreading through her body, until the mounting longing within her was almost out of control. But fear and common sense were stronger, and she looked up at him and said, 'If you don't stop I'll scream and the soldiers from the army camp will come running!'

He released her and as she scrambled to cover her legs and maintain some respectability, he said, 'You are just a prick teaser, Kitty Simmons! But one day, you'll see, I will have the pleasure.'

They continued their relationship for a further two months, but eventually Gerry's constant nagging about giving herself to him, and her insistence that she was saving herself, erupted into a mighty row one night when Gerry had suggested their walk home from the pictures could be via the Common.

'If you loved me you would!' he said angrily.

'And if you loved me, you'd wait!'

'I've no plans to marry for a long time,' he stated vehemently.

Kitty faced him, her eyes flashing with anger. 'In that case you'd better find yourself another girl!'

'That's just what I will do!' he said and, turning, he stormed away from her.

It was several months later that Kitty was introduced to Brian Freeman by a mutual friend as they all queued together to see a film. She remembered him vaguely from school but had never really noticed him before. When she agreed to go out with him, she discovered Brian couldn't have been more different from Gerry. He was more mature in his ways. He knew where he was going in life, knew exactly what he wanted and when he kissed Kitty, he made no further demands on her.

There was such a stability about him that Kitty felt secure. He wasn't as dashing or handsome as Gerry Stubbs, but was not bad-looking, with his firm-cut features. Comparing Brian with Gerry was a bit like comparing Gary Cooper with Errol Flynn, she thought. To her, Brian seemed ideal husband material – a strong man with high principles – and when he proposed, she accepted without hesitation. She felt he was a man with whom she could build a safe future.

But eighteen months into her marriage she realised she was not in love with her husband, nor he with her. There was no burning passion between them. Affection and respect – but love? Kitty wasn't at all sure what that was. It was nothing like the emotion on the silver screen at the cinema, which they visited once a week. She often mused what it would be like to be held in a man's arms and kissed until she was breathless. How wonderful that must be. Her favourite film star was Clark Gable and she would often fantasise about him lifting her into his arms and carrying her up a broad flight of stairs to a luxurious bedroom and ravishing her as he had done when playing Rhett Butler to Vivien Leigh's Scarlett O'Hara in *Gone With the Wind*. Brian could never compete with that!

Some of her married girl friends told her how wonderful sex was, but she didn't think there was much to be enjoyed. Brian huffed and puffed and moaned above her every Saturday night, until he was satisfied, leaving her irritable and frustrated. Where was the romance? Would her life have been different, she wondered, if she had stayed with Gerry Stubbs? She was certain it would. When Brian made love to her, she often wondered what it would have been like to have shared a bed with Gerry. She saw him from time to time and there was still something, a certain chemistry, between them, and a *frisson* of danger about the man.

'You married the wrong man, Kitty,' he told her one time, with a smile. 'He's too staid for you. Let me take you out one night and show you what a real man is like.'

She refused, telling him it was time he settled down, and he laughed.

'Why buy a book, darling, when I can go to the library?' he said, and walked away.

But she'd heard disturbing rumours about him. He was deeply involved with the black market for one; and another, that he was running a gang of villains to whom the law meant little. But when he looked at her with those teasing eyes, and wore that sexy smile, she found the bad things hard to believe. Or perhaps she just didn't want to.

Forgetting the past, one morning in early 1943 she stared out of the kitchen window on to the small garden, with its vegetable patch and Anderson shelter, and saw nothing. Her mind went blank. That morning after Brian had left for work, the postman had delivered the small brown envelope marked O.H.M.S. They had been expecting his call-up papers, of course; after all, Brian was not in a reserved occupation and was in the age group the Government had now stipulated for conscription.

Dragging herself back to the present, Kitty tried to analyse her feelings. Naturally she was upset at the thought of her man going to war, facing untold dangers, like her younger brother, Eddie, who at nineteen, was a single man and already in the army, but she knew that she would welcome the freedom. She felt her life was uneventful and dull.

How she longed to go dancing again, but whenever she suggested it to her husband, the idea was met with little enthusiasm. A weekly visit to the cinema was the only moment of excitement for her. She wished she'd been able to continue to work as a shop assistant; at least then she'd have seen new people every day. She felt starved of company. Brian, who worked for the Southern Railway, had insisted, when they married, that she give up her job and be 'a proper wife', as his mother has been to his father. Not that Kitty wanted to emulate her mother-in-law in any way. Gladys Freeman was a harridan, whereas her husband, Frank, was a quiet, kind man who seldom got his say in anything. Sadly for Kitty, Brian had inherited more genes from his mother than his father, inasmuch as he could be quite dictatorial at times. During their courtship, Kitty had thought it masterful but, after eighteen months of married life, did not appreciate it any more.

Had she known what the future held for her, she would have been more content with her humdrum existence.

Brian Freeman looked at his watch and realised it was time to go home. He clocked off and made his way to the bicycle shed of the docks station where he worked in the administrations office, making sure the trains ran to schedule. He was a great organiser. He himself was never late, used to running to a timetable every day. It had become second nature to him and it carried on in his home life. He expected his supper on the table at a quarter to six, which gave him time to get home, have a wash, and change out of his suit into comfortable attire. With clothes rationing, he had to take care of the two suits he wore to the office if he was to keep up his appearance.

He put on his bicycle clips, mounted his trusty steed and whistled to himself as he rode home, wondering what Kitty had cooked for him. She was a good housekeeper, kept the home sparkling clean and ironed his shirts with just the right amount of starch. All was well with his world, he thought – until he arrived home and glanced at the sitting-room mantelpiece, where he saw the brown envelope addressed to him, waiting to be opened.

'Hello, love,' said Kitty as he picked it up. 'That came by the morning post.'

He didn't reply, but ripped it open and read it. She waited expectantly as he studied the contents.

With a stricken expression he said, 'They want me to report for training in ten days' time!'

For a moment Kitty didn't know what to say. As a married man he'd not been called earlier. First it was the reserves, single men, and then various age groups, but now, with murmurings of a second front, the Government were recruiting more men.

'Well, we knew it was bound to happen sooner or later,' she said, trying to be comforting.

'It doesn't mean I have to like it!' he snapped.

She turned on her heel and went into the kitchen. As she mashed the potatoes she tried to put herself in his position. How would she feel? She'd be scared. After all, no one but a fool would be pleased to be facing an enemy, under fire, going off to some foreign land – living with strangers. Without knowing it, she was echoing her husband's thoughts.

Brian took a Woodbine out of a packet and lit it, sucking in the nicotine, blowing it out slowly as he tried to calm the tension growing inside him. Bloody hell! Just as things seemed fine. He'd have to let them know at the office in the morning; they were already short-staffed as it was. And he was doing so well, making a name for himself. There would be no guarantee either that his job would be waiting for him when he returned . . . if he did return. He suddenly faced his own mortality. His safe, nicely ordered world suddenly collapsed around him. He sat down at the table, put his hands to his head and murmured, 'Bugger!'

Kitty saw the dejection in the slope of his shoulders as she came back into the room and went over to him. Putting her arms around him, she said softly, 'The war can't last long.'

He caught hold of her hand and said, 'If only that were true, but I'm afraid we have a long way to go yet.' He stood up and said, 'I'd better go round and tell Mum and Dad.'

'But your supper's ready. I'm about to dish it up!'

'Put mine in the oven, will you, Kitty? I'm not very hungry. I'll not be long.' And he left her alone.

She was livid. After all, there was a lot to talk about. How

7

would she manage financially? What was she expected to do whilst he was away? She couldn't possibly sit around in an empty house waiting! He had looked stricken . . . If only he would unleash his feelings instead of keeping them locked inside, maybe, just maybe, they could get really close. Then she could help him, be of comfort . . . but she knew her husband. And by now his bloody mother would be fussing over her boy. How sick Kitty was of hearing 'my boy' this, and 'my boy' that! What a shame she didn't make the same fuss over Frank, her husband, a man who certainly deserved better.

Kitty turned on the wireless and picked up the paper.

Gladys Freeman was all aflutter. 'I'd have thought your job at the railway was important enough to keep you home!' she said. 'There's plenty of other men who don't have a job with such responsibility – why don't they take the likes of them? What will I do when you're not around?'

Her husband intervened. 'You carry on like everyone else,' he snapped. 'Knit socks, write letters – look after your husband!'

For Frank to take a stand was so unusual, it took the wind from Gladys's sails.

'Come on, son,' said Frank, 'this calls for a drink at the pub.'

'I'll get my hat,' ventured his wife.

'No need,' said Frank, putting on his jacket. 'We need to talk, Brian and me, man to man.' He opened the door and walked into the street. 'Women don't understand war, son,' he said, dismissively.

In the public bar of the Anchor Inn, war was on everyone's lips. Frank ordered two pints of bitter and took them over to a quiet corner. Once he and Brian were seated, he picked up his drink and said, 'Cheers, my son.'

After taking a long swig of his, Brian asked, 'You've been in a war. What was it really like, Dad?'

'Bloody awful! But that was then. This war, things have moved on. The tanks we had in the First World War were useless; today things are more modern. Then it was largely horsepower, the four-legged kind. Yes, you have a laugh with your mates, but you watch your back all the time. It is not a time to be careless if you are involved with the fighting.'

'I'm not one for mixing with the lads, as you know, Dad. I like being on my own.'

'Then get used to it! Your life could depend on a mate. A company is a team, Brian. Discipline makes a team; you'll train together, play together, and fight together. Keep each other going. You become like a family. In the forces, friendships are carved between men that last a lifetime.'

Their conversation was interrupted as Gerry Stubbs paused in front of them. 'My God! You two look as if your favourite aunt died and crossed you out of her will!'

'Brian's just received his call-up papers,' explained Frank.

'Ah, well, that explains it. When do you have to go?'

'In ten days' time. How is it that you, a single man, are still hanging around, anyway?' Brian demanded. He had no liking for Stubbs.

'Failed my medical, didn't I? Never mind, Brian, someone has to stay at home and look after the ladies!' Gerry walked away, laughing loudly.

'Take no notice of him,' said Frank, seeing the rush of anger flush the cheeks of his son. 'He's just a wide boy and will probably end up behind bars one day.'

'I've never liked him. Even as a boy he was full of himself.'

'So how did Kitty take the news?'

'To be honest I didn't hang about long enough to find out. She was trying to be comforting, but I'm sorry to say I did brush it aside.'

'Well, you were no doubt a bit shocked, but let me tell you, you have a good lass there, you should take care of her. God knows what the men whose wives are cavorting around town with the Yanks would think if they could see. Your Kitty wouldn't behave like that, I know.'

'She'd better not!' Drinking the remainder of his beer, Brian rose to his feet. 'Best be getting back, Dad.'

'All right, son. I'll stay and have another. By then your mother will have calmed down.'

That night in bed, Brian drew Kitty into his arms and kissed her. 'I'm sorry about earlier, rushing off like that.'

This was so unlike her husband that Kitty was touched. 'That's all right. I understand. But tomorrow we must sit down and talk about the future.'

'We will, but now I have other things on my mind.' And he slipped his hand between her thighs.

Chapter Two

The following morning, Kitty was washing the breakfast dishes, listening to the eight o'clock news on the Home Service. The dilemma of how she would be spending her time whilst Brian was away had been solved by Ernest Bevin, the Labour Minister. He decreed that all women between the ages of eighteen to forty-five should be in part-time employment, helping the war effort.

She welcomed the idea. Apart from wanting to do her bit, she was bored at home. She wanted to use her brain, needed to be with other people, and as it was now compulsory, Brian could do nothing about it and she would be earning money of her own. She longed to be independent again, not to have to account for every penny that went out of the housekeeping. How wonderful – freedom at last! Then she was overcome with guilt. Her husband was about to go to war and she was feeling great!

The next ten days passed quickly. The news in the papers was good. The German army in North Africa had surrendered, so folks hoped that maybe the war would soon be over. Whole areas of Southampton had been destroyed, and many lives lost during the relentless air raids of 1940, but now, in 1943, the town was trying to get back to normality. Bombsites were still being cleared, one-storey buildings had replaced the damaged shops in Above Bar, and life continued. But the constant movement of troops through the town heading for the ships in the docks was a reminder to all that war still raged just across the English Channel.

Brian was issued with a train pass and instructions to present himself at Norwich barracks by noon the following day. Kitty had hoped they might have spent their last night together quietly, but Gladys had other ideas.

'We'll all go to the Anchor and give my boy a good send-off!' she had declared, and no one could change her mind.

Frank had suggested that Brian and Kitty would prefer to be alone – 'After all, she *is* his wife.'

'And *I'm* his mother!' Gladys snapped. In the end they all gave in for a quiet life, but it was an evening fraught with tension. Kitty had invited her parents to join them. They wanted to say goodbye to their son-in-law, and Kitty felt she needed someone in her camp to counteract the flack that would be coming at her from Brian's mother.

Brian was edgy, Gladys was tipping back the port and lemon at a furious rate, getting more maudlin with every one, Frank was trying to control her, and Kitty was furious that their last night together, for goodness knew how long, was wasted on the whims and demands of such a dreadful woman. Amy and Jim Simmons tried their best to keep the conversation flowing, but Mrs Freeman wasn't having any, and dominated the evening. Unable to listen to Gladys any longer, Kitty made an excuse and headed for the ladies'.

As she came out of the door, Gerry Stubbs was waiting. He smiled at her. 'Hello, Kitty. I've been watching you, wondering how much longer you were going to sit there. You flew across the bar as if you were escaping.'

'That's exactly what it felt like!' she said, and laughed. 'Was it that obvious?'

'Not to a stranger, but you forget how well I know you.' He caressed her cheek. 'Look, there is a back entrance here – come outside for a break. We'll have a quick smoke before you face that old hag again.'

And without giving his invitation a second thought, Kitty

followed him. They sat on a concrete step together with only the glow of a crescent moon to pierce the night sky. There were no streetlights because of the blackout, and it made for a tranquil feel to the night.

'That's better,' he said as he lit two cigarettes and passed one to her. She took it gratefully. 'So, pretty Kitty, your old man is off to the war?' he said.

'Yes, in the morning.' She felt his arm slip around her shoulders.

'If you were my wife I wouldn't leave you alone. I'd sneak you into my haversack, under my tin helmet.'

She chuckled. 'It would be a bit cramped.'

'Come now, Kitty darling, don't tell me you've lost all those romantic notions since you were married?'

She sighed. 'I don't know what I've become since I got married.'

There was a such a wistful note in her voice, that Gerry stared into her eyes and softly said, 'I told you he was the wrong man for you. You need someone to love you to death, hold you close every night, buy you flowers, cosset you . . . spoil you.'

'Oh, that *would* be nice.'

It was a cry from the heart and Gerry could not resist her. He cupped her face in his hand and kissed her very gently. As he felt her respond, he moved his mouth over hers with a sensuality that made her head spin. Then he gathered her to him, running his fingers through her hair. He caressed her soft neck, but when he reached for her bosom, she put her hand over his, stopping him from exploring further.

He released her and chuckled, 'Darling Kitty, you're still a prick teaser!'

She quickly ran her fingers through her tousled hair, and smiled. 'No, I'm not, I'm a married woman now and I shouldn't be here.'

He helped her to her feet. 'You and I should be together, you know that.'

13

'No, I don't, so don't you go getting any daft ideas, Gerry.'

He held up his hands in surrender. 'All right, but when you get too lonely, you know I'll be there . . . if you want me.' He eyed her expectantly, seriously, and Kitty knew he meant it. He took her hand in his. 'If you ever need me for anything, Kitty – anything – you let me know. All right?'

She nodded. 'All right,' she said, and walked through the door he held open for her, confused as to why she had, in a moment of madness, allowed Gerry to kiss her, but at the same time admitting it had been exactly what she'd needed. It was just such a pity, she thought, that her husband never showed her such affection.

Gerry didn't follow. Instead he sat back down on the step, lit another cigarette and thought of the soft lips that he had tasted, and the ardour with which Kitty had responded. The girl was obviously starved of love. He meant love, not sex. He wasn't surprised: that Brian Freeman had always seemed a cold fish, even at school. He never really mixed with the others, as one of the lads. And now he was off to war. Well, bloody good luck to him!

'You were a long time,' Brian accused, as Kitty sat beside him.

'Excuse me!' she said. 'Since when do I have to account for my time spent in the ladies'? For goodness' sake!'

Gladys leaned over and asked, 'What time's your train tomorrow, Brian?'

'Why?'

'I want to see you off, of course.'

'That won't be necessary,' said Kitty firmly. 'I'll be there and we want to be alone. I'm sure you can understand that?' She was damned if she was going to let her mother-in-law intrude again.

Gladys made to argue but Frank intervened. 'Of course we do, love. Besides, goodbyes are awful. Come along,' he said to his wife, pulling her to her feet, 'it's time to be off home.'

'But—'

'Come on, woman, for heaven's sake!' He looked at Brian and

held out his hand. 'Good luck, son. Keep in touch and take care, you hear?'

'Thanks, Dad.' Brian turned to his mother and kissed her cheek. 'You take care too. I'll write.'

Filled to the brim with port and lemon as well as emotion, Gladys had tears welling in her eyes. 'My boy!' she began.

'Now, Mum, that's enough!'

'For God's sake, woman, let's leave here with a bit of dignity,' admonished Frank and he firmly led her away.

Kitty's parents rose to their feet. 'We'll be off too,' Jim said. 'Give you time to yourselves.' Holding out his hand, he said, 'Good luck, son. Take care of yourself.

Amy kissed Brian's cheek. 'We'll see you soon, Brian. Take care.'

After promising she'd visit them soon, Kitty waved goodbye to her parents.

Brian sat back down. 'Whew! Thank God that's over. Do you fancy a walk, Kitty? I need some fresh air.'

'So do I. Let's go.'

They strolled through the park in the moonlight. Despite all the railings having been taken away and melted down to make things more necessary for the war effort, and the odd trench dug here and there, Southampton parks were well maintained, and in the light from the moon, the flowerbeds could be seen, the remnants of the spring bedding waiting to be renewed. They found a bench and sat in companionable silence for a while.

'I wonder what I'll be doing this time tomorrow night,' Brian remarked.

'Getting ready for bed, perhaps. If you have an early morning start, I imagine that lights out won't be late.'

'You sound very knowledgeable all of a sudden.'

'Not really,' said Kitty. 'I was only going by what we've seen in the war pictures at the cinema, that's all.'

'I'm sure real life will be far removed from the films,' he said wryly.

Turning to him she asked, 'How do you feel at this moment? I wish you'd tell me.'

'Mixed up! My life is all upside down. Everything I know is changing and I'm not in control of it. I don't know if I'm coming or going, and that's the truth!'

'Oh, Brian, how awful for you . . . but maybe once you're settled in, you might enjoy the change.' It was all she could think of to try to cheer him.

'I don't like change,' was his reply, and he withdrew inside himself again.

She tucked an arm through his. 'Tonight is our last night together for a while, and here we are sitting in the moonlight. Let's make the most of it . . . kiss me.' She turned up her face in expectation.

He looked at her for a moment, then gave her a peck on the cheek. 'Come on, we'd best get back as I have a lot to do in the morning.'

What did she expect, she asked herself as they walked home. Brian was never a man to show his feelings. It was something that, tonight, he'd told her his thoughts, but she had hoped that he'd feel a little more emotion, under the circumstances.

Later, in bed, as he made love to her, she felt it was just to satisfy his needs – topping up, as it were, before he went away. There was not a word of love, nothing to say she would be missed.

The following morning, on the station platform, there were several couples who were obviously in the same position, as well as the troops already in uniform, in transit to some place or other. Brian found a seat, stowed his small brown suitcase and leaned out of the window.

'I'll write as soon as I can. I'll have some money transferred to you. Take care of yourself. Best take my seat before someone else pinches it,' he said, and moved forward to kiss her quickly.

As Kitty stood on the platform waiting for the train to pull out she watched other couples. Men leaning out of the carriage doors, arms wrapped around wives and girlfriends, making the most of every last moment . . . and her husband was sitting inside the carriage, making sure he was travelling comfortably! She turned on her heel and left the platform before the guard had blown his whistle. What was there to wait for?

In the carriage, Brian was fighting to keep his stiff upper lip, as the saying went, when all he wanted was to hold Kitty and tell her he'd miss her. He wasn't one for expressing such sentiments, he thought, but today, by God . . . He jumped to his feet, pushed his way to the window in the corridor of the train and eagerly looked out – but there was no sign of her. His smile faded and he returned to his seat.

Kitty walked back through the town. After all, there was no reason to rush, she only had herself to please, and she felt the need to do something cheerful.

Southampton, although sorely battered, now had a cosmopolitan air about it, with troops from many different countries passing through to the docks to be shipped out to wherever they were needed. The French navy had docked for a while. Dashing sailors with red pompoms on their hats eyed the girls, flirting with them in accents only normally heard at the cinema. They sounded so romantic, very like Charles Boyer, which made them extremely popular. There were also Poles, Scots, Australians and, of course, the Yanks.

Kitty passed a small group, leaning against a wall, chewing gum and smoking. 'Hiya, honey,' called one. 'Want to make a lonely solider feel at home?'

She laughed and as she walked by she said, 'You look quite at home to me!'

His friends laughed and teased their buddy and another applauded her quick retort. 'I told you these limey chicks were smart,' he said.

There was a sudden lightness in Kitty's step. Naturally she

17

worried about her husband – Brian was entering a strange world from today and she hoped he'd be able to settle – but she felt as if a load had been removed from her shoulders. She could now be her own woman, and she would take full advantage of the opportunity whilst she could.

Lieutenant Jeff Ryder, emerging from a newsagent's shop, heard the rapport between his men and the pretty English girl, and smiled. She had such an air about her. There was a bounce in her step as she responded to their teasing. He admired the slim legs, small waist and ready smile. She was synonymous with his idea of an English rose, with her clear complexion, her soft-modulated voice. The English were indeed different. There was a quaintness about them as a race that was rather endearing, he found.

As he walked past the men they stood and saluted him smartly. He returned their salute, wondering just how long it would be before they were all posted across the water to face the enemy. At least, unlike many of his men, he had no wife to worry about, which in wartime he felt was an advantage.

For his part he knew that it would be some time before he'd be sent from the camp in Southampton. His job at the moment was to organise the companies in transit, but his time would come, eventually. Clutching his newspaper, he made his way back to his office.

Chapter Three

Brian Freeman duly arrived at the barracks in Norwich, where he was sent to line up with the other conscripts. They were a mixed bunch, he thought as he looked around. Some were quiet, others were nervous and showed it, and there were a couple who thought they were comics, trying to make smart remarks to cover their inner feelings. Eventually they were told to stand to attention by a sergeant major with a loud voice that belied his stature.

It was then that Brian recalled Kitty and her war films, because this scene echoed very much of what they had watched on the screen at the local cinema, with the sergeant throwing insults at the men, telling them he could never make soldiers of such crummy specimens of the human race.

'If Jerry could see you lot, he'd know without a doubt he could win the bloody war!' he yelled. 'Well, gentlemen, that just isn't going to happen. I'm not losing my bloody life through such a miserable bunch as you. You'll learn to be soldiers in the six weeks that you are here, or die trying.' He walked up and down, eyeing them with utter contempt.

'It's your mothers I'm sorry for. All that pain to produce something as worthless as you.' He stopped in front of them. 'In a moment you will be dismissed and Corporal Burgess here will show you to your quarters. You will then collect your uniforms, have a medical and go to the mess hall for a meal. After which you will be shown how to stow your gear, make your beds and keep a tidy billet. Then you will learn to be soldiers. Understand?'

There was a low murmur of assent, which made the sergeant glare at them. 'Now I know I'm not going deaf,' he said with heavy sarcasm. 'When I ask you a question I expect you to answer "Yes, Sergeant," in a voice loud enough that your Auntie Maud back in the Isle of Wight can hear. Understand?'

'Yes, Sergeant.'

This time there was no complaint. Calling his corporal over, the sergeant major said, 'Take this bunch away. I'll see them later.'

Brian and eleven others were taken to a billet where twelve bunks were laid out, six either side of the room.

'Not exactly the bloody Ritz, is it?' remarked one of the wags.

'How would you know?' snapped Corporal Burgess. 'You'd never be allowed over the doorstep! Right – choose a bed, leave your cases on top and come with me. You'll be supplied with bedding and uniforms.'

The day was never ending. The camp barber cut their hair, then they showered and lined up naked in front of a doctor to be medically examined. Their uniforms, mess kit and bedding were issued. Back at their billet they were shown how to stow their things, and how to make a bed to the corporal's rules and regulations, and after, instructions were received on how to clean their boots and their equipment. When eventually they did fall into bed, they were exhausted.

'Tomorrow you learn to be soldiers!' warned the corporal. 'When reveille sounds you don't linger in bed, you jump to it or the sergeant will have your bollocks!'

As Brian lay on his bunk, he came to a decision. He didn't like the army, he'd be much happier back in Southampton, but as he had no choice, he would make the best of it. The only thing he did feel comfortable with was the regimentation. After all, he'd lived his life by routine, it suited him and maybe he could get used to it in this alien environment. He thought of Kitty and wondered how she was feeling. A bit lost, he supposed, without him to cook for and care for. After having two meals in the mess, he missed her cooking already.

Kitty was indeed feeling lost. It was odd, being in this empty house, knowing that Brian wasn't coming home for his supper. She tidied up, dusted and vacuumed; put aside clothes to be washed, tidying those to be ironed. She would see about getting a job in the morning, and she blessed the Labour Minister who insisted that women should work. She would pop round to her parents' as soon as she had time and tell them of her plans. The last person she wanted to see was her mother-in-law. But now she would have more time for her married friends, some of whom were already coping with husbands away in the forces. Yes, she'd get in touch with them later when she was more settled.

Whilst Brian was sleeping in his barracks that night and Kitty was slumbering fitfully in her bed, Gerry Stubbs was taking delivery of black market goods. It was a good haul, he thought with a smile of satisfaction as he checked off the latest addition to his stock.

He had started his business in a small way during the Blitz, looting bombed-out property – emptying gas meters, finding a couple of safes in two business premises, which were opened by using gelignite, obtained by nefarious means. The contents had given him the finance to buy illegal ration books. Then he and his gang plundered NAAFI stores, depleting their stocks. Now he had a warehouse, which was supposedly used for housing building materials, which he supplied to the council and private builders for rebuilding the town. Much of his stock was now legally requisitioned from bombsites where the remains were to be demolished, materials such as staircases, fireplaces, bricks and roof tiles, which earned him a pretty penny. It was also a good front for his other activities.

Way in the back, out of sight of prying eyes, was a refrigerated unit that held horsemeat and various cuts of lamb and beef, which were sold to businesses that were not too concerned as to the origins of the goods, as long as they were fresh. Hotels and restaurants were all merely scraping livings during the shortages, and it was all part of the game of knowing the right person for the right materials. Gerry dealt in everything that was in short supply and was able to help many – and make a stash of money into the bargain. He was a smart man with good looks and charm, a quick mind and an ability to get out of a tight corner should the need arise.

He was surrounded by like-minded men who had been rejected by the armed services for various reasons, who didn't mind breaking the law and who were capable of using force if necessary. And there were occasions when it was necessary. Criminals ran the black market, and sometimes the various gangs clashed. Behind the smile and the charm of Gerry Stubbs, was a character who was calculating, devious and dangerous.

He picked up a packet of nylon stockings that he had bought from an American soldier, and put them aside in his office. He would give those to Kitty. He fully intended seeing her again, especially now that her husband was away. He'd give her a little time to be alone first – and then he'd call.

After the first week, which seemed interminable, the following five passed surprisingly quickly, it seemed to both Brian and Kitty. Brian had settled to army life and found he quite enjoyed it after all. He was reasonably fit when he joined his company and the rigorous physical exercises had improved his fitness. He enjoyed learning about small arms. He was soon adept at cleaning, loading and firing his 303 Enfield rifle and the Bren gun.

The army didn't allow them to use real bullets at first, of course. As Sergeant Green said, 'I let you have the real stuff, you'll all be shooting one another and I don't see why I should deprive the Germans of the pleasure!'

Despite his father encouraging him to mix with his fellow recruits, Brian still kept himself apart for most of the time, but he had joined in the odd game of darts and cards. He was good at following orders, appreciating perhaps more than the others the need for regulations. To him they made sense.

Kitty had also settled in her own way. She soon adapted to living alone, and where she used to visit the cinema once a week with Brian, she now did so with various girl friends, and, if she were honest, they were better company. She also spent time with her parents whenever she could. Not that her mother, Amy, was demanding, unlike Gladys Freeman. Amy was a bright lady with a sense of humour and very supportive of her daughter during these troubled times, as was Jim, Kitty's father.

Kitty now had a job in one of the local factories, working on different shifts, making parts for engines. She soon became proficient at working on a line of girls with a specific routine. She wasn't at all sure what she was handling, but it didn't matter as long as she did it correctly.

The banter between the women was fun and sometimes very crude. In time she wasn't shocked any more by the revelations made on the factory floor. It just made her realise what a quiet life she'd led. And tonight she'd been persuaded to go with some of her colleagues to a dance given by the Americans.

'It's great, Kitty,' said Jean, her friend whom she'd known since they had shared a school classroom. 'They have loads of food – stuff you and I only dream of. Besides, these Yanks know how to dance – and they have their own band. They play all of Glenn Miller's music.'

And so, later, dressed in her best frock, Kitty met the girls as arranged and, with some excitement and trepidation, she walked into the Nissen hut where the dance was to be held.

Kitty was surprised at the size of the interior. At the far end was a stage with a band already playing. Flags of all nations were draped around the walls, chairs were placed for those who wished to rest, and at the other end of the room was a bar with tables and chairs. Beside this was a long trestle table crammed with food. She couldn't believe her eyes. There was ham, not

Spam, sandwiches, sandwiches made with real eggs, not the usual powdered stuff, and vol-au-vents filled with what looked like tinned red salmon! Beside these there were plates of cream cakes, chocolate éclairs, cream puffs and a bowl of fresh fruit.

'We are fortunate. We have supplies sent over from the States.' At the sound of the American voice she spun round and saw the smiling face of an officer. He held out his hand. 'Lieutenant Jeff Ryder,' he said.

Shaking his hand she replied, 'Kitty Freeman. I haven't seen such a spread since before the war,' she laughed. 'I thought for a moment I was dreaming.'

'Can I get you a drink?' he asked.

'That's very kind of you. I'd like a gin and tonic.'

They sat together at a table. 'I've seen you before,' he said.

She was surprised. 'I'm sure we've never met.'

'No, we haven't, but I saw you in the shopping centre the other day. Some of my soldiers were teasing you.'

'Oh yes, I remember,' she said, chuckling. 'You Yanks are a cheeky lot!'

'We're just not quite as reserved as you Brits.' He glanced at her wedding ring. 'Your husband in the forces, Kitty?'

'Yes, he's only just been called up,' she explained. 'The girls I work with persuaded me to come tonight.'

He laughed and said, 'You sound guilty about being here. Are you?'

She looked rueful. 'I suppose I am.'

'There's no need you know. We are all in this war together and, after all, this is an innocent dance. Nothing untoward is going to happen to you.'

'I suppose not. Tell me about yourself,' she said. 'Do you have a wife back home?'

Shaking his head he said, 'No, I'm free and single.'

Looking at his fine features, wide blue eyes, smiling face and sleek dark hair, she wondered why on earth some girl hadn't managed to snap him up. 'No one back home waiting?'

'No. I didn't think it was the right time, with the war and all, and besides, I haven't met the right woman yet.'

His accent wasn't as strident as many she'd heard. It was soft and cultured – and she was curious. 'Where do you come from?'

'Boston, Massachusetts. In civilian life, I'm a lawyer.'

'And what is a lawyer doing in the army?'

'Like your husband, I'm serving my country . . . But enough of me. Would you care to dance?'

'I'd love to.'

Jeff led her to the dance floor and took her firmly in his arms. They danced effortlessly around the room, their steps matching, their bodies flowing together to the music as the band played Glenn Miller's 'A String of Pearls', followed by 'Elmer's Tune'.

As they left the dance floor, Jeff said, 'You'll have to excuse me, Kitty, but I must see that everything is going well. But please save another dance for me.'

'I will,' she promised, and made her way back to her work-mates.

'Bloody hell, Kitty, you struck lucky, girl!' said Jean. 'What a gorgeous bloke. He looks just like a film star! I got some smart aleck from New York who promised to get me into the films if . . . well, you can imagine what. Do they think we're stupid?'

'What did you say to him?'

'I told him my father was a lord and would cut off my inheritance if I agreed.'

Everyone laughed. 'Did he buy it?' someone asked.

'Of course he did. You mention the aristocracy or the Royal Family to the Yanks and they go goggle-eyed.'

'I'm surprised he's not after you for your title and money,' said Kitty.

'Ah well, I thought of that. I told him that next week I was being presented to the King and Queen, just after the announcement of my engagement to Sir James Bartlett!'

'Now you can't tell me he swallowed that!'

'As a matter of fact he did,' she said, tossing her head and laughing. 'I told him I was travelling incognito tonight, otherwise he would have to follow protocol and bow to me and would you believe it, he looked at me and bowed from the waist and said it had been a privilege and he would have something to tell his folks back home.'

Everyone fell about laughing at Jean's audacity.

'I wish I could be like you,' said Kitty, wiping the tears of mirth from her eyes.

'The trouble with you, Kitty, is you've been married too long. I remember you at school. You had all the boys after you, especially that Gerry Stubbs.'

'I went out with him for a while after,' said Kitty.

Jean stared at her in surprise and said, 'You've got some courage then. Everyone knew he was fast,' and she looked at Kitty with a certain amount of speculation.

'No I didn't! But I sometimes wanted to!'

'I heard he's been going around for some time with that Nancy Brannigan,' said Jean. 'And you know what she and her family are like!'

Everyone who lived around their area knew about the Brannigans. They were a family who left Ireland during the potato famine and who had settled in Southampton. The old man was a stevedore in the docks, the mother known for her loud mouth, and Mick, the son, had served time in prison. Nancy, the daughter, was a real firebrand and troublemaker, but good-looking, with flowing red hair and a bust that many a woman would die for. She had cut a swath through the town's young men in her teens.

'I wouldn't have thought she was his type,' Kitty ventured.

'You are joking! With her reputation? Gerry wouldn't have much persuading to do to get her on her back!'

As Kitty made her way to the ladies', she couldn't help but be disappointed to hear of Gerry's liaison with the redhead. She thought he would have had better taste.

The rest of the evening passed off enjoyably. The band took a rest and the girls thoroughly enjoyed the food, which was served to them by the Americans. They were urged to eat up, which they did with great relish.

'God,' said Jean, as she bit into a chocolate éclair. 'I have to tell you, this is better than sex!'

Kitty laughed at her. 'That's only because you've forgotten what it's like.'

Jean pulled a face. 'Too right. My Harry's been in North Africa too bloody long. Still, now the Germans have surrendered, maybe he'll be sent home.' She sat munching slowly, wiping a bit of cream from her mouth, lost in thought. 'At least he's still alive,' she said quietly.

Eventually, as the bandleader announced the final number, Jeff Ryder appeared beside Kitty. 'I'm sorry I couldn't get back sooner,' he said, 'but would you have the last dance with me?'

'I'd be delighted,' she said. As they moved around the floor, Kitty found herself trying to compare Jeff with Gerry Stubbs. Both had charm, but the American was a gentleman and had class: that was the most obvious difference. She couldn't imagine the officer making a pass at her, unlike Gerry, and this was proved to her when Jeff offered to run her home.

When he pulled up outside her home in Harborough Road, he jumped down to assist her, and said, 'Thank you for making the evening so enjoyable.'

'But I hardly saw you!'

'I know, but when we did spend time together, I found you delightful company.' He walked her to the door and waited until she'd unlocked it before he bade her good night. 'You take care, Kitty. I hope we meet again.'

She watched him drive away and for a moment wondered why she was disappointed that he'd not asked to see her in the future, and then she scolded herself. For God's sake, you're a married woman, she thought. But it had been so nice to be in

27

the company of a man who had paid attention to her. Was that such a sin? Her Brian was a gentleman too, and a good man, but however she tried, she couldn't honestly say he was as interesting as either Gerry Stubbs or Jeff Ryder.

Chapter Four

It was now mid-July and Kitty had received a letter from Brian telling her he would be home towards the end of the month for a week's leave. He was no great correspondent, but managed to write a letter every week. He'd told her a little about his training, but words didn't come easily to him, either spoken or written, though he had made it quite clear he didn't like her working in a factory. She'd ignored his remarks when she wrote back. It didn't matter what he said, she'd decided, she wasn't going to change her job to please him. She enjoyed the camaraderie of her working day. It helped to fill what would have been many lonely hours. After all, he was living his life, following orders from the Government, and so was she!

It was fortuitous that she was on a shift that allowed her to be at home when Brian arrived. She looked at him with some surprise as he came through the door. After all, it was the first time she'd seen him in uniform.

'Hello, Brian. It's good to see you.' She felt awkward and wondered why, but as she looked at him dressed in his khaki, he was like a stranger.

He threw his kitbag down and took her into his arms. As his mouth covered hers, she was taken aback by the fervour of his kisses. When he released her she chuckled and said, 'You missed me then?'

'Six weeks is a long time, Kitty.'

'So it would seem.' Staring at him she said, 'You look so

different! What does that mean?' she asked, pointing to the insignia on his uniform.

'I'm in the Royal Engineers, commonly known as Sappers.'

She detected a note of pride in his voice. 'And what do Sappers do?'

'They build bridges; look after the maintenance of search-lights, rail construction and railway operation and control. Which is why they put me there, what with my experience.'

He was quite unlike the man she knew; he was animated as he explained, and she couldn't help but conclude that the army was good for him. 'Would you like a nice cup of tea?' she asked.

'That would be lovely.' He followed her into the kitchen, saying, 'My, Kitty love, I've really missed your cooking.'

Turning to him, she said, 'Is that all you missed about me?'

He put his arms about her waist and looked into her eyes. 'No, Kitty. Sleeping with a lot of men isn't much fun.'

'Neither is sleeping alone,' she murmured. And she entwined her arms around his neck.

He covered her mouth with his again, and kissed her with a longing that said far more than words. 'Never mind the tea,' he said softly. 'Let's go upstairs.'

She turned off the gas beneath the kettle. 'Are you going to carry me up to the bedroom, like Rhett Butler?' she whispered.

'Who?'

'Never mind,' she said as she took his hand and walked towards the stairs.

They had been on the bed but a few minutes when there was a loud rapping on the front door. They both stopped in mid-embrace.

'Who the hell is that?' asked Kitty.

'You in, Brian . . . Kitty?' called Gladys Freeman, loudly through the letter box.

'Did you write and tell her you were coming home?' asked Kitty angrily.

'Yes, didn't you tell her?'

'No, I bloody well didn't, because I knew she'd be on the damned doorstep within a few minutes of your return – and I was right.'

He made to get off the bed.

Kitty held him back. 'You go down to her now, and you can take your kitbag and spend the rest of your leave with that bloody woman!'

He lay back in her arms until the insistent knocking stopped and they heard the heavy footsteps walk away. But the moment had been lost.

'I'll go and make the tea,' Kitty snapped. At the bedroom door she paused. 'You need to make up your mind, Brian, which one of us you are married to!'

The following morning, Kitty rose early, as she was on the eight-to-twelve shift. As she pulled on her dungarees and tied her hair up in a turban, she looked at the sleeping figure of her husband and felt a pang of guilt. He'd reached for her in bed later that night, but she was still so peeved, she pretended to be asleep. Even now, she was still bristling with indignation. When she took her wedding vows, she hadn't expected there to be more than two of them in the marriage and it was time that Brian explained that to his mother. She'd put up with her interference long enough. Now, with the war, she wouldn't see a great deal of him, and although she realised Brian would have to see his parents, which was only natural, she wanted them to have some time, which was now so precious, to themselves. Why couldn't his mother understand? She hastily scribbled a note telling him where she was, and quietly left the house.

When Brian awoke a little later and found the house empty, he wasn't pleased. Why wasn't his wife here waiting for him? He had wanted to sit down to breakfast with her and catch up on local events. When he read Kitty's note and learned she was at the factory he was even more incensed. He'd looked forward to this leave so much and it was all going down the drain. His mother's arrival on the doorstep yesterday had started it all. Well, he'd call on her now and put a stop to that.

Gladys was washing clothes in the scullery of her home when Brian pushed open the back door. With a wide smile she said, 'Hello, son, you're a sight for sore eyes. How are you?'

'Fine, Mum. You look well.'

'I came round your house yesterday,' she said, 'but no one was home. I wanted to see how you made out with the training. Never mind, I'll cook a meal tonight and you can tell me and your dad all about it.'

Brian felt as if he was being smothered. 'No, Mum!'

She gave a puzzled look. 'What do you mean, no?'

'I've been away for six weeks—'

'And don't I know it!'

'So does Kitty. She's missed me and I want to spend as much time as possible with her.'

'I see, and not with your parents. Been complaining, has she?' Gladys snapped.

'No,' he lied, 'but you must realise that Kitty is my wife. We have our own life to lead. I'm a man now and not tied to your apron strings any more!'

Gladys flushed with anger. 'How could you say such a cruel thing?'

'I don't mean to upset you, Mum, but just stop organising things for us. You do it out of kindness, I know, but just leave us to make our own arrangements, that's all I'm saying.'

With a loud sniff and an angry toss of her head, Gladys said, 'Fine! I'll just forget I have a son.'

Brian closed his eyes and counted to ten. The last thing he wanted was a row with either of the women in his life. Putting his arm around his mother's shoulder, he kissed her cheek and said, 'Don't be daft. I'll call and see you before I go back to camp.'

He caught a tram to the High Street and walked slowly towards the waterfront. Here he watched as American trucks lined up, full of troops, waiting to be allowed into the docks and shipped across the English Channel. Being a part of the fighting forces himself now, he took more interest in his surroundings, wondering when he would be making the same journey and what he would find on the other side – hoping it wouldn't be anything like the failure at Dunkirk.

The Allies had just invaded Sicily after severe bombing had paved the way for them, and Brian thought: well, at least I've missed that. He wondered if that was where Kitty's young brother was, as they'd not heard from him for a while. Last time Eddie was in touch with the family he was at Catterick, waiting to be shipped out, destination unknown.

He ambled into a pub and sat quietly drinking a glass of ale, puffing on a cigarette, watching the locals. There were several old codgers giving their opinion on 'that bloody man Hitler'. At the bar, several American soldiers sat, exchanging quips with the barmaid, handing out gum as bait for a date, but she'd heard it all before.

'You think I can be bought for a stick of gum? What a cheek!'

One of the Yanks laughed and said, 'Are you trying to up the ante, babe?'

'I'm not your babe. You lot are full of bull! You come waving your nylons and Hershey bars and think you can buy everything.'

Brian admired her stand, but he'd seen several girls strolling around the town with other American troops and wondered what they had been offered. He looked at the material used for the men's uniforms and silently compared it with the roughness of the khaki uniform he was wearing. There was no comparison, and as for the officers' attire, with their dark green jackets and beige trousers – well, how could any British army man compete? He certainly wished the Tommies were paid as well. It made for bad feelings among many British troops and that led to trouble.

Glancing at his watch, he decided to meet Kitty as she came off her shift and to try to make up for the unfortunate start to his leave. He swallowed the dregs of the beer and left the bar.

Kitty greeted Brian warmly and with surprise when she saw him waiting at the factory gates. She kissed his cheek and said, 'This is unexpected.'

He said, 'I thought we could have something to eat quickly, then go to the cinema, and then this evening go out somewhere for a meal.'

'Just the two of us?' she asked guardedly.

He smiled with amusement and said, 'Just the two of us.'

She beamed at him. 'I'll have to get home and change first. I can't eat out like this.' She pulled at her dirty dungarees. 'The oil from the machines gets everywhere.'

When they eventually reached home, he said, 'You go and get washed and dressed, and I'll make us a sandwich and a cup of tea.'

'My goodness, how you've changed!' she remarked. When Brian had been at home, he'd never helped that much, but then she'd always been there to look after him.

'Well, things are a bit different now,' he said.

'Yes, I suppose they are.' And as she was washing Kitty realised that Brian had changed considerably during the six weeks he'd been away. He didn't seem to be so dictatorial as before; he'd softened somewhat in his ways . . . seemed less stuffy! She chuckled at her own thoughts. My God! She'd made him sound old. But then she realised that when he worked for the railway, he was very set in his ways and at times he had seemed just like an old man. Kitty had often thought as they sat at the table together – he's fifty already! Yet when he'd taken her into his arms on his return yesterday, there was this young man, filled with desire. Maybe there was hope for him yet, she thought, and hurried downstairs.

The evening went well. After the cinema, they found a small restaurant and sat enjoying their meal. Brian told Kitty about his life in the army.

'You know, I really didn't think I'd enjoy it the first few days, but actually it isn't at all bad.' He grinned at her and said, 'You wouldn't believe the sergeant. He isn't that big a bloke but he could make himself heard for miles if he had a mind to – and sharp! He doesn't stand any nonsense . . . but I would think he's an excellent soldier. Certainly the sort you'd want beside you when there was any fighting!'

His words chilled her to the bone. They made the war all too close. 'Will you be posted abroad?'

He shrugged. 'I suppose so, at some time.' Then, seeing the worried look on her face, he quickly said, 'Now don't you fret, Kitty. I'll take good care if I am, don't you worry.'

As they were walking home, they called into a local pub for a nightcap. 'To round off the evening,' suggested Brian.

To Kitty's surprise, standing at the bar was Jeff Ryder with another officer. He saw her as she walked in and as he was leaving a little later, he passed by, smiled at her and said, 'Good evening, Kitty,' nodded to Brian and walked on.

'Who the devil was that?' asked Brian.

'An American I met a few weeks ago.'

'Met? Where did you meet him?' he asked angrily.

'Some girls at the factory and I went to a dance at the American base.'

'Do what? You've been out dancing with the Yanks! What sort of game have you been playing whilst I was away?'

Kitty was furious. 'How dare you talk to me like that? It was a perfectly decent dance given by the American troops, that's all.'

'Maybe so, but he seemed to know you pretty well. He addressed you by your name.'

'That's because he asked what it was. All we did was dance a couple of times; he was on duty, for goodness' sake! I hardly saw him, yet the way you're carrying on you'd think I'd slept with him!' Her cheeks were flushed with anger.

'Did he know you were married?' Brian demanded.

'Of course he did. I told him you had only recently been called up.'

This seemed to mollify him and he said, 'I'm sorry, love. I didn't mean to go off the deep end like that, but the Yanks seem to think they can come over here and lord it over everybody.'

'Well, Lieutenant Ryder wasn't like that. He was a gentleman and was only doing his duty. Come on, let's go home.'

Once they were home and in bed, Brian tried to make amends. 'It's not that I don't trust you, Kitty, but sometimes I think I'm not really the husband you hoped I'd be.'

'Whatever do you mean?'

'You're a woman who wants life to be like the great romances you see at the cinema, and I can't be like that. It's not how I'm made.'

This was such a revelation coming from him that Kitty was deeply touched. Putting her arms around him she said, 'I know you find it hard to put your feelings into words, but a woman likes to be told things.'

'Like what?'

'That she looks nice, she's attractive to her husband and that she's loved.'

'Oh, that,' he said. 'Well, I married you, didn't I?'

She had to smile. He hadn't changed that much. 'Come here,' she said.

When it was time for Brian to leave, Kitty insisted on accompanying him to the station again. 'Goodness knows when next I'll see you,' she said wistfully, 'so I want to be with you.'

The train arrived, belching out steam along the platform. When it stopped, Brian tossed his kitbag on a seat and returned to hang out of the window.

'You take care,' he said. 'It was good to be home.' He leaned forward and kissed her as the guard blew his whistle.

'Write soon,' Kitty said, waving at him until the train rounded the bend and he was out of sight. Well, that was more than he did last time, she thought as she left the station. The army was certainly doing him good – and their marriage, for that matter. After the first rocky moments, they really enjoyed each other's company. Brian kept his mother away by visiting her when Kitty was working, and he was more relaxed than she'd ever known him. He evidently missed life at home and seemed to appreciate her more and that made her happy. Rhett Butler he wasn't, but he was learning.

Chapter Five

Nancy Brannigan wandered through the tall stout iron gates of Stubbs and Co., Builder's Merchants, and made for the office. The door was open but Gerry was nowhere to be seen. It was hot and stuffy inside and she fanned herself with a sheaf of papers taken from a somewhat cluttered desk. She stood at the window. Through the open doors of the warehouse she could see Gerry Stubbs railing at one of his workers. She could tell by the waving of his arms and the threatening stance that Gerry was in a foul temper. His bad moods never bothered her, for wasn't she used to such things at home? The Brannigans were a volatile Irish family in which nothing was ever said quietly.

Gerry stomped back to his office, muttering beneath his breath, and when he saw her standing there he snatched the papers from her hand and threw them on the desk, asking abruptly, 'What are you doing here?'

She leaned against the wall and, thrusting out her chest, said invitingly, 'I thought I'd come and see you, darlin'. I was in need of company.'

'Then take yourself off and go and find some lonely Yank instead of bothering me.'

'That's not what you said to me last night!' she retorted.

'That was last night. Today I'm busy and I don't want you hanging around!'

'You bastard! I'm good enough for you in bed, but not at any other time, is that it?'

He gave her a hard stare and said, 'Exactly! I couldn't have put it better myself!'

'That is no way to talk to a lady, Gerry Stubbs!'

He laughed loudly. 'A lady! You wouldn't know what a real lady is, my dear Nancy, so don't start getting ideas above your station. You are what you are – a tramp. A good-looking one, I'll say that for you – you have a great body and you know how to use it – but a lady? Never in a million years.'

She flew across the office, hurling herself at him, fists raised ready to strike the smiling face. But he was ready for her and grasped her wrists tightly. 'You really must learn to control that Irish temper of yours,' he said.

'Let go of me! You're hurting!'

He propelled her towards the door and pushed her outside. 'Go away and bother someone else,' he said as he released his hold. 'I'll be in touch when I want you.'

'You arrogant bugger!' she yelled. 'Don't bother. I wouldn't touch you with a bargepole.'

He grinned broadly. 'Now you know that's not true.' He pulled her to him and kissed her roughly, almost bruising her mouth as he did so. 'Off you go now, like a good girl.' He playfully slapped her buttocks, then closed the door on her.

She heard the bolt slip into place as she rubbed her tender wrists, and she knew better than to disturb him further. Running her hands through her riotous red hair, she walked away, a sly smile on her face. Their spats were legendary, the relationship on and off, but she knew he would call on her again and she would go with him. They were good together – or bad together – and she loved it.

Gerry was a good lover and made no other demands on her. He was a free spirit, as was she. They both went their own ways. She had a good time with the Yanks and any other man who took her fancy, but no one was like the charmer Gerry Stubbs. When she lay in his arms, she forgot all other men. He was a villain, she knew that, and she didn't care. Everyone was on the fiddle these days, though perhaps not in such a big way as he was, but when he called on her it was always with some gift: nylons, perfume, foodstuffs. He was a generous man.

For his part, Stubbs had already dismissed her from his mind. Nancy Brannigan to him was just a butterfly who fulfilled his sexual needs when he felt like it. Today he had other things to think about. An order for a client had not been put together by one of his men and it was due for collection. As they were black market goods, he didn't like either them or the punter waiting around once they'd been brought here from one of his secret storage places, in case the Old Bill got too interested. He glanced at his watch; they would just about make it in time.

Ten minutes later a small builder's van pulled into the yard and he hurried out to see the loading of the cartons of cigarettes, jerry cans filled with petrol, bacon, and a box of tinned fruit bought from an American who had purloined it to sell to cover his gambling debts.

How these Yanks liked to gamble! Crap games, poker . . . they had to do something, he supposed, as they waited to be shipped out. They had too much money, in his opinion, but at least he was the beneficiary. To his mind, gambling was a mug's game.

The driver, a rough-looking individual, glanced around nervously. 'You sure we're safe to do this in broad daylight?' he asked.

'As long as you don't take too long,' Gerry snapped, 'and don't forget to load those two fireplaces in front of the goods. Then if the police see you they won't be suspicious. After all, a builder's van collecting materials from a builder's yard is normal enough. So hurry up. I don't want you hanging around.'

He returned to his office and picked up the nylon stockings he'd planned to take to Kitty Freeman, but he'd been so busy he'd forgotten. Now there *was* a lady, and he still lusted after her. He felt beneath that polite exterior there was hidden fire. Fire he doubted her husband had ever discovered. But perhaps *he* might, if he was lucky. It was something to think about. He'd pop round and put his toe in the water. He wouldn't give her any warning either; an unexpected visitor would be a nice surprise.

But Kitty already had an unexpected visitor. She'd been cleaning the living room when she heard the back door open. Hoping it wouldn't be her mother-in-law, she walked into the scullery in time to see her brother closing the door . . . and locking it.

'Eddie! How lovely to see you.'

But as he turned to face her she was shocked at his appearance. He was dishevelled and unshaven and he looked shifty. 'What on earth is the matter?' she asked.

Grabbing her by the arms, he said, 'You've got to hide me, our Kitty.'

'Hide you? Whatever for? What on earth are you on about?'

'I'm not going back to the army; I don't care what anyone says. I've had enough.'

'Come and sit down,' she said, thoroughly alarmed by now. 'I'll put the kettle on and you can tell me all about it.' Then she looked at the state of him again. 'Why don't you go upstairs first and wash? You look filthy.'

'I've been sleeping rough,' he said. 'I smell to high heaven!'

'Come on, I'll get one of Brian's clean shirts out for you. Are you hungry?'

'I haven't eaten for two days,' he said.

Upstairs, she opened a drawer and removed a shirt and some underwear. Laying it out on the bed she said, 'Here, put this on when you've washed. I'll be in the kitchen.'

'You won't open the door to anyone, will you?'

'No, of course not.' And she left him alone.

Downstairs in the kitchen she wondered what on earth had happened. If her brother was absent without leave, he was in serious trouble; the Military Police would be looking for him. What was she to do if they called on her, asking for him? If only Brian were at home . . . but then when she thought about it,

Brian would probably insist he give himself up!

Eddie had always been a bit wild and impulsive, and when he was called up, she had been relieved, thinking a spell in the army would do him good, make a man of him. He'd been away for some time now and she wondered what on earth had happened to make him take this step.

She warmed up some leftover shepherd's pie she'd saved for her meal that day, made a pot of tea for them both, and waited to hear her brother's story.

'I was in that mess at Dunkirk,' Eddie explained. 'I can't make you understand what it was like on those beaches. Many of us were seasick going in. Men drowned who were landed too soon in deep water. The endless bombardment whilst we were on the beach was horrendous – either side of me my mates were being blown apart. And then the hours waiting waist-deep in water to be evacuated, wondering if you would live that long.' His voice was choked with emotion.

'Oh, Eddie . . . ' Kitty said.

'Then, months later, they sent my company out to the desert, to Tobruk. The desert, Kitty. The heat, the flies, the dysentery. How the bloody Arabs live there, I don't know. I was eventually sent home. My insides were a mess because I'd caught some bug or other. I was in hospital for three months.'

'None of us knew this,' Kitty declared.

'Well, you know me. I didn't want to worry Mum and Dad. Besides, I'm not much of a home bird, you know that.'

She did. Her mother used to despair of her irresponsible son who wouldn't write and let her know how he was or where, until she gave up worrying saying, 'If anything's wrong, we'll soon hear.'

He took a long swig of his tea and declared, 'I'm through, Kitty. I've had enough. I've done more than my bit for King and country; they can do without me now.'

'You'll go to prison as a deserter if they find you!'

He grinned at her. 'I'll make bloody sure they don't!'

She was exasperated with him. 'You're not a child any more,' she told him angrily. 'You can't sit in a corner and sulk when things don't go your way! Good heavens, Eddie, there are thousands of men going through the same things as you – where would we be if they all threw their hands up and ran away?'

'Now don't get all sanctimonious on me, our Kitty.'

'Sanctimonious! You've got a nerve. I've pulled you out of more scrapes than soft Joe when you were a kid, but now it's time you stood up to your responsibilities.'

'Are you telling me you're turning me down?'

'You can stay the night, that's all, and don't you go running to Mum.'

'Don't be stupid, that's the first place they'll look. Why do you think I came here?'

'But eventually the MPs will come here too. They'll check all the family and as I'm your sister . . . '

'Let me stay a few days until I sort my head out. I'll think of something.'

How many times had she heard him say that when he'd been in some sort of scrape or other as a youngster?

'What time is Brian due home? Do you think he'll give me any grief?'

'He's been called up; he's away right now at Catterick. He recently had a week's leave so I don't expect him in the near future.'

'Couldn't be better!'

'You take a lot for granted!' said Kitty angrily. 'If I'm found harbouring you, I too could be in serious trouble!'

'It's only for a few days, Kitty. Surely that's not asking too much?'

'Well, you can't be seen. You certainly can't leave the house.'

He smiled at his sister, knowing he'd won her over.

'I'll be as quiet as a mouse,' he said. 'You won't know I'm here, nor will the neighbours. If I need fresh air I'll wait until it's dark.'

Kitty looked at the clock. 'I've got to go to work. I work in a factory these days,' she said, 'but I'll be back just after four o'clock. We'll talk about it all then.'

'Do you mind if I get my head down in the spare room?' he asked. 'Only I haven't slept much these past few nights.'

'How long have you been on the run?'

'Five days.'

'Oh, my God! The redcaps are bound to call here soon.' She rose from her chair and said, 'We'll talk about this when I get home.'

During the following four hours, Kitty found it very hard to concentrate on her work, worried as she was about the dilemma facing her. If she turned Eddie out, what would become of him and if she let him stay, what might become of her? He was her brother, after all, and she'd seemed to spend her life getting him out of some fix or another. Even as a small child, he and trouble came together.

At the end of her shift she was no nearer a solution. She went to wash her hands, then made her way home. Just as she opened the front door, she was grabbed around the waist from behind and lifted into the air.

'You're still as light as a feather,' said Gerry Stubbs. 'Married life hasn't changed your figure, I have to say.' And he carried her into the room before she could stop him.

She looked around frantically but, to her relief, there was no sign of Eddie.

'Put me down,' she snapped.

'Now then, pretty Kitty, that's no way to talk to an old friend – and one bringing gifts.'

'What the devil do you want?' she demanded.

Knowing her as well as he did, Gerry immediately sensed there was something amiss. 'What's the matter?' he asked, dropping his jocular tone.

'Nothing's the matter. I just don't like being crept up on like that.'

'Then why are you so tense? It's only me, after all. Now, if I were a complete stranger I could understand you being nervous.'

'Brian could come home at any minute. What do you think he would say if he found you here?'

'I know your old man's away because in my local last night, your mother-in-law informed everyone that she hadn't seen much of her boy when he was on leave. You are not her favourite person at the moment, Kitty – so what's going on?' He walked to the table and picked up an army beret. Holding it up he looked at her and raised his eyebrows. 'Are you entertaining another man? That's not like you at all!'

'That's mine.' Her brother appeared at the bottom of the stairs.

'Eddie!' she exclaimed in horror.

Gerry looked from one to the other and immediately caught on. 'Have you deserted?' he asked.

'That's right!' He looked defiantly at Gerry.

Her legs suddenly seeming to give way beneath her, Kitty lowered herself on to a nearby chair.

'Then what the bloody hell are you doing here, putting your sister in danger with the law?'

'I've been sleeping rough and I needed to clean up. Where else could I go?'

'Back to your unit, that's where.'

'It's all very well for you!' said Eddie aggressively. 'You have no idea what I've been through.'

'You gutless little creep. Other men are going through the same; they don't run away.'

Eddie sneered at him. 'I don't see you in uniform!'

This really riled Stubbs. He'd failed his medical because of flat feet, which to this day was a great embarrassment to him, but had he been passed fit, he would have willingly gone into one of the forces, despite the fact he was making a fortune on civvy street. In many ways he regretted the position he was in. He had an adventurous spirit and would have liked to have gone abroad to another country to see what it was like, and here was a young lad snivelling about his lot.

'How long do you intend to hang around?' he asked, ignoring the barb.

Eddie shrugged. 'Dunno.'

'You can't stay long,' interrupted Kitty. 'If I'm found hiding you, what will Brian have to say? He'd be furious.'

Gerry looked at Kitty and saw the anguished expression. He couldn't have this. 'Have you got a couple of old pairs of Brian's trousers and another shirt?'

'Yes, but why?'

'I once told you that if you ever needed me I'd be there. Well, now you do. I'll take Eddie off your hands. I can't stand by and see you putting yourself out on a limb for him.'

'But where will you take him?'

'It's best you don't know. Then you won't have to lie. Look, Kitty, before long the MPs will knock on your door. You can say you don't know where he is without lying. Now go on, get some things together, I want to talk to your brother.'

When they were alone, Gerry turned to Eddie and said, 'I'm only doing this for the sake of your sister.'

With a sneer, Eddie said, 'You always fancied her!'

Gerry caught him around the throat. 'Now listen to me, you little pipsqueak. I won't stand any of your bloody cheek. You had better know now that if you don't keep your nose clean and do everything that I tell you, I'll hand you over to the authorities without a minute's hesitation.'

'I could always tell them you've been hiding me.'

Gerry looked coldly at him. 'You could and it would be your word against mine. Do you think they would care? All they would care about is having you back in custody.'

The younger man paled as he looked into the steely glare of the other's eyes.

'All right,' he conceded reluctantly.

Taking a flat cap off the peg behind the front door, Gerry handed it to Eddie and said, 'You wear that and keep your head down. If we see anyone, make sure you don't make eye contact. I don't want anyone remembering you. Right?'

'Right.'

Kitty returned with a small bundle. 'I've put some clean underwear and socks in here too,' she said, and went to the cupboard under the stairs and took out a large shopping bag. 'I'll put them in here.'

'We'll go out the back way,' said Gerry. 'Say goodbye to your sister.'

'Bye, Kitty. Sorry to cause you trouble.'

She hugged him. 'Take care,' she said.

'He'll be in safe hands,' Gerry assured her. He put his hand in his pocket and withdrew the pair of nylons. 'I bought these for you,' he said. 'I'll be around again to let you know how this little bugger is. All right?'

By now Kitty didn't know if she was coming or going. She just nodded.

The two men left by the back door and she carefully looked out of the window to watch them walk up the street, thankful that Gerry Stubbs had been around to solve her problem. After all, he had said if she ever needed anything, to call on him, yet she felt uneasy. Would there be a price to pay for this great favour?

Chapter Six

Gerry Stubbs took Eddie to a lock-up garage, which he used, among others, to store some of his illegal goods. There was a small room above it with a barred window and a camp bed in it.

'I'll bring you some blankets later,' said Gerry.

'And how about a Primus stove to brew some tea?'

Gerry glared at him and said, 'Definitely not. For one thing, I don't want you accidentally setting fire to the place, and secondly, where are you going to get tea? I don't suppose for one moment you have a ration book?'

'No, of course not, but I'm sure you can put your hands on some spare.'

'I don't think you get the picture,' said Gerry. 'You are seeking refuge from the law, hiding out to save your scrawny little neck from the glasshouse. This is not a holiday hotel, and you need to keep your head down for a while. I'll send you a flask of tea and some food later. Here you'll stay until I say so.'

'What if I need the lavatory?'

'You'll get a bucket and some torn newspaper.'

'I might as well be in prison!'

'You have a choice,' said Gerry threateningly. 'And frankly I'd as soon turn you over to the military as not. I'm only doing this to save your sister any aggravation, but you give me any, believe me, that's where you'll finish up – or floating in the docks. Take your pick!'

'Kitty would never forgive you!'

Laughing derisively, Stubbs said, 'Don't be ridiculous. All I'd have to say was that you left my safe haven and tried to make it on your own. She'd certainly believe me, so don't give me any old bull.'

Eddie stood quietly weighing up his options. No way did he want to return to the army, and Stubbs was his only hope. Otherwise he'd be running scared and forever looking over his shoulder.

'Whilst you're here,' said Gerry, 'don't bother to shave. A beard will change your appearance. And grow your hair longer. That army cut gives you away. Then in a few weeks' time—'

'A few weeks!' exclaimed Eddie.

'In a few weeks' time, when you've changed your appearance and I think it's safe for you to be seen, you can work for me.'

'Doing what?'

'Whatever I want!' He walked towards the stairs. 'No noise, understand? I don't want anyone getting nosy.'

'Fine. But bring me a paper to read, will you, or I'll go crazy without something to do.'

Gerry ignored him and walked down the stairs, locking the garage door behind him. As he made his way down the street, he wondered just what he'd taken on. Young Eddie was going to be a headache until he realised that Gerry meant what he said. He could see that the boy needed a short sharp lesson in the near future. Well, that wasn't a problem, and at least now Kitty owed him a favour. If he played his cards right, he could use this to his advantage.

Left alone, Eddie decided to explore his surroundings. Walking down the stairs he tried the door to the front of the garage and found it locked securely from the outside, which didn't surprise him. Turning around he began to study the contents of the place. Boxes were stacked one on top of another. Some contained tinned food – corned beef, Spam – others, packets of tea, coffee – army supply, marked on the outside he noticed. Others, with American markings, had tinned fruit and cigarettes. There was an open case filled with torches and batteries and an unopened one of bourbon.

'Damn!' he muttered. He could do with a drink, but thought it unwise at the moment to try to open the case. Gerry would go mad if he did, and looking at all this stuff, Eddie knew he was surrounded by goods worth a small fortune . . . and Gerry had said later he would let him work for him. Well, if he was dealing in all this there had to be some perks to be had. Money to be made. He could perhaps make enough to take himself up to the Smoke. Hiding in London would be far easier. He wasn't going to hang around down here a minute longer than was necessary, being his hometown, but he would need cash to tide him over. Yes, he thought with a satisfied grin. He could well have landed on his feet here. He walked back upstairs, lay on the bed and fell asleep.

At his new camp at Catterick, Brian, unaware of the situation at home, was undergoing some specialist training. He and a group of others were studying the French railway system. He had no idea why – a need-to-know basis, they were told. But there were rumours of a second front, of landings in France, though no one knew the specific destination. They were also being trained to use explosives, which he found fascinating but wondered just what they would be blowing up.

'I reckon they're planning another invasion,' one of his pals remarked that evening as they stood outside their billet, smoking.

'What makes you say that?'

'Well, it stands to reason, don't it? They're planning to take the railways to move troops, or why are we studying them? And, of course, this sudden exercise, using explosives – they wouldn't bother otherwise.'

'Yes, it makes sense,' Brian agreed. 'Especially now the Yanks have taken Palermo in Sicily.'

'Yeah, I reckon the powers that be are planning a big offensive, and we'll all be in it, mate!' He stubbed his cigarette out, saying, 'Well, I'm off to get me 'ead down.'

Left on his own, Brian mulled over the conversation. In one way he was anxious to try out his new skills. What was the use of months of training if you didn't put them to good use? But, of course, he knew that it wasn't as simple as that. All of them would be in mortal danger from enemy artillery fire. He rubbed his finger up the bridge of his nose to his forehead, to ease the sudden tension he felt. And yet . . . he wanted to go, to be involved. The army had given him a sense of adventure, which was really very strange, considering that he had been perfectly content in his carefully orchestrated world before he was called up.

His horizons had been widened; some of his natural aloofness had left him. His father had been right: the army was like a family. Although he hadn't made a close friend of anyone in particular among the men, they were slowly banding together. There was a certain camaraderie. They shared private jokes about the sergeant, the officers. It became second nature to judge the men who were weak and who were strong in command. The young officers who had come straight from a military academy were certain targets.

'He couldn't bloody well lead a scout troop,' it had been said of one young officer, recently arrived. 'Christ, he can't even grow a beard. What he's got on his chin is nothing but bum fluff!'

'I bet he had a bleedin' nanny to change his nappies,' remarked another. 'He's just a bloody chinless wonder!'

Brian turned his thoughts to home and wondered just how Kitty viewed her life these days because for her too, and other wives, things were very different.

Kitty was wandering around her house like a lost soul, and no matter how she tried, she couldn't gather her senses. The sudden appearance of her brother and his equally sudden departure was like a bad dream, and she couldn't help but think that Eddie might be in as much trouble with Gerry Stubbs as with the might of the military police. With either, her brother could end up behind bars! It was good of Gerry to come to her aid, she admitted, but what did he plan to do with Eddie?

A visitation from Stubbs early that evening gave her the answer.

'He's holed up in a safe place,' he said. 'When a few weeks have passed, he can work for me.'

'Is that wise, keeping him in Southampton?' she asked anxiously.

'You won't know him, Kitty, in a few weeks. By then his hair will be longer and he'll have a beard. After all, he won't be going to the local pubs where people know him. I'm not that stupid.'

'You'd best make sure he knows that,' she warned. 'Eddie is very wilful and pig-headed.'

'Not with me he isn't!'

She didn't like the menace in his voice. 'You won't hurt him, will you?'

'That's up to him, Kitty. As long as he toes the line and doesn't give me any trouble then he'll be all right.'

'And if he does give you trouble?'

'He'll regret it!' Catching hold of her hand, he said, 'Look, Kitty, I wouldn't give the boy houseroom if it wasn't for you, because I think he's bad news, and I'm really sticking my neck out here. I will keep him in check, but you must know, *if* he lets me down – I'll deal with him.'

There wasn't much she could say to that. After all, he was being honest.

'Don't look so worried, Kitty darling. The kid is my problem now, not yours.'

'Thanks, Gerry. I don't know what I would have done had you not been there.'

He said softly, 'I told you if ever you needed me . . .' He leaned forward and kissed her cheek.

As he did so, the back door opened and Gladys Freeman walked in. 'Well!' she exclaimed. 'Such carrying on – and behind my Brian's back!'

Completely unfazed Gerry said, 'There is nothing going on
here at all, Mrs Freeman, to my deep regret, I have to say. Kitty is
always telling me she's a happily married woman.' He walked
towards the door, with Kitty following him.

'I'd keep the back door locked if I were you,' he said quietly.
'I'll be in touch.'

Kitty turned on her mother-in-law. 'How dare you come in
here without knocking?'

'It's my son's house!'

'And it's mine too. I would never dream of doing that when I
call on you.'

'You come so seldom I wouldn't notice,' Gladys snapped.

And it was true. Kitty only visited when she had to, usually
with Brian, and if she could make an excuse not to do so, she
would. 'Was there some reason for your visit?' she asked coldly.

'I just happened to be passing, and I thought I'd call in and see
if you'd heard from Brian. Your husband!' she added pointedly.

'I don't need to be reminded, thank you! I had a letter last
week. He's fine.' Kitty could see Mrs Freeman was about to make
herself comfortable and said, 'You will have to excuse me but I'm
just on my way out.' Picking up her handbag, she asked, 'Which
way are you leaving, by the front or back door?'

'Well, I never! My Brian won't be pleased when he hears how
I've been treated today.' And turning on her heel she slammed
out of the scullery door, which Kitty immediately locked behind
her, leaving the house herself a few minutes later by the front.

She was steaming as she walked up the road. That bloody
woman forever meddling in her life. No doubt the old devil would
write to her son, complaining, and would, of course, tell him of
Gerry's visit. She would have to think up some story or other
about him being there, because she obviously couldn't tell Brian
the truth. Neither could she tell her parents. Her mother would
be beside herself with worry.

She would go window-shopping, she decided, to take her mind
off things. She headed for the Bargate, the remains of a medieval

gateway, now surrounded by modern commerce. Just as she was passing the American Red Cross Club, who should she see coming out of the entrance but Jeff Ryder.

'Hello, Kitty. This is an unexpected surprise. How are you?'

'To be perfectly honest I'm in a foul mood!'

He looked so surprised, she started to laugh. 'What's the matter?' she asked him.

'I was taken aback, I guess.'

'Well, I'm perfectly human, you know. I have all the vices and not all of the virtues.'

It was his turn to be amused. 'So tell me, what has caused this bad mood?'

'My mother-in-law!'

'Oh dear. Look, how about coming and having a quiet drink and telling me all about it? I have broad shoulders for you to cry on, if necessary.'

'I don't feel the need to cry, but a drink and some company could be just what I want,' she said gratefully. He was such a nice polite man; she had no compunction about accompanying him. They settled in a quiet corner of the lounge bar of the nearest hotel and started to talk.

'Was that your husband I saw you with a while ago?' Jeff asked.

'Yes, he was home on a week's leave after his initial training period.'

'How's he liking the army?'

She thought for a moment. 'You know, even in six weeks, it's changed him.'

'In what way?'

'Well, Brian lived his life by the clock and he was quite rigid about it. In fact, his life was rigid.'

Jeff looked puzzled. 'How do you mean?'

'Oh, you know, supper on the table at a certain time. Shirts starched to a certain degree. The pictures once a week on a Friday,' she raised an eyebrow and sardonically added, 'and made love every Saturday night!'

54

Jeff tried unsuccessfully to hide a smile. 'No surprises then?'

'No surprises. But I have to say when he came home it was different.'

'Well, he had been away for a while.'

'No, it was more than that. When he spoke about his work, he was excited. Animated even.'

'Kitty, I hate to say this but you make him sound like a bit of a bore.'

She grimaced. 'I suppose I do, but when I think about Brian I'm afraid that is the truth. He's a lovely man really, very loyal, upstanding, but he has no romance in his soul. That's what I really miss, and a bit of spontaneity.'

Looking at the lovely girl sitting next to him, Jeff thought what a great pity it was that her husband seemed such a disappointment. 'Why did you marry him?' he asked.

'I suppose because he was reliable, strong, capable . . . and I may have been on the rebound from another man.'

'Was he exciting?' asked Jeff.

'Too much so!' Kitty laughed. 'They couldn't be more different.'

'Do you wish you'd married the other guy?'

'Good God, no! I had a lucky escape.' She looked wistful for a minute and said, 'But he was spontaneous, and romantic, and a little bit dangerous, and that made him exciting.' She suddenly looked embarrassed. 'I'm sorry, Jeff, I really don't know where all that came from.'

'Sometimes it's easier to talk to a stranger and get this kind of thing off your chest.'

'Tell me about yourself. I know you're a lawyer from Boston, but what else?'

'There's nothing much to tell, Kitty. My dad is a lawyer too; Mom was a teacher. I have a sister, Marie, who is married.'

'They sound a nice family. And you haven't found the right woman yet?'

'That's right.'

'Have you looked?'

He started to laugh. 'You are very direct, Kitty, and yes, I have looked and had a fine time searching!' His eyes twinkled with amusement.

The next hour flew by as they exchanged their views over a million different subjects. Looking at her watch, Kitty said, 'Good heavens, look at the time. I'd better be getting home.'

'I'll walk you there.'

'No, that's all right, you don't need to do that.'

'Oh yes I do. I asked you out, I'll see you home.'

They walked back through the Polygon area until they reached her house. 'Thank you for a very stimulating time,' said Kitty. 'It was just what I needed.'

'It was my pleasure. I was going to ask you a favour,' he said.

'And what's that?'

'Whilst I'm stationed here, I would love to look around the area. There are so many interesting places nearby. Like the New Forest.'

'And Bucklers Hard.'

'What's that?'

'It's where, years ago, boats used to be built. And then you could see the stone in the forest where Rufus the Red was killed.'

'Was he a king?'

'Yes.'

'If I could get the transport would you come with me as my guide? I can assure you it would all be strictly above board.'

'I'm sure it would be, and I'd be delighted.'

'I'll be in touch then. So long, Kitty, and thanks.'

As she climbed into bed that night, Kitty thought what a very strange day it had been, but what had started badly had ended pleasurably. Jeff Ryder was a stimulating companion, a true gentleman, and it would be fun to show him around. There was no harm in that, although she thought it prudent to keep it to herself. The girls at the factory would make much of it and Brian certainly wouldn't understand.

Chapter Seven

During the next few weeks, Brian and his company went off on manoeuvres. This meant no leave for the men, and when they complained the sergeant had a field day with them.

'What's the matter with you, you miserable lot? Missing your oats? I'll have to have more bromide put in your tea. How do you think you'll manage in a field of war? There are no wives or girlfriends around then!'

'What about those sexy French women?' asked one of the men.

'There's plenty of them and you'll probably end up with a dose of the clap if you start dipping your cock, my lad. That's supposing any of them fancied you . . . which I doubt, seeing as you're as ugly as sin!'

'He didn't say we weren't going to France,' whispered the man standing next to Brian, who had already noted the fact. But when?

They were all sleeping under canvas whilst they took part in war games, each company taking turns to be the enemy. Brian found his adrenaline pumping as he slithered across wet grass with twigs and foliage on his tin hat and camouflage mud on his face. But when it came to the real thing, how would he fare? Would he be found wanting, too scared to act? This thought was terrifying, knowing it could mean life or death to him or the men serving with him. He felt a little better at the service on Sunday morning when the army padre gave his sermon, telling his small congregation out in the open, 'It's no sin to be frightened. Without fear, men take stupid risks.'

★　★　★

Unlike his brother-in-law, Eddie Simmons was really scared. He'd become so bored holed up in his small room that he'd broken into a case of bourbon and consumed most of the liquor from one of the bottles during the long night. He'd passed out on the bed, which is where Gerry found him the following morning. He was rudely awakened when Gerry had thrown the unsavoury contents of the bucket over him.

He sat up, covered in his own faeces and urine, stinking to high heaven. He heaved when he sat up as his stomach rebelled.

'You throw up, you bastard, and you'll sit in it!' threatened Gerry. 'I should have known you couldn't be trusted.'

'I'm sorry,' Eddie whined. 'You don't know what it's like sitting here day by day with nothing to do, all on your own. No wireless for company.'

'And whose fault is that? If you'd stayed in the army like a man you wouldn't be here. Look at you – you're disgusting!'

'I need a wash and a change of clothes,' said Eddie. 'I can't stay like this.'

'I'll fill the bucket from the outside tap and you can clean up as best as you can, but clean clothes, forget it. You can sit in your own filth because that's all you're fit for.' Gerry left him, return-ing shortly with a water-filled bucket. 'Here. And you can clean the floor as well. There's a mop downstairs at the back of the garage and a bottle of disinfectant. Use it because this room smells like a fucking cesspit! I'm taking the bourbon away. You tamper with any more of my stuff and I'll break all your fingers!' He glared at Eddie. 'I'm in two minds to have my men chuck you into the briny. That'll clean you up, just enough for the fishes to enjoy you when you sink to the bottom.'

'I can swim,' was the angry retort.

'Not with a lump of cement tied round your ankles you can't!'

Eddie froze with fear. 'You wouldn't do that, would you?'

'Don't push me too far or you'll find out!'

★ ★ ★

Gerry was livid as he walked away. If the boy wasn't Kitty's brother he would have him dumped. He would give him one more chance, but if he misbehaved again, that would be it! He didn't have the time for all this aggravation. Besides, he had far bigger fish to fry. He was meeting up with a mate of his soon, who ran a gang in London and who had a proposition for him. He was the only man he really trusted. They'd grown up together, started thieving together, and when the war started they both found their niche in the black market. Only Ken went up to London to settle, despite the bombing. He'd survived the German bombardment of the city and started his own lucrative business, and they helped each other out on occasion. Gerry was very curious about this meeting. It must be pretty important, as Ken wouldn't discuss it over the telephone.

Kitty was sitting in the passenger seat of Jeff's Jeep as they drove through the New Forest. In early September the leaves were tinted with autumn shades, the forest ponies grazed and wandered slowly across the road, unconcerned by the odd passing car. With petrol rationing the traffic was very light these days, so the animals were reasonably safe and any driver who knew the forest well was always on the lookout for them, though during the dark of night there was, sadly, the odd accident.

Jeff drove the Jeep off the road on to a grassy patch just outside the town of Lyndhurst and suggested they walk up the small hill and sit on the seat at the top under a small cluster of trees. It was quiet and peaceful, surrounded by the flora and fauna of this beautiful place.

'This reminds me a lot of New England back home, especially at the beginning of fall.' He turned to her and explained, 'That's what we call the autumn back home. You know, the fall of the leaves?'

'That's rather a nice expression,' Kitty said, 'and very descriptive.'

59

As they sat down on the beach he asked, 'Have you heard from your husband recently?'

'Yes, he's on exercises at the moment,' she said, and with a frown added, 'He thinks there is going to be an invasion soon. Do you think he's right?'

'I really don't know, Kitty. Italy has signed an armistice, which surprised the Germans, but they still occupy Rome.' He didn't tell her about Overlord, the code name for the plan to invade France in the future. It was still in its conception at this time, and in war things could change. He couldn't give away classified information, anyway.

They spent an enjoyable time exploring the countryside. They drove to Lyndhurst, then on to Brockenhurst and ended up at Rufus' stone, marking the spot where Rufus the Red was shot in the eye with an arrow. Jeff was very impressed.

'America is such a young country in comparison,' he said. 'What really gets me is the history here, the heritage, how through hundreds of years various kings and queens have reigned – the plots and intrigues that took place.'

'For an American, you seem to know a bit about it,' Kitty remarked.

He grinned at her. 'I have been reading up on it because the history of the country is so fascinating,' he explained.

'You should go to the Tower of London,' said Kitty, 'and there you'll see where some of the wives of Henry the Eighth were beheaded! England also has a very bloodthirsty past.'

'I know,' he laughed. 'Well, we've had a few presidents assassinated, so we too have blood on our hands.'

They drove back to Southampton after stopping for lunch at a quaint little old world restaurant they found.

'I've had such a lovely time, Jeff,' Kitty said when they arrived outside her home. 'Thank you so much.'

'Thank you,' he said. 'Would you let me take you to the movies one evening to repay you for being such a delightful guide?'

She hesitated, knowing that Brian wouldn't approve, but she so enjoyed the company of this charming man, who was always a perfect gentleman and who knew she was a married woman, so she told herself that she really couldn't see the harm. 'I don't need any repayment, but I'd like that, thank you.'

They arranged to meet the following week.

The life of Kitty's brother had at last taken a turn for the better. Having now grown a beard and his hair, and kept his nose clean by staying out of trouble, clearing up the small room to the satisfaction of his benefactor, he was surprised when Gerry called late one evening and let him out.

'Come on,' said Gerry, 'I've got lodgings for you with a couple of my men. When you get there, you'll find some different clothes. You have a strip wash and get changed, then you can burn the stuff you're wearing because, frankly, you stink.'

'Thanks, Gerry. I'll be glad to get out of here.'

'Let me warn you, young Eddie, that these two are hard cases. You do as you're told because they won't hesitate to deal with you if you don't.'

'What do you mean?' he asked fearfully.

'Let's hope you don't have to find out!'

It was dark outside and Gerry led him to a narrow street in the dock area where the houses were built close together. Stopping in front of a shabby door, Gerry knocked. It was opened just a little to allow the occupant to see who was on the doorstep. Then it opened wider to let the two of them inside.

In the living room were two men who gave Eddie baleful glares.

'Hello,' he said. They both ignored him.

Gerry introduced them. 'This is Ernie and Jack,' he said. 'You do as you're told by them. All right?'

Eddie nodded.

'Right, take yourself into the scullery where on the side are some clothes. There is a piece of soap and a towel. Strip down and have a wash, then get changed. Put your old clothes on the side to be burned. I'll see you tomorrow.'

Left alone with the two strangers, Eddie was filled with a certain dread. These two blokes looked very tough, he thought. Best do as I'm told until I know what's going to happen. 'I'll go and get washed then,' he said. Again there was no response.

One of the men followed him into the kitchen and Eddie tensed.

'Here,' the man said, 'you'll need some hot water to get you clean. We don't want you polluting the air here, so make sure you have a good scrub. Put your clothes outside, they stink to high heaven.' The man poured the water into an enamel bowl in the sink, refilled the kettle and returned to the living room, putting the large brown kettle on the hob of the range.

Whilst he was washing, Eddie could hear them talking in low tones, but he couldn't make out their conversation no matter how hard he strained to listen. He didn't like them, he knew that, and by the looks they gave him they didn't welcome his presence at all.

When he'd finished his ablutions and changed, he walked back into the room. 'If you show me which is my room, gents,' he said, 'I'll go to my bed.'

They looked mildly amused. The older man spoke. 'There's only two bedrooms here, sonny, and we have one each. There's a camp bed folded up in the corner – you can put that up in the scullery 'cause that's where you'll be sleeping. You'll find a couple of blankets with the bed.' And he turned back to his companion.

The camp bed was army issue like the one he'd used in the garage. Muttering under his breath, he unfolded it and tried to settle himself for the night. At least he was clean, and he had a bit more room to move about, but he wondered just what Gerry Stubbs had in store for him now. If he didn't like the setup at least he could take a runner, but of course he had no money. He'd just have to bide his time.

Gerry was sitting in a small sleazy club in Southampton's docklands with Nancy Brannigan. He was quietly celebrating a delivery of goods that would make him a small fortune. He put an arm around her shoulders and nuzzled her neck. 'You're looking very tasty tonight,' he murmured.

But Nancy was preoccupied. 'Gerry,' she began, 'our Mick is coming out of prison next week.'

'Before you go any further,' he said, 'I'm not interested.'

Mick Brannigan was a hothead who would spend his life in and out of the nick and Gerry didn't want anything to do with him.

'Couldn't you find him a job or something?'

'What, and have him nicking stuff within five minutes of working there? Not likely.'

'Mum doesn't know what to do with him. And Dad won't give him houseroom.'

'Ah, well, your dad has principles, unlike his children.'

She flared up at him. 'You're in no position to talk!'

'Just because I make a bit of money the way I do, doesn't mean I am without principles, Nancy darling.'

'Don't you darling me,' she snapped.

He stroked the back of her hair. 'Don't get moody on me, girl, just because of your brother. I admire your parents, but young Mick is a waste of space. He'll continue to break your mother's heart until he dies.'

'Don't you mean until *she* dies?'

'No, love, I don't, because I don't see your brother making old bones. He'll rub the wrong person up the wrong way and one day he'll end up in a dark corner somewhere – dead.' Seeing the gathering fury in her eyes, he said, 'It's no use you blowing a gasket because if you're honest, Nancy, you'll admit I speak the truth.'

She gave a sullen look and said, 'Maybe so, but did you have to put it into so many words?'

'Come on home with me,' he whispered. 'I'll make you forget about your brother.' Dear God, he thought, wasn't he having enough trouble with Kitty's kin without taking on a Brannigan?

Nancy rose from her seat. 'No, thanks,' she snapped. 'I'm not in the mood!' and she walked out of the bar.

Gerry was surprised. Nancy was always ready for a tumble with him, and after a few drinks he was in the mood for a bit of affection tonight. He emptied his glass. He'd call on Kitty Freeman, tell her how well he was looking after her brother – maybe she would be inclined to show him a bit of gratitude.

The house was in darkness when he arrived, with the back door locked and bolted. Damn! He didn't want to knock at the front door and alert the neighbours. He got out a small torch from his pocket and shone it on the ground, searching for some grit or pebbles. Gathering a handful, he started throwing them up at her bedroom window. Eventually his bombardment was successful and the window opened at the bottom.

Kitty leaned out. 'Who's there?'

In a loud whisper he said, 'It's me – Gerry. I've news of your brother.'

The window closed and after a few minutes, the front door opened. 'You'd better come inside,' she said softly.

Chapter Eight

As soon as Gerry walked past her and she caught the smell of alcohol on his breath, Kitty knew she'd made a mistake.

'Hello, Kitty my darling,' he said, eyeing her up and down. 'How very enticing you look.'

She pulled her dressing gown tighter around her. 'What do you want? You said you had news of Eddie.'

'What?' He couldn't take his eyes off the rounded shape of her breasts. 'Oh, yes. I came to tell you he's fine.'

'You didn't come here for that at all – you were lying!' she accused.

Putting out his hand, he caught hold of her gown and pulled her slowly towards him. 'How right you are, darling,' he said softly. 'I came to see you. To fill your lonely hours while your husband's away.'

For the first time since she had known Gerry, she was afraid. 'You've been drinking,' she said, trying to pull herself free – but he wouldn't let go.

'I've had a few; I don't deny it . . . but not *too* much, I can assure you. I felt in need of some affection and thought of you, pretty, pretty Kitty.' He put his hand behind her head, holding her firmly and forced his lips on hers.

She struggled like an eel beneath him and managed to free herself, running round the table until it was between them.

He just laughed. 'You didn't used to be so shy with me, darling. I remember when we used to kiss and cuddle. You liked it then.'

'For Christ's sake! That was years ago! I'm a married woman and you shouldn't be here. Now get out! Go home and sleep it off.'

'You should be nice to me, Kitty. After all, I took your brother off your hands, didn't I? You and I are good friends – so come and be friendly.'

She was terrified. How on earth could she get rid of him? Facing him bravely, she said, 'You did that as a friend to help me, you said. If I needed anything, you said, I only had to ask.'

'And I meant it.'

'You didn't say that there was a price to pay, did you?'

'Well, there isn't a price, not really. I just want you. I've always wanted you. Come on, darling, let's help each other. You are lonely, and I'm sure that Brian doesn't satisfy you in bed, whereas I certainly can. Come on, Kitty, let's find out just how much of a woman you really are.'

She tried a different tactic. 'I can't believe you would force yourself on me, Gerry. After all, you are always saying how successful with the fairer sex you are – or is that because you force them into submission?'

'Of course not! I don't need to!'

'Then why do it with me?'

'You really don't know how I feel about you, do you? When we split up I was sick. It wasn't what I wanted at all.'

'Well, we all know what you wanted!' she retorted.

'That's true and I don't deny it. I wanted you more than I have ever wanted any woman. There's something about you, Kitty – and I've never lost that feeling.'

There was a look of longing in his eyes that told her she was really in trouble. Sober, Gerry Stubbs was malleable, but he'd had just enough to drink to make him stubborn. She tried pleading. 'We're still friends, and I'm grateful for that. Please don't make me hate you.'

'What makes you think you would hate me, darling? I would be gentle, loving. I'd make sure that you enjoyed it too. Don't be

66

afraid.' He held out his hand. 'Come to me, Kitty.'

She was suddenly furious. How dare he come to her house and threaten her? Who the hell did he think he was? She glared at him and, fuming, she gave vent to her anger. 'You bastard! What gives you the right to enter my house with an excuse, then threaten to make love to me, or rape me if I won't agree? What sort of a monster are you?'

He grinned and said, 'I love it when you're angry. Your eyes are like saucers. Beautiful blue ones.' He suddenly made a grab for her, catching her by her wrist. 'Gotcha!' As much as she struggled, she was no match for him and he slowly drew her round the table until he held her firmly in his arms.

'Relax, darling,' he coaxed as he kissed her. He had pinned her arms to her sides so there was no escape from him. His mouth slowly assaulted her senses even as she struggled, until the pent-up emotions inside took over and, despite everything, she began to relax. Gerry had always been able to awaken within her feelings she had never experienced with her husband – and he was doing that now. He was being gentle, persuasive. Had he been brutal it would have been different – she could have fought him – but his caresses were wearing down her inhibitions until at last she had no fight left in her. Her body betrayed her . . . but her conscience didn't.

'Please don't do this to me,' she pleaded as she felt him lift the hem of her nightdress. 'Please, Gerry. I'm begging you.'

He looked at her, her eyes brimming with tears. And as they began to trickle down her cheeks, he said, 'For God's sake, don't cry, Kitty!' But the tears continued to fall and he let go of her gown.

She began to cry quietly, like a child. 'Leave me alone. Just leave me alone. Go away . . . please just go away.' She slumped on to a chair, burying her head in her arms.

'There will come a time, Kitty. I will have you – and that's a promise!'

A moment later, she heard the front door close. When she

looked up, she was alone. And then, filled with relief and guilt that she had all but succumbed to Gerry's advances, she began to sob.

The following morning, when she joined the workforce at the factory, Jean asked, 'Are you all right? You look dreadful.'

'I didn't sleep well,' Kitty said, and set her machine going. The noise precluded any further questions and she was still battling with her own guilt. For one moment last night she almost gave in: her body had ached for her former boyfriend and she couldn't understand it. She believed in her marriage vows. For better or worse, she had said at the altar. She had been so frightened, yet still Gerry had managed to stir her and she was ashamed.

During the lunch break in the canteen, she and Jean sat together. Her friend was excited as she heard that her husband, Harry, was on his way home.

'I can't wait to see him,' she declared, her eyes shining brightly. 'It's been such a long time.' Turning to Kitty she confessed, 'I'm feeling really nervous. It's like being a bride on her wedding night all over again!'

'I know how you feel,' said Kitty. 'When I first saw Brian in uniform it was like being with a stranger. I felt almost shy for a while.' Then she asked, 'Is marriage all you thought it would be?'

Jean thought for a moment. 'Not really, I suppose. Living with a man is different from when you're courting. We all have funny ways, I suppose, but my old man is a good husband, so I've no complaints. How about you?'

'My biggest problem is my mother-in-law!' said Kitty ruefully. 'Although I have to say the army has changed Brian a bit, but for the better. I suppose absence makes the heart grow fonder.' But as she said it she knew that if she was honest, marriage for her had been a bit of a disappointment. As Brian had said, he couldn't be the romantic type of husband she really wanted, but in her heart she knew he was a better man than Gerry Stubbs.

The man in question was suffering from a hangover. He was also feeling somewhat guilty about his visit to Kitty and his actions when he was there. He hadn't meant to upset her at all, and he knew that he had scared her, yet for one moment last night he thought she was going to give in. Then she'd spoiled it all by crying. It had killed his passion. He had never forced himself on any woman – there had never been the need – but he still desired her, so he must try to make amends. He went into the local florist's and had them send her a large bouquet.

Kitty was at home when the flowers arrived. She answered the knock on the door to be presented with a large bouquet by the florist's messenger. She read the card. 'I apologise. Gerry.' Shaking her head, she thought, at least he has a conscience. As she put the flowers in water, she made up her mind never to put herself in a compromising position with him again. It was far too dangerous and, knowing him, he would persist until he wore her down.

Shortly after, as she was arranging her flowers, there was another rap on the door – a very decisive one – and she opened it with a retort ready, thinking that Gerry had called personally to make amends. She was therefore surprised and horrified to see two Military Policemen standing waiting.

Her heart gave a leap as one of them enquired, 'Mrs Kitty Freeman?'

'Yes,' she answered, trying to appear unconcerned. 'Can I help you?'

'We're looking for your brother, Edward Simmons.'

'I'm sorry but I have no idea where he is,' she said. 'The last my mother heard he was somewhere abroad, but I can't remember where. My brother doesn't write often, I'm afraid.'

The soldier held her gaze and said, 'He hasn't called here then?'

'Good heavens, no. I've not seen him for a very long time. But I don't understand – why don't you ask his company where he is?'

'They don't know,' said the other man. 'Your brother's done a bunk, miss. Now that's a very serious offence.'

'Whatever do you mean, he's "done a bunk"?'

'He's absent without leave. And the army doesn't like its soldiers disappearing, especially in wartime.'

'Could he have been killed? God help me for thinking it, but isn't it possible in some battle or other?'

'Not young Simmons. It seems he was a reluctant soldier, didn't like it in the army. Now if he calls here, you would be wise to report him. If you hide a deserter, you too will be in trouble. I hope I make this clear to you, Mrs Freeman.'

'Yes, indeed you do. I hope you find him. I'll be worried until I know where he is.'

'Then you won't mind if we have a look around inside, will you?'

'No, of course not,' Kitty said, stepping back. 'Go right ahead.' She waited with bated breath as they searched the house and garden before returning to the front door.

'Thank you. Remember what I said if he shows up.'

'I will,' she assured the MP. And breathed a sigh of relief as they left. With trembling hands, she put the kettle on the stove and lit a cigarette to calm her shattered nerves. She hoped that she was convincing. Her heart was still pounding. How right Gerry had been about them, and thank God Eddie was no longer here. No matter what Gerry had done the night before, he'd saved her neck and for that she was grateful.

Later that week, Gerry Stubbs went to London to meet his old friend Ken. They sat in a quiet corner of an East End pub and exchanged pleasantries. There was a lot of reminiscing about their younger days when they used to go thieving together.

'Who'd have thought those small beginnings would have led to this, eh?' remarked Ken. 'I'm doing really well, making lots of dosh. Yeah,' he said smugly, sitting back, puffing on a large cigar, 'war isn't all bad is it, me old mucker?'

Laughing, Gerry said, 'There is always an ill wind, if you know what I mean. But what did you want to talk to me about?'

Ken leaned forward and in a low voice said, 'I've heard about a consignment of diamonds being delivered to a place in Hatton Garden, and then sold on. There will be a courier calling to collect them, carrying a great deal of money. You interested?'

'Bloody hell! Well, you'd better tell me a bit more about it. What do you want from me?'

'Someone I can trust, for a start. This thing is big, worth thousands; I need a small team only. The fewer that know, the better. This is what I had in mind . . .'

The two men huddled together and made their plans.

When he returned to Southampton, Gerry was elated. If this deal came off he'd be made for life! He began to dream of a rosy future. After the war he could stay in England, buy a large house and live the life of Riley – or he could go off to America and live there. It was supposed to be the land of opportunity. Just the sort of place for him, with his flair for making money. There were endless things he could do with so much money. But he must be careful to keep the plan all to himself. He would need just one of his own men. One who would be ideal for the job in hand, who could be trusted, and who was handy with a shooter. It was unfortunate that they would have to go tooled up, but there was no alternative in this case. With a bit of luck they wouldn't have to use guns. It was always so messy when that happened. He only used them when it was absolutely necessary and his men knew that it was as a last resort only that they put them to use. Fortunately, none of them was trigger-happy and that was a blessing in his business. He lit a cigar and puffed contentedly on it, toying with his various ideas for the future.

Chapter Nine

Kitty kept her appointment to visit the cinema with Jeff Ryder. *Gentleman Jim*, starring Errol Flynn and Alan Hale was a light-weight film with plenty of action, which Kitty enjoyed.

'I love the American films, especially the ones with such glamorous leading roles,' she said as they walked down the steps from the circle to the foyer. It was unfortunate timing because Gladys Freeman was making her way out of the stalls. The two women met face to face.

Gladys looked at Kitty and then at her companion, who was holding Kitty by the arm, steering her through the crowd. The expression on the face of her mother-in-law was a mixture of disbelief and anger.

'Well, I can see you're not one to stay at home and worry about your husband!' snapped Gladys.

Kitty bristled. 'Fortunately at the moment I have no need to worry about Brian,' she retorted. 'He's only in training and not fighting.' Turning to Jeff, she said, 'I'd like you to meet Brian's mother.'

'How do you do, Mrs Freeman? Good movie, wasn't it?'

'Well, I never!' she said, taken aback.

'I was going to suggest that I take Kitty for a drink – would you care to join us?' asked Jeff with a polite smile.

'No I would not!' And she pushed her way to the exit.

Feeling totally embarrassed, Kitty said, 'I'm so sorry. I wouldn't have had that happen for the world.'

'Will she make trouble for you and your husband?'

'You can bet on it. It will give her the greatest pleasure.'

By now they were outside the cinema, and Jeff said, 'I think perhaps you need that drink. Come on.'

When they were settled in the nearest public house, he said, 'I am sorry to cause you trouble, Kitty. We know we're doing nothing wrong, just keeping each other company.' He sipped his beer and said, 'Perhaps it would be best if we didn't meet again.'

'No one, certainly not that old battle-axe, is going to tell me how to run my life!'

Laughing at her indignation he said, 'As long as you're sure. I don't want to come between you and your husband.' He looked thoughtful and said, 'Seriously though, Kitty, if I was married to you, I'm not at all sure I'd be pleased to hear you'd been out with another man.'

But she was adamant. 'If Brian can't trust me then what basis do we have for marriage?' Besides, she admitted to herself, she loved being in Jeff's company. He was a very intelligent man and they had such interesting discussions.

'I'll come and meet him when he's next on leave, if you like, and assure him that I have nothing but the best intentions,' he suggested.

Kitty didn't think that would work at all. Brian had set views about most things and in her heart she knew that he would object strongly. It was bad enough when Gladys had written telling him about finding Gerry in the house. She'd explained that he had just called in to tell her about some tinned fruit on sale at the local grocer's. Such things were so hard to come by that eventually he'd believed her.

In answer to her questions about life in the United States, based on what she had seen in Hollywood films, Jeff began to describe the southern states of America – the difference that still existed between North and South. 'The civil war may have been won by the Yankees,' he told her, 'but there is a saying below the

Mason-Dixon Line: "Save your confederate money, the South may rise again!" '

'Oh dear,' she said.

'Don't look so worried,' he assured her. 'It will never happen. But if a Southern belle falls for a Yankee from the North, I can tell you there is hell to pay within the family.'

As he walked her home he said, 'I was going to ask you out to dinner, but perhaps I shouldn't.'

'Don't be silly! You have never so much as laid a finger on me. Our friendship is entirely innocent so why can't I enjoy talking to you?'

'If you are quite sure?'

'I am.'

'Then how about Wednesday of next week? I will be away until then, touring other camps. I'll pick you up at seven thirty, if that's all right.'

'That'll be fine,' she said, 'and thank you for a lovely evening.'

Later that night, as he climbed into bed, Jeff wondered if he had made the right move, asking Kitty out again, after this evening's meeting with her mother-in-law. He felt that she would meet with opposition from Brian, but he really liked her and looked forward to her company. And although she was right in saying he hadn't touched her, it wasn't because he hadn't wanted to. He had desperately wanted to take her into his arms tonight and kiss her. Had she not been married, he would have done. Yes indeed. Mrs Kitty Freeman was one hell of a woman.

When Brian read the letter from his mother, with elaborate details of Kitty and her Yank, he was furious. What sort of a game was she playing in his absence? Well, he was going to put a stop to it! He wondered if it was the same American who had spoken to her when they had been out together during his last leave. No matter, the same man or a different one, she was his wife and he would not permit her to go cavorting with other men.

Consequently when he came home that weekend, he and Kitty had a terrible row. Almost as soon as he walked in the front door, Brian began.

'I think you've got some explaining to do,' he snapped.

Guessing that his interfering mother had written to him, she asked, 'What do you mean?'

'You know damned well what I mean. How do you think I felt when I heard you were out with a Yank? I won't have it, do you understand?'

Kitty blazed right back at him. 'No doubt your mother wrote to you! God knows what she implied. I was with Lieutenant Ryder, the American who spoke to me. It was all very innocent, I can assure you!'

'Innocent! You are a married woman – or have you forgotten?'

She tried to calm down. 'No, of course not, and he knows that.'

'That only makes it worse. Doesn't the man have any principles?'

'Indeed he does. In fact, he said he didn't want to cause trouble between us so we had better stop meeting.'

'What do you mean, *stop* meeting? Have you seen him often?'

'No, not really. We bumped into one another and went for a drink and then another time to the pictures, that's all.'

Brian was livid. 'You're behaving like a trollop!'

'Excuse me – I am not!' Her eyes flashed with anger. 'It was a pleasant evening in pleasant company, nothing more.'

'You're not to see him again, understand?'

'Don't you trust me?' she asked angrily.

'It's not a case of trust, it's a case of what is right. You are married to me, which means you are my property.'

'Your property? How dare you? I'm not a piece of merchandise, I am a human being and I don't belong to anyone! I am me – a person.'

'Who made her wedding vows, to honour and obey. You will obey me in this matter or there will be trouble. Do I make myself clear?'

'Perfectly.' Kitty walked into the kitchen, silently fuming.

Brian came to the door and quietly asked, 'How would you feel, Kitty, if you heard I was keeping company with another woman in Catterick? Would you like it?'

'That's different,' she said stubbornly.

'No it isn't. You know you wouldn't like it; it's not the done thing.'

She remained silent. Brian was right, of course, and she could see his point of view. 'I'm sorry,' she conceded eventually. 'I didn't think I was doing any harm.'

Knowing her as he did, Brian didn't think she was lying about her friendship with this man but as he said, 'It's not that I don't trust you, love, I do; it's the man I don't trust.'

'But he has never ever made a pass at me,' she argued.

'Maybe not, but, Kitty, you are a fine-looking woman and if this was to continue, who knows what might happen?'

For Brian to pay her a compliment was so unusual that she was touched by his sentiment and her anger faded. 'You think I look all right then?'

Seeing the soft smile he said, 'Oh yes. Come here.' And he took her into his arms and kissed her.

As they sat down to their supper she thought about her date with Jeff the following Wednesday, when he was supposed to take her to dinner. She would go, but that would be the last time they would meet, she decided. She would explain the situation to him. Brian was right: she was his wife and had no right to be meeting another man.

Sitting in the train on his way back to the army camp, Brian pondered over his time at home. He had sorted out the situation with the American, and Kitty had been made to see the error of her ways, right enough. She sometimes was such an innocent. She hadn't realised the danger of such a liaison, of that he was sure, but he did suspect the Yank's intentions. Was the young officer waiting for an opportunity to take advantage of his absence? You couldn't trust any of them. Overpaid, oversexed and over here, was the popular saying, and in many cases, proven to be right. Well, no soldier of any nationality was going to tread on his territory!

Kitty had every intention of explaining to Jeff that she couldn't see him again, but as the dinner progressed and he held her attention, talking about living in America, his personal life and expectations for his future, the moment never seemed to arise where she could stop the flow of conversation.

Their discussions were on a different intellectual level from everyday chitchat with friends. He questioned her opinions, made her think, search her heart and mind for answers. No one had ever before sought her thoughts and feelings about serious matters, like the war, education, the death penalty, children and their upbringing. It was, for her, heady stuff, which stimulated her mind, made her think and, more important, made her realise that she did have her own opinions and some she discovered were very strong.

'Yes, I do think people should get the death penalty when they have committed murder! Why should they not pay the ultimate price? God said, "An eye for an eye," after all.'

'But Christ said you should turn the other cheek,' Jeff suggested.

'I'm sure He didn't mean in such circumstances,' Kitty said. 'He probably meant for the likes of my mother-in-law. Now there I think the death penalty would be justice!'

He rocked with laughter. 'Oh, Kitty. What a hard woman you are.'

She grinned at him and said, 'Well, of course I don't mean it, not really. The loss of her power of speech, though, would be entirely acceptable.'

'Has she been in touch with Brian after seeing us, do you know?'

This was the moment she could tell him what Brian had said, but she answered, 'I've no idea.'

As they drank their coffee she thought she must be mad, crossing her husband this way, but she just couldn't give up this man for no good reason. She admired him so, and he was teaching her so much in his own way. Opening her eyes to life – widening her horizons. It was like an education and she felt she would be a lesser person if she gave up such an opportunity to improve herself.

During the lunch break at the factory the following day, Kitty's friend Jean sat beside her. 'You're a sly one,' she said.

Taken by surprise Kitty asked, 'What do you mean?'

'I saw you coming out of Gatti's restaurant last night with an American officer. You kept that pretty quiet, I must say!'

Kitty felt the colour rise in her neck and face.

'Oh, you look quite guilty – what *have* you been up to, you naughty girl?'

'Absolutely nothing! Jeff is a perfect gentleman. We just enjoy each other's company that's all . . . and that really *is* all!'

'If that's the truth it seems a great pity; he's so good-looking. Is he married?'

'No, as a matter of fact he isn't, and before you say anything, I know I am – and so does he, and he treats me with respect.'

With a sly grin Jean asked, 'Don't you fancy him, just a little bit?'

'Oh, for goodness' sake! We're just good friends.'

Jean gazed at her and said, 'That's all very nice, but in my experience platonic friendship between a man and a woman never lasts. Either he wants more and you become lovers or he wants more and the woman doesn't, and it ends. Just take care, Kitty, and for goodness' sake don't let Brian find out. He'll do his nut!'

When her shift had finished, Kitty stopped in Watt's Park on her way home and sat on a bench. In her mind she was thinking over Jean's remarks about Jeff. Yes, he was good-looking, and if she was really honest, she did find him attractive, and if she weren't married, yes she would fancy him. Then she began to wonder how she appeared to the American. He hadn't tried to kiss her or even hold her hand. Perhaps she didn't appeal to him in that way. And then in true female fashion she wondered why not! Why did people have to make judgements? Gladys Freeman had jumped to conclusions; so had Jean. At least Brian had believed her . . . but if he knew she was still seeing the lieutenant, he would also think the worst! Oh, why did life have to be so complicated?

She entered her house through the back door and just as she was closing it the garden gate opened. A stranger walked in. His beard gave him a menacing look and her heart missed a beat.

'What do you want?' she asked sharply.

'It's me – Eddie. Don't you recognise your own brother?'

Chapter Ten

Mindful of the recent visitation from the Military Police, Kitty said, 'Get inside quickly.'

Eddie sauntered past her as if he didn't have a care in the world. 'No need to get your knickers in a twist. No one recognises me these days. You certainly didn't!'

Shutting the kitchen door behind her, she said, 'I had the MPs here looking for you. They even searched the house.'

He wasn't in the least concerned. 'I wasn't here so what's all the fuss about?'

'But if Gerry hadn't helped you, you might have been. Where would that have left me?'

'You worry too much,' he said as he made himself comfortable in an armchair.

'So, where are you hiding out now?' Kitty asked.

'I'm in digs with a couple of Gerry's men. I work in his builder's yard, moving stuff, stacking wood, anything that needs doing. I can even venture into pubs now I've grown this,' he said, stroking his beard. 'Not any of my old locals, of course – that would be foolish. I'm all right, Kitty – I've even got a girlfriend.'

'What? Are you mad? Does she know who you are?'

'Don't be bloody silly, of course not.'

'Don't you think you are taking unnecessary risks, going out with a woman?'

He shrugged. 'Why? If Nancy doesn't know the truth, she can't tell anyone.'

'This wouldn't by any chance be Nancy Brannigan, would it?'

He grinned broadly. 'Yes, do you know her?'

Kitty looked at him in despair. 'I thought she was going out with Gerry Stubbs.'

Her brother lit a cigarette and with a sly grin said, 'Yeah, well, he hasn't been around much lately.'

'What is it with you?' she stormed. 'You go looking for trouble. You have always been the same. Christ, Eddie! Gerry is the one man who is keeping you out of the glasshouse and you go behind his back and take his girl.'

'Nancy is anyone's girl, Kitty. I'm just borrowing her. She likes a good time with any man who takes her fancy – and she fancies me.'

'I'll give you some advice – drop her, because when Gerry gets back and finds out you've been dallying with his girl, he'll blow a gasket! Now I think you'd better go. I don't want you coming here. I have enough to contend with without you muddying the waters any further.'

He rose to his feet, a sulky look on his face. 'That's not very sisterly of you, I must say.'

'Why should I care about you, Eddie? All you've ever cared about from the day you were born is yourself. Now go.'

When she was alone, she tried to calm down but, as always, her brother had upset her. He was playing a dangerous game – well, she couldn't help him, and anyway he was a man now. At twenty, he was no longer a child. *He* decided to run away from the army, so he must be prepared to face the consequences; he was not her responsibility. She'd be like Pontius Pilate in the Bible: she'd wash her hands of him.

That night, as Nancy lay in his arms, returning his kisses with great passion, Eddie smiled to himself. Give this woman up? What was his sister thinking? Nancy was as wild as he was. She loved a risk. At this moment they were making love in Gerry's bed. Without Stubbs' knowledge, Nancy had had a second key cut to his house and whilst he was away in London, they had taken advantage of his absence. It gave an added *frisson* to their lovemaking.

'When Gerry comes back, we'll have to be careful,' Eddie said, burying his head in her ample bosom.

'Don't worry, darling, we'll find a way. After all, how will he find out? I'm not going to tell him – and you certainly wouldn't dare!'

The reason for Stubbs' absence was his involvement in the heist being carried out in London. It had all been meticulously planned, with just four of them involved: Gerry and one of his men, Ken and one of his. They had bought an old black cab and done it up with false plates. The courier had been identified, and his expected time of arrival – all information sold to them from a man working inside the jeweller's. A man who, through his gambling, owed a lot of money to one of the heavy mobs in the East End. A man who was desperate.

The cab was parked a block away from the jeweller's, waiting. Ken's man was the driver with a lifetime's knowledge of the backstreets of London. The other three were sitting in the vehicle like passengers, wearing gloves, with black facemasks at the ready. No one spoke and the tension inside the vehicle was tangible.

The driver, looking in his side mirror, said quietly, 'Here he comes.'

Everyone stiffened.

The unsuspecting courier walked past the taxi, which was slowly moving forward ahead of him. He took no notice; it was just another taxi on the streets. As he drew level the back door opened, someone jumped out and, putting a pad over his mouth, heaved him inside the vehicle, which sped off, before the man knew what had happened to him. All the courier remembered was a masked face, as his senses reeled and he blacked out.

'Quick!' said Ken. 'Use the cutters!'

Gerry cut through the chain that was attached to handcuffs around the courier's wrist and the briefcase he carried, whilst his man held the pad of chloroform over the victim's nose and mouth.

The driver sped through the backstreets, yet keeping within the speed limits so as not to bring unwanted attention upon them, until he drew up in a dead end. They all piled out of the car leaving the unconscious courier behind, and walked quickly away in different directions, Ken hiding the briefcase inside his coat.

Later that evening, the four of them met in a back room of a decrepit building on London's East End docks, excited, tense and filled with expectation. All waiting to see the colour of their ill-gotten gains.

'Well?' asked Gerry. 'Was it worth it?'

'It bloody well was,' grinned Ken, and opened the case. Inside, neatly packed in bundles of one hundred pounds, was a stack of money. 'A pretty picture, gents, wouldn't you say?' he said.

'How much?' Gerry asked.

'Twenty thousand smackers! Sixteen grand split between you and me, Gerry. Four grand between the other two.' There were cries of exultation and much backslapping.

'Lovely grub!' Gerry said with a satisfied smile.

As they stacked the money in four piles, Ken gave them a warning. 'This will hit all the papers tomorrow, so for the foreseeable future for Christ's sake don't go spending a lot of money – and hide what you have somewhere safe. Tell absolutely no one. We couldn't be identified; there are no fingerprints, so box clever, my friends. Understand?'

They all muttered their agreement.

'Now I suggest we split up. Don't get in touch with me for anything until this blows over. Good luck, and thanks.' He shook each of them by the hand. To Gerry he said, 'Thanks, mate. See you around.'

As they left the building, Gerry said to his man, 'I'll hang about the city for a bit, you go straight back to Southampton. It wouldn't do for us to be seen together here in the Smoke. When you come to work tomorrow, say we've been around the salvage yards looking for stuff. OK?'

'Fine. I'll catch the Underground now. See you in the morning, and thanks, guv. This little pile will really set me up.'

'Don't get your pocket picked en route, will you?' Gerry grinned at him and winked.

'Anyone tries, I'll break his fingers – before I push him under a train,' the man said laughingly as he walked off.

The national papers the next day contained full reports of the robbery. Gerry read them thoroughly. The courier had been unable to give any identification, apart from a masked man pulling him into a vehicle. But Gerry was outraged when he read that the total amount of money stolen was claimed to be thirty thousand pounds! Had Ken pulled a fast one on them all, or was it an insurance scam? Whichever it was, there was nothing to be done about it. If his pal had double-crossed him, he would get even some time in the future, but this was not the moment to make waves. Eight grand was a small fortune, which eventually he could use to his advantage. Just how, he hadn't yet decided. He left his office and walked down to the warehouse.

Eddie, unaware that Gerry was back, was leaning against a pile of wooden planks, smoking.

'Put that fucking cigarette out, you stupid bastard! How many times have you been told about causing a fire? The stuff in here will go up like the fifth of November! And why are you standing around when there's work to be done, anyway? Go and move those fireplaces; they need stacking one against the other.'

Eddie made a rude gesture to the back of Stubbs as he muttered angrily to himself, 'You jumped-up little spiv! I'm screwing your girl, and she loves it, how do you like that?' But he knew he dared not say this loudly. And later, as Nancy swept into the yard and ignored him, he grew even more belligerent.

The next two months seemed to fly by and soon the shops were full of Christmas gifts. Despite the shortages and the rationing, the windows looked festive, although at night they were in darkness, which Kitty thought was a shame for the children. She remembered walking through the streets as a child with her mother, gazing in awe at the displays, the twinkling lights, the spectacle of it all.

Brian had been home on the odd weekend, full of his life in the army, and the rumours of a second front, but he was bitterly disappointed that Christmas leave had been cancelled. 'You can go round to Mother's house,' he said, 'then I know you won't be on your own.'

'If you aren't going to be here,' Kitty said quickly, 'I'll go to Mum's. It will be a good opportunity to spend some time with her and Dad.'

He shrugged. 'If that's what you want.'

'Yes it is,' she said firmly. No way was she going to pacify him by going to *his* mother's house.

Brian no longer questioned her about seeing Jeff, the American, taking it for granted that Kitty had obeyed his wishes, which, of course, she hadn't. They saw each other whenever Jeff was free. They went to Winchester to see the cathedral, visited art galleries, walked, talked, laughed and began to know each other even better.

With Jeff, Kitty felt she was a different woman. She felt alive, vibrant, interesting, a person in her own right – Kitty Freeman – not just somebody's wife or daughter . . . an appendage. She grew in stature and in confidence, but the more time she spent with the good-looking officer, the more fond of him she became. He still treated her with respect, giving her a chaste kiss on the cheek whenever they parted, when Kitty found herself wanting him to sweep her into his arms, to feel his mouth on hers. She hated herself for her perfidy as she performed the duties of a wife when her husband came home.

She had even taken Jeff to meet her parents.

Amy and Jim were very sociable and inquisitive. They made Jeff welcome and plied him with questions about the American way of life. He was quite at home with them and when, later, they all walked along the beach together, wrapped up against the wind, Amy walked with Kitty, leaving the men together.

'Nice young man, this lieutenant,' Amy said. 'I imagine that Brian knows nothing about him?'

'He does know about my knowing him,' said Kitty, carefully choosing her words, 'but not that I am seeing him still.' She looked at her mother and asked, 'Is it so wrong, Mum? Jeff is so interesting, such good company.'

'And away from home. Is he married?'

'No, he's unattached.'

'But you aren't. Be very careful, Kitty,' Amy said. 'Jeff is a charming young man, different from Brian in every way, but it is Brian you are married to.' She made no further comment, for which her daughter was very grateful.

On the way back to Kitty's house, Jeff said, 'Strange, isn't it, how different people are?'

'What do you mean?'

'Your delightful parents, for instance. I see them and then I see Mrs Freeman and I wonder just how you became involved with that family.'

'My parents have always lived in Southampton. Brian and I went to the same school, although we didn't meet properly till I was nineteen. Simple really. We grew up in the same area, although Mum and Dad were never friends with the Freemans.'

'No,' he said, 'I can see they would have nothing in common.' He gazed at Kitty and said, 'The more I get to know you, the less I understand how you came to marry Brian.' He immediately apologised. 'I am sorry, I had no right to make that observation.'

'You are entitled to an opinion,' she said. After a moment's hesitation she said, 'Brian is a good man, a good husband.'

'Why is it that when you mention him, there is always a "but" in the sound of your voice, Kitty? Can you tell me you are really happy being his wife?'

What could she say? Her marriage had never lived up to her expectations, but that was life, wasn't it? Full of disappointments, but you made the best of what you had. But if she were honest the answer was no. And the more time she spent with Jeff, the more she realised it. For the first time in her life, she was truly falling in love. She looked up at the man who had come into her life so unexpectedly and couldn't answer.

'You must know by now how I feel about you, Kitty?'

Her heart leaped as she said, 'But you have never said anything. You have never even kissed me properly.'

'You don't think I've never wanted to? Jesus! You have no idea how hard it's been for me not to take you into my arms.'

Kitty was filled with happiness. And looking up into his eyes she said, 'Please don't wait any longer.'

Jeff gathered her to him in a close embrace and kissed her slowly and longingly. When he released her he caressed her face and said, 'You are beautiful, Kitty darling, and I think I'm in love with you.' And he kissed her again.

Chapter Eleven

When they arrived home, Jeff said, 'I'll be in touch. You need to decide if we should continue to see one another, because if we do, we are both looking for trouble. You know that, don't you?'

She nodded, too confused and happy to answer.

He didn't touch her other than to squeeze her hand before walking away.

Kitty went into the kitchen, filled the kettle and lit the gas beneath it. Now what was she to do? She knew she loved Jeff, more than she could have ever imagined. To be in his arms today and to feel his mouth on hers had been heaven. And he felt the same! That in itself was wonderful. This lovely man, who was so well bred, so very intelligent, such good company . . . was in love with her. She found it hard to believe. She danced around the kitchen and into the living room, until she stopped in front of the mantelpiece and looked at the framed photograph of her husband, dressed in uniform. She suddenly came down to earth.

Picking up the picture she sat in a chair and studied it. Brian was wearing his superior expression, which she knew so well. He used to look like that frequently before he went into the army, usually when he was giving orders about the starch in his shirt or what he'd like for supper if she could manage to find it in the shops. Yes, he looked – condescending – that was the word. And pompous . . . like his mother. Folk always tell a prospective bridegroom: look at the mother; that will be your wife, down the line – but who warns the bride? And what would happen when the war was over and Brian came home? Would he go back to his old ways? He was so pleased with his life in the army, but when that was over he would miss it – would that make him more self-important and more demanding . . . ? And she wondered if she could bear it!

Making a pot of tea and pouring herself a cup, she continued to ponder her problem. It wasn't only Brian who was different since he'd joined the army: so was she. She had blossomed, thanks to Jeff. But he could be sent overseas at any time and she would never see him again. ''Tis better to have loved and lost, than never to have loved at all.' She remembered the quote from somewhere – but was it true? Ignorance is bliss, it was also said. To honour and obey – *she* had said. She went to bed, her head spinning.

She had continued to see Jeff and their love had grown, and now he was going to spend Christmas with her at her parents' home. She had approached her mother first.

Amy had stared at her daughter and asked, 'Kitty, do you know what you are doing?'

'I love him, Mum,' she said. 'I can't help myself. I long for every minute to pass until we're together again.'

'What about Brian? How can you be a wife to him and love another?'

Wringing her hands Kitty said, 'I know, and when Brian is at home I am filled with guilt. When he takes me in his arms, I don't want him to touch me.'

'Dear God! Whatever do you do?'

'I pray for it to be over.'

Holding Kitty close, her mother said, 'This can't go on, you know that. You have to make a decision.' She paused. 'Have you slept with Jeff?'

'No I haven't! I'm not that bad . . . but to be honest, if he'd suggested it, I would have.'

'Oh, Kitty, Kitty. Whatever will become of you? If Brian finds out I can't begin to think of the consequences.'

'Let me have this Christmas, Mum, and then I'll make a decision.'

'I'll have a word with your father. I don't know what he'll say! I'll let you know.'

Now it was Christmas Eve and Kitty was huddled inside the Jeep that Jeff had borrowed. It had been a dry but cold day and outside, as they spoke, their breath misted on the air. But neither of them minded the cold as they drove, the back of the vehicle packed with Christmas parcels and their suitcases.

'I can't tell you how much I'm looking forward to this Christmas. I really miss my folks at such times – I guess we all do – so to be with you and yours is wonderful.'

As he glanced at her, her heart swelled with happiness. 'Mum will be in the kitchen cooking mince pies, I expect, and preparing the vegetables. She was thrilled when you said you would get a turkey. They are like gold dust this year.' She knew also that there was a large carton in the back of the Jeep packed with goods that they were unable to buy during these difficult times, but Jeff wouldn't tell her what they were.

'It's a surprise,' he said; 'my contribution for your parents' kind hospitality.'

She sat back looking at the passing scene, content to be with the man she loved. She looked over at him and he gave her one of his heart-stopping smiles. She leaned across and kissed his cheek.

'Hey, steady, young lady, we don't want to have an accident,' he chided with a grin. 'At least wait until I can enjoy it.'

When they eventually arrived, Jim came to meet them, smiling all over his face. He shook Jeff by the hand. 'Merry Christmas,' he said. 'What can I carry?'

Between the three of them they toted everything into the kitchen, where the aroma of cooking filled the air. 'This reminds me of my mom's kitchen,' said Jeff as he searched for a place to unload his carton.

'Put it over there,' said Amy.

Kitty staggered in with a huge parcel and a small suitcase. 'This is the turkey, Mum. Can you take it before I drop it, please?'

Her mother took the bird and unwrapped it. 'Good gracious!' she exclaimed. 'This will feed an army.'

Jeff laughed. 'That was the general idea, but the camp cook was very obliging. We had a shipment in time for Christmas, so the troops certainly won't go short without this bird, I can assure you.' He undid the carton. Inside were tins of fruit, big red apples – 'From Canada,' he said – sugar, tea, coffee, two tins of ham and a dozen fresh eggs. He then handed Jim a bottle of bourbon. 'I thought you might enjoy this, sir.'

Looking at the label, his host beamed. 'My word, yes. We'll enjoy it together.'

Amy looked at the pile of stuff in front of her and with twinkling eyes asked, 'Are you sure you're not Father Christmas in disguise?' They laughed at her obvious delight.

In the army camp at Catterick, the atmosphere was entirely different. Discipline still reigned, although on Christmas Eve there was a cessation of exercises, and in the evening there was to be entertainment put on by the troops themselves. Then at midnight a choir from one of the local music societies was coming to sing carols during the midnight mass, conducted by their own chaplain. But beneath every army uniform was a man whose thoughts were of home. So there was for some a subdued air about their jollity. Others decided to just get on with it and enjoy the moment when the officers and sergeants seemed a little more human and approachable.

At the appropriate time, the men gathered inside a Nissen hut, where a temporary stage had been built, and prepared to watch the pantomime called *Puss in Hobnail Boots*.

Brian settled into his seat and waited for the opening, but his mind was back in Southampton, thinking of Kitty. She would be at her mother's now. It was just as well she was with her own family. The Christmases spent with his were always filled with tension, his mother taking digs at Kitty whenever possible, despite he and his father trying to keep her in check. The one Christmas he had enjoyed had been when he and Kitty were engaged and had spent it with Amy and Jim, before Kitty left home. Never mind, he would make up for his absence when he next had his leave.

Christmas morning was cold and crisp. The Simmons household was up and about early. Amy had stuffed the bird and put it into the oven, and Jim was lighting a fire in the living room as Kitty came downstairs, dressed in her father's dressing gown, which she pulled round her to keep warm. Walking into the kitchen she heard unfamiliar sounds outside and, peering through the window, she could see Jeff sawing logs from some stout tree trunks. He was wearing dark brown trousers and a cream sweater. It seemed strange to see him out of uniform.

Her mother watched Kitty and said, 'He's a useful lad. He offered to do that for your father.'

'He looks so different,' said Kitty.

'Well, now you are seeing the man and not the uniform. Does it make any difference to how you feel?'

Kitty laughed and said, 'I didn't fall for the uniform, Mother!' And as Jeff came into the kitchen carrying logs she kissed him. 'So this is really what you look like.'

'You have no idea how much I longed to discard the army,' he replied, and carried his load into the other room.

'We've not had a Christmas card from Eddie,' Amy said wistfully. 'I hope he's all right. If only we knew where he was and that he was alive.'

Kitty's heart ached for her mother. How could she tell her that Eddie had deserted? It would break her heart. 'I'm sure he'll be keeping his head down, Mum. You know he never writes. If there was bad news, you'd have heard by now.'

'I'm sure you're right,' said Amy cheerfully. 'I'd better get on.'

In the living room, the men busied themselves with the fire and when they had finished their chores and the women had said they were no longer needed, they settled before the hearth and talked.

'I heard on the news today that Eisenhower is to be supreme commander of the Allied forces and Monty his field commander. There's going to be an invasion, isn't there?' Jim asked. 'Well, that's what everyone is saying.' He looked expectantly at his guest.

It was no longer a secret so Jeff wasn't breaking any rules when he answered, 'Yes, sir, I'm afraid there is, but no one knows when as yet. We have no choice if we are to beat the Hun, otherwise he will try to invade these shores.'

'I suppose you'll have to go then?'

'Yes, I will. The future is full of uncertainty for us all, but that's war, I guess.'

'After the bombing of Berlin last month, I would have thought the Germans would be ready to cave in,' said Jim, 'but that man Hitler is obsessed with power. Surely he can't expect to win?'

'I'm sure he doesn't doubt that he can. Such men never do. We will just have to make sure he doesn't.'

After the King's speech, they all sat down to enjoy the fruits of Amy's cooking. Kitty's father opened a bottle of wine and the time seemed to speed by. Jeff regaled them with tales of his childhood, of his sister and her family and about his hopes for the future. He wanted to open his own law firm in Boston. He described his life before the war, his days at university, his favourite baseball team, the Boston Braves, the pranks he and his friends got up to, and how most of them, like him, were scattered around the world, fighting against oppression.

'But one day, hopefully, we can all get back to leading a normal life,' he finished.

'We'll all drink to that,' said Jim, and filled their glasses.

After the meal, Jeff and Kitty helped to clear away and wash the dishes, ignoring Amy's pleas to leave it to her. 'No, ma'am, you have done so much,' insisted Jeff. 'It's the least I can do.' But after, he and Kitty put on their coats and went for a walk.

Arm in arm they found a small park near by and sat on a low wall. Jeff put his arm around her to keep her warm and said, 'That was such a great day, one I will always remember.' He tipped up Kitty's face and kissed her. 'When I was telling your folks about my hopes for the future, I didn't say that I wanted you to be a part of them, but I do.'

'Whatever do you mean?'

Looking earnestly into her eyes, he said, 'Darling, you're not happy with Brian but I believe you could be with me. I want you to divorce him and marry me.'

She was stunned. 'Divorce?'

'Yes. I love you, Kitty. I want us to spend the rest of our lives together. Is that what you want?'

'Of course it is, but divorce . . . ? It isn't something that you do lightly – well, certainly not in England.'

He started laughing. 'Well, it isn't the norm in my neck of the woods either, I'll have you know.'

'I didn't mean that, but here it is something that is very much frowned on.'

'Are you expected to stay with a man you don't love?'

'Yes, I suppose you are.'

'And is that what you want to do?' There was such a note of disappointment in his voice that she immediately cried, 'No, that's the last thing I want. I want to grow old with you.'

'You had me worried for a minute,' he said, with a look of relief.

'It just seems the wrong thing to spring this on Brian at this time, with talk of the invasion. I wouldn't like to send him a Dear John letter. That wouldn't be fair.'

'But is it fair to be at home waiting for him, knowing you love me?' Jeff asked softly.

'No, and I hate myself for it.'

'And I hate the thought of you sharing a bed with him. Of him making love to you when you love me and I want to be the one to hold you in my arms, to love you. It drives me crazy when he is home on leave . . . and I know I don't have the right to be this way. The man is your husband – and I feel a heel!'

'We couldn't help falling in love! We were not looking for someone else, it just happened . . . it wasn't anyone's fault.' She caressed his cheek. 'I for one am not sorry. I've never been so happy in my entire life.'

Kissing her gently Jeff said, 'Neither have I, and I'm not going to lose you.' Gazing into her eyes he asked, 'Will you mind living in Boston, away from your family?'

'What?'

'If you marry me, darling, we'll have to live in the States. That's where I earn my living.'

This took Kitty totally by surprise. Everything seemed to be happening at once. And of course Jeff would have to stay in his country to carry on with his law practice; he certainly wouldn't be familiar with the laws of this country. But to leave England – her family? America – Boston – it was thousands of miles away.

'I don't know,' she said. 'It is all so much to think about.'

He held her close and said, 'I'm sorry, I'm rushing my fences. It's all been too much too soon, but I love you, Kitty.'

'And I you, but we have to wait. If there is to be an invasion, I can't tell Brian, can I? It wouldn't be fair to send him into a field of battle, knowing I was leaving him. That would be cruel.' She looked at him, pleading with him to understand.

'When I'm sent over there, I need to know that eventually we'll be together,' he said.

She couldn't even bear the thought that he too would be in danger. What if he was killed? To lose this man would be terrible. She clung to him. 'Please don't talk like that.'

'We have to face facts,' he said. 'And before I go, I'll open a bank account for you, in case I don't return. Then you will have enough money to get out of this marriage and be independent, able to lead your own life the way you want to.'

'Stop it!' she cried, and got to her feet. 'If I lost you I wouldn't want to live.' She ran off, tears streaming down her face.

Jeff ran after her, took her in his arms and held her tightly until her sobs subsided. 'I'm such a fool!' he said. 'I've ruined your Christmas – how stupid of me. I am *so* sorry, please forgive me.'

Flinging her arms around him, she smothered him with kisses. 'You are here, my Christmas is perfect, but no more talk of war, I beg you.'

They walked slowly back to the house hand in hand, and for the rest of the holiday they didn't speak of the future again, but just enjoyed their time together.

Chapter Twelve

Christmas for Eddie, Kitty's brother, was the worst he'd ever known. Before he joined the army, he and his mates would go down to the pub on Christmas morning and have a skinful of beer, go home to his mother's cooking, then sleep it all off in the afternoon. In the army there had been friends of sorts who would at least have a few jokes and a beer in the mess, but in hiding he had no one.

Nancy had been hanging around Gerry's neck all the time, clinging to him like bloody ivy. It made him sick! Especially when she flaunted her new and expensive watch, a present from Gerry, under Eddie's nose.

'When are we going to get together again?' Eddie demanded when she came to the builder's merchant's yard one day just after Christmas. Gerry was out at the time.

'When you can afford to give me this sort of thing,' she taunted.

'You said, when he came back we'd find some time together,' he reminded her.

She laughed in his face. 'I did, didn't I? Well, who knows, I may be able to fit you in somewhere soon.'

He was enraged. He grabbed her arm and pulled her close to him. 'Don't think you can treat me like a piece of dirt and get away with it, you bitch!'

'You listen to me, Eddie whatever your name is; I can do what I bloody well like. What are you going to do – complain to Gerry about me?'

'You'll be sorry you treated me this way, I can promise you that!' He thrust her away from him.

Nancy fell back against the wall and grazed her arm. 'Don't you threaten me, you bastard. I only have to tell Gerry how you forced yourself on me when he was away and you are in real trouble.'

'Forced myself? That's a laugh. You couldn't wait to open your legs, as I well remember.'

'But he doesn't know that,' she smirked. 'You were all right as a stopgap. If it hadn't been you, it would have been someone else. You were handy, that's all, panting like a dog every time you saw me.'

Eddie clenched his fist, but Nancy saw this and said, 'Now that would be really stupid. You lay a hand on me and Gerry will kill you.'

He watched her walk away, his eyes glued to the swing of her shapely hips, and cursed. He'd pay her back some time in the near future. Little tramp! Who did she think she was to talk down to him like that! The sooner he could gather enough money together to make his way up to the Smoke, the better.

On the other hand, Gerry Stubbs had enjoyed the festive holiday. His stash of money was well hidden in several places. He wasn't stupid enough to put all his eggs in one basket. He'd treated Nancy to a decent watch, bought a couple of suits on the black market, but apart from that, he'd been careful. Nancy and he had gone to the Polygon Hotel for their Christmas lunch and then they had gone to the room he'd booked, where they drank champagne and spent the rest of the day in bed. Pleased with her present, she'd been more than a willing partner between the sheets.

Gerry had wondered how Kitty had spent her time, and assumed her husband was home on leave. He'd thought of taking a few things round to her to help out with the rationing, but had decided against it. After their last meeting, he thought it wiser to wait a bit longer before he called. He hoped the flowers and apology sent with them would have helped her to think a little more kindly towards him after his drunken behaviour, but he still desired her. He could wait; he was a patient man.

But Lieutenant Jeff Ryder was the man to win over the lovely Kitty. Their love and need for each other eventually overcame the rules of society. When Jeff had a two-day pass, they planned to spend this time in a hotel in the New Forest.

When Jeff had approached her about them spending these precious days together, Kitty hadn't hesitated. Working part time at the factory had enabled her to take the time off without causing any problems or explanations.

'Are you sure you want to do this, darling?' he asked.

'I can't think of anything I'd like more,' she said, winding her arms around his neck and kissing him passionately.

'I can't wait to make love to you,' he whispered as he nuzzled her neck. 'I can't believe it is going to happen after so long. It has been hell for me just to hold you when I have longed for so much more.'

It was 3 January, and the hotel was still festooned with decorations from Christmas and New Year's Eve. 'These will all have to be taken down by Twelfth Night,' she told him. At his puzzled look she said, 'It's an old English custom. To leave them any later brings bad luck.'

'That's what I love about this country,' he said, 'its quaint ways.' He signed the register and, picking up their cases, said, 'Come along, Mrs Ryder.'

Kitty felt her cheeks flush.

Jeff laughed at her. 'This is your honeymoon, my darling.'

As she followed him to the lift, she felt just like a bride. She was nervous, excited, and desperately in love.

They didn't wait to unpack. Jeff had arranged for champagne in an ice bucket to be served in their room. He took Kitty's coat and then opened the bottle, and poured two drinks. Handing her a glass he said, 'To two wonderful days.'

'I'll definitely drink to that,' she said.

They gazed out of their bedroom window, which overlooked the forest. Many of the trees were devoid of leaves, and there was a stark beauty about the scene, with the gorse bushes and conifers in the distance and the ever-present New Forest ponies.

'It looks very cold out there,' said Kitty.

Taking her glass from her, Jeff held her tightly and said, 'Then let's stay here in the warm. We can have lunch sent up to the room, if you like.'

'That sounds very tempting.'

'You are tempting, my darling.' He kissed her slowly and deliberately, moving his mouth sensuously over hers, unbuttoning her frock as he did so, letting it fall to the floor. Caressing her smooth shoulders, he said, 'God! You're beautiful.'

They moved to the bed and undressed. Without his clothes, Kitty could see that Jeff had the build of an athlete, with broad shoulders and tapered hips. There was not one bit of spare flesh on his body.

As he held her in his arms, she was thrilled by the closeness of him, the warmth from his bare skin against hers. Their bodies entwined, and as they made love, neither was constrained by shyness, but liberated by love for the other.

With his expertise, Jeff brought Kitty to the height of her passion with gentle caresses, exploring her body, as he told her how much he loved her. It was as if she'd never been made love to before. There was tenderness in his touch, passion in his kisses and she was taken on a journey of complete sexual satisfaction.

After, she lay back against the sheets, wonderfully weary and relaxed.

'Oh, Jeff,' she murmured, 'that was so good.'

He kissed her gently. 'I can't spend the rest of my life without you, Kitty, I really can't.' They curled into one another until they fell into a deep sleep.

Later, they had lunch served in their room on a table in front of the window, where they could watch the beautiful rural scene before them, delighting in the antics of the ponies and a few visitors who were brave enough to face the cold, in order to enjoy this pleasure at close quarters. It was such an interesting picture that, after eating, they decided to don their coats and venture forth themselves for a walk, returning to the hotel some time later, to take tea in the cosy and comfortable lounge.

That evening they dined, and to the music of Glenn Miller records they danced on the tiny dance floor. But it mattered not that there was hardly room to move, as they were content to hold one another close and sway to the music until, after a nightcap, they returned to their room and made love once more.

The following day, after eating breakfast in the dining room, they walked around the shops in Lyndhurst. Jeff took Kitty into a little jeweller's and bought her a gold chain with a small pendant, made with a beautiful amethyst, delicately surrounded by scrolls of gold.

'I can't give you a ring, darling,' he said, 'but you can wear this as a token of my love and our hopes for the future.' He put it round her neck whilst they were still in the shop.

The assistant smiled at her delight and said, 'It suits you, madam.'

'I'll always wear it,' she said.

'What if Brian asks about it?' Jeff asked, as they walked back to the hotel.

'I'll tell him my parents gave it to me for Christmas,' she said, vowing she would never take it off.

Brian was due home on leave and Kitty was dreading it. How could she pretend, after the wonderful weekend with Jeff? The thought of performing her wifely duty in the bedroom filled her with horror. But what choice did she have? The imminent invasion was on everyone's lips, and she couldn't tell Brian she was in love with someone else, not now, when at any moment he could be sent over to France. Should she do so and he was killed, heaven forbid, she would have it on her conscience for evermore.

The front door opened and her husband walked in, a smile on his lips. Throwing down his kitbag, he pulled her into his arms and said, 'Come here, Kitty love, I've really missed you.' His mouth crushed hers in his eagerness.

She wanted desperately to push him away.

Brian released her and asked, 'What's wrong, aren't you well?'

'I'm fine, why do you ask?'

'It's been so long since I saw you and that welcome was tepid, to say the least!'

'I'm sorry,' she said quickly. 'I'm just a bit tired, that's all.'

'Perhaps we should go to bed, then,' he said softly. 'Then after, you can sleep.'

'Good heavens, Brian! You've only just come through the front door – can't we at least sit down and have a cup of tea and a chat? I'm your wife, not some whore!'

'It was my wife I was inviting to share my bed,' he snapped. 'What's got into you, woman? I'd have thought you would have been pleased to see me.'

'I am pleased to see you,' she said, trying to keep the panic from her voice. 'Just don't treat me like some sexual object, that's all.'

'Well, this is some welcome home, I must say.'

Trying to make amends, she said, 'I'm sorry, but you must realise that when you've been away, it takes me time to get used to you again. I just feel a bit shy, that's all.'

His anger evaporated 'I'm sorry, Kitty, I didn't understand. You women do have strange ways and I'll never understand them in a million years. Put the kettle on and I'll unpack your Christmas present and you can tell me what you've been doing.'

She breathed a sigh of relief. 'I spent Christmas with Mum and Dad, as you know. It was a lovely break. It was very quiet, but very enjoyable. How about you?'

'Christmas in the army wasn't as good as being home, of

course, but they put on a concert for us, and we didn't have to go out on exercises. It was all right, I suppose. I missed you, Kitty.'

She was filled with guilt.

He handed her a small package. 'Merry late Christmas, darling.'

Inside was a silver bangle. 'It's lovely,' she said, and kissed him. Going to a cupboard she took out a long box and gave it to him.

Brian opened it and saw it held a new watch. 'This is just what I need,' he said, delighted with his gift. 'I broke the strap on mine only yesterday.' He pulled her on to his knee and kissed her. 'It is so good to be home,' he said as he cuddled her. As he did so he noticed the pendant that Jeff had given her. 'That's nice,' he said. 'Where did it come from?'

'Mum and Dad gave it to me.'

'I like it. It suits you.'

She could have cried. Here was the man she married, happy to be home, admiring her lover's gift, pleased to see his wife – who could hardly bear him to touch her. She felt like a traitor.

Later that night as, in the marital bed, he took her in his arms, she gritted her teeth and pretended, until his clumsy lovemaking was over, and as he slept beside her, she looked at his tousled hair and wondered what he would say if and when she told him the truth. Did she have the right to destroy their marriage? Probably not. But didn't she have the right to a happy life with the man she loved?

It was the longest week in Kitty's life. She was grateful for the times when she was able to escape and go to the factory, and, of course, she was unable to see Jeff at all. She was utterly miserable. Jean noticed that something was amiss, and when they finished their shift she invited her to pop into her house – which was on the way to Kitty's – for a cup of tea.

Kitty jumped at the chance. Anything to delay her return to her home and husband. She sat at the kitchen table, making small talk until Jean poured the tea and sat beside her.

'All right, Kitty. What's the matter?'

103

She was taken completely by surprise. 'Whatever do you mean?'

'Something is wrong. You look utterly miserable, and sometimes it's good to get it off your chest. You know anything you tell me will stay between these four walls.'

Kitty burst into tears. The tension of the last few days was all too much and the kindness of her friend was her undoing. She poured out her sad story.

'Was Jeff the American I saw you with that time?' she asked.

'Yes, and I am in love with him. He wants me to get a divorce and marry him.'

'Bloody hell! What are you going to do?'

'I want to spend the rest of my life with him, even if it means going to the States.'

'But divorce!' exclaimed Jean. 'That's a really big step.'

'I know, but I can't do this to Brian, not yet. It wouldn't be fair.'

'But are you being fair to him now?'

'What he doesn't know won't hurt him,' said Kitty desperately.

'I have to say this, although it might hurt,' said Jean, 'but Jeff could be sent to France and be killed – then what? You'd be left without anyone.'

'I know. He wants to open a bank account for me just in case that happens, so I can be free if I want.'

Jean was speechless for a moment. 'He must really love you to do that.' She hesitated and then asked, 'You are being careful, I hope? You don't want to get pregnant with one man and be married to another.'

'Jeff is careful; he is aware of the difficulty.'

'And Brian?'

Kitty shook her head. 'He never has taken any precautions, but nothing has happened ever since we've been married.'

'Christ! You're taking a chance, aren't you?'

'I know, but what on earth can I do? I use a douche without him knowing, but it is a bit haphazard, I realise that.'

'You really have a problem, girl.'

'I know.'

'You could ask Brian to wear something, saying you don't want a child while the war is on,' suggested her friend.

'Yes, I could. Perhaps I'll broach the subject when he comes home again.' She rose from the table and said, 'Thanks, Jean. It was good to be able to talk to you.'

'You take care,' she said as she showed Kitty to the door, 'and for goodness' sake, be careful.'

The last evening of Brian's leave was a nightmare as Kitty was forced to spend it in the local pub with his parents. When she asked couldn't they do something else, Brian grew angry.

'Mum says you never go and see her these days and that she didn't see you even at Christmas,' he accused.

'How could I visit her over Christmas when I was away? I did slip round one afternoon with a present each for them.'

'Yes, when she was out.'

It was true. Kitty had chosen her time well. She knew that Gladys went shopping on a Friday and that was when she'd visited, knowing Frank would be by himself. She'd stayed on a short while, chatting to him, before making her escape.

'Well, we are meeting them for a drink,' said Brian. 'As I go back to camp in the morning, it is the last opportunity I'll get – and try to be nice to Mother.'

'I'll do my best,' Kitty said drily, 'but I don't make any guarantees!'

'I don't know why you two can't get on.'

'Because your mother is interfering and domineering,' she replied, 'and don't tell me she isn't because you know damn well she is!'

He didn't answer.

Kitty thought the evening would never end. It wasn't long before Gladys began.

'You all right, Kitty? You look a bit peaky. Not pregnant, are you?'

'No I'm not, and I'm fine, thank you.' She ignored the hard stare that Brian cast in her direction.

'It's about time you had a family anyway,' Gladys declared.

'Well, I'm doing the best I can,' said Brian smugly.

'Do you both mind!' Kitty was furious. Turning to her mother-in-law she said, 'When I want a family it will be because *I* want one not because *you* think I should.'

Gladys sniffed her disapproval. 'I don't want to interfere, of course,' she said.

'That'll be a first!' snapped Kitty.

'Brian! Are you going to let your wife talk to your mother like that?'

Before he could answer, Kitty stood up. 'I'm going home.' Looking at Brian she said, 'You stay with your mother; after all it is your last night. She'll prefer to have you to herself.' And she walked out of the bar.

She was so angry that she walked very quickly, cursing quietly to herself. 'Bloody woman,' she muttered. 'At least when I marry Jeff I won't have to put up with her.' It was almost worth getting a divorce for, she thought, and then laughed, wondering if an interfering mother-in-law was grounds for so doing. Some divorce court judge might think it was. Oh, if only it were true.

Chapter Thirteen

Whilst Kitty was battling with her personal problems, men of importance and esteem were dealing with problems of gigantic proportions – how to win the war against the common enemy, Germany.

Plans were well under way for the invasion of France, code-named Overlord. False rumours and disinformation were being spread, in the hope of fooling the enemy into thinking the invasion would take place at Pas de Calais, the shortest crossing from the English coast, instead of the beaches of Normandy, the planned landing place, which intelligence reports stated were less well defended than the area around Calais.

Technical planning for D-Day had started early in January 1944. The beaches were secretly surveyed, allowing the Allies to find whether the beaches were sand or shingle – vital information to allow the right vehicles and tanks to land with the least trouble. An artificial harbour had to be built as there was no natural one for the troops to make use of. An underwater pipeline would have to be laid to carry fuel. All of which had to be done before any consideration could be made for the actual landings.

Brian was posted further north with his company, to start building the Mulberry harbours, as they were known. At last he felt that he was doing something worthwhile, pushing to the back of his mind that soon he and his company would be going to war. It meant that there was little leave and what there was, was sometimes too short a time for him to make a trip home. And when he did manage, he felt that Kitty was feeling the strain. She appeared to be distant most of the time, and he put this down to his prolonged absence and the threat of his being sent to France. Everyone was suffering in some way or other. She'd even asked him to take precautions when they made love, saying she didn't want to get pregnant whilst the war was going on – it was too much of a worry, especially with him being away. To placate her he had agreed, although he didn't enjoy the sex as much.

He wrote to her once a week, but his letters were short as he was not good at putting words on paper. Kitty's letters too were fairly short. She wrote: 'There isn't much to tell you. I go to work, sometimes to see a film with one of the girls, clean the house and I occasionally go to Bournemouth for a change, to shop. You wouldn't believe how difficult it is travelling by train these days! The train schedules are changed and then when the trains come, they are so full of troops it is difficult to get a seat.'

She obviously didn't tell him about her affair with the American officer!

Jeff was kept pretty busy at these times, of course, as Britain was becoming one huge army camp with large-scale military exercises taking place in different parts of southern England. He was organising troop movements, sending supplies to various camps, knowing also that his time with Kitty was getting shorter and shorter with every passing day. But he saw her as often as his time permitted. He would take her some stores from the PX to help eke out her rations. Sometimes he would give her nylon stockings, which were always received with great delight.

'I have to get mine repaired when they ladder,' she told him. 'And in the better weather we girls paint our legs with cold tea and draw a line with a brown pencil down the back for a seam.'

'I've never noticed that!' he said.

'Ah well, when I go out with you, I wear my best stockings, that's why,' she laughed.

'When we are married, I'll buy you a dozen pairs at a time.'

Although she wanted to, Kitty could never quite allow herself to think in these terms. There were too many problems ahead of them before they could even begin to consider such a step.

Whenever possible, they would spend the night together at the hotel in the New Forest where the staff now greeted them as regular visitors. During dinner one night the waitress crossed to the table.

'Everything all right for you, Mrs Ryder?'

Kitty assured her that it was and when the woman had walked away, she said to Jeff, 'The staff must know we're not married.'

'Probably,' he said, 'but it's wartime, Kitty. Things are different.'

She would cling to him when they were in bed, feeling she had to make the most of every moment, dreading the time when they would be parted. Jeff would try to soothe her troubled soul. 'One day, sometime in the future, we'll be together all the time, darling. I'll sell my apartment and buy a nice house and you can choose the furnishings. You'll get sick of the sight of me,' he joked.

'Never!' she cried, kissing him with a certain desperation.

Gerry Stubbs was living the life of Riley. There were so many shortages that he could charge what he liked for his ill-gotten goods. With the masses of troops around, the NAAFI was having to be restocked on a regular basis and he and his band of villains had a field day, stealing stores en route, holding up the lorries and their drivers, clearing the contents, leaving them empty, raiding stores – hiding their loot all over the place to fool the police who, so far, hadn't been able to catch them. Kitty's brother, Eddie, had come on some of these raids and had proved to be helpful, which pleased Gerry, as he didn't like the man. He was always hanging around whenever Nancy came to see him and he suspected that they might have had something going between them at some time, but he had no proof – so let sleeping dogs lie, he thought, at least for the time being.

Eddie was pleased with himself as he was making good money from the raids. He put some by for the time that he lit out for the big city. He was fed up with Southampton, and Nancy

Brannigan. Gerry was making so much money that she never seemed to leave his side these days, paying Eddie no heed at all. Indeed, she made a point of ignoring him!

He paid her back in full one evening when she called just as the builder's merchant's was being locked up and Gerry wasn't around. Eddie saw her going into the office and ran over quickly, letting himself in just as she turned to leave, pushing her back inside, closing the door behind him. With the blackout curtains up, he knew that no one from the warehouse could see them. He pushed her up against the wall and held her there.

'Let me go, you bastard. Gerry will be here in a minute and he'll bloody kill you if he finds you!'

He laughed at her and said, 'He's away.' He saw the sudden fear in her eyes. 'I have you all to myself, now isn't that nice?'

She struggled but was helpless against his powerful build. 'Let me go!' she cried.

'When I've finished with you,' he said, pulling up her skirt and tearing at her underwear. He pressed his mouth against hers hard and she bit his lip. 'You bitch!' he said, as he tasted the blood. Thus enraged he undid his flies and, lifting her off the floor, put her legs around him and thrust his manhood into her again and again, holding her hands behind her back until with one final thrust, he came.

She cried out in pain. 'I'll get you for this, you bastard, see if I don't!'

He let go of her and she slumped to the floor in tears.

Hauling her to her feet, he opened the door. 'Get out!' He spat the words at her and pushed her down the steps, locking the door behind him after dousing the lights. He pushed her through the gates on to the pavement. 'That'll teach you to treat me like dirt.'

'You are dirt!' she screamed at him, trying to straighten her clothes. 'I've stepped in better things than you.'

He laughed at her. 'You loved it really.'

Nancy Brannigan was from Irish stock and not without spirit. 'You think you're some great lover, don't you? Well, let me tell you, you're the worst fuck I've ever had and I've had a few. You, you're useless in bed!'

She couldn't have insulted him more. With an angry cry, he clenched his fist and punched her, knocking her off her feet. She curled up in a ball and covered her head to try to protect herself from the rain of blows that followed.

When eventually Eddie stopped battering her, he looked at the figure on the ground and saw the blood. He kneeled down and quickly called, 'Nancy?' There was no answer. He lifted her head and saw she was unconscious. Getting to his feet he panicked. Looking around and seeing the road was empty, he took to his heels and ran.

The following morning, as the other two men left the house, he feigned illness, wondering what to do. Perhaps this was the time to leave Southampton because if Nancy told Gerry he was the one who had raped and attacked her, he would be in serious trouble. Whilst he was contemplating his next move, one of Gerry's men returned to pick up some tools he'd forgotten. As he was gathering them together he said, 'Nancy Brannigan was attacked last night. She's in hospital.'

'Is she all right?' asked Eddie fearfully.

The other man shrugged. 'She hasn't regained consciousness,' he said. 'They say she may be in a coma.'

'Good God,' muttered Eddie, 'how dreadful.' Thinking rapidly, he decided he was safe for a while. 'I'm feeling a bit better,' he said. 'I'll think I'll come back with you.'

Gerry Stubbs was an angry man. Nancy was a girl without morals, but she had charm and he'd grown used to her ways. 'If I ever find the person who did this,' he said to Eddie, 'he's a dead man!'

Eddie felt a chill run down his back. If Nancy regained consciousness, she would be able to tell Gerry that he was the guilty party, but it didn't seem likely at the moment. He needed to be on the spot. If she was to recover enough to talk, he needed to know; then he could quickly disappear. He cursed his temper and

Nancy for goading him like she did. He hadn't meant to hurt her; he'd just lost his rag. What if she died? But if she did so without regaining consciousness, he'd be safe, as there had been no one around at the time. She wasn't worth swinging for and he vowed not to become involved with one woman again. He'd pay for sex – it was safer.

Nancy remained in a coma for the next seven days. Eddie was so on edge that he decided to go to see the state of her for himself. Buying some flowers, he headed for the South Hants Hospital.

The sister on the intensive care ward told him, 'There is little change.'

He was shocked when he saw her. Tubes and machines surrounded her. Her bruised face was half covered by an oxygen mask. My God! What had he done? He placed the flowers on the locker and left, his hands trembling as, outside, he lit a cigarette. Before, he'd been trying to plan for all eventualities, but actually faced by his victim, the seriousness of his situation hit him. Whichever way you looked at it, if discovered, he could be facing imprisonment or, if she died – the rope! He felt sick in the pit of his stomach.

Nancy Brannigan was the topic of conversation in the canteen where Kitty worked.

'Poor cow,' said Jean. 'Whatever she is, she didn't deserve that.'

'Do the police have any leads at all?' asked Kitty, filled with dread, knowing that Eddie had been keeping company with the unfortunate girl.

'Apparently not, but Gerry Stubbs is also looking for the culprit, so whoever did this will pay dearly one way or another if he finds him. She was found just outside the gates of his builder's yard, but he was away at the time. Just as well as, who knows, he may have been a suspect.'

'Gerry? Surely he wouldn't be capable of such brutality?'

'Well, she was his bird, even though she got around. I can tell you I wouldn't like to upset him!' Jean exclaimed. 'He may have charm, but there is a very cruel streak in that man.'

Kitty paled at the thought. He had promised he would have his way with her, eventually. If she found herself in such a situation again, would he use brute force when she refused him? But even worse was the notion that her brother may have been involved with Nancy Brannigan's attack. He had been going out with her and she knew well that he had a temper. Hadn't it caused him enough trouble, even when he was growing up? But she couldn't bring herself to believe that he would have done such a foul deed – not her brother.

It was a further week before Nancy came round, but she was so poorly, she was unable to speak. Unaware of her slight recovery, Eddie decided to pay her another visit. When he got there it was to see Gerry Stubbs sitting beside the bed. Eddie turned about to make his escape when Gerry saw him. He beckoned him over.

'What are you doing here?' he demanded.

'Just thought I'd bring some flowers,' he said. 'How is she?'

'She regained consciousness last night.'

Eddie felt his senses reel and for a moment he felt dizzy with shock and grabbed hold of the back of Gerry's chair to steady himself. 'Did she say anything?'

Shaking his head Gerry said, 'No. The doctors say it's too early to tell, but she may have sustained some brain damage.'

'How would that affect her?'

'Who knows? She may never be able to talk. We have to wait and see.'

At that moment, Nancy's eyes flickered open.

'Hello, Nancy, love, it's Gerry,' he said quietly 'Squeeze my hand if you understand.' He felt a slight pressure and was elated. 'She did it! She squeezed my hand.' He looked at Nancy but her eyes were now closed. 'I'll go and find a doctor. Stay with her, will you?' and without waiting for an answer he rushed off.

Eddie stood beside the bed, his heart racing. He leaned over the patient and said, 'I don't know if you can hear me, Nancy. It's Eddie. I'm really sorry for what I did.' He hoped this might appease her, thus serving his own interests.

Nancy opened her eyes . . . and as Eddie gazed at her he could see the hatred in the look she gave him. He stepped back with shock just as the doctor came back with Gerry. As soon as they were occupied with the patient, he made a hasty retreat.

Chapter Fourteen

It was now the month of May and troops were still pouring into Southampton. All around the county of Hampshire, marshalling camps were being set up. Along the dock roads it was difficult to move for armoured vehicles, tanks and troops. There was a large assembly of landing craft in the Eastern Docks. Rhino float units and pier heads were being prepared to tow the Mulberry harbours across the Channel.

Jeff knew that it would soon be time for he and his company to move out. Kitty was devastated when he told her, trying to prepare her for the inevitable.

Holding her close he said, 'Now come on, honey, it will all be over soon. The Allies are winning. It can't be long before the Germans have to concede that they are beaten.'

Tears brimmed her eyes. 'I know, but you still have to go and fight. I don't know what I'd do if anything happened to you.'

He tilted her chin. 'Now listen, Kitty. I need you to be brave. I need to know my girl is keeping that stiff upper lip the British are renowned for. I *will* come home. I *will* marry you. We *will* have a life together. You have got to believe me.'

She gazed into his eyes and saw the determination gleaming in them. Taking a deep breath she said, 'Yes, I do believe you.'

'I'll write to you as often as I can,' he promised, 'and you must write too. When men are away from home, they look forward to mail.'

Trying to put on a brave face she summoned a smile. 'I'll tell you all the gossip. Mind you, when you lot leave, there won't be any!'

He grinned and said, 'Now that's a bit unkind.'

'Surely you've seen the curtains lift from my neighbour's windows when you've called here?'

He looked surprised. 'As a matter of fact I've never noticed. But at least I've only called in the daytime. Does that make a difference?'

'The fact that you've not stayed the night here won't make a bit of difference,' she told him. She didn't tell him about the looks of hostility and disgust she'd seen on the faces on some of her close neighbours. She didn't care! She loved this man deeply and she knew she was breaking her marriage vows, but she was also aware that when Brian came home, all the neighbours talked about her behind her back. And she knew that eventually she would have to tell him that she wanted a divorce. She had decided to take this gigantic step, but the timing had to be right. She hated her own duplicity in this, but she was mindful that she did owe him some loyalty at the time when he needed it most. No way would she send him off to the war with any more worries than were necessary. At least she could do that much for him.

There were no such noble thoughts in the mind of her brother. Nancy Brannigan was still very ill and unable to speak, and Eddie was a bundle of nerves. He could have taken off to London but then he would have worried himself to death, wondering if she had recovered enough to name him. This way he was on top of things. It was a bit chancy, he knew that, but he felt it was the only way he could handle the situation, and Nancy wasn't yet out of the woods; she was still on the danger list. With a bit of luck she would croak, which, he'd decided, would be safer for him, despite then being guilty of murder. Then he could take off, change his name, start afresh. He was learning how to wheel and deal, he could keep his head above water and, if he wanted to, he could get a job. It was only that bitch that was a spanner in the works.

116

Gerry Stubbs was having to watch his step at this time. The police were clamping down on crime in a big way. The police commissioner was adamant that he would put an end to all the racketeers on his patch. He told a parade of the force, 'All these men passing through our town are ready to give their lives for their country, whilst this rotten core are making money on the back of the war. It is obscene and I'm going to put a stop to it.'

Consequently, Gerry was having to move his stuff around pretty frequently. He had a few police in his pocket, who tipped him off when a certain area was to be searched, which had saved his bacon up to now. But he was edgy these days.

'You'd think they'd allow a man to make a living!' he exclaimed. And of course he was still trying to find out who had attacked Nancy. 'The bloody police are useless,' he complained.

'It must be difficult for them if no one saw anything,' Eddie ventured.

'Surely she must have screamed? Someone must have heard her.'

Eddie knew she hadn't made a noise as his first blow had knocked her down and dazed her, but he wasn't saying any more.

'You were around at the time – didn't you hear anything?'

'No,' said Eddie calmly. 'It happened outside, apparently, according to the police. I was probably in the warehouse. I don't remember.'

'I can't believe that nobody knows anything,' grumbled Gerry, and he got up and walked away, to Eddie's great relief. He had to watch his step when Gerry talked about Nancy. It was too easy to say the wrong thing, let something slip.

Stubbs made his way to his office and sat contemplating, wondering who on earth could have attacked Nancy in such a violent way. And why was she just outside his gates? Was she coming to see him? He hadn't told her he would be away that day. If she was calling to see him, and he surmised that was her reason for being on his doorstep, had she been inside and found him

117

missing? He'd questioned his men but none had seen her, or had she been attacked as she was about to enter his establishment? According to the hospital reports, she'd been raped. Her money was still in her handbag, which was surprising, so maybe the man had been disturbed – yet no one came forward as a witness. Knowing that Nancy Brannigan was well able to take care of herself, he'd been surprised that she had been a victim at all. He'd seen her temper in a local pub when a drunken seaman had approached her and been sent off with a flea in his ear and a well-aimed punch to the chin that a fireman would have been proud of.

He shook his head in despair and picked up a load of invoices that needed his attention.

Brian Freeman was coming home on leave. Some of the Mulberry harbours were being shipped down to Southampton and he was coming with them. He was really looking forward to being home again. He too was aware that all the troops would be leaving to go to France in the near future and he wanted to make sure that Kitty would be all right. Knowing from her letters which shift she was working, he wasn't surprised to find the house empty on his arrival. He had a wash and a shave and went to meet her.

Kitty walked out of the factory with Jean, who was the first to see Brian standing across the road. 'Your old man is waiting for you,' she said.

Kitty's heart sank. She hated her own duplicity when he was home, playing the part of the faithful wife, and every day she was with him she was filled with guilt. But she couldn't give up Jeff. He was like life's blood to her, necessary for her very existence, but when Brian made love to her she felt no better than a woman of the streets.

She bade her friend goodbye and crossed the road.

'Hello, Kitty, love,' said Brian, and kissed her cheek.

'You're looking well,' she said. And he did. His face was tanned from working outside and the army had shed the loose poundage from his body and he was more alive in his demeanour than she had ever known.

He took her home and said, 'Put your glad rags on, I'm taking you out to dinner.'

'That'll be nice,' she replied, thinking: thank God! At least he doesn't want to drag me into the bedroom as soon as he's stepped inside the door. After their contretemps about this very thing when he was on leave before, he hadn't made the same mistake again.

As they sat at their table in the restaurant, he smiled across at her. 'I've looked forward so much to coming home and seeing you. It seems such an age since we spent time together.'

'How long have you got?' she asked.

'Three-day pass, then I've got to go back up North, but I'll soon be here again in Southampton.' He paused, looked down at his plate and thought about his words carefully. Then, looking up, he said quietly, 'We'll soon be shipping out, Kitty.'

Her heart sank. Despite the fact that she loved another, this man was her husband and although she wasn't in love with him, she did care about him. 'Oh, Brian . . .' was all she could say.

'Now I don't want you to worry,' he said.

'Of course I'll worry.' She wasn't lying – she would worry about him, of course she would. 'Just you keep your head down, that's all, and wear that damned tin hat at all times. Do you know where you are going?'

He joked, 'Really, Mrs Freeman! Don't you know that careless talk costs lives?' But his jollity faded as he said, 'France, I expect, but I don't know when.'

'War is so useless,' she raged. 'Men fighting and dying – all for what? Just to please some jumped-up little dictator who craves power!'

He looked at her in surprise. 'Well, I never! I didn't know you had any interest in politics and current events.'

'How can anyone not be interested in what's happening? Good heavens, haven't we been through enough with the Blitz? Surely you remember having to spend nights in the shelter, ducking every time there was an explosion? And can you imagine what it would be like if the Germans won the war? Life wouldn't be worth living. Thank God we have such a man as Churchill leading us. I listen to all his speeches; he's an amazing man. He is the heart of the British public!'

Brian looked at her with astonishment. 'Well, I must say you have changed since I've been away.'

She let out a deep sigh. 'Everyone has changed and after the war is over, nothing will ever be the same.' She looked at him and said, 'You too have changed, Brian. You're a different man from the one who left the railway to join up.'

He gave a wry smile. 'It's true. Strangely enough, I enjoy the life . . . not the going to war part, of course, but the regimentation, the discipline. It suits me. And I've learned new skills.' Pulling a face he said, 'I was living in a bit of a rut, I now realise, and to be honest I'm not at all sure I want to go back to the old way.'

'What are you saying?'

'Well, if I come out of all this unscathed, I quite like the idea of staying in the army.'

Kitty couldn't have been more surprised. 'You'd better not tell your mother that. She'd have a fit!'

He did laugh at her quip, which he wouldn't have in the old days. 'My mother has nothing to do with what I do with my life, but how would you feel about it?'

She didn't know what to say. What could she say? 'I think we'd better wait until all this is over and then talk about it,' she said in the end.

In bed later that night, Brian was in a contemplative frame of mind and instead of making his sexual overtures to his wife, he lay back on his pillow, hands behind his head and said, 'We have to face all eventualities, Kitty love.'

'Whatever do you mean?'

'It is possible that I could be killed in action.'

She went cold. It wasn't that she hadn't already thought of the possibility – every woman with a man in the war had to at some time or other – but now that her husband had actually put the thoughts into words, it chilled her.

'You mustn't talk like that,' she said hastily.

He ignored her. 'Should the worst happen, I've got an insurance against my life, so you'll not be without money. It's only for six hundred pounds – I couldn't afford the payments for a higher one – but . . .'

She stopped him. 'Don't! I can't bear to hear you talk this way.'

He took her in his arms and said tenderly, 'You are very sweet. If I do come back—'

'*When* you come back . . .' she insisted.

'When I come back, things will change. If I sign on for several years, of course, it will be a change, but I mean I'll change too.'

Now she was really puzzled. 'What do you mean?'

'I was a bit of an old stick-in-the-mud, I know that now. Being in the army has opened my eyes. We'll live a more interesting life, I promise you.' He grimaced. 'I can't be your film star-type hero – I'm no Errol Flynn – but I will change.'

Kitty thought her heart would break. Brian was doing his best, facing up to the things that had been missing in their marriage, promising a brighter future for them . . . but she wouldn't be here. She would be with Jeff – thousands of miles away!

He kissed her softly. 'I'll miss you, Kitty love,' he said as his hand started caressing her breast.

She couldn't answer, but let him make love to her, pretending to reach an orgasm to please him and hating herself every second, until it was over. She lay on her pillow and listened to his even breathing as the tears trickled down her cheeks. How much longer could she keep this up? Each time Brian came home it was harder than before. She was leading a double life, which was a nightmare. Several times she almost called him Jeff! Her nerves were in shreds and her feeling of guilt was a heavy burden. Sometimes she wondered if it was worth it; then she thought of her lover and she knew it was. Brian, if he came home safely, and she prayed he would, would get over her betrayal, in time. His mother would certainly do everything for him and welcome the opportunity! Sometimes Kitty tried to blame it all on the war. If it hadn't been for the war, she wouldn't have met Jeff . . . but she knew that indeed the choice had been hers in the very beginning and the blame for it all was on her own shoulders.

The day that Brian had to return to camp, Kitty was working, and she was grateful not to have to say goodbye as a faithful wife at the station, compounding even further her duplicity. Jean came over to her before she started her machine.

'Brian all right?' she asked.

'Yes, fine. He says he'll be sent to France soon.'

'So will your Yank, I suppose,' Jean said softly.

Kitty just nodded.

'Oh, Kitty, what are you going to do?'

'Nothing until this is all over. Then I'm going to Boston with Jeff, after the divorce.'

Jean pursed her lips. 'Well, rather you than me,' she said.

'What do you mean?'

'You say that Jeff is a lovely man, but here and in a glamorous uniform is one thing. Home in the States, among his own people, he will be different. If you find you've made a terrible mistake, what then?'

'You don't know him,' said Kitty defiantly, and switched on her machine, leaving Jean to return to hers.

As she worked, Kitty thought about her friend's remarks and knew she was only trying to be helpful, but the one thing in this whole messy business Kitty was sure about was Jeff. She didn't doubt him for one minute. Wherever he was, he was the man she loved. The man for whom she would go through fire and water. Then she grinned. I hope his mother is not like Gladys Freeman, she thought. That would be too much!

Chapter Fifteen

The beginning of June was fast approaching and the plans for D-Day were all but complete. It only remained for the powers that be to choose the day for landing and this was determined by the weather.

Brian was now stationed at Marchwood, and had spent twenty-four hours with Kitty before all leave had been cancelled. It had been a traumatic experience for her. He had been quiet and withdrawn, knowing that it was now a matter of days before the big move across the Channel and, as all men in this situation, he was feeling very tense. He didn't want to go out to a pub for a drink, didn't want to see his parents, although he felt he should. He just couldn't stand the idea of his mother wittering on.

'It's more than I can handle,' he told Kitty.

Instead he'd written a letter to Gladys and asked Kitty to give it to her after he'd left. She said she would, but dreaded doing so, knowing that Gladys would be livid that her son had chosen this way of saying goodbye.

'I'd just like a quiet evening at home with you,' he said.

She'd made a shepherd's pie, his favourite, and they'd sat and listened to the wireless. Tommy Handley's ITMA had at least brought a smile to his lips, but when during a variety programme the resident singer had sung, 'Now is the Hour', he had withdrawn inside himself even more.

Kitty was at a loss to know how to help him and any conversation between them had been very stilted. Then, when they retired to bed and he made love to her, it was with a desperation, lacking love and tenderness. After, she held him close in her arms like a child until he fell asleep.

The following morning she cooked his breakfast and as they sat at the table together she tried valiantly to bring a touch of lightness to the situation.

'Now you be careful of those French women,' she said. 'They're a different kettle of fish from us.'

He tried to match her effort. 'I'm more worried about their quality of beer. As you know, I'm not into all that wine muck!'

'You never know, you might get to like it.'

He couldn't go on. Quietly he said, 'I'll just be glad to get this all over with and come home safely.'

Reaching across the table, she gave his hand an affectionate squeeze. 'You'll be fine,' she said. 'I can feel it in my water!'

He rose from his chair. 'Well, best be off, I suppose.' He held her tightly and said, 'You take care. I'll write as soon as I can.'

Kitty kissed him goodbye and walked to the front door where he picked up his kitbag. Standing on the doorstep she watched him walk down the road, turning at the corner to wave. She went back inside and wept.

Jeff was rushed off his feet in his office. There was such a massive movement of troops that he felt he didn't have time to breathe. He wanted to see Kitty but hadn't had a moment to himself, which had been very worrying, as he desperately wanted to tell her his news. Eventually he managed to find two hours of freedom and had jumped into the Jeep and driven to her home. When she had opened the door, she flew into his arms.

Lifting her off her feet, he carried her into the house. 'The neighbours will certainly have a field day now, darling,' he said.

'I don't care,' she replied defiantly. 'They don't run my life. I do!' She ushered him into the living room, where they kissed each other passionately.

'I've got some news for you, Kitty,' he told her.

She looked stricken. 'You're leaving!' Wringing her hands in despair she said, 'I can't stand these goodbyes.'

He took her into his arms. 'It's good news, darling. I'm needed here for a bit longer so we still have time together. My replacement has been sent elsewhere and can't get away.'

The relief was overwhelming, and she held on to him. 'Make love to me, Jeff, please,' she begged.

There was no way he could resist her.

They lay together, naked. As he caressed her body and kissed her, he murmured, 'I love you so much. I can't wait to make you my wife. To take you home to my folks, introduce you to all my friends, to spoil you, love you, and grow old with you.'

'I'm going to miss you so much when you do go,' she told him as he moved over her and entered her gently. She matched his rhythm, twisting with pleasure beneath him. 'Oh, Jeff,' she whispered as he took her to the heights of passion. 'I love what you do to me.'

After, they lay in each other's arms. He eased himself away from her and said, 'Darling, I'm sorry. I have to go but at least I'll see you again soon.'

Before she opened the door, Jeff took her into his arms and kissed her until she was breathless. 'Remember that I love you, that I *will* come back and then together we can sort out our future.' Reluctantly he began to open the door. 'Be careful, darling,' he said. 'We don't want to give the neighbours anything more to talk about.'

'Sod the neighbours!' she said, but she didn't touch him again, just watched him climb into his Jeep and drive away after he lifted a hand to wave.

As she turned, she noticed the twitch of a curtain in the window of the house next door and, glaring, she tapped her nose to the hidden observer and, walking into her own home, slammed the door.

Gerry Stubbs stood by the cigarette kiosk in Latimer Street and watched the lines of American and British troops march past, heading for the docks, tossing money and KP rations to watching children, who scrambled to pick up their bounty from the pavement. All he could think about was his loss of revenue. Now the Yanks were leaving, his supply of nylon stockings was finished, American cigarettes would no longer be available and the NAAFI would not be bringing in such a load of supplies. Still, he couldn't really complain. He still had the bulk of his eight grand from the raid in London and he'd made a killing these past few months. There was the local need for foodstuffs, which were still on offer, but not in any great quantity. The fact that the men were putting their lives on the line didn't bother him that much. He felt he was doing as much for the war effort in his own way. He threw the cigarette away and returned to the warehouse.

D-Day had been delayed for twenty-four hours because of bad weather, but in the early hours of 6 June, Eisenhower gave the go-ahead for the invasion. The plan was to land about 135,000 men and about 20,000 vehicles on the beaches of Normandy. The attack would be on five beaches, the British to take Gold and Sword beaches, the Americans, Utah and Omaha beaches and the Canadians, Juno beach.

The inhabitants of the South Coast of England were well aware the invasion had started as hordes of bombers and fighter planes droned overhead, towards Normandy. Paratroopers and the French maquis were creating chaos in the immediate interior of Normandy, capturing vital bridges and destroying rail lines to stop the Germans bringing in reinforcements.

The sea was rough during the crossing and in the landing craft carrying Brian and his company, many of the men were sick, hanging over the side, retching. And although the Germans were taken by surprise, thinking the landings, when they happened, would be at Pas de Calais, there was heavy opposition as the troops poured from the landing craft.

Holding their rifles above their heads, Brian and his comrades ran down the ramps and jumped into the water. The chill of it took their breath away, but their anxiety to reach dry land safely was uppermost in their minds. Beside him, a soldier who wasn't very tall sank beneath the waves. Brian grabbed his collar and hauled him to the surface, dragging him onward until the soldier could touch the bottom. Screams came from others around him as they were hit by enemy fire.

Heavy shelling of the beach had started, and the congestion of the troops arriving made it difficult to find an exit. Brian's heart was pumping wildly as he staggered out of the water and ran up the beach. He heard the whine of bullets and threw himself flat. The man beside him wasn't as fortunate. He was caught by several bullets and fell beside Brian, eyes wide open, without expression, blood pouring from chest wounds. Looking at him, Brian knew he was dead. Getting to his feet, he ran as fast as he could until he found shelter.

One of his mates landed beside him. 'Christ! That was bloody hairy! You all right?'

'I think so,' Brian answered. 'Come on,' he urged, 'we can't stay here,' and moved forward.

In Southampton, Kitty made her way to the Freemans' house, clutching the letter Brian had written to his mother. She was dreading the inevitable confrontation. Walking round to the back door, she knocked on the pane of glass and waited.

Gladys, wearing a wraparound apron, her hands covered in flour, opened the door. 'Oh, it's you,' she said. 'You'd better come in, I suppose,' and she walked away.

'I've got a letter here for you from Brian,' Kitty said.

'Why did he send it to you and not me?' Gladys demanded.

'He wrote it when he was at home and asked me to deliver it,' she explained.

'What do you mean, he wrote it at home? Has he been on leave then?'

'He had just twenty-four hours before he was sent overseas,' Kitty informed her.

'Sent overseas!'

'Yes, his company is part of the invasion force. I'm not sure when he left. He didn't know that himself.'

Gladys slumped into a chair, opened the letter and read it slowly. Then she glared at Kitty. 'I suppose you kept him away. You rotten bitch!'

Although she felt sorry for Brian's mother Kitty was furious at her verbal insult. 'I certainly did not! It was the way he wanted to do it. He was feeling apprehensive about going to France; he didn't want to see anyone. Surely you can understand that?'

Gladys stood up and raged at Kitty. 'You think my own son wouldn't come and say goodbye to his mother? My boy would never do such a thing; this is all your fault. You're jealous, that's the whole truth of the matter. You hate it when he spends time with me.'

'That's not true.'

'Then why don't you come and visit me with him? You are not like any daughter-in-law that I know. All my friends have theirs visit, but not you. Not good enough for you, is that it? Got ideas above your station, you have, and anyway, what sort of a wife are you, going out with a Yank?'

Kitty paled and wondered how much Gladys Freeman knew.

'Remember,' the woman continued to rail, 'I saw you coming out of the cinema with your fancy man! I told my Brian all about you.'

'And I'm sure it gave you great pleasure!' Kitty snapped, her patience at an end. She walked to the back door and, turning, said, 'If I have any news from him, I'll let you know.'

As she walked down the street she thought, what did you expect? Her mother-in-law had behaved exactly as she had imagined. She was mindful of her motherly feelings towards her son at such a time, but in fact it was Gladys who was the jealous one. She wanted to control Brian. There was no way she wanted to cut

128

him loose from her apron strings. Letting out a deep sigh, Kitty walked on. It had been a strange time, with Brian leaving for France and Jeff staying on. She was in fear for Brian's safety and prayed every night that he would come home unscathed, but then her problems would really begin.

The problem for Eddie, Kitty's brother, however, was growing. Nancy Brannigan had been taken off the danger list. When Gerry Stubbs imparted this news to him, he felt sick.

'Yes,' said Gerry, 'the doctors are now more hopeful. She's still got a long way to go, of course, and they have to wait to find out if she has suffered any brain damage.'

'Brain damage?'

'She still can't speak, you see. They say it may be only temporary, or at the worst she may never be able to talk properly again – and, of course, she's still very weak. It's a matter of time. I'm calling into the hospital this evening; maybe there will be some better news.'

'Poor girl,' said Eddie, secretly relieved. 'We'll have to hope for the best.' But the more he thought about it the more he realised that Nancy Brannigan had to be silenced. He remembered vividly the look of hatred in her eyes when she looked at him. To him that proved that although she was robbed of speech, her brain was very much alive.

That afternoon, he made his way to the hospital, knowing that Gerry wouldn't be there until the evening. Perhaps he'd be lucky to catch her alone. He had to try.

The sister showed him where Nancy had been moved to now she was out of danger. The bed was at the end of the ward. With slow deliberate steps, he walked up the ward until he stood at the bottom of her bed.

'Hello, Nancy,' he said quietly. 'I hear you are getting better.'

She was sitting propped up with pillows. When she saw who her visitor was, she made to press the bell to summon the nurse, but Eddie was too quick for her. He snatched the cord out of her hand, pulling the curtain around; he sat on the bed and said, 'Now I don't think that would be very wise.'

The patient glared at him, her mouth moving in an effort to speak, her hands clenched in frustration as no words came forth.

Eddie gripped one of her hands and said menacingly, 'I've just come to warn you, Nancy my dear, it would be very unwise of you to let anyone know that it was me who put you here.'

She struggled weakly to remove her hand and he laughed. 'Oh dear, not very strong yet, are we?' Leaning over her, he said, 'It would be so easy for me to slip out one of your pillows and hold it over your face. Who would know? It would be quick and easy, and when I left the nurses would think you were asleep. Then when they discovered differently they would think it had all been too much for you and you had gone to a better place.'

Now there was a look of fear in the patient's eyes.

'I see you have got the message,' he said. 'Just remember I don't make idle threats.' Standing up, he pushed the curtain back and, smiling at her, said, 'I'm so pleased you're getting better. Let's hope you live a nice long and peaceful life.' He nodded to the nurses as he walked out of the ward.

Chapter Sixteen

Walking down the road away from the hospital, Eddie pondered over his future. He felt that at the moment he was reasonably safe from any allegations Nancy might make, were she able. If she couldn't speak she would be able to write when she was stronger, although he felt she wasn't able to do so at the moment. Holding a pen would be too much for her. He could tell that when she tried to struggle with him. But he was also aware that the Irish girl was unpredictable and normally bloody-minded. Should he cut his losses and run now, or should he hang around a bit longer? If he did take off, would Gerry wonder why and put two and two together? It was a predicament. He remembered one of his father's sayings: 'When in doubt, don't.' He'd hang about a bit longer.

When Gerry called at the hospital later that evening, the nurse told him that they had given Nancy a sedative as she'd been upset and overwrought and she was now sleeping.

'What brought that on?' he asked, full of concern. 'She hasn't taken a turn for the worse, has she?'

'We don't think so. She had a visitor earlier this afternoon – perhaps he upset her.'

'A visitor. Who was it, do you know?'

The nurse shook her head. 'It was some man, I believe.'

'What did he look like?'

Apologising she said, 'I'm sorry, Mr Stubbs, but I wasn't on duty.'

'This afternoon, you say, so if I drop by tomorrow afternoon, will the same people be on duty?'

Looking at the nursing roster, she told him this was so.

'Then I'll be back tomorrow,' he said, and strode out of the hospital. Who on earth could it have been? Perhaps it was her father or that no-good brother of hers. He was still around, living off his parents, unable to find work with a prison record. Well, he'd ask tomorrow for a description. He'd soon sort it out.

The following afternoon Gerry carefully questioned the young nurse before him. 'Now describe this man,' he demanded.

'Tallish, his hair was dark and a bit long, really – looked a bit scruffy, if you ask me.'

'Anything else?'

'Yes, he had a beard so I couldn't see a lot of his face.'

'And what exactly happened, do you know?'

'I told him where Miss Brannigan was and he went up the ward. I was busy after that but I did notice he pulled the curtain round a bit. I thought he wanted a bit of privacy – you know how difficult it is to talk when someone's in the next bed.'

'Yes, yes,' he said impatiently. 'Then what?'

'I didn't see the going of him, but I noticed the curtain pulled back, so I went to see if she needed anything. A right state she was in, I can tell you. Crying, tossing about. I called the sister.'

'Thank you,' Gerry said, now knowing the identity of the visitor. 'I'll just pop along and see Nancy.'

'She's much calmer today,' the nurse told him.

Gerry walked up the ward, fuming to himself. What the hell was Eddie doing coming in here and upsetting his girl? Well, when he got back to the warehouse, he'd bloody well find out.

'Hello, Nancy,' he said as he reached her bed. 'How are you, darling?'

She just looked at him and turned away. He decided then and there not to mention Eddie to her in case it triggered another episode. The girl looked pale today and unwell.

'I've bought you some grapes,' Gerry said, putting them on the

132

side. Sitting beside the bed, he nattered on about everyday events for a while but didn't linger, as Nancy looked so tired. 'I'll call in tomorrow,' he said, and rose from the chair. He kissed her forehead and said, 'You take care now and no flirting with the doctors.' But there was no reaction from his quip and, feeling more than a little concerned, he left the hospital.

When he reached his warehouse Gerry entered his office and looked out of the window. Across the yard through the open doors, he could see his men at work, sorting tiles, loading new stock, sweeping up. As he watched, Kitty's brother came outside and lit a cigarette.

Gerry went to his door, opened it and yelled, 'Eddie! In here – now!'

Ambling over, Eddie climbed the wooden stairs and entered the office. 'You wanted me?'

'I believe you went to the hospital yesterday?'

With his senses immediately alert he answered, 'Yes, but I didn't stay very long.'

'How did you think Nancy looked?'

'Pale, thinner, but that's to be expected, isn't it, after what she's been through.'

Gerry watched the man in front of him very carefully, noting the watchful expression in his eyes. He was hiding something, the bastard. 'What did you say to her?' he asked coldly.

Shrugging nonchalantly Eddie said, 'Not a lot really – talked about the weather, the war, work. It's really difficult to make conversation when Nancy can't talk.'

Gerry's eyes narrowed as he listened. 'And that was it?'

'Yes, I left after.'

Walking around his desk, Gerry stood in front of him and said, 'Liar!'

With a startled look Eddie said, 'What the hell are you talking about?'

'After you left, Nancy was so upset they had to give her a sedative.'

133

'Why would she be upset? It was just idle chitchat, that's all.' Eddie could feel his heart beating wildly.

Grabbing the front of Eddie's overalls, Gerry said, 'There was more to it than that. You're hiding something. What else did you say?'

'Nothing, I swear! Look, Gerry, how would you feel in her place? People visit, she can't talk back to anyone, she's bound to be upset. Wouldn't you be?'

There was a certain logic in his argument, and Gerry released his hold. 'Keep away from her in future.'

'Yes, all right. Is there anything else?'

'Get out!' Gerry snapped. He wasn't absolutely convinced, but what could he do? Nothing. There was only one person who could tell him what really transpired and she couldn't utter a word – not yet, anyway. When she was able to speak he would ask her if anything was said to upset her so, and if there were he would deal with Eddie then.

As he walked back, Eddie wiped the perspiration beading his forehead. Christ! That was a close call. He hadn't bargained for Nancy getting in a state. He smiled slowly. He must have scared her, though, and that was a good thing. But he felt that his days were now numbered in Southampton. In case he had to take off suddenly he thought he'd better call to see Kitty; find out how the family was, as once he went to London there was no way he could keep in touch, because as soon as Nancy was better, Gerry would know he was the culprit and be after him. Him and the Military Police!

Kitty was ironing when he arrived at the open kitchen door. He tapped on it and walked in calling, 'Kitty! It's only me,' remembering the shock she got before at his changed appearance.

'What on earth are you doing here?' she asked.

'That's not very welcoming, I must say.'

'You'd better come in.' She carried on working. 'I've been wondering about you since I heard about Nancy Brannigan.'

Although he was taken by surprise he asked, 'And why's that?'

Putting down her iron, she said, 'Because you told me you were seeing her. Did you beat her up, Eddie?'

He was shattered by her perception. 'Why on earth would you think such a thing?'

'Because I know you. As a child you had a temper, and a streak of cruelty. I remember the terror you put Mum's cat through until one day it scratched you. You were only seven at the time and as far as I can see you haven't changed a bit.'

'When have I been cruel?'

'The way you've ignored our parents in the past is cruel. Mother especially. You've just used her over the years without any thought for her feelings as a mother. How do you think she would feel now if she knew what you'd done?'

'For God's sake, Kitty! I'm a man. It's different. Girls cling to their parents more. I'm no different from other men.'

'Did you hurt Nancy Brannigan?' she asked again.

'No, of course I didn't, I've told you that already. She was just a bit of fun, that's all. As soon as Gerry came back it was over.' The lies tripped off his lips effortlessly.

'Why are you here?'

'I may be moving on soon. Thought I'd come and say goodbye before I do.'

'Where are you going?'

He grinned at her. 'London, but I won't tell you where exactly in case the Military Police call.' He paused and asked, 'How are Mum and Dad?'

'As if you really care!'

'I didn't come for a fight, Kitty. I thought we could have a cup of tea together like two civilised people. Once I've gone, I doubt I'll be back.'

There was something in his voice that touched her – a certain sadness, a finality – and she put down the iron and filled the kettle. 'All right,' she said.

'I suppose Brian has gone off with the invasion forces,' he said.

'Yes. He wasn't happy about it, as you will appreciate.'

Lighting a cigarette Eddie said, 'Yes I do, and I know you think I'm not much of a man for running away, but if you had seen what I had, you might understand a little more.'

She ignored his remark. 'I see the news all the time, of course, but naturally it's a worry.'

'I do know, Kitty. But the Allies are slowly getting the upper hand. He'll be home before you know it.'

'He's thinking of signing on permanently when the war is over.'

'Bloody hell! Why would he want to do that?'

'He likes the life – not during wartime, but he enjoys the regimentation.'

Eddie started to laugh. 'Yes, I could see that he would. You know, Kitty, I never ever could understand why you married him.'

Her brother hadn't said anything like this to her before and she was intrigued. 'What makes you say that?'

'You're bright and capable of so much more than just being his wife. He dominated you and, what's more, you took it in your stride. What happened to you? You used to be so fiery as a child. I remember you bawling me out many a time . . . and saving me a few as well. Once you married Freeman you changed.'

Every word was true. Once she was married she lost her personality. It became smothered by that of her husband. 'Well, now I've changed. I want much more out of life.'

'What, like being an army wife?'

'No, I would like to go to America after the war.'

Eddie nearly choked on the tea she had poured for him. 'America? Have you lost your marbles? How are you going to afford to do such a thing?'

But she wasn't going to discuss her future any further with him, and passed it off. 'We must all have a dream otherwise life wouldn't be worth living!'

He finished his tea and got to his feet. 'Best be off. I hope you achieve your dream, Kitty. I've screwed up my life; it would be nice if one of us achieved something.' At the back door he paused. 'I won't be back again. Take care of yourself and when next you see the folks, give them my love, will you?'

'Of course. Eddie, are you sure that you're all right? Is there anything wrong?'

He laughed. 'And if there was, would you get me out of it again?'

'No I would not! You're a grown man now, responsible for your own actions.'

Looking at her, he said wryly, 'That I am. I am what is known as a survivor, Kitty, my dear. I'm a past master at ducking and diving. I'll be fine.' He paused. 'If you go to the States, leave Brian behind, make a life for yourself whilst you can.'

As she folded the blouse she'd ironed, Kitty wondered what was in Eddie's mind as they chatted. Normally he was entirely self-centred, but today he had been different. There was evidently something on his mind, probably some kind of trouble he'd made for himself. If so, she really didn't want to know. It was better that way.

Eddie's plans for a final departure were unexpectedly delayed. Gerry called him into his office the following morning with Ernie and Jack, the two men he lodged with, and shut the door behind him.

'Eric's the furrier's, in Bedford Place, has a nice little stock of fur coats, I've heard,' he said with a sly smile. 'I intend to rid him of them. Now here is the plan.'

As Eddie listened he became excited. The money forthcoming to them all would swell his fund, giving him more than enough to finance him for his stay in London. It would allow him time to establish himself. Another week would do it, then he'd be gone.

Three days passed, then in the early hours of the morning, a small van pulled into the side road next to the furrier's. Not a soul was about. Gerry stepped out of the van and, walking round the back, quietly undid the doors. The three men stepped out, all wearing gloves, with scarves across their mouths, covering part of their faces. They made their way silently to the side entrance where they broke the lock and chain on the gate, entering and closing it behind them.

Jack moved forward to pick the lock as Gerry told Eddie to keep watch. 'We'll go inside,' he whispered. 'Let us know if you see or hear anyone.'

It was a dark night with heavy clouds blotting out any moonlight, for which Eddie was grateful. His heart was pounding, his adrenaline pumping. He strained to listen but all he could hear was the occasional hoot of an owl. It seemed as if he was waiting an age and he became nervous. 'For God's sake, hurry, will you?' he muttered, and then stiffened as he heard footsteps in the distance, approaching slowly. He slipped out of the gate and up to the corner and peered around. To his horror he saw an air-raid warden ambling along the small parade of shops, stopping at each one, flashing his torch at each shop interior and walking on, coming closer to the furrier's. Eric's front window was huge and Eddie knew that if the warden shone his torch inside he would probably see Gerry and his men. He turned quickly, entered the gate and made to run into the back entrance of the shop. He tripped over a heavy lead pipe on the ground, which hit an old tin watering can by the back step. The rattle seemed to echo around the empty streets. He cursed, picked up the pipe and ran inside the shop.

'Someone's coming,' he warned the men. 'Hurry!' As the others gathered together a pile of fur coats, Eddie rushed to the exit and stepped outside.

'What's going on here then? What are you doing on private property?'

The light from the torch was shining in his face and, without thinking, Eddie gripped the lead pipe and took a hefty swipe at the man. He heard a loud groan; the torch dropped and the man's body hit the ground.

Gerry came running out and, flashing his torch, saw the man prostrate on the garden path, blood seeping from a wound. 'Jesus Christ! What have you done, you bloody fool?'

'Let's get out of here,' urged Eddie, and fled to the van. The others quickly followed. Throwing the coats into the back, they climbed in as Gerry started the engine and drove away, cursing loudly.

Back at his own warehouse, behind locked gates, Gerry let rip. 'You stupid bastard! What if that man is dead? We're all in the shit.'

'I couldn't help it. He came out of nowhere.'

Looking at the others, Gerry asked, 'Did you see if he was badly hurt?'

They all shook their heads.

Ernie said, 'It was all so dark. There was some blood but I don't know where it came from.'

Turning to Eddie, Gerry said, 'Where did you hit him?'

'I don't know. He was shining his fucking light in my eyes and I just lashed out.'

Gerry paced up and down, trying to work out what was the best thing to do. 'I'll have to get rid of the stuff,' he said. 'If I drive up to London now, I can move the coats.' He glared at Eddie. 'I'll have to sell them for next to nothing all through you losing your bloody nerve.' Turning to Ernie, he said, 'Come and help me put some petrol in the van. There are a couple of jerry cans in the warehouse.' To Jack he said, 'Take him back to the flat and behave normally tomorrow, because no doubt the police will be nosing round. I'll get back as soon as I can.'

Eddie felt himself being shoved in the back. 'Come on, let's go.'

Once safely at home, Eddie found himself up against the wall, being held by the throat in a grasp that scarcely allowed him to breathe.

'I never liked you,' Jack said. 'I always knew you were trouble. Well, let me make one thing clear, I'm not going down for murder if that bloke dies. That's down to you, mate. You had better keep your nose clean over the next few days 'cause if you don't, Gerry will have you and if he doesn't, I will!' He let go and Eddie slumped to the floor, gasping for breath.

When he'd recovered he went into the scullery and poured himself some water. Now he really would have to go. He couldn't afford to wait and see if he was a murderer. He'd wait only for Ernie to return and when he and Jack were both asleep, he'd sneak out. Hiding out in London was his only chance now. His luck had run out and, if he wasn't careful, it would be the hangman's rope he would feel around his throat.

Chapter Seventeen

Brian Freeman was now in Arromanches, constructing the Mulberry harbours, which were to be a crucial lifeline to the troops. There had been losses, of course, but the men with whom he had shared a billet had all come through the landing safely and he began to realise just what his father had meant about comradeship. During the hand-to-hand fighting, as they fought their way through villages to reach their destination, they became a small brotherhood.

Sitting quietly near the beach one evening having a cigarette, Brian was joined by one of his mates. Bert Ford and he had become friends of a sort. They shared similar views on life, they had discovered during the odd chat. Both were married, with decided ideas about most things, but Bert was a father with a two-year-old son.

As he lit a Woodbine Bert said, 'I only hope my kid doesn't have to go through this sort of thing when he grows up.'

'Surely this is a war to end all wars?' Brian remarked.

'I bloody well hope so, or why the hell are we here?' Bert puffed on his cigarette and said, 'I wonder when we'll get some mail from home. I want to know that Christine is all right.'

'I know what you mean. I'd give anything to see Kitty right now.' And Brian sat ruminating about his last night at home. He knew he'd been withdrawn and regretted the wasted opportunity. It couldn't have been much fun for her either . . . but that was war.

In the near distance, the sound of a heavy bombardment could be heard. The next main objective was to liberate Caen. Caen opened the direct route to Paris and would be heavily defended – they all knew that and they all knew that it would be a hazardous journey. If I come out of this alive, thought Brian, my life will be very different. He would make the most of it. No more being cautious, calculating every little thing. Life was to be lived and he was going to live it to the full.

During the days that followed, he wondered if he would ever get home in one piece. Once the Mulberry harbours were in place, Brian's company moved on. The fighting was intense. The Germans were pushing everything they could towards Normandy, trying to protect Caen and keep the Allies out. Every night Brian silently thanked God for his safety. He wasn't a religious man, although he believed in the Deity, but during the dangerous times, he made promises to his Maker if he was to come through this ordeal alive, as did many others. He also told himself that if his name was on the next bullet there wasn't a lot he could do about it, which was of no comfort at all. He had written a letter to Kitty during the odd quiet moment. This he found a comfort. Not that he told her about the danger that surrounded them every day; instead he tried to sound cheerful. He told her about Bert and his family, and that when he, Brian, got home he'd like them to start a family of their own.

Gerry Stubbs was in a fighting mood when he was told at the start of the working day that Eddie was missing. 'What do you mean, missing?'

'When we got up this morning, guv, the little bleeder had done a runner! His clothes had gone and everything.'

'That bastard has been nothing but trouble from the start!' Gerry stormed. 'I managed to get rid of the fur coats in London and sold them for a bloody song all because of him. If I ever get my hands on him I'll kill him!' He paced up and down his office. Pointing to Jack he said, 'Right! You hang around the coach station, and you,' he pointed to Ernie, 'go to the railway station. Maybe someone will have seen him. Ask around. I'm off to see his sister, see if she knows anything.'

Kitty was startled by the loud hammering on her door, and even more surprised when she opened it and Gerry Stubbs pushed his way in, shutting it behind him, forcibly propelling her into the living room.

'Right, where is he?'

'Where's who? she asked, rubbing her arm where he'd held her.

'Your bloody brother, that's who.'

'I've no idea, and who the hell do you think you are, barging your way in here like this?'

'Your brother has landed me right in it and now he's taken a powder. Buggered off! I might have a murder hanging over me because of him.'

Kitty felt her blood chill. 'Why, what's happened?'

'We went out on a job last night and he clobbered an air-raid warden with a lead pipe.'

'Oh my God!' Kitty sat down in the nearest chair as her legs almost gave way with the shock. 'Is the man dead?'

'You think we stayed around to find out? Has Eddie been here?'

She shook her head. 'He called unexpectedly last week, said he was going to London.'

'Did he! Last week, you say?' He thought for a moment and said, 'I suppose he stayed on to do this job. Crafty little sod – after all I've done for him too.' He glared at Kitty. 'I rue the day I took him off your hands, I can tell you. I should have dumped him in the dock then and there.'

Kitty looked at him, eyes filled with horror. This was a Gerry she hadn't seen before, because he was not joking. 'What are you going to do?'

'Find him, that's what. I've got plenty of contacts in London. He won't get far.'

'And then what?'

'You don't want to know.' He leaned towards her with a menacing stare. 'You had better keep this to yourself, Kitty my darling, because if you breathe a word of it, it could be your last!'

'It's nothing to do with me!' she retorted, fear giving her strength. 'If you choose to live beyond the law, that's your lookout. I want nothing to do with it.'

'If he comes here, Kitty, you had better tell me, if you know what's good for you.'

'He won't come here. If what you tell me is true, he'll be miles away by now.'

'Yes, he's good at running away, is your brother.'

Getting to her feet she said, 'I think you'd better go.'

He held her tightly by the shoulders and said, 'Don't you tell me what to do, lady. I'll do as I bloody well please. You owe me and don't you forget it. And one day I'll be back to settle, that I promise.' He kissed her savagely, bruising her mouth, ignoring her struggles. When he let her go he said, 'And when I come back, tears won't stop me next time.' He sent her staggering as he pushed her away and went to the front door, which he slammed behind him.

Kitty found she was trembling. She put her hand to her mouth: it felt swollen. She walked to the scullery and ran the cold tap, soaking a cloth in the water, holding it to her lips. But when a little later she looked in the mirror, her lips were puffy and bruised.

When Jeff called later, he took one look at her and said, 'What on earth has happened to you?'

'I opened the cupboard door and forgot,' she lied. 'I walked into it.'

He took her into his arms and said, 'You poor darling. Is there anything I can do?'

'Just hold me tight,' she said quietly as she fought back the tears.

Gerry Stubbs had put the fear of God into her. She had bought a copy of the *Southern Daily Echo* and read the headlines. 'DARING RAIDERS KILL WARDEN' stared her in the face. Her brother was a murderer. And she was almost certain that it was he who had attacked Nancy Brannigan, although he had denied it. She had always known when he was lying and he had lied to her about the girl, she was sure.

'Let me take you out,' suggested Jeff. 'You look very pale – is everything all right?'

'I'm fine,' she assured him, although she felt unwell. It was the shock of it all. Her brother! How could he do such a thing? Her mother would be heartbroken if she knew. And now there was the added threat from Gerry. He wasn't joking when he said he would be back. What was she to do?

'Let's go for a walk,' she suggested. She needed to get out of the house, although she didn't really want to be seen in a public place with a swollen mouth.

They strolled up Wilton Avenue to Bedford Place and looked in the shop windows. Then she realised that she was standing opposite the furrier's where in the paper it said the raid had taken place. This was where the man had been killed. Oh my God, she thought, and started to walk quickly away.

Jeff called after her, 'Kitty, wait.' When he caught up with her and took her arm he could feel her trembling. 'Darling, whatever is the matter?'

'A man was killed here last night,' she said. 'I just couldn't bear to be near the place, that's all.'

'Come along,' he said, 'let me take you home.'

Once there, he fussed around her, making her coffee with some he'd brought with him. Handing her the cup of steaming liquid, he said, 'Here, drink this. This is proper American coffee, this will put you right.' He watched her as she drank, then he said, 'Kitty, what really is the matter? Something's worrying you, I can tell. Won't you share it with me so I can help?'

She longed to share her troubles with him, but how could she?

Jeff was a lawyer; he would realise the seriousness of her situation and no doubt want to do something about it – maybe insist she go to the police. She dare not. Gerry had threatened her life if she did.

'I haven't heard from Brian,' she said in desperation, 'and I'm worried.'

It was like a slap in the face for Jeff. 'I see,' he said quietly.

What a stupid thing to say, she thought. Yes of course she worried about Brian's welfare, but now her lover was hurt and that was the last thing she wanted. She caught hold of his hand. 'I'm sorry,' she said, 'it's not just that, it's the whole damned war. You could be going away soon. It's a lot to bear.'

'And, of course, Brian is your husband.'

'But it's you I love!'

He stared intently into her eyes.

'It's you I love,' she whispered.

He gathered her into his arms and held her. 'I'm frustrated and worried too, honey. After all, I'm a free man without ties, and I'm asking a great deal of you, I realise that. I'm asking you to give up your husband, your family, your country – your way of life.'

'And I'm ready to do all that,' she insisted, 'to be with you.'

He tipped her chin and asked, 'Are you really sure?'

'Yes, yes I am, please believe me. I love you more than I can say. I have never ever felt this way before.'

He kissed the tip of her nose. 'That's all I need to know.' He glanced at his watch. 'I'd better get back,' he said. 'I'll be tied up for the next couple of days, but the following evening, we'll go out to dinner somewhere.'

'That would be lovely. My mouth should be better by then.'

'I'll try and work out a weekend pass if I can. It would do us both good to get out of town for a while, walk in the forest, be together all day . . . and night.' He smiled. 'Especially the night.'

She walked outside with him. As he left she sensed, yet again, someone behind the curtains of the house next to hers and poked out her tongue before closing the front door.

146

★ ★ ★

Eddie Simmons sat in a small café in Smithfield Market and ordered breakfast. He'd caught the milk train that morning, creeping out of the house with his things whilst Gerry's two men slept.

London was awash with troops from all nations; the buildings heavily sandbagged against air raids. It was a teeming metropolis, just the place to lose yourself, he thought. He'd find a little bed-and-breakfast place somewhere and stay a while. Get himself a job of sorts. With so many men away at the war, it shouldn't be difficult to find something that would pay cash in hand, no insurance cards. He'd have to tidy himself up a bit, because he knew he looked a bit of a scruff with his long hair and beard. He would have it shaved off – he was tired of it – and he'd buy some spectacles in Woolworth's to use as a disguise. There were bound to be some without strong lenses. He'd have his hair trimmed, but not short. That should be enough to throw the MPs off the scent. No, he'd be fine. He had a little stash of money and, with some more coming in if he were working, that would be enough to keep him. All he needed was enough for some grotty room. If he could get a job in a restaurant he would be fed. He wouldn't mind just washing up, anything would do. When you were on the run, you couldn't be fussy. He wasn't too worried about Gerry Stubbs finding him here. After all, where would he start looking?

Eddie would not have felt quite so confident if he had known the extent of Gerry's connections in London. They stretched over the city like a large spider's web, and Gerry had already made several phone calls to London to friends, business colleagues and members of the underworld who owed him a few favours. It was just a matter of time before someone came up with something. Gerry knew this. He could wait.

Chapter Eighteen

It was the month of July and Brian had been sent to Dieppe as a member of staff of the Movement Control Officer, who belonged to the Royal Engineers. The main railway station had been taken over and made into his headquarters, placing all the employees of the French *chemin de fer* under military control. Rolling stock and other railway equipment had been requisitioned from the French, and as the troops arrived, they could now be marshalled and moved on. Brian's previous experience had stood him in good stead and he was grateful to be out of the front line and settled for a while. He was housed with the previous station master, who didn't seem to mind at all being taken over by the Allies.

'Anything to get rid of the Boche!' said Monsieur Pallier in his deeply accented English, as he showed Brian to a small bedroom at the back of the house. 'My wife, she is dead, but my daughter, Lisette, she cooks good.' He shrugged his shoulders and gesticulated continuously as he spoke. 'We don't 'ave much, but we manage,' he said.

Later that evening, Brian was introduced briefly to the daughter and discovered for himself how well Lisette cooked, as he sat down at the table with the two of them. He looked at the contents of the large soup plate in front of him with a certain suspicion.

'It is a poor man's bouillabaisse, monsieur, a fish stew, but only with 'alf of the ingredients,' Lisette explained.

Brian looked up at her and for the first time realised what a good-looking girl she was with her shoulder-length fair hair. She was simply dressed in a bright skirt, which showed off her small waist. Her white blouse was open at the neck, showing the deep cleavage of her full breasts. He also noted that her mouth twitched as she tried to hide a smile at his reaction to the strange dish. Her hazel eyes twinkled as he quickly said, 'You must forgive me, miss. I'm a meat-and-two-veg man myself.'

'Ah, the British with their roast biff! They 'ave to 'ave food that is far too 'eavy. Eat – and taste real cooking!' And she laughed.

It was the laugh that did it. It was soft, girlish, infectious – and Brian was smitten. During the meal he couldn't take his eyes off her. He chatted to her just to hear the delightful fractured English. She seemed utterly uninhibited. It didn't matter that there was a stranger at the table, she chatted away as if they were old friends. He even accepted a glass of white wine . . . and enjoyed it!

During the days that followed, he worked hard in the station, moving trains when and where they were required, organising the loading and unloading of both troops and equipment, then rushing home to wash and shave, ready to spend his time, when he was able, with Lisette.

She was twenty and unmarried, she told him, as they went for a stroll after dinner one evening. 'I 'ave not met the man I love enough to marry. With the war, it is difficult. The young men are away fighting or are in the Resistance, but I 'ave Papa to look after anyway.'

'Would you like to be married?' Brian asked.

'Only to the right man – and then I will 'ave lots of babies!' Her laughter echoed down the lane.

'You like children?'

'I love children.' She danced away from him like a child herself, then came back to his side. 'I want to 'old a baby to my breast and feel it suckle – 'ow wonderful that must be.' She stroked her breast as if trying to visualise it.

As he saw her taut nipple against her blouse, Brian felt himself harden. He wanted to reach out and touch the soft mound. Oh,

149

how he wanted her! His feelings were so strong they surprised him. What on earth was he doing? He was a married man! But as they continued their walk, the need for her was so great, it was painful.

How he wished he could shed his English constraint – be free with his feelings and emotions as was Lisette. How liberating it must be. He was far too controlled, had never been able to give free rein to his thoughts, unable ever to put those he had into words. Damn it, he couldn't even put them down on paper when he wrote to Kitty . . . Kitty! He hadn't given her a thought for days. How dreadful! Whatever was happening to him? He, with his rigid outlook and beliefs. He realised that since he'd been in the army he had changed – but fundamentally he was the same, surely? Yet here he was, lusting after a French girl! He glanced at her and she smiled at him. At that moment he felt he would die for her if necessary! Was this love?

'And you, *monsieur*, you are married?'

'Yes.'

'Do you 'ave babies?'

Shaking his head he said, 'No, and because of the war, my wife didn't want to start a family.'

'If my 'usband was in the war, I would want 'im to give me a child.'

'You would? Why?'

She looked up at him with tears misting her eyes. 'In case 'e was killed, then I would 'ave something of 'is, for ever. I would look at the baby and remember 'ow it was made with love – it would be my most precious belonging.'

Later that night, standing in his darkened bedroom, curtains pulled back, Brian studied the night sky, which was clear, and filled with stars. A crescent moon shone. In the distance were the sounds of trucks and the rattle of trains pulling out of the station under supervision of the night staff. Further afield explosions lit up the sky momentarily. He puffed on his cigarette and knew that despite the war – indeed, because of the war – he was more content at this moment than he had ever been in his whole life.

As the days passed, Brian began to lose a little of his English reserve, all due to Lisette, who would tease him. 'Are all Englishmen like you?' she asked.

'What do you mean?'

'We French are so, so . . .' she struggled to make herself understood, 'we show our feelings. If I am angry, I shout, if I am 'appy, I laugh, if I am in love, well . . . but you English, you never show anything!'

He chuckled. 'That's not true.'

'*Oui*, it is. You do not see the beauty of the simple things around you!' she exclaimed.

He was both puzzled and intrigued. 'Like what?'

She looked about her, then swiftly picked a wild flower and held it up for him to examine. 'What do you see 'ere?'

Shrugging, he said, 'It's a flower.'

'That's what I mean! Look at it closely, see the shape of the petals, see 'ow the colour deepens in the centre. It is so delicate, so beautiful.' She gazed at him with her soulful eyes. 'Can't you see it?'

And as he looked closely at the small bloom, he saw what she meant and, looking up, said, 'Yes, I see.' Then somewhat awkwardly he said, 'I see too the colour of your eyes. They're brown with flecks of hazel in them. They also are beautiful.'

She gave a cry of delight and said gleefully, '*Exactement!* There you are! You can do it if you want to . . . don't you want to?'

Slightly abashed at his own words, he said, 'I've never thought of things that way, I suppose.'

'Then it is time you did,' she said, and walked away.

Whilst the war was raging in Europe, the Germans were sending their V-1 bombs or doodlebugs, as they were commonly known, over England. You would hear the steady drone of the engines and then suddenly there would be silence as the bombs plummeted to earth, exploding on impact. Troops continued to pour into the

151

port of Southampton on the way to France. The ships transporting the troops did not return empty. They were used to bring home the wounded, who were sent away in fleets of ambulances, which were waiting at the docks, to hospitals around the country. Increasing numbers of German prisoners were brought back also, many of whom were temporarily housed in an improvised pen in Mayflower Park, much to the fascination of the locals.

Jeff Ryder was kept busy with the steady influx and departure of American troops. 'I wonder there are any men left in the States!' he declared to Kitty one evening as they sat in her living room, listening to the wireless.

'Are there many casualties?' Kitty asked.

'We are at war, darling, what else can I say? Have you heard from Brian?'

'I had a letter yesterday,' she told him. 'He's in the Dieppe railway station, working.' She paused. 'He seems quite happy.'

'That's good. Then you have nothing to worry about.'

It was a strange letter, Kitty thought. He sounded different somehow, but perhaps it was because he was staying in one place and doing work that was familiar to him. At least he wasn't with the troops that were fighting.

She and Jeff were like a married couple these days. Kitty had long since lost her interest in her neighbour's gossip. If Jeff were able, he now stayed the night, but, out of respect for Brian, the couple used the spare room for their lovemaking, which improved as the weeks passed, both aware that they had to snatch every moment they could as, eventually, Jeff would be sent to France. Every time he had to return to camp, Kitty was in fear of him receiving his orders to go, and longed for the days when they could be together properly, in their own home.

Gladys Freeman had also received a letter from Brian, which she read over and over and insisted on reading it several times more to her husband until, with exasperation, he said, 'For Christ's sake, woman, will you shut up!'

'Well, I never did! I thought you'd have been thrilled to get a letter from your son.'

'Of course I am, and I'm pleased that he's safe and seemingly enjoying himself, despite everything, but if you insist on reading it aloud one more time, you'll send me off to the pub!'

'Then go to the bloody pub!'

Frank got to his feet, grabbed his jacket, said, 'What a good idea,' and walked out of the house.

He welcomed the stale smell of the beer as he walked into the bar. He ordered a pint and sat chatting to one of his mates.

'Heard from your Brian?' the man asked.

'Yes, we heard today. He's holed up in Dieppe at the railway. Lodging with a French family, by all accounts. Well, the father and daughter – it seems the mother is dead.'

With a sly wink his friend said, 'He'll be all right then, nice little French mademoiselle, eh?'

'You forget he's a married man.'

'As long as he doesn't forget it.' And the man laughed.

Frank wondered if Kitty had forgotten she was married. He'd seen her in the town on the arm of an American officer. Nice-looking chap too. He wasn't too happy about it either but hadn't mentioned it to Gladys. My God no, she'd have been round there like a shot. It wasn't his place to interfere, he felt. War made strange bedfellows, but it usually all worked out in the end. Brian would come home, the Yanks would leave and they could all get on with their lives.

Nancy Brannigan was getting on with hers. She was slowly making a recovery and was able to get out of bed and walk a little. Gerry sometimes borrowed a wheelchair to push her around the hospital to give her a change of scene. She was still a little weak, but she especially enjoyed visiting the children's ward and watching those who were able, playing with the toys. She would look at those wearing bandages and look at Gerry, her eyes expressing pity for their plight.

To Gerry's delight she had uttered a few words, but the doctor had taken him aside and warned him, 'We don't think there is any brain damage. What she has suffered is severe shock, which has robbed her of her speech. It is imperative that she is kept calm and free from any further trauma. I have explained this to the police. It would be unwise to question her about the attack until she's stronger.' He frowned and added, 'She may well have blocked the whole incident from her mind anyway.'

'I see,' said Gerry. 'Thanks.' As he walked back to the patient he was frustrated beyond measure. He wanted to know if Eddie Simmons had anything to do with the assault, but he would have to wait. All he was doing was waiting, it seemed. There had been no sighting of the bugger anywhere. But he was bound to come up for air sooner or later.

Eddie, in fact, was enjoying himself. He'd got a job washing dishes in a smart hotel, cash in hand, which suited him. He had a small room in Earls Court, and after work, he went to the cinema, or out to a pub. He was fed at the hotel, so he didn't have to worry, which was a godsend, as he didn't have a ration book. If he was hungry he went to a café somewhere. He even went dancing, finding some girl there to fill his sexual needs. He became less of a fugitive, and stopped looking over his shoulder to see if anyone was watching him. One night, in need of female company, he went to the Palais de Dance, and spent the evening dancing with a girl who invited him back to her flat.

'Do you serve breakfast in the morning?' he asked cheekily.

'It depends on how well you perform, darlin,' she told him.

'In that case I might be there for lunch as well!'

What he didn't know was that the girl worked for one of London's villains, who was a friend of Gerry Stubbs.

Chapter Nineteen

Betty, the girl that Eddie was seeing, worked as a prostitute for Big Tommy Hanson, who ran several bawdy houses in the East End of London – and a black market ring. He was a massive man who ran his businesses with an iron rod. Everyone who worked for him had been given the details of the army deserter who his mate was looking for, with instructions to tell him personally if they thought they had found the miscreant. Betty was unaware that she had bedded the missing man, as the description was of someone with a beard. She liked Eddie and had arranged to see him again.

Eddie himself was extremely happy. He had a job and now a girlfriend who was good in bed. What more could a man ask for? During the following two weeks, they met frequently, between Betty's clients. He was well aware of how she made her money, but he didn't mind. Why should he? Live and let live was his motto.

The more he saw her and the closer they became, the more his male ego overcame his natural caution. He started to try to impress her. 'I was at Dunkirk, you know,' he told her one night in bed. 'Bloody terrible it was.'

'Why aren't you still in the army?' she asked.

He grinned broadly at her and said, 'I was invalided out. You, my dear, are sleeping with a hero! I saved a couple of men's lives, pulling them out of a foxhole, but I got shot in the leg for my trouble.'

She frowned as she'd not seen the signs of any wounds on him and she'd become very familiar with his body. 'Was it serious?' she asked.

'Enough to send me to hospital and get me out of the army.'

'Show me,' she challenged.

'No, no,' he said quickly. 'It makes me embarrassed to show my war wound. Come here, I've got a better idea as to how we can spend our time.'

After they had made love, she questioned him further about his life in the forces. He began to elaborate his fictional tale. So carried away was he that he became careless and when Betty asked, 'Do you have any brothers or sisters?' he answered without thinking.

'Yes, a sister in Southampton.' As soon as the words were out of his mouth, he cursed beneath his breath. How could he be so stupid? But as Betty continued with her caresses, he thought, why am I worried? I'm in London, among the thousands thronging the streets, passing through. This woman doesn't know I'm a deserter and, after all, she only knows my first name. No one is going to find me, he told himself. Where would they even begin to look?

Betty ran her finger across his mouth and then his chin. 'You know you'd look very handsome with a beard,' she ventured. 'I love a man with a beard; it tickles in all the right places when you make love. Or even a moustache, like Errol Flynn.'

He became watchful. 'Got no time for either, myself,' he said quickly.

She cuddled into him. 'Then I'll have to be happy with what I have. Kiss me,' she urged, wanting to take his mind off the conversation and allay any suspicions he might have. By the time she'd finished with him, Eddie had forgotten everything, except the feel of her voluptuous body and the gyrations it made beneath him as he satisfied his sexual needs.

The following day, Betty paid a visit to her boss.

156

'I have recently got to know a man who is a bit suspicious, and I wonder if he might be your missing deserter, as he told me he has a sister in Southampton. When he told me that, I began to wonder,' she said and proceeded to relate the tale of the missing war wound and beard. 'He got right twitchy when I mentioned him growing one,' she said.

'Have you arranged to meet him again?' asked Tommy.

'Yeah, in a couple of days' time. I'm to meet him outside the restaurant where he works, then we're supposed to be going to the pictures.'

'Right,' he said. 'Give me the time and place. I'll get in touch with my mate. Good work, girl. If it is him, I'll see you all right.'

Gerry Stubbs was delighted to get the call from London. 'Thanks, Tommy,' he said. 'I'll catch a train to the Smoke, and be there just a bit earlier on the day. Give me the address and the time this girl is supposed to meet him.' He picked up the pen and started to write.

It had been a busy day in the restaurant and Eddie thought he would never ever get through the piles of washing up. He cursed beneath his breath as even more dishes were carried out of the dining room. At this rate he would be late for his date with Betty, but he was sure she would wait.

At last he finished his chores and disappeared into the men's toilets to change into some clean clothes. 'See you tomorrow,' he called as he left the restaurant.

Outside, he looked around, but Betty was nowhere to be seen. 'Women!' he muttered. 'Always bloody well late.' He lit a cigarette and watched for her coming from the direction opposite. He finally saw her in the distance and waved, then he glanced to his left as a taxi hooted and caught his attention. He froze as, to his horror, he saw Gerry Stubbs and the two men with whom he shared lodgings approaching rapidly. He glanced back towards Betty, but she was no longer there. 'Bitch!' She had set him up.

He moved quickly, but not quickly enough. From his right side, he felt an iron grip on his arm and a voice he thought never to hear again said, 'Well, Private Simmons, this is a surprise. Who'd have thought that as we cast our net for deserters, you would land in it. You've made my day. The army will be pleased to have you back – you rotten little bastard!'

A sergeant was standing holding him, flanked by two tall Military Policemen. 'Take him away, lads,' said the sergeant. 'We don't want this little bleeder to take off again, do we?'

Gerry Stubbs and his men stopped in their tracks and watched as their quarry was taken from them.

'I don't bloody well believe it!' stormed Stubbs. 'Weeks I've waited for that bugger, and now he's going to be behind bars where we can't get at him.'

'If they court-martial him, guv, he'll be run out of the army at some time, even if they put him in the glasshouse for a while. You'll just have to wait.'

'Whenever he surfaces you have my promise, I'll be his welcoming committee. Glasshouse! He'll wish he stayed there when I'm through with him!' He turned on his heel and walked hurriedly away, swearing beneath his breath.

Inside the military vehicle, Eddie sat, hands cuffed, stunned by the unexpected turn of events. His blood had run cold at the sight of Stubbs and his thugs, and it was almost a relief to be taken by the MPs, even if he had to take an ear-bashing from the sergeant.

'A right case you are, Simmons,' began the NCO. 'I can stomach anything, except a coward.' He looked at Eddie with undisguised disgust. 'Some of your mates were killed in action. Brave men who had principles, who were prepared to lay down their lives for their country . . . and look at you! Living it up. Swanning around like you have the right. Well, I hope they throw the book at you!'

'At least I'm alive!' Eddie retorted.

'By the time I've finished with you, believe me, you will wish you were dead! I hope you know that soldiers have been shot in the past for deserting?'

At Eddie's look of horror, he smiled. 'Yes, think about it. That would be a turn-up for the book, wouldn't it? You running away from enemy fire only to be topped by your own! Well, let me tell you, I would be very happy to be in charge of the firing squad if asked.'

The rest of the journey was taken in silence.

On the arrival at the barracks, Eddie was put in a cell and told, 'You will be brought up before the commanding officer in the morning, who will decide your future. He may give you the choice of accepting his punishment or go before a court martial, but whichever it is, you will serve time, my son!' And the door slammed shut.

Eddie sat on the camp bed and ran his fingers through his hair. There must be some way to get himself out of this trouble, but if he was to squeal on Stubbs, he could be fingered for the murder that took place during the robbery at the furrier's, and that was the last thing he wanted. Here, he could spend a month in the glasshouse – or if he went for trial, goodness knows how long he would serve. Whichever it was, it was better than being taken by Gerry Stubbs and his men. If they got hold of him, he was liable to end up dead and his body found floating in the drink somewhere.

Gerry Stubbs returned to Southampton in a furious temper. He wanted Simmons so badly it was almost unbearable. For one thing, Eddie could finger him and his gang for numerous robberies – and a murder. Although it was Eddie who actually struck the blow that killed the warden, the others could be charged with being accessories, and Gerry had no intention of going down for something he didn't do. If he could dispose of Eddie, they would all be in the clear . . . but he had been cheated at the last minute.

His anger didn't abate after visiting Nancy that evening. She was running a temperature and was fretful. As he sat with her he thought of the vibrant feisty girl he had once known and wondered if she would ever fully recover. It only fuelled the anger boiling inside him. And later, after a few drinks, all he wanted was revenge. He knew just the place to get it.

Jeff had taken Kitty out for the evening and they had ended up at the Guildhall at a dance. As they left the building and made their way back to Harborough Road, he said, 'I can't stay tonight, darling. I must get back to the camp. But I can stay for a quick cup of coffee and a cuddle.'

As they arrived at the house, in the darkness, lit only by the torch that Kitty carried, they were unaware of the shadowy figure lurking in the front garden next door.

Kitty went into the kitchen to fill the kettle. Jeff followed her and put his arms around her waist, nuzzling the back of her neck.

'Now stop it!' she admonished. 'That isn't fair, you have to leave soon so don't start something you can't finish.'

'True, and every time I have to leave you, it becomes more difficult.' He turned her to face him and said, 'I love you so much, Kitty. I want to be with you every minute of the day.'

'I'm glad you aren't. My goodness, we would get heartily sick of each other if that was the case,' she teased.

They sat and drank the coffee and chatted and kissed one another until Jeff looked at his watch and said, 'Sorry, honey, but I really must go. I'll try and pop around sometime tomorrow. What shift are you on?'

'I don't go in at all tomorrow.'

'Then perhaps I'll come for breakfast,' he said. 'I could maybe get away for an hour.'

She snuggled into him and said, 'That would be lovely.'

She showed him out of the house, and walked back to the living room. Just as she was picking up the empty cups, she heard a knock. I suppose he's forgotten something, she thought, and glanced quickly around the room. There didn't seem to be anything. Opening the door, she began, 'What have you—'

Gerry Stubbs pushed her back inside, closing the door behind him. 'Hello, sweetheart,' he said. 'I've come to collect!'

Chapter Twenty

Kitty was frozen to the spot with fear as she saw the expression in Gerry's eyes. There was a wildness about the look he gave her and his mouth was tight with anger.

'How dare you push your way into my house?' she blazed, thinking that this was not the time to let him see she was terrified.

He smirked. 'Well, well, Kitty, entertaining the Yanks now . . . who'd have thought it? And there was me thinking you were faithful to dear old boring Brian, when all the time you've been lifting your skirts to the Allies.'

Kitty could see he was drunk. 'Don't you talk to me like that. You make me sound like some kind of tart and I'm not!'

'I bet your husband doesn't know his home is being used for the comfort of other men.'

'It's not a case of other *men*. That one officer and I are just friends, I'll have you know.'

'Yes, and my old dad is the Pope! I wasn't born yesterday, but I'm only too happy to see you are capable of passing your favours around, because now it's my turn!'

There was a tightening in the pit of her stomach as she asked, 'What do you mean?'

He caught her by the front of her blouse and pulled her towards him. 'Tonight you will lie with me, Kitty. Tonight I'll find out just how much of a woman you really are.'

She knew that this time there was no escape. She tried to move her head away but Gerry held it firmly as he lowered his mouth to hers. She felt the invasion of his tongue as he forced her lips open. She wanted to be sick. He scratched her as he tore the front of her blouse, exposing her firm breasts encased in a lace brassiere.

With a lustful gaze he said, 'Beautiful. Full and rounded, just the way I like them.'

'Don't you touch me, you bastard!' she cried.

'I haven't even begun,' he said, and lifted her up, carrying her, kicking and struggling, until he found the bedroom, pulled back the covers and threw her roughly on the bed. He held her down, lifting her skirt and tearing at her knickers, throwing them aside. He then undid his trousers and stepped out of them.

Kitty sickened at the sight of his swollen member. 'Don't do this, please, Gerry,' she pleaded.

'Now come the tears, I suppose. Well, don't waste your time. You are paying for the misdemeanours of that fucking brother of yours!'

'I'm not responsible for Eddie. *You* took him off my hands – I didn't ask you to.'

He was livid. 'I did that to help you, or have you forgotten? That was my first mistake, keeping him was the second – the third was letting you off the hook when I was drunk.' There was such a note of menace in his voice as he spoke it chilled Kitty to the bone. 'The army picked him up the other day, by the way, but when they're done with him, he's mine . . . and now – so are you.'

Despite her struggles, she was helpless against Gerry's superior strength as he spread her legs and thrust himself into her, again and again. She tried to scream, but he smothered her mouth with his. He grasped her breast in a brutal manner, and she flinched as he pinched the pink nipple, moaning softly to himself, until eventually he came. He slumped on top of her, his breathing heavy, his body at last still.

Kitty lay silent, tears trickling down her cheeks – her body violated.

Stubbs eventually got to his feet and dressed, staring at her partly naked form, until she tried to cover herself, averting her gaze from his.

As he put on his jacket he said, 'It would have been better if you had been a bit more co-operative, darling, like you are with your Yank, but I'm not one to complain.' He straightened his tie. There was a look of disdain on his face as he glared at her. 'You know, Kitty, you have really disappointed me. I kind of put you on a pedestal, you know. Always fighting me for your honour, and though I complained bitterly, I respected you for it. But you are no better than any of the whores walking around Southampton with their Yankee boyfriends. You had me fooled for a while, I must say.' He buttoned his coat. 'I'll be off then.'

Kitty turned her head and glared at him, her voice filled with hatred. 'If you ever come near me again, Gerry Stubbs, so help me – I'll kill you! she threatened. She could hear his laughter as he walked down the stairs and out of the house.

As soon as she heard Gerry leave, she got to her feet, stumbled to the door and bolted it, then slumped to the floor, trembling from head to toe. Hugging her aching and bruised body, she sobbed until she was exhausted. Eventually she struggled to her feet and ran a bath, filling it, ignoring the five-inches-only rule of the day, climbed into it and scrubbed herself from top to toe until she made her skin red and sore.

She tore the soiled sheet from the bed and rolled it into a tight bundle, casting it aside with disgust. After, as she lay on the bed, she tried to shut out the ugly scenes that had taken place, but they wouldn't go away, until, desperate for peace of mind, she got up and made herself a strong cup of tea and laced it with a large shot of brandy from a bottle that Jeff had given her. After a while she slept – albeit fitfully – under a blanket on the settee.

Early the following morning, Kitty woke. She felt stiff and sore. Her eyes were puffed from weeping, her mouth was tender and there were bruises and scratches on her body. She closed her eyes in despair as she saw her reflection in the long mirror of her wardrobe. One moment she was filled with rage, the next uncontrollable tears. Her hands shook as she filled the kettle and tried to light the gas. She cupped her hands beneath the cold tap and splashed the water on her face, trying to pull herself together, when suddenly she remembered that Jeff was supposed to be calling that morning! She was panic-stricken. There was no way she could let him see her like this. She hastily scribbled a note.

'Friend not well. Gone down to Bournemouth to look after her. Will contact you when I return,' it read. She quickly and furtively pinned it to the front door, shut herself out of sight in the kitchen, and listened for him. She heard the sound of his Jeep's engine outside, his footsteps coming up the path, then silence, footsteps receding and thankfully the sound of his vehicle leaving.

In the kitchen, Kitty breathed a sigh of relief. She couldn't possibly contact Jeff until her bruises were healed, and then it would be lie upon lie to hide the real truth. But she had another more serious concern: Gerry Stubbs had not taken precautions when he'd raped her. Now she would be on pins until she had her next period. My God! The very idea that he could have made her pregnant was almost too much to bear. Jumbled thoughts filled her mind as she tried to cope with the possibility. If that happened, she'd have an abortion! She buried her head in her hands.

All this was through her bloody brother. She recalled the fact that Gerry told her the army now had Eddie. She wondered how that could be and wished she'd had the good sense to contact them herself and hand her brother over when he'd first called on her. Life was full of ifs. If the war hadn't happened – if Eddie hadn't deserted – if she hadn't known Gerry Stubbs, if she had never met Jeff . . . She took two aspirins, hoping they would relieve some of the pain, and staggered to bed as a means of escape, curled herself into a ball and tried to shut out everyone and everything.

Kitty remained like this for two days, unable to leave the house, unable to let the factory know she wouldn't be in, but she couldn't worry about that. She would think up some explanation when eventually she was able.

The front and back doors were firmly bolted – not that she really thought that Gerry Stubbs would return. He'd taken what he had always wanted, but she was still frightened. At least she knew that Brian wouldn't come marching in. He was still in France, according to his letters.

Brian's last thoughts these days were of home; apart from the time he read letters from his mother and Kitty. He was concerned about the Germans' new weapon, the flying bombs, now descending on England. Southampton, however, was not suffering from them too much; London seemed to be the main target. One or two of his mates had families there but they were being evacuated, it seemed. The battle for Caen was still raging, and there were constant raids by German bombers all of which the troops trying to run a railroad had to contend with. The most exciting news was the attempt on Hitler's life in late July.

'Pity the bugger wasn't killed,' Brian said to Lisette as they stood in the darkness of the garden, watching the flashes of the guns in the distance. 'The war would have been over in a few months.'

'And then you would be sent 'ome,' she said quietly.

He glanced at her. Their friendship had grown as the weeks passed. 'You sounded sad when you said that,' he said tentatively.

'I will be sad when you go. I 'ave got used to 'aving you around.'

'I'll miss you too.' He took her by the hand. 'I think you are the most beautiful girl in the world.'

'Take care, Brian,' she teased. 'You are forgetting that you are an Englishman; they don't say things like that.'

'Because the English don't say much, it doesn't mean they don't think them,' he protested.

'So, what are you thinking?'

She was teasing him, he knew that, but there was a certain invitation there too. 'I'm thinking I would like to take you in my arms and kiss you.'

'Then, *chéri*, stop thinking about it and do it!'

As he held her, he could feel the soft round contours of her body as she pressed against him, offering her mouth willingly to him. Never had he felt like this before, not even with his wife. He was swept away with passion . . . with love. He loved this woman and had done so from the first moment he saw her. All else was forgotten in their ardent embrace.

'Oh, Lisette, how can I leave you and go back to England. I want to stay here with you always,' he murmured against her hair as he held her.

Gently stroking his face she said, 'But you 'ave to go back eventually: you 'ave a wife to go 'ome to.'

Gazing into her eyes he said, 'I thought I loved Kitty, but since meeting you I now know what real love is. Don't misunderstand, Kitty's a good woman and we're fond of one another, but I am not the man of her dreams.'

Lisette smothered him with her kisses. 'We 'ave today, Brian, never mind tomorrow. We don't even know if we will survive this war. The Germans could come back. Let's take the time we 'ave together. I love you, let's make the most of it.'

Brian looked bemused. 'How can you love me? I'm a staid Englishman, you are full of life.'

'It is because you are what you are, *chéri*. You are a – 'ow you say? – a solid person. But now you are blossoming into an exciting man also, *non*? I like that too.' She gazed at him from beneath lowered lashes. 'Papa is working tonight, come with me to my room.'

He was both excited and a little shocked at her suggestion. 'Do you know what you are saying?'

She laughed at him. 'Brian, I am a Frenchwoman, I know what I want. I want you. I am not in'ibited like your English girls.'

It was his turn to be amused. 'If you saw some of our women

with the Yanks, you wouldn't call them inhibited!'

'There you are then.'

'You are sure about this?' he said.

'I am sure,' she said and, taking his hand, she led him inside the house and upstairs to her room.

In the low light from the bedside table, he watched her undress. She was slender and lithe and completely natural as she shed her clothes. He did the same and they lay together, their naked bodies entwined as they made love. Lisette was not shy and told him what she wanted from him. He was being schooled in the art of lovemaking, and it was an enlightening experience.

As they lay back against the pillows, he said, 'That was not the first time you have done that.'

Chuckling softly she said, 'That good, was it?'

Pulling her closer he said, 'It was wonderful.'

Later, as Lisette slept, Brian lay thinking how great life would be if he was married to this crazy woman, living here, helping with the railway, instead of being in Southampton. He felt a pang of guilt when he thought of Kitty. He had been unfaithful to his wife, broken his marriage vows, but he had been with the woman he truly loved. This must have been what Kitty had looked for in their marriage. How disappointed she must have been, yet he had thought what he had was fine, was all it should have been! Never did he realise it would feel like this. This wasn't lust, this was true love. He even considered getting a divorce after the war. My God! How his mother would carry on if he did! How would Kitty feel? Would she feel betrayed, or would she be relieved? All these muddled thoughts . . . He turned towards Lisette and took her in his arms. She murmured softly in her sleep and he kissed her forehead. He closed his eyes and slept.

Five days after her attack, Kitty returned to work. She used makeup to disguise the bruising on her face. Her clothes covered those on her body. She made up an excuse to the foreman that she had a touch of influenza, which he accepted, especially as she didn't look particularly well, but Jean, her friend, was not so easily fooled.

'Whatever has happened to you?' she demanded when she first saw Kitty.

'I've not been well. I'll talk to you later.'

But Jean had seen her wince once or twice at her machine and when they took their lunch break she didn't accept Kitty's excuse. 'Hurt yourself, have you?' she suddenly asked.

Shaken, Kitty said, 'Whatever do you mean?'

'You are obviously in some sort of pain. Now the flu doesn't do that. What's been going on, Kitty?'

'Nothing, nothing at all.'

'Your Yank hasn't been heavy-handed, has he?'

'Good heavens, no.'

'Just asking. Some of the girls have found a few bad 'uns, that's all.'

'Jeff is a perfect gentleman, and a gentle man,' Kitty insisted. 'I'm fine, really.'

Jean didn't pursue the subject further.

Kitty would have given anything to have confided in her friend, but the offence was so serious, she dare not. Anyone in their right mind would have reported Gerry Stubbs, but she couldn't. Her brother had killed a man. He was in custody now and would probably serve time, and Stubbs knew all this. She couldn't be the one to put a hangman's noose around Eddie's neck.

How Gerry had changed! There had been none of the old chemistry there. Now he was hard and unforgiving. Never would she have believed it possible that he could have treated her so harshly – telling her she was no more than a whore. Now he frightened her. Before, the sense of danger about him had been exciting. Now it was terrifying.

Chapter Twenty-One

Jeff Ryder was getting worried. It had been over a week now since he'd called on Kitty and found the note pinned to her door, yet there had been no word from her. The silence was driving him mad. He felt helpless. And, moreover, word had come through that he would soon be posted to France, to continue his work there. He had no idea how soon and he was desperate to see Kitty before he went. Jumping into his Jeep, he headed for Harborough Road to see if perhaps she'd returned.

Kitty had been hanging out her washing when she heard a knock on the door and, thinking it was the postman, she opened it.

'Kitty, honey, you're back!'

She tried to cover her surprise and shock at seeing her lover, praying the bruise on her face was no longer visible.

'Jeff! Yes, I got back late yesterday.'

'How's your friend?'

She quickly tried to gather her thoughts. 'Much better, a touch of flu, that's all.'

He looked at her with a bemused expression and asked, 'Are you going to ask me in or are we going to feed the local gossip out here?'

She stepped back. 'Sorry, yes, of course, come in.'

Once he stepped inside and shut the door, Jeff took her into his arms and held her. 'God, I've missed you.' He tilted her chin and kissed her gently. But all she could feel was Gerry Stubbs' mouth assaulting hers, and she eased Jeff away, saying, 'Come into the kitchen and I'll make some coffee.'

'Is something wrong?' he asked.

'No, nothing, why should there be?'

'You don't seem that thrilled to see me, that's all.'

'I'm sorry,' she said, 'I've been so busy, what with looking after my friend and getting back late last night, that I'm exhausted.' He didn't answer but she felt him watching her closely as she made the coffee. It began to unnerve her and turning to him she said, 'Why don't you go and sit down and I'll bring this through?'

He didn't move. 'Have you heard from Brian? Have you had bad news?'

Gazing at him, she said, 'No. I heard last week; he seems fine.'

'Then what is it?' he persisted.

'What on earth are you talking about?'

There was a sharpness to her voice as she answered that didn't escape his notice. 'Kitty, you are on edge, nervous. Don't you think I know you well enough to sense that? Now what the hell is it?'

How on earth could she tell him? She wanted to – oh, how she wanted to. She needed to be comforted by the man she loved, to be told by him that everything would be all right, but she couldn't. Neither could she stand the hurt expression as he looked at her. Putting down the coffee, she went to him and wound her arms around his neck.

'Hold me, just hold me?' she asked.

He took her into his arms, and Jeff could feel the tension in her body begin to relax as they stood in a gentle rocking embrace. Neither spoke, but he was deeply concerned. Something was radically wrong; what on earth could it be? This was so unlike Kitty he couldn't even begin to imagine. But he wouldn't press her; she would tell him in her own time.

They eventually sat at the table with their coffee. 'How have you been?' she asked.

'Busy. Troops and supplies are still being shipped abroad.' He

171

looked at her and said, 'I'm so pleased you're back because I will be shipping out with them myself quite soon.'

Her heart sank. She was devastated; this was almost too much to bear. Whatever else was going to happen? Her world was falling apart around her, it seemed, and she was helpless to stop it. She put out her hand and took his. 'Have you any idea when?'

He shook his head. 'It will only be a matter of weeks now.'

'Oh, darling, I'll miss you so much,' she said, biting back the tears.

He rose from the table and, taking her hand, led her to the settee. As they sat he put an arm around her and held her close. 'I know, I'll miss you like hell too, but it was bound to happen. We have been more than fortunate to have this long together.' He gazed into her eyes. 'Do you still love me, Kitty?'

'How can you ever doubt it? Of course I do.'

'Enough still to come to the States and live with me as my wife?'

'I'll go anywhere to be with you.'

'It won't be easy for you, divorcing Brian.' He grinned and added, 'You will take some flack from his mother, that's for sure.'

This made her laugh at last. 'That miserable old biddy would be grounds for divorce if the law was fair!'

Jeff said, 'I have to go but I'm off duty tomorrow night – can we spend it together?'

'Of course.'

'I'll take you out somewhere for dinner first, how's that?'

'It'll be lovely.'

She saw him to the door and waved goodbye as he drove away. Back in the living room she wondered how she would feel when they went to bed. At the moment the very idea of having sex was absolutely repugnant to her, but Jeff was her true love and soon he'd be leaving. There was no way she could refuse, but secretly she was dreading it.

Meanwhile, her attacker was feeling very pleased with himself.

Nancy Brannigan was coming home! As far as the doctors could tell, there was no brain damage. Her power of speech was returning, but when the police were eventually allowed to question her, she told them she couldn't remember anything other than being grabbed from behind and then waking up in the hospital ward.

'It's the shock of it all,' the doctor explained to Gerry. 'She may never remember because she doesn't want to. The trauma may lie buried for ever or it may come back suddenly, if something or someone triggers that secret button.' He patted Gerry's arm. 'The main thing is she's pulled through. She just needs building up, a bit of cosseting. My advice to you is don't probe. Forget it, put it behind you, that's what Nancy has done. Now she needs to get on with her life – let her do so.'

It was all very well for him, Gerry thought. He wanted to know if Eddie was behind the assault – not that he could do anything about him for the moment. He had heard that he was going before a court martial. Well, he should be swinging from a thick rope and if he had his way, when the bastard eventually was free, he would sort it – once and for all.

It was deemed best for Nancy to return to her family for the first week. As Gerry explained to her, 'I can't be around all the time to look after you for the first few days. You can move into my place after that, if you like.'

She smiled at him. 'Won't I be in your way?'

Grinning at her, he said, 'No, Nancy. I never take other women back to my place, only you. When you are a bit stronger, we'll have a great time, you'll see.'

'Have all the Yanks left town?'

He saw the laughter in her eyes as she asked, which cheered him. At least there was a bit of the old spark left.

'By the time you are fit enough for Yanks, my wild Irish girl, the war will be over. Then what?'

'I'll have to make do with you,' she said.

173

'Cheeky monkey! Look, I'll have to go. I'll send a taxi for you in the morning. I've left some food at your mum's to feed you up. I'll pop in to see you in a couple of days' time.'

As Nancy watched him walk away she wondered just what he would do if he knew that Eddie Simmons was the man who'd put her in hospital. Had Simmons not been in custody, as Gerry had mentioned one evening during visiting hours, she would have told him. Time enough for that when Eddie was out of prison, because it seemed certain that he would serve time. She wondered how long he would get. However long, she hoped he'd have a hard time. She'd wait for her revenge. It would be all the sweeter for the wait. She would insist on watching him get what was coming to him. She would stand where he could see her. She wanted him to know why he was being punished.

Kitty Freeman stood naked before her mirror, turning this way and that, searching for telltale bruises. There was a slight yellowing here and there, which could easily be explained away if necessary. She felt desperately unhappy. Jeff would soon be leaving and she should want to be close to him during the few precious moments left to them, and that bastard Gerry Stubbs had spoiled it for her: for that alone she would never forgive him.

During dinner with Jeff, Kitty tried to be normal, to make him laugh, to enjoy him, but despite everything, there was a certain atmosphere between them. Kitty was worrying about being a loving bedmate and Jeff was puzzling over whatever it was that was still worrying her. Perhaps her sick friend was worse than she suggested, but if this were the case she would have told him. The thought had occurred to him that she had met someone else. This he dismissed almost as soon as it entered his head. Kitty was no fly-by-night. No, it was something very deep and therefore serious. If only she would share it with him.

Later in bed, he didn't rush her but held her in his arms, stroking her hair, telling her how much he loved her; teasing her, trying to make her relax because in his arms she was tighter than a spring.

'Kitty darling, we don't have to make love if you don't want to,' he said.

She burst into tears.

He rocked her like a child until her sobs subsided. He reached for his jacket and took out a handkerchief. Handing it to her, he said, 'Well, I've never found a woman so relieved at not having me make love to her.' He smiled down at the tear-stained face and asked, 'Am I that bad in bed?'

She did manage a smile. 'Don't be ridiculous. It just me. I'm so sorry. But don't think it's because I've stopped loving you. I love you so much I can't find the words to explain.'

'Couldn't you try?' he teased.

Chuckling, she said, 'Now you're fishing for compliments.'

'Jeff, I'm really tired – could we just go to sleep?'

'If that's what you want, of course, we'll just cuddle up together. As long as I can just hold you, I'm happy . . . not as happy as I might have been,' he said, grinning wickedly, 'but I'll settle for that.'

As she lay quietly in his arms, Kitty counted her blessings in finding such a man. She would make it up to him next time. Yes, next time it would be all right, but as she lay there, she couldn't help wonder what would happen if she found she was pregnant with Gerry's child. The waiting was driving her crazy.

Chapter Twenty-Two

Eddie Simmons was kept under close arrest awaiting his court martial. He had been marched before his commanding officer on his return and was given a strict talking to.

Lieutenant Colonel Humphries looked at him coldly before saying, 'Men like you, Simmons, give the army a bad name. The nation needs real soldiers on a battle front, not miserable wretches like you.' He looked down at a report lying on his desk and said, 'You have a bad attitude, according to your sergeant. You have never liked discipline, but discipline is what makes not only a good regiment but also a good man. You have failed both, miserably. You disappear for months on end, showing complete lack of responsibility, and now you will pay the price for letting me down, the regiment down – but, most of all, your country. You will be informed of the date of your trial. In the meantime you will be allocated an officer to defend you. He'll contact you later this morning. Take him away!'

As Eddie was marched back to his cell, his heart was beating nineteen to the dozen. He was really in the shit now, he thought, and had no idea how long a sentence he would receive, although he knew he would be sentenced. There was no way he could get away with this. But one thing he did know: when, eventually, he was a free man, he would have to lie low. If only he could leave the country, but with the war still on, it wasn't possible. Nor was it legal. Ireland and Switzerland were the only safe places, being neutral, but he just couldn't get to either. When the war finished, he'd get a job on a ship and leave it at some foreign destination, anywhere that was out of the reach of Gerry Stubbs.

Stubbs was being very careful these days. Yes, he dabbled in the black market still, but in a very minor way. His legitimate business was still ticking over and he was still sitting on his pile of money, but he knew the case of the air-raid warden was still open and the local police superintendent was very keen to clear up the mystery. Thank God that Simmons was locked away, Gerry thought. Eddie wasn't going to say anything to incriminate himself, therefore there was no one who could incriminate *him*, apart from his own men, and he trusted them. They didn't want to be accused of murder either.

Now that Nancy was home, his anger had abated, but he felt no remorse about Kitty. To think she was consorting with a Yank when he had thought her such a lady. She was no better than any of the other girls around town! He wondered just how Brian would take the news if he were ever told. He took a perverse pleasure when he thought about it. Freeman was always a bit high and mighty, even at school. Well, he wouldn't be so now if he knew about his wife carrying on, would he? Gerry laughed loudly to himself at the thought, as he walked into his office.

Brian was far from being high and mighty. In fact, low and lustful would describe him better as he straddled his French mistress, the sweat breaking out on his brow as his passion was being spent. He rolled off Lisette and lay beside her, completely exhausted.

She threw an arm over him and stroked his now limp phallus. '*Chéri*, you are a changed man in bed these days. You 'ave become like Casanova!'

He looked a mite embarrassed; nevertheless he smiled with pleasure because it was true. Lisette had been a good teacher. He had learned how to please a woman as well as himself because she had demanded it, telling him what she wanted and showing him how to be more adventurous. He'd discovered the pleasures of other positions instead of the usual missionary one. And now sex was synonymous with love as well as desire.

He fondled and kissed her. 'You have made me that way,' he said.

'Making love is an art, *chéri*. Never to be rushed, but to bring enjoyment and satisfaction.'

The corners of his mouth twitched with amusement. 'I'm very satisfied, how about you?'

''Ow very English,' she chortled. 'Never would a Frenchman ask such a question. 'E would know; 'e would expect his partner to 'ave an orgasm – every time.'

Brian still found it strange that Lisette could talk so freely about sex. How very different life was here. Although the war was still being fought, and they had suffered raids that had sent them flying for cover, the living was honest, uncomplicated, without pretence. Lisette was without pretence ... about anything! It could be disconcerting at times. After one particularly hard day he'd returned to the house and taken her into his arms, only to be pushed away.

'*Merde*. You stink like a pig!' she had exclaimed. 'Go and strip off your clothes and wash.'

He had slunk away to do as he was told. Kitty would never had said such a thing. Sex with his wife, he remembered, had never been exciting and this was his fault, he now realised. He'd not been much of a lover; he'd only satisfied himself. Now he wondered if she had pretended to enjoy it and thought she probably had, and even knowing it was he who was at fault, it annoyed him. Why had she not been honest about her expectations, like Lisette? But, of course, it wouldn't have been very British!

As the weeks had passed, Monsieur Pallier had accepted that his daughter was having an affair, and turned a blind eye. This would never have happened back home, Brian mused. He found it all so liberating but worried how it would be when at last the war was over. He didn't want to go home, he wanted to stay here with the beautiful, wanton and sexy girl to whom he had lost his heart. The very idea of leaving her was painful. He was a changed man from the soldier who had sailed from Southampton into uncertainty. The army had changed him but, more so, being with Lisette had changed him into a real man with feelings, feelings he was learning to put into words. Through this wonderful woman he was quickly casting aside his inhibitions. He liked who he was these days and didn't want anything to change.

While Brian was living a contented existence, across the Channel, Kitty was devastated that Jeff would be certain to be sent to France with only minimum notice at any time. She was desperately unhappy and clung to him.

'It won't be for ever,' he said, trying to bring her some cheer. 'We are breaking through the German defences all the time. We are only forty miles from Paris now, and before you know it the war will be over.'

Gazing into his eyes she said, 'Don't you go getting yourself killed over there!'

'Not me, honey, I'm fire-proof! Listen, I can get an overnight pass for tomorrow. I'd like us to go to the hotel in Lyndhurst just one more time before I leave. Can you manage it?'

'Of course I can,' she said.

'I'll have a twenty-four-hour pass from ten o'clock in the morning. We'll drive to Lyndhurst, leave our stuff and walk in the forest, have lunch somewhere, go back to the hotel and later, have some dinner. How's that sound to you?'

'Wonderful!'

'I have to go now, so I'll collect you just after ten in the morning.' He kissed her soundly and left.

Knowing that Jeff was bound to be leaving soon, Kitty put aside all her fears of making love to him after her experience. She refused to let that bastard Stubbs rob her of the time spent with the man she loved. She wanted to be close to him, because heaven knew when she would ever see him again. She wouldn't even let herself dare think that he might never return. That was too dreadful to contemplate.

He was on time and Kitty ran out to the Jeep, carrying a small suitcase, and jumped into the vehicle, completely unaware that her mother-in-law was coming down the street and had seen her leave.

Gladys stood dumbfounded. Well, the brazen hussy! That was the same American she'd seen her with at the pictures. She turned sharply on her heel and made for home.

When her husband arrived home from work later that day, she gave full vent to her feelings. 'You'll never believe what I saw today with my very own eyes!'

With a deep sigh Frank asked dutifully, 'What did you see?' He sat at the table and removed his heavy shoes.

'Her! That wife of Brian's. She's nothing but a whore.'

Frank looked up and said, 'Good heavens, woman, is there any need to use such language? And the girl's name is Kitty.'

His heart sank as she said, 'I saw her getting into a Jeep with that Yank, the one at the cinema. And she was carrying a suitcase.'

'Now don't you start jumping to conclusions,' he warned.

She was puffed up with outrage. 'Do you think I'm simple or something? She was off to stay somewhere with him. I really don't know what the world is coming to. I'll write and tell Brian what's going on.'

'You will do no such thing!'

'He has a right to know.'

Frank got to his feet and glowered at her. 'For once in your life, you will mind your own business. Do I make myself clear?'

'How can you say such a thing? A man has a right to know what his wife is up to.'

He was angry and it showed. 'Now you listen to me. You don't know for sure that anything is going on.' He put his hand up to stop her interrupting. 'And another thing, you only want to cause mischief. That's why you want to write to him.'

She exploded with rage. 'How dare you say such a thing?'

'Because it's true. You have never given Kitty a chance from the day your dear son told you they were getting married. She put your nose out of joint!'

'Rubbish! I'm only thinking of him.'

'Like hell you are! If you were thinking about him you would realise that a man away fighting the enemy doesn't want bad news of any kind. Bad news can make a man careless; he could get himself killed. Would you like that on your conscience? If you were a decent mother you would want to protect him.'

He had deflated her sails. 'I wouldn't want anything to happen to him,' she conceded.

'Good, at least you have some sense. Now get my supper, woman, I'm starving.'

Gladys retreated to the kitchen, mumbling to herself. Well, maybe it wasn't wise to inform Brian whilst he was in a war, but she would soon tell him the truth when he came home . . . and she'd be round there in the next few days to give that wife of his a piece of her mind. No one was going to stop her doing that!

Completely unaware of the commotion she was causing, Kitty was blissfully happy. She and Jeff had booked into the hotel, then wandered through the forest, stood and watched the ponies, were enchanted by the squirrels gambolling around, hunting for food, and enjoyed their moment together. They sat on the bench under the trees on top of the small hillock – their favourite spot – and talked.

'I'll always remember this place, with you sitting here beside me. It is so beautiful, so very peaceful, like a small slice of heaven here on earth. I'll carry this picture with me wherever I go.'

She snuggled into him. 'In another month or so, the leaves will start to turn, then it is really glorious – and in the spring, when the buds appear and new life begins.'

'I have been so happy in Southampton since we met, and I can't wait to return so we can really start planning our future together. I'll have to go to the States to leave the army – they can't do it here – but I'll be back for you. Of course, I'll return to Boston first to see my folks and prepare them for an English daughter-in-law.'

She frowned and asked, 'Do you think they'll like me? Won't they expect you to marry some American woman?'

Laughing he said, 'Don't be an idiot, honey. They want what makes me happy. They'll adore you as I do. Come along; let's walk back to the hotel. We'll have some lunch and then we'll go to our room where I can show you how much you mean to me.'

As she lay in his arms, Kitty closed her eyes and breathed in the scent of the man beside her. She caressed his broad chest, ran her finger along the sensuous mouth and kissed the fingers that had just given her so much pleasure. She loved Jeff unreservedly. With him she felt a whole person. Complete. Here in his arms she shut out the ugly pictures of her rape and relaxed. She knew when he went away it would be like losing a limb and she would be in pain until his safe return. But pain meant love, and if she had to suffer to be able to live the rest of her life with him, she would happily do so.

'You will write to me often, won't you?' she asked.

'As often as I can, darling. But if you don't hear for a while, or regularly, please don't worry. It can be difficult to send mail sometimes.'

She stretched like a cat. 'I feel so contented, I don't want to move.'

He kissed her gently. 'I'm going to take a bath, then we should get dressed for dinner. It may be the only chance we get and I've ordered champagne, so we will dine in style and celebrate our future together.'

It was a memorable evening. The chef had done them proud, after Jeff had told him that he would probably be leaving for

France shortly. They sat at a table in a quiet corner, away from most of the other diners, like two honeymooners, enraptured with each other. They walked in the grounds of the hotel in the moonlight before they retired to their room where they finished the night with coffee and cognac. It was as if this was their wedding night as they made love and vowed to be true to each other.

They drew back the curtains and stared at the stars in the clear sky. Jeff pointed to a line of three and said, 'I think that is part of the Plough, but whatever they are, and wherever I am, I'll look for them in the sky and think of you, here beside me.'

'And I'll do the same,' she promised. 'Until you come back to me.'

Chapter Twenty-Three

Gladys Freeman walked along Harborough Road with a determined air. She'd been building up to this meeting with her daughter-in-law for days and, if she were honest, she was looking forward to it. Ever since Brian had first met the girl who later became his wife, things between her and her boy had never been the same!

Kitty, getting washed and dressed ready for her stint in the factory, was unaware of the old warhorse approaching and when there was a knock on the front door, she assumed it was the milkman.

Gladys rudely pushed past her when the door opened.

'Do come in,' said Kitty angrily, 'and why the front door – you usually come round the back?'

Without invitation, Gladys strode into the living room and, turning on Kitty, said, 'It's time somebody spoke to you about the way you're behaving and as Brian's mother, it's my right to do so.'

Immediately the hairs on Kitty's neck stood up, raised by anger. 'You have absolutely no right to interfere with my life; I don't give a damn who you are. You had better leave now.'

Gladys drew herself together. Imperiously she said, 'I will not tolerate your behaviour when you are married to my son!'

'*You* won't tolerate my behaviour! Who the hell do you think you are to barge into my house and tell me how to live my life? My own mother wouldn't do that.'

'I saw you getting into a Jeep the other day with your American, suitcase and all. What have you to say to that?'

'It's none of your bloody business, you interfering old biddy. Look to your own marriage before you come trying to sort out mine.'

Taken aback by this accusation Gladys asked, 'What on earth do you mean?'

By now Kitty's dander was up. 'You have a wonderful husband and how he puts up with you I'll never know . . . do you ever think about him and his needs? No. You only think about yourself. You and "Your Boy". It's your husband you should be considering instead of poking your nose in other people's business.'

It was now the older woman who was on the defensive. The sudden flush of outrage started at her neck and rose until her face was puce. 'I'll have you know I've been married for thirty years and never looked at another man.'

'And I don't suppose one has looked at you either,' retorted Kitty cruelly. 'You are a monster! Just think how lucky you are to find a man who would put up with you for so long. Now I suggest you take yourself and your nasty little mind back to that saint of a man who has the misfortune to have married you!' Taking Gladys by the arm, she pushed her to the front door and opened it. 'Don't bother to call again.'

At a loss for words for once in her life, Gladys stepped over the threshold to have the door slammed behind her. She walked slowly away, deflated by the slating she'd had. She had been so ready for battle but Kitty had hurled her own accusations at her. Had she been right?

For the first time in years, Gladys took a close look at her life. She couldn't accept the slurs thrown at her. Her Frank had never complained. She'd always done what was right for the family, and now she was only trying to protect her son's marriage. She straightened her shoulders and walked away.

Kitty was fuming. She could have cheerfully strangled Gladys

Freeman, but now, it would seem, her affair with Jeff was out in the open. Well, she didn't care. Her love for him was something she had no control over. She had a chance at a new life in a new country with a man who felt the same about her, and no one – especially an embittered old woman – was going to spoil it for her. She grabbed her handbag and left the house.

On the way to work, Kitty made a detour and called at her mother's. Tapping on the kitchen door she walked in. 'Anyone home?' she called.

'Here!' called Amy from the living room. She took one look at her daughter's face and asked, 'Whatever is the matter? I can almost see the steam coming out of your ears.'

Throwing her handbag on the table, Kitty stormed about her mother-in-law, telling Amy what had transpired.

When Kitty had run out of angry words and had stopped to draw breath, her mother said quietly, 'You can hardly blame her, dear.'

'What?' Kitty couldn't believe what she was hearing.

'Brian is her son, and when she sees you swanning off with an American officer . . . what do you expect from the woman?'

'But you don't carry on like her.'

'No, you are my daughter, but you know I'm not entirely happy with the situation. I'm worried you will give up your marriage only to find out too late that it was a mistake. However, I do know Gladys Freeman and she is an interfering woman. There are tactful ways of doing things.'

'She couldn't even spell the word. They should stand her on the front line and let her have a go at the Germans!'

'You think that would stop the war?' asked Amy with a broad grin.

'No. They'd fire a cannon at her and blow her to smithereens. Deservedly so.'

The women both started laughing, which relieved the situation, and when Kitty clocked in at the factory a little later, her temper had cooled.

When she arrived home, Gladys, to her chagrin, was still upset. She began to wonder just what her husband really thought of her. Was he a happy man? Did she interfere a lot? She supposed that she did really but only when she thought she was right. She had ruled the roost she supposed, but that was because she was a strong woman and Frank was easy-going. She was in a state of confusion and decided to work it off. It was the only way she knew how to cope with her feelings of uncertainty.

When Frank Freeman arrived home that evening, the house gleamed and the smell of lavender furniture polish assailed the senses. The brass ornaments shone and the stove was gleaming from the black leading that had been polished with vigour. Gladys was strangely quiet, he thought, as she waited for him to wash. She placed before him a plate of stew topped with dumplings and mashed potatoes, which she knew he liked.

'You all right?' he enquired.

'Fine,' was the succinct reply.

Knowing her so well, he was certain that eventually he would be told what was on her mind at great length, therefore he enjoyed the unusual peace as he ate his fill, slowly, to prolong the interlude.

Clearing his plate, he said, 'That was lovely, dear, thanks. Just what a man needs after a hard day.'

'Am I a good wife, would you say?'

He looked at her in astonishment. 'Good heavens, where did that come from?'

'You haven't answered me.'

He was suddenly aware of the terseness in her voice. 'I've never complained, have I?'

'No, you haven't, but that doesn't mean that you think I am.'

'Whatever is biting you, woman? Out with it. Something is obviously eating away at you. Tell me and stop beating about the bush.'

It was the only invitation she needed. Gladys poured out the whole sorry story of her visit, word for word from beginning to end. He listened in silence until she'd finished.

'You never cease to amaze me with your stupidity!' Frank snapped.

It was like a devastating blow to Gladys. 'What the hell do you mean?' she cried.

'You just can't help interfering in things that don't concern you, can you? Brian and Kitty have to take care of their own lives. They're not children, you know!'

'I can't stand by and see my son made a fool of by that girl.'

'How do you know that he is being a paragon of virtue?'

She glared at him. 'How could you even think such a thing?'

'For Christ's sake, woman! Brian is a man; he's away from home and may be so for much longer. It's wartime, things happen.'

'Did they happen to you? You have been in a war.'

'That was before I married you, Gladys, and I was very young, but yes, I had a good time.'

She looked at him as if he were a stranger.

'You don't think you were the first woman I slept with, do you?'

Not knowing what to say, she gathered together the dirty plates and took them into the kitchen, but she couldn't get out of her head the mental picture of her husband with another woman. That was hard to accept. This was not the Frank that she knew; the man, she realised with great clarity, she had taken so much for granted.

Nancy Brannigan was now well enough to go out and about. Her bruises had healed, her ribs still a little tender from the beating she took, but apart from the occasional headache, she was back to normal. Well, almost. She still flirted with anything in trousers, but she stopped short of having sex with them. Her bad experience had affected her inasmuch as she didn't want any man to invade her body – as she thought of it – except for Gerry. She felt safe with him and he was considerate whenever she consented to have sex with him. Nevertheless, she was no longer as voracious as she used to be.

As each day passed her hatred for Eddie Simmons became increasingly obsessional. She wished he was free because she would have shopped him to Gerry and delighted in his come-uppance. In fact, longed for it. Now the bastard was safe behind bars, but she would pay him back eventually, even if she had to wait a lifetime. She had heard he was awaiting trial and wondered if he had been sentenced. So desperate was she to know, she decided to visit his sister. Surely she would know, and then she, Nancy, could plot her revenge.

Kitty was approaching her house when to her surprise she saw Nancy coming from the opposite direction. She waited.

'Hello,' she said, 'I was sorry to hear about your trouble. Are you better?'

'In some ways, not in others. Could we have a word?'

Taken by surprise and somewhat cautious, believing that her brother had been the cause of Nancy's beating, she said, 'Of course. Would you like to come in and have a cup of tea?'

'Thanks.'

Whilst Kitty was boiling the kettle, Nancy looked around the living room. She admired the neatness and the furnishings. Nothing was expensive but obviously it had the feminine touch and good taste to make the most of it. The room was cosy and inviting. As Kitty smiled across the room at her, Nancy had to admit the girl was attractive, with her dark hair and blue eyes. There was a softness about her that was lacking in her brother.

Kitty brought the teapot, cups and saucers to the table. 'I'm sorry I've no sugar. I've used up my ration until next week.'

'That's all right,' said Nancy. 'I'm used to going without it now. I wondered if you had any news of your brother?'

Kitty paused for a moment as she poured the tea, then

continued. 'No, I've not heard from Eddie for a while.'

'I know he's in an army prison!'

'Do you?' She stared at Nancy and asked, 'What exactly are you here for?'

'I want to know when that bastard is coming out.'

'Why are you so interested?' Kitty asked, although dreading the answer.

'Because it was him that beat me up, that's why!'

Kitty's fears were realised. 'I am sorry to hear you say that.'

Picking up her cup, Nancy looked over the brim at Kitty and said, 'You don't seem that surprised.'

Meeting her gaze, Kitty said, 'Well, I knew that he was seeing you whilst Gerry was away. I told him it was stupid and would lead to trouble. I did ask him if he was the one that hurt you but he denied it.'

'So you thought he was capable, then?'

'I hoped I was wrong. Does anyone else know this?'

With a smirk Nancy replied, 'Not yet, but when the time is right I'll tell Gerry and he'll sort him out.'

'Oh yes, Gerry Stubbs is good at taking revenge,' snapped Kitty.

'Did you know that your bloody brother raped me?'

Kitty was shocked and horrified. 'No, I certainly did not!'

'No, well, it isn't the sort of thing a man should be proud of, but he did. In the office, before he beat me up.'

'I am so sorry to hear this. How dreadful for you. Does Gerry know about it?'

'No, it's not something I want anyone to know but you. I want you to understand why your brother will be paid back.'

Remembering her own misfortune at the hands of Gerry Stubbs, Kitty felt compassion for the girl. 'I understand your bitterness,' she began.

'How can you understand? I'm no angel, but to have a man force himself on you leaves a mark. If it hadn't been for Gerry's kindness, I don't know what I would have done.'

To hear Gerry held up as a paragon of virtue was more than Kitty could take. 'Oh, he can be kind when it suits him, but you should be very careful. He is as big a bastard as my brother!'

'At least he wouldn't rape a woman.'

Seething inside, Kitty glared at Nancy. 'No?'

It took a moment for the girl to recognise the significance of the remark. Frowning, and with an expression of disbelief, she said, 'Oh my God! You're not telling me that he did that to you?'

'Yes I am! Because he thought it was Eddie who had attacked you, he took his revenge out on me, here, in my own house. So you see – I do know just how you feel.'

Muttering expletives under her breath, Nancy said, 'Men are such bastards!'

'Not all of them,' argued Kitty. 'Some are gentlemen through and through.'

'I've yet to meet one,' remarked Nancy ruefully, 'but I expect a lot of that is my own fault.' She grinned broadly. 'If I'm honest, I use the buggers.'

'But rape is something else, isn't it?'

With a look of despair the Irish girl agreed, 'Yes, it is. I felt dirty afterwards. Used, like a piece of dirt. Worthless.'

'I do understand, and I can't tell you how sorry I am that it was my brother who is to blame. He never was any good.'

Rising to her feet, Nancy said, 'I'd better be off. Thanks for asking me in. Is there anything I can do for you? After all, you suffered on my account.'

'It wasn't your fault, but if you do have any influence at all, make sure that Gerry doesn't come back. He is one to hold a grudge, as I'm sure you know.'

'You don't think he will return, do you?' asked Nancy, startled by the very idea.

Shrugging, Kitty said, 'No, not really, but I keep all my doors and windows locked just in case.'

'You poor bitch! I'll see what I can do.'

Kitty didn't confide in her her fear of pregnancy. Her period was due in a few days' time and she was praying that everything would be all right.

As she walked home, Nancy Brannigan went over in her mind everything that had been said between her and Kitty Freeman. She felt real sympathy for her, knowing what she'd been through, the feeling of degradation afterwards, and she wondered how she could ever approach Gerry. He had been really good to her but now if he knew for certain that it was Eddie who was the culprit, would he go back to seek his revenge on Kitty again? She couldn't let that happen.

Chapter Twenty-Four

Private Eddie Simmons stood to attention in front of the officers acting as judges at his court martial. It had been fairly straight-forward. The officer defending him had done his best to plead on his behalf, but there were no mitigating circumstances that led to his desertion, which didn't give his man much of a chance.

The officers sitting at the long table facing him muttered together for a few minutes and all nodded their agreement, before one of them spoke. 'You have been found guilty as charged and will serve a six-month sentence. Have you anything to say?'

'No, sir.' What was the point, Eddie thought. It wouldn't make a bit of difference.

As he was marched away he mused that six months in the glasshouse was a lot safer than being in France or the hands of Gerry Stubbs. Whatever they threw at him inside would be a breeze compared to either alternative.

He was bundled into an army vehicle with a couple of other miscreants and driven to Aldershot to serve out his term. They, it appeared, were to serve a month each for insubordination. Eddie didn't converse with them. Although he felt he was safe inside, it was just beginning to dawn on him that he had lost his freedom. Even with the threat of Stubbs hanging over his head, he had enjoyed being in London, wandering around, pleasing himself. This would be very different. He knew enough about the army to know that whatever was ahead wouldn't be easy. Discipline and order never had sat well with him and he knew he'd be in for a tough time. It had been said that a sentence could be shortened for good behaviour, and he could be free in three months if he had a mind to behave himself. He'd heard of criminals getting 'stir crazy' from being shut up, but he didn't think that would bother him. It would be having to obey orders that would give him the most trouble.

As the vehicle entered the barracks and was driven to the correction unit known as the glasshouse, he saw that the area they were now in was surrounded by barbed wire. They drove through the main gates, which were closed sharply behind them.

The three of them were bundled out and marched in double-quick time to their room. 'You've got fifteen minutes to stow your gear, and I mean fifteen. Not sixteen, not eighteen,' bellowed the sergeant, a bruiser of a man with a mean look about him. 'Get used to it. Everything is done to time here, every minute of every day. Get on with it!' Looking at his watch, he walked out of the room.

There was an unspoken air of urgency among the prisoners, and in silence they did as they were told, but when the sergeant returned he turfed all their belongings on to the floor and told them to do it again in less time, and properly. 'You will learn to be fast and efficient if you want to last in this place,' he said.

They duly tried again, but this time the sergeant stood and watched, his timepiece in his hand. 'Sixteen minutes isn't good enough!' The belongings once more were in a bundle on the ground.

By now Eddie was fuming inside but he knew enough about the army to know this was their first test. The glasshouse was there to break the rebellious spirit of a man and Eddie knew that he would really have to control his temper if he was to earn remission for good behaviour. He would be sorely pushed to achieve that.

The following morning, the inmates were stood to attention on the parade ground where they were put through their paces, marching to double-quick time throughout. Eddie's muscles in the back of his legs ached until he stumbled and was given a great deal of verbal abuse by the sergeant before being sent to have breakfast. 'You will be given half an hour and no more!' the prisoners were warned.

As Eddie stood in the queue, he became very impatient at the slowness of the serving. 'Can't you lot hurry up?' he called. 'By the time you've got your fingers out, we'll have no time to eat.' He was completely ignored and was forced to bolt down the food in front of him when he eventually sat down.

After their hurried meal, the men were given their duties for the morning and handed buckets of hot water, mops and tooth-brushes. Eddie looked at his and asked, 'What are we supposed to do with these?'

The NCO told him they were to clean the latrines and the toothbrushes were for scrubbing the edges and nooks and crannies of the place. 'I don't want to find a scrap of dirt anywhere when I do my inspection,' the men were told, 'or you will do the whole place again.' Eddie swallowed the words of anger rising in his throat.

While Eddie was on his knees cleaning, Jeff Ryder was busy sorting out the papers in his office, ready to hand over to another officer who would be taking his place, as he had received orders telling him he was being shipped over to France three days hence. He had been expecting such a move for some time, but now the notification had arrived he found that, mentally, he wasn't pre-pared for it. He had become used to his life in the camp at Southampton, and his affair with Kitty, the woman he loved and intended to marry. It had all become cosy and safe. Now he had to face the fact that he was going into a battle zone and there was a possibility that he might not return. He also knew that it would put added pressure on Kitty, having her husband and her lover in France. He hadn't been free to see her for several days as it was, and tonight he had only a few hours to spend with her. He was at a loss how to handle the situation.

★ ★ ★

Kitty was delighted to see him when later that evening he arrived at the house. Throwing her arms around his neck she kissed him. 'I've missed you these past few days,' she said.

He held her close before saying, 'I'm sorry, darling, I can't stay for too long. I've a lot of packing up to do.'

She looked at him with anxious eyes. 'Why are you packing?'

He held her face and said softly, 'I'm being sent to France.'

'No!' She clung to him as the tears ran down her cheeks.

Leading her over to the settee he tried to comfort her. 'We have been so lucky to be able to spend so much time together. We knew it would happen eventually.' Kissing her eyes, her cheeks, her mouth, he said, 'It won't be for long. The Germans can't hold out much longer. Paris has fallen to the Allies now. It's just a matter of time.'

'Where are you going?'

'France is all I can tell you, Kitty. I'll write to you as soon as I can, but if you don't hear for some time, don't worry. In wartime, mail can be difficult.'

'Don't you dare go and get yourself killed,' she said.

'What, and leave you to the tender mercies of other men? I'll be back, have no fear.'

She quietly reached beside the settee and touched a piece of wood for luck. 'How long have we got?' she asked.

'Long enough for me to make love to you,' he whispered. 'I want to hold you in my arms to give me something to remember during the lonely nights ahead.'

'And they had better be lonely!' she teased.

Gazing into her eyes, he said, 'There's only one woman for me, Kitty, and that's you. You are my night, my day . . . my life. Without you I am nothing.'

'Oh, Jeff. I do love you so much.'

Their love that night was full of tenderness. Knowing he was leaving gave an added poignancy to their caresses, their murmured words. And when it was over, they lay in each other's arms, silent, lost in their own thoughts, until Jeff said, 'I have time to have a cup of coffee with you and then I must go.'

Kitty told herself she must put on a brave face. She didn't want Jeff's last moments with her to be marred by tears. Those she would shed when he had gone and she was alone.

Whilst they sat together at the table in the kitchen, he handed her a bankbook. 'I have opened a bank account for you,' he said. 'There is five hundred pounds in it.'

She gasped with speechless amazement. This was a great deal of money to her.

'This is to give you something behind you for emergencies.'

In case he didn't come home, she thought. He said he'd leave her money to get out of her unhappy marriage if she so wanted. 'I don't know what to say.'

'There is nothing to say. At least I know you have a certain security, should you need it.' He cupped her face in his hand and kissed the tip of her nose. He looked at his watch and rose to his feet. 'I have to go, darling.'

They walked to the door together. Jeff took her into his arms and kissed her soundly. 'I love you and I'm coming back.'

'I'll be waiting,' was all she said as she opened the door.

He climbed into his Jeep, stared long and hard at her, then drove away.

She stood at the door, tears silently trickling down her face, watching the vehicle until it rounded the corner and was lost from sight.

Kitty returned to the kitchen, picked up the bankbook, held it to her breast and sobbed.

The following day, Kitty confided in her friend Jean. 'I feel as if someone has died,' she said woefully.

Jean, being a realist, snapped, 'But no one has, you silly bitch! Jeff is just going to France with thousands of others. He'll be fine. You just have to have faith, that's all. I can see you haven't changed your mind about him then?'

197

Kitty shook her head. 'I never knew how much love one human being could have for another. I adore him.'

'Well, I have to say, he's a good-looking bloke from what I saw of him.'

'But it's not for his looks that I love him,' said Kitty. 'He's just such an interesting person to be with. I have learned so much from him during these past months. He taught me to think for myself, to be my own person. With Brian I was his wife and that was it. We never sat and talked about anything but domestic matters.'

'Well, my old man isn't any Einstein but I still love the old bugger. Have you heard from Brian lately?'

'I get the occasional letter, not that he's any great writer, but he's safe and well, and he seems strangely happy.'

'Not desperate to get home?'

'Funnily enough, no. He doesn't say he misses me or his home, and definitely not his mother!' Both girls laughed. 'He writes mainly about being in France. He loves the place, imagine that? Brian, a thorough Englishman, beer and meat pies his staple diet, but now he writes about French cooking . . . and drinking wine. He used to call it foreign muck. Well, I guess the war has changed us all.'

'Yes, it certainly has,' agreed her friend. 'I just wonder how we will all settle down when it's over.'

Kitty, knowing that when the war ended and Brian came home her problems would begin, didn't want to think too much about that, yet she wanted the war to come to a close so that everyone would be safe. What a muddle life was! She had definitely changed – Brian too – and she imagined that in every household there would be difficult days to face in the future, one way and another. But when her period was late, she was faced with yet another dilemma.

Chapter Twenty-Five

Kitty was in despair. Her period was now almost a week late, which was unusual. A day, maybe two, had been known, but never as long as a week. She tried to make excuses. It was the drama of being raped, of Jeff leaving: all these things could have taken their toll and she couldn't be certain. She would have to wait another four weeks. Then what the hell was she to do? She walked up and down her living room, beside herself with worry. She had sworn she would have an abortion if this happened, but she had heard so many sordid stories of backstreet abortionists and even a couple of girls dying as a result. Who could she confide in? No one at this stage. Oh God, what a mess!

Gerry Stubbs was a nervous wreck. One of the men who had been on the fur heist with him, and had been a witness to the accidental killing of the air-raid warden, had been picked up by the police whilst burgling a house. The house owner had returned unexpectedly and had overpowered him during a scuffle and summoned the police.

Stubbs' main concern was that Ernie, who had a long crime sheet, would ask for several other cases to be taken into consideration, and thereby be given a blanket sentence. Gerry was afraid that he might grass on him in exchange for time off. He knew for a fact that, although Ernie had worked for him many times over the years, there really was no real honour among thieves, as the saying went, and when it came down to personal survival, anything could happen.

He walked up and down his office like an animal in a cage, snapped at his staff and nearly bit the head off Nancy Brannigan when she called to see him.

'What do you want?' he demanded, scowling at her.

'Thanks very much,' she retorted. 'A nice welcome that is, I must say.'

'I've got a lot on my mind.' Putting a hand in his back pocket he pulled out a wad of notes and peeled off two fivers. 'Here, go and buy yourself something.'

She glared at him. 'When will you learn that money doesn't buy everything? I came here just because I wanted to see you. To be with you.'

He didn't have the patience for such niceties and said, 'Fine!' and went to put the money away.

She snatched it out of his hand and said, 'I'll bloody well take it because you were so rude, but don't expect me to be all lovey dovey when you come home.' She tossed her hair angrily. 'Anyway, I may not even be there.'

'Please yourself,' he snapped, and strode out of the office.

She walked towards the shopping centre, deep in thought. She had been living with Gerry ever since she'd recovered from her ordeal with Eddie Simmons. When she'd first moved in, Gerry had been very kind and solicitous, but as she improved, he reverted to normal. He was loving whenever he wanted sex, but treated her like a skivvy around the house, expecting her to keep the place clean, do his washing and ironing, cook his meals and meet every demand he made – and she was sick of it. I'm not his bloody wife, she thought, and now he doesn't even treat me like a mistress. Besides, she still had the mental picture in the back of her mind that he had raped Kitty Freeman, and she hated him for it, despite the fact that in bed, he treated her with gentleness.

She was stronger mentally now and certainly didn't need him

as a crutch. She was better off living at home and leading her own life. She would get a job, she decided, be independent, and if he called on her as he used to and she felt like it, she'd go out with him; if she didn't, she'd tell him to take a hike!

When Stubbs eventually arrived home, he put the key in the door and called, 'Nancy!' There was no answer. He yelled her name again. He was hungry and wanted something to eat and was in no mood to be messed about. He stopped and listened and realised the house was unusually quiet. Nancy normally had the wireless blazing, but not tonight. He went up the stairs two at a time and looked in the bedroom. The bed was unmade and several drawers were open – and empty, the clothes removed from the wardrobe. Then he realised she'd left him. He cursed under his breath, not because of any deep feelings he had for her, but for the inconvenience it caused him. He slammed out of the house and made for the nearest café.

Ernie Byers was sitting in the interview room facing two detectives, watching them very carefully, being economical with his answers. There was no way he could deny the break-in, as he'd been caught in the act, but he was trying to decide which of the other jobs he'd pulled he could lay before them.

'Come on, Byers,' one of the policemen said. 'Help us clear up the crime sheet. I know you haven't been keeping your hands in your pocket. We have a list of burglaries and we would dearly like to tick a few off.' He started to read down the list.

Ernie sat listening as he sipped a cup of tea he had been given, but when they suddenly said, 'Eric's, the furrier's in Bedford Place,' Ernie spluttered tea all over them.

The detective who had just been reading from the list looked at the prisoner with eyes that narrowed as he said, 'Was that down to you, my son? Bit out of your league, isn't it?'

Shaking his head vigorously Ernie denied it. 'That weren't nothing to do with me, guv, honestly.'

201

The detective glared at him. 'Now why is it that I'm convinced that you're lying?'

'No, I'm not. That sort of heist isn't my game. Burglary, yes. Like I did that one you mentioned in Hill Lane and the other in Wilton Road.' He rattled off a couple more addresses in his haste to convince them. 'You know my record as well as I do.'

'Then why did you react the way you did?'

'I was so surprised that such a serious crime was listed with the others. A bit of breaking-and-entering is one thing, but that – well . . .'

'The warden was killed,' said the detective, watching Byers closely.

'Yeah, I read about it in the papers.'

The two policemen looked at each other and this time the second man spoke. 'Yes, of course we know about you, and we know that violence isn't your game, and you certainly don't want to be sent down for murder, but if you gave us a name, it would really help your case. We'd put a good word in the right ear.'

Ernie paled. 'You're not laying this at my door. I had nothing to do with it. No way.'

'Where were you on that night?' asked the other man suddenly.

'How the hell do I know? It was some time ago.'

They told him the date.

'I can't remember,' he protested.

'Well, we'll take you back to your cell and give you a bit of time to think,' he was told. 'Solitude is good for concentrating the memory.'

As he was led back to his cell, Ernie Byers was sweating. He would continue to lie about the furrier's. If he did then there was no way they could pin it on him. There were no witnesses, he knew that. He would just have to watch what he said and deny everything.

Later that evening Nancy Brannigan was in the ladies' room at the local pub. Just as she was about to open the door, which led back to the bar through the snug, she heard the voice of Gerry Stubbs, who had entered with his mate Jack. Not wanting to see him, she closed the door to, listening to their conversation, wondering when she could make good her escape.

'I'm worried about Ernie,' said Gerry. 'I only hope he keeps his mouth shut about the fur coats and Eddie snuffing out the old geezer.'

'The last thing we expected was the air-raid warden, guv. If only the stupid bastard had chinned him, knocking him out instead of using the lead pipe, the old man would have made it.'

Nancy was shocked. Eddie Simmons had killed the air-raid warden! She felt suddenly nauseous as she realised how near to a similar fate she had come at his hands. She bent her head and listened further.

'He won't cop for that,' said Jack. 'He certainly won't want to go down as an accessory to murder.'

'Neither do I,' grumbled Gerry. 'But you know what it's like: if the Old Bill get wind of anything they wear you down. I'm not sure he's strong enough to withstand such pressure.'

'The idea of a long stretch inside will keep him shtum. He don't like doing porridge – but then who does?'

'If I could get my hands on that bloody Eddie I'd do for him myself. Worst mistake of my life, taking him off his sister's hands.' He smirked to himself. 'Still, she paid for the error.'

Nancy felt a chill down her back at his words, knowing full well what he meant. Anger coursed through her at his casual dismissal of such a dreadful action – and now *she* knew about Eddie, and this was dangerous knowledge. Certainly something that could get her killed if Gerry ever found out . . . but at the same time, maybe it could be useful. The police would be very pleased to have a lead and it could be a way to pay Eddie back for the beating he gave her, but she would be involving Gerry too. It would be a very hazardous thing to do, because if he got away with it, he would come after her if he discovered she was the one to grass on him. She decided to keep well clear of him in the future. She waited until the two men had time to have left the pub before daring to come out. She then ordered herself a double Scotch to settle her ragged nerves.

Jeff Ryder was driven to Paris where he was to be posted at the headquarters the American Seventeenth Army had set up. Despite the fact that the Germans had been driven out, there was a taut atmosphere in the newly liberated city. Snipers were still picking off targets. Women, crudely named 'horizontal collabora-tors', who had been friendly with the Germans, had their heads shaved and were paraded in disgrace wearing placards telling all of their shame. General de Gaulle and other leaders of the Free French had walked up to the Cathedral of Notre-Dame to celebrate the liberation as the church bells pealed.

It was in the aftermath of all this that Jeff had arrived. He was given a room in a hotel and set up in an office, faced with a mountain of paperwork, for there was much to be done.

It was several days later that he had any time to sit and write to his beloved Kitty.

My Darling, [he wrote]
I am now in Paris, a romantic city in normal times, and I so wish you could be here with me. We could walk along the Seine in the moonlight, stroll down the Champs-Elysées, and sit at a table drinking coffee and watch the world go by. Of course, it isn't quite such a peaceful picture at the moment as the city is full of French and American troops and naturally there are the usual shortages, yet the beauty of Paris shines through all this mayhem. I miss you more than I can tell you and long for the day when once again I can hold you in my arms.
Love
Jeff xx

When Kitty received the letter, she was overjoyed and read it repeatedly. He was safe and still loved her. It lifted her spirits for a moment, but then the thought that she could be carrying Gerry Stubbs' child filled her with despair. If this was the case she had two choices: to have an abortion, or to have the child. Then what? Would she put it up for adoption and pretend it had never happened? Live with Jeff and this lie? If she kept it, how could she possibly explain to him and to Brian? How would they feel? Would Jeff understand and stand by her?

Ever since he had taken his leave of her, she'd read the papers avidly, listened to every news broadcast, wondering where he was and was he still alive, now at last she knew he was safe. She would put her other troubles behind her until they were proved one way or another. It was with a bounce in her step that she walked up to Bedford Place and into Eastman's the butcher's to buy a shilling's worth of meat to make a stew. She had been off her food, but now she felt ravenous.

The butcher looked at her happy smile and said, 'You look all perky this morning, Kitty. Had some news from your old man, is that it?'

'Yes,' she lied.

'You'll soon have him back safe and sound, you'll see, and hopefully rationing will soon be over too. Got to feed up our men when they come home, haven't we?'

They continued to exchange polite conversation until Kitty left, clutching her parcel. She supposed she should feel guilty, she thought, but nothing could mar her happiness, not even the sight of her mother-in-law coming towards her. The last time they had met, Kitty had ordered her out of the house. Today Kitty walked up to her and said, 'Hello, Mrs Freeman. How are you?'

Gladys glared at her. 'You have no shame, have you? You walk up to me as if nothing has happened, yet I know for a fact that you have been unfaithful to my son.'

'You know nothing for a fact!' retorted Kitty. 'You only think you know, and I suggest that you be very careful of what you say in case I have you up for defamation of character.' And she strode away.

205

So the old devil was right about her and Jeff but she wasn't going to give her the satisfaction of knowing. Anyway, she didn't want the interfering busybody writing to Brian. It wouldn't be fair for him to learn of her infidelity through a letter from his mother. But it did occur to her that if she had a child, how Gladys would crow at the top of her voice. It completely ruined her morning.

Chapter Twenty-Six

The love affair between Brian Freeman and the lovely Lisette Pallier had increased in its intensity. Monsieur Pallier, as a concerned father, had taken Brian aside one night and had asked him some very pertinent questions.

'Monsieur Brian, do you love my daughter?'

Although startled by the direct way he had been approached, Brian didn't hesitate. 'I adore her,' he said.

'That is all very well, but what 'appens when the war is over? You leave my girl with a broken 'eart and go 'ome to your wife!'

Brian met his piercing gaze and declared, 'I will have to go home, *monsieur*, but it will be to ask my wife for a divorce. I want to come back to France and marry Lisette.'

The Frenchman wasn't convinced. 'All soldiers make promises, then they go 'ome, see their families, and poof! All else is forgotten. What if Lisette 'as a child?'

With a wide smile, Brian said, 'I would be so happy. I want children. I would care for them both.'

''Ave you told this to Lisette?'

'Of course, and she is happy to wait for me.' He looked earnestly at the other man. 'This is no sordid affair, Monsieur Pallier. I didn't expect to fall in love, but I will never betray your daughter.'

'You 'ave betrayed your wife!'

A frown creased Brian's brow. 'It's true and she doesn't deserve it, but the feelings between me and my wife are nothing compared to the love I have for Lisette.'

'You 'ave a bad marriage?'

'No, I can't honestly say that. My wife is a good woman, but our marriage is a disappointment to us both, if I'm honest. I feel sure she will be happy when I suggest we part.'

The Frenchman looked worried. ''Ow can you be so sure?'

'It makes little difference,' said Brian. 'I am coming back to France and Lisette. No matter what.'

'I 'ope you are a man of your word,' stated the Frenchman firmly.

'You have my promise on it.'

Monsieur Pallier rose to his feet and said, 'I 'ope so.'

Later that evening, when Brian was with Lisette, he asked her, 'You do believe me when I say that I'll return to France after the war, don't you?'

She wrapped her arms around his neck and said, '*Oui, chéri*, why do you ask?'

'Because your father doubts my word.'

'Of course, 'e is my papa, but 'e is only looking after me.' She started laughing and said, 'Are you worried that 'e will come after you with 'is shotgun?'

With a chuckle Brian said, 'I wouldn't put it past him if the need arose.' Pulling her closer he added, 'But it won't be necessary. I'll be back, we will be married and have lots of babies.'

Lisette smothered him with kisses. 'I want your babies. Little half-English Brians, running around.'

'We may have girls.'

Gazing at him with a smouldering look she said, 'What a delight it will be trying to make them.'

'You are a shameless hussy!' he laughed.

'What is a 'ussy?'

'A sexy girl,' he explained. 'One without shame.'

'Sex is shameful? I don't think so, and neither do you, *chéri*, not the way you are when we make love. The way you drive yourself inside me.'

His laughter rang out. 'You don't have any inhibitions at all. My mother would have a fit if she could hear you.'

'I would not say this to your mother, but she 'ad sex at least once, or you would not be 'ere!'

The mental picture of his mother and father copulating sent Brian into fits of laughter. 'What a ridiculous idea!'

'Not at all!' protested Lisette. 'Just because it is our parents doesn't mean that they don't 'ave the same needs.'

'I know and you're right, but it just seems strange.'

She gave a wicked grin. 'A little bit dirty, I think you mean.'

'Something like that.'

'*Chéri*, don't go all English on me. You 'ave that look in your eyes like you 'ad when you first arrived.' She caressed his face. 'Those closed thoughts don't belong in France. You are learning to be open, don't shut your mind again.'

He suddenly smiled. 'You're right. Sex is wonderful, no matter who does it!'

She clapped her hands together with glee. '*Voilà!* That's better.'

As they walked on, Brian couldn't help but wonder just what his mother would make of this young woman, should they ever meet. She certainly wouldn't know how to cope with her, and that gave him a certain satisfaction.

Kitty was in despair. She had missed a second period. It seemed almost certain now that she was with child and she didn't know which way to turn. She walked up and down her living room, trying to picture every scenario. Brian arriving home and finding a baby in the house; Jeff discovering the same thing. Would he still want her, even if she explained how she became pregnant? Would he be sympathetic . . . would he even believe her? If he didn't, then she would have to stay married to Brian . . . but maybe he too wouldn't want her and her bastard child. Her thoughts were driving her crazy. How she was filled with loathing for Gerry Stubbs. It was all his fault. She had to make a decision very soon.

The following morning in the factory, she suddenly felt nauseous and, shutting down her machine, made a hurried dash to the toilets where she vomited. She rinsed out the foul taste from her mouth and splashed cold water on her face, as she felt feverish. Then taking a drink of water, she returned to her workbench.

Jean was watching her carefully, worried about her pallor, and as they finished their shift and clocked off, she approached her friend. 'Not feeling well?' she asked anxiously.

'What are you talking about?' asked Kitty.

'I saw you dash out. I just wondered if you were all right.'

Kitty looked at her friend and hesitated. She had to confide in somebody. 'I'm pregnant!'

'Oh my God! What on earth will you tell Brian?'

'I really don't know.'

'Well, anyway, Jeff will be pleased. He'll have even more of a reason to want to marry you.'

Kitty's gaze lowered as she murmured, 'It isn't Jeff's child.'

Jean looked stunned. 'What?'

Tears welled in Kitty's eyes. 'The baby is Gerry Stubbs'.'

'What kind of a fool are you, Kitty?' Jean raged. 'Don't you have enough trouble without letting Gerry make love to you?'

'I didn't let him. He raped me!'

Jean ushered her outside away from eavesdroppers and when they were alone, Kitty told her friend everything.

'Come on, love,' said Jean, 'we need a drink to help us think,' and she took Kitty into the lounge bar of the nearest public house. They sat drinking gin and tonic in a quiet corner. 'How far gone are you?'

'I've missed two periods.'

'Does anyone else know?'

Kitty's eyebrows rose. 'Are you kidding?'

Jean, ever practical, said, 'Well, Kitty, you have two choices, keep it or have an abortion.'

Kitty cringed. It made it all seem so sordid.

'If you keep it,' her friend reasoned, 'it causes so many problems, with Brian but most of all with Jeff. Men are a bit strange when it comes to rape. You would think they would be full of sympathy, but for many it is too big a problem for them to handle. If you get rid of it, no one will ever know.'

'*I'll* know!'

'Of course, and you will never forget it, but if you do get rid of it, you will never ever be able to tell Jeff after you marry him. It will have to be a lifelong secret. No confessing after.'

Kitty put her hand to her head. 'Christ! What a bloody mess!'

Watching her friend's distress, Jean hesitated, then said, 'I do know of a woman who will do it for you. A friend of mine got in a mess like you and went to her.'

Kitty looked at her in horror. 'But isn't it dangerous?'

Shrugging, Jean said, 'It's a chance you take, I suppose, and if you have the money. It costs twenty quid.'

White-faced and shaking, Kitty thanked God for the money that Jeff had left her and said, 'I don't have an alternative, do I?'

'Of course you do, but there will be consequences. It all depends which chance you want to take the most.'

Kitty lit a cigarette and, deep in thought, slowly sipped her drink.

Stubbing out the cigarette, eventually she said, 'Can you arrange for me to see this woman and soon?'

'If you're sure.'

'I'm not sure of anything so don't question me any further. Please just do it!'

Swallowing the last of her drink, Jean said, 'Fine, I'll go round now and ask my friend to make an appointment for you. I'll see you tomorrow at work.' Patting her friend's shoulder she said, 'I'm sure you have made the right decision.'

Kitty sat alone for a moment longer thinking: I wish I could be sure.

The following morning, Jean told Kitty that the appointment had been made for two days hence. 'Would you like me to come with you?' she offered.

Shaking her head, Kitty said, 'No, thanks, and I do appreciate it, but I have to do this alone. Just give me the address.' She read the piece of paper and saw the house was in the Chapel area, which didn't bode well. What did you expect, she thought, some nice house in Bassett? Nice locations didn't go in for illegal abortion!

On the appointed day, with trepidation in every step, she made her way to Nelson Street. The normally run-down area of the town now looked much worse as it had suffered during the Blitz and many houses were boarded up whilst others were just wrecks after the bombing with the debris cleared away. Kitty's heart sank as she searched for the number she required. Taking a deep breath, she knocked on the door.

The woman who opened it was wearing a grubby wraparound apron. Her greasy hair was scraped back with Kirby grips. 'Come in,' she snapped. 'I don't want the neighbours poking their noses in my business!'

As Kitty followed her, the air was filled with the smell of cooked cabbage, which, when she was led into the kitchen, she could see was being boiled in a pot on the stove.

Sweeping a pile of soiled children's clothing off a chair, the woman said, 'Sit down whilst I gets ready.' Looking at Kitty she remarked, 'Got yourself in a bit of trouble, 'ave you? Well, never mind, I'll soon sort you out.'

Kitty felt sick as she watched the woman clear the kitchen table and wipe over the oilcloth that was on it with a damp dirty rag, but when she saw the long metal knitting needles produced from a knitting bag and thrown carelessly on to the table, she wanted to scream.

'Take your skirt and knickers off and lie on the table,' she was told.

Getting to her feet, her eyes bright with horror, Kitty picked up one of the knitting needles and asked, 'What are these for?'

Looking exceedingly irritated the woman snapped, 'I'm going to shove one up inside you, you silly girl. That'll get things going, have no fear.'

Kitty, now rigid with fear, glared at her and said, 'You are not laying a finger on me, do you hear?'

'Please yourself, dearie. You're the one in trouble. You came to me, I didn't invite you.'

Kitty turned on her heel and almost ran out of the house. Outside, her feet hardly touched the ground as she ran as fast as she could, until she had to stop, she was so breathless. Leaning against a wall, she gasped for air. Whether she liked it or not, she would have the baby rather than let anyone like that dreadful woman mess with her. She would have to face whatever the future held. Come what may.

She continued slowly, her mind in a turmoil, until she reached her home, where she lay on top of her bed, still wearing her coat, and slept through pure exhaustion.

The next few weeks, for Kitty, passed in a sort of haze. Jean had been horrified at the tale of the trip to the woman in Chapel and had been as supportive as she could during this difficult time. But as the days passed and the morning sickness thankfully stopped, Kitty realised that very soon she would be unable to hide her pregnancy for very much longer, and decided to visit her mother – the only other person she felt she wanted to confide in. Up until now, Kitty had kept her secret during her visits to her parents. She chose a time when she knew her father would be at work.

Amy was delighted to see her and rushed to put the kettle on the hob, but as she turned back and saw the look of anxiety on her daughter's face she came and sat beside her and asked, 'What is it, dear? What's the matter?'

Kitty told Amy everything. Her mother looked shocked when she heard what Eddie had done but was even more horrified when she was told that Gerry had raped Kitty out of spite and revenge.

'You must go to the police and report this!' she exclaimed.

'No, Mum! I couldn't possibly tell them what happened. It was too humiliating. I just want to forget it.'

'How can you when you are pregnant?' She paused and said quietly, 'At least you didn't go to some backstreet abortionist, thank God!'

Kitty was filled with guilt as she'd kept this part of her experience to herself.

'Gerry Stubbs shouldn't be able to get away with this!' Amy was angry but, seeing the distress on Kitty's face, she took her in her arms and tutted to her as she used to do when Kitty was a small child. 'There, there. Everything will be all right, one way or another.'

Kitty burst into tears.

'It's all Eddie's fault!' Amy cried. 'If it wasn't for him, none of this would have happened. I blame myself.'

'No, no, you mustn't.'

'I should have had a firm hand with him as a youngster.'

'It would have made not a jot of difference, Mum. Eddie always was a wild one.'

Looking crestfallen, Amy said, 'That's all very well, but look what he has brought about. How you have suffered because of him. It just isn't fair. I'm glad the army have got him. I never want to have anything to do with him, ever again.'

'What am I going to do when Brian and Jeff come home?' asked Kitty with desperation in her voice.

'I don't know, dear, but things have a strange way of working out, one way or another. The main thing is for you to look after yourself.'

'Oh, Mum, I wish I had your optimism.'

'I'll tell your father when he comes home.'

'Whatever will he say? I don't want him going round to Gerry's to sort him out!'

Her mother looked surprised. 'What can he say? You were raped; this was in no way your fault. He is your father, and he'll stand by you, of course. And I'll make sure he doesn't do anything stupid.'

Kitty flung her arms around her mother and said, 'I do love you.'

Chapter Twenty-Seven

The next two months passed by. In September the failure of the attack on Arnhem put paid to hopes of ending the war that year. The heavy raids on Cologne made sure the city wasn't used as an advance base for the Germans, but the Germans retaliated by sending the new V-2 rockets to England. They were so fast that no warning could be given. The first anyone knew was a sudden explosion. And so the war continued. At least the blackout was no longer the rule. Ordinary curtains could be pulled – except in a raid, when, of course, blackout was observed – and streetlighting was stepped up. Then in November, the Home Guard was finally stood down.

'Surely that's a good sign?' Kitty's mother remarked when she visited her daughter one late autumn afternoon.

'I'd like to think so.'

'Have you heard from Brian?'

Kitty nodded. 'Well, three weeks ago. He doesn't write that often now, which makes it easier for me as I don't have to write back every week.' Placing a hand over her swelling stomach she added, 'I find it very difficult to sound as if everything is normal, but he seems happy, so that's good.'

'And Jeff?'

Kitty's expression softened. 'He writes as often as he can. I do miss him, Mum.'

The plaintive tone in her voice touched Amy and she walked

over to her daughter and put her arms around her. 'Of course you do, dear.'

'I'm so frightened that he won't want me when he knows about the baby.'

Amy pursed her lips and said, 'Only time will give you the answer to that, Kitty. We will just have to wait and see.'

'Brian will go mad, I know he will.'

'Kitty darling, stop worrying. It isn't good for you. No one knows what will happen but we will face all these problems together.'

Christmas 1944 came and the war raged on. There was no news of Glenn Miller, the American bandleader whose plane had disappeared on a trip to France. Kitty was deeply saddened by this, as she remembered dancing to his music with her beloved Jeff and knew this man's melodies would always hold memories of the happiest times of her life.

She stayed with her parents as she had done the previous year, but this time without Jeff, and she felt desperately lonely. She had sent a Christmas card to her in-laws, but had bought them no presents this year. She disliked Gladys so much she felt she would be hypocritical to do so, and she had so far managed to keep away from her dreadful mother-in-law, knowing that if Mrs Freeman saw her pregnant state she would have a field day with her!

Kitty had left the factory and got a part-time job in a grocery store. There had been a lot of gossip among her factory work-mates, which had been difficult to ignore, but here in the small shop, the owners assumed she was carrying her husband's child so there was no pressure on her. But there was no doubt that sooner or later Gladys Freeman would hear about her pregnancy. Kitty didn't relish the thought.

The papers continued to be full of the battles for supremacy that were still taking place, but the news of the Russians discovering the death camp of Auschwitz shocked everyone. The black and white pictures of the skeletal prisoners silenced those who looked at them. It was difficult to believe that any race could wreak such cruelty and misery on other human beings. Kitty and Jean shed tears as they sat together reading the papers.

'How could they do this?' cried Jean.

Kitty was saddened beyond words.

'Poor bastards,' murmured Eddie Simmons, sitting in his cell in the glasshouse at Aldershot, reading the same articles. He wouldn't have liked to be among those who had discovered such atrocities.

He had three weeks more to serve to complete his sentence. He had been unable to keep out of trouble and therefore had to serve the full six months. The constant time regime drove him crazy. Wake-up call at 06.00 hours, then half an hour to wash and shave, under escort all the time. 'You can't even take a piss without being watched,' he complained to another offender one day. And sometimes you were only given five minutes to visit the toilet. Knowing someone was watching you could seriously affect your being able to perform and this caused him some discomfort at times. Any misbehaviour would mean your name was entered in the Punishment Book. He couldn't remember the number of extra drills that had been imposed on him during his incarceration. On top of that, everything had to be done at double time, which was hard, but his leg muscles eventually got used to it. Visiting days were the worst, as he had no one, which gave rise to much taunting from his superiors.

Christmas had been the hardest time. There had been no change in the routine; as the prisoners were told by an NCO, 'Christmas isn't happening this year for you lot. Father Christmas will not be calling!'

Eddie thought how nice it would have been to have his father at least come to see him, but as he'd not informed his parents of his present abode, what could he expect? Even if they did know where he was, he doubted they would want to see him, after all he'd done.

Now as the time to leave drew nearer, he wondered just where to go. Certainly not back to London. He thought he might take himself off to Glasgow. He felt he would be far enough away from the reaches of Gerry Stubbs there. He'd get a job and when the war was over he would get a ship, perhaps one going to Australia, and take off once they docked. Now all he had to do was keep his nose clean for three more weeks and he'd be a free man. So he would have a dishonourable discharge from the army . . . so what? He was only too pleased to get out of it.

Fate, however, was conspiring against him. Several of the stolen furs had fallen into the hands of the Metropolitan Police and intense enquiries were taking place. Gerry Stubbs was not aware of this, but the Chief Constable of Southampton had the bit between his teeth. These coats had been stolen on his patch and a murder committed. He wanted action.

The local force had a list of suspects for the robbery and Gerry Stubbs was one of them.

'He's a small-time racketeer,' said the detective in charge, 'who has been too crafty for us in the past. We've yet to discover any goods on his premises. He's had someone in his pocket, I would say, but this sort of caper is just up his street. He probably had to ditch the furs in a hurry when the old boy was killed. We'll watch him for a while and see if he makes a mistake.'

Unaware that he was being followed, Gerry went about his business as usual, and all the time the police were building a file against him. But Gerry's main aim was to be waiting for Eddie Simmons when he was released. He was the one weak link in the chain. Ernie, the other man, now inside for burglary, had held up during the questioning and proved his worth. He had been sent down for a few months, and Gerry had got word to him that he would be rewarded for his loyalty. It was now only Eddie who could place him at the scene of the crime, and he planned to remove him.

The police got wind of his hatred for Simmons and waited to see what was afoot. It was at this time that Nancy Brannigan made an anonymous call to police headquarters.

Ernie Byers, the burglar, was very surprised to be told he had a visitor. It wasn't the usual visiting day, so it was with some curiosity he followed the prison warder to the private room. He became wary when he saw the two detectives who had questioned him after his arrest sitting waiting. He said nothing.

'Sit down, Ernie,' said one, pushing a packet of cigarettes and a box of matches across the table towards him. He took one and lit it, drawing in the nicotine in an effort to calm the feeling of tension rising inside.

'How are you keeping?' asked one.

'Cut the crap,' snapped Ernie. 'Get to the point. Why are you here?'

'No flannelling you, Ernie, is there?' laughed the other.

The prisoner didn't answer.

The detective watched him closely and said, 'Tell us about Eddie Simmons.'

Byers was no fool, he'd been living by his wits all his life. 'What about him?' he asked casually.

'You admit that you know him then?'

'Of course I know him! He works for Gerry Stubbs, same as I do.'

'Doing what, exactly?'

Shrugging, Ernie said, 'Moving stock from the warehouse. Delivering, collecting goods, whatever is needed.'

'How much do you know about Simmons?'

'I don't know anything about him, really. He turned up at work one day; nothing was said about him except he was an extra hand, that's all. I wasn't interested in him enough to ask,' said Ernie nonchalantly.

'You didn't know he was an army deserter then?'

The prisoner looked surprised. 'No – he never was?'

'Indeed he was. Been on the run for months, but he was picked up some time ago by the Military Police in London.'

'I didn't know anything about that,' said Ernie. 'He just up and left our place unexpectedly one day. No one saw him go. I had no idea where he went,' and, grimacing, he added, 'He was no great loss. Workshy he was.'

'Did he have a temper, would you say?'

'Wouldn't know. I never mixed with the bloke socially.'

'Capable of knocking off old guys – like an air-raid warden?'

Byers froze. 'Don't know what you're talking about.'

'Oh, come along now, I think you do,' said one of the men. 'I think you know precisely what we mean.'

Byers shook his head but said nothing.

The chief detective said, 'You went to Eric's, the furrier's, with Gerry Stubbs, Jack Baker and Eddie Simmons, to knock it off. The warden discovered you and Simmons hit him, killing him. Then you all took off, leaving the poor bugger lying there.'

Ernie was completely thrown. How the hell did they find all this out?

The man waited and said, 'Some of the coats have turned up, you know, and what's more, we have a witness that can put the three of you on the spot.'

In his confusion, Byers spoke without thinking. 'There were no witnesses!' Then realising what he had said, he cursed loudly.

In the glasshouse at the garrison in Aldershot, Eddie Simmons was escorted to the washhouse and told to change into his new demob suit, shirt and tie. He decided to take the trilby on offer. Why not? It was all for free. He looked at his reflection in the window and tilted the hat at a jaunty angle. He looked pretty fit, he thought. All the forced marching he'd endured had honed his body. Great! There were two things he was longing for. A pint of beer and a woman. The money that he had on him when he was arrested was returned to him, so he had the readies for a few days of fun. Once he stepped out of the gates of the garrison, he would celebrate his freedom. Then after a couple of days he'd head for Glasgow and start again. He was resourceful, if nothing else, he told himself. He'd soon be on his feet, living the life of Riley!

He was escorted to the front gate and as soon as he passed through, he looked back at the barracks, put two fingers up to the sentries and, laughing, walked off down the road. He was free! The army had done with him and he with them. There was no longer any danger of him being in the forces, fighting the enemy. He was on home ground in dear old England. He could stomach an air raid or two; compared with the strict regimentation of the glasshouse, that was nothing.

He turned into the main road where, after a while, walking in the direction of the town, he heard a car approaching. Now this *was* a bit of luck. He stood, held out his thumb and was delighted when the vehicle stopped.

'Going into Aldershot by any chance, mate?' he asked the driver.

'Yes. Hop in.'

So pleased was he as he climbed into an empty seat beside the driver, Eddie hadn't taken any notice of the figure in the back seat until someone tapped him on the shoulder.

'Hello, Eddie. Had a nice holiday, have you?'

His heart sank as he recognised the voice of Gerry Stubbs. He made to grab the car door handle, but he felt something hard and cold pressed in the nape of his neck.

'I'll blow your fucking brains out if you try,' Gerry snapped. 'Maybe that would be a good result. It would save me a great deal of trouble – but it would only make a mess of the car.'

Eddie thought about trying anyway, but by then the vehicle had speeded up and he decided it would be foolish: he could get hurt. Perhaps another opportunity would present itself. He would remain alert. But as they stopped at a set of traffic lights, a car that had been behind them passed them and suddenly swerved in front of them, blocking their way.

'What the bloody hell is going on?' Stubbs asked, keeping his revolver at Eddie's neck.

He saw the two men who quickly emerged from the vehicle, running towards them, and immediately had them nailed as plain-clothes coppers. You could always pick them out in a crowd. At the same time a marked car arrived from behind, jamming them at the rear. Four uniformed police tumbled out. Gerry's car was surrounded.

All the doors were opened and the occupants were told to get out. Gerry stuffed the revolver in his pocket, but it was quickly confiscated as the men were pushed up against the vehicle and searched.

'Dear me,' said one of the police officers, 'dangerous thing to be carrying about, and illegal. Possession of this alone should take you off the streets for a while.'

'What's all this about?' Gerry demanded, but as one of the detectives said, 'Edward Simmons, I'm arresting you on suspicion of murder,' his heart sank.

'You're all coming down to the nick for questioning,' he was told. 'Anything you say . . .'

Gerry glared at Eddie and cursed him as he listened to the caution and was shoved into the police car.

Nancy Brannigan was working in the newsagent's and, knowing that today was the day Eddie Simmons was supposedly due out of the glasshouse, wondered if the police would be waiting for him. It had taken considerable courage for her to make the anonymous phone call, but she felt she had to do something. At least she had given them the names of the men who had burgled the furrier's. After that it was down to them. She couldn't do any more – she had to protect herself – but she was very edgy all day long.

The following day in the *Southern Daily Echo*, there was an article that made her very happy: 'THREE MEN HELD FOR QUESTIONING OVER DEATH OF AIR-RAID WARDEN.' So the police had taken her seriously. She read on, but there was little more information. No names were mentioned. The men were helping the police with their inquiries, it said. Word would soon get round, though, and it wouldn't be very long before she discovered the names of the men. She'd go to her local, which was always the source of any scandalous news.

She was absolutely correct. Everyone was talking about the arrest of Gerry Stubbs, his sidekick Jack and Eddie Simmons. Nancy wondered if Kitty knew of the arrest of her brother. Perhaps she ought to tell her, but she wasn't entirely comfortable with the idea, especially as she had been the one to shop him. It was Kitty's brother, after all, so she decided against it. At least she'd been the means of getting Gerry out of the way. Now Kitty wouldn't have to be frightened of him calling again.

Kitty Freeman learned of her brother's arrest when Gladys, her mother-in-law, barged in the back door of her house that evening.

Kitty was washing up at the sink when the back door burst open. 'Don't you think it would be polite to knock?' she said angrily.

Gladys ignored her and shook the newspaper at her. 'Your brother is being questioned at the police station,' she said, and handed the paper over.

Kitty read the headlines and the report with trepidation, then said defiantly, 'There is nothing here to say my brother is one of these men!'

'My neighbour's husband is a constable – he told his wife and, knowing you were married to my son, she came and told me,' stated the older woman triumphantly. 'I knew you and your family were no good. I was right all along.'

Knowing of her brother's guilt because Gerry had told her about it, Kitty was at a loss to argue, but there was no way she would let this old harridan get the better of her. 'You be very careful what you say, Mrs Freeman. You are making a lot of accusations here. Should you be misinformed, you could be had up, then *your* name would be in the papers. Think about that, and kindly leave. I don't want you in my kitchen or my house.'

Gladys Freeman had been so full of vengeance that it wasn't until now that she noticed the pregnant bulge of her daughter-in-law. 'My God, you're pregnant!' Looking back up into Kitty's face she gave a malevolent smile. 'You talk about my character when you are no better than a slut. My boy will get to hear about this, you see if he doesn't!'

'Then you'd better rush off and write to him. Goodbye!'

But as the woman left, Kitty sat down and tried to collect her thoughts. She couldn't be bothered that Gladys was aware of her condition – it was inevitable; she was more concerned as to how on earth the police had discovered the truth about the robbery. She picked up the paper from the floor where it had dropped and read the article. Three men, it said. Could that mean Gerry Stubbs as well? She certainly hoped so. He had told her about the murder, which had been very dangerous knowledge, and he'd threatened her if she told. Oh my God . . . she wondered if he thought she had? If he was released on bail, he could come after her. Well, she wouldn't stay in the house alone; she'd throw a few things in a bag and go round to her parents'. They might know more about the arrests. As she packed she cursed her brother.

When she arrived at her mother's, Kitty found Amy was reading the *Echo*. 'Have you seen this?' she asked Kitty. 'It says the police are questioning three men about the murder of the air-raid warden. Your father's gone down to the police station to see if Eddie is one of them.'

'I'm afraid that Gladys Freeman thinks he is. She couldn't wait to come and tell me, but let's wait and see what Dad says. I've brought my things, Mum. I thought I'd come and stay for a few days, if that's all right? This business has shaken me up,' she added.

'Of course it's all right,' said Amy. 'Your father and I will welcome the company. And we should stick together at a time like this.'

Just then Jim came in through the kitchen and into the living room. His face was white. He looked at Kitty but didn't say a word. Taking off his hat and jacket, he sat opposite his wife. 'Eddie's there, all right. He and two others are being held at the station. It doesn't look good, I'm afraid.'

'Do you know who the other men are?' Kitty asked her father.

'It seems one of them is Gerry Stubbs. I hope he gets what's coming to him. Eddie should have known not to get mixed up with him. Even if he did desert, he had other choices.'

'Where did we go wrong?' asked Amy, gazing with tear-filled eyes at her husband.

'You didn't do anything wrong!' exclaimed Kitty. 'Eddie was always trouble. Even as a child. You gave him a good home and a lot of love, always.' She kneeled beside her mother. 'Nothing is your fault! If it's anyone's, it's mine. I let Gerry take him off my hands!'

'It's no one's fault but Eddie's. I hoped that being in the army would make a man of him,' ventured Jim, 'but even there he couldn't face up to things and ran away. Imagine – a son of mine doing such a thing! I couldn't believe it when the MPs called round here.'

Amy looked startled. 'I didn't know they came here!'

Putting an arm around his wife, Jim said, 'What was the point of upsetting you?'

'I was always afraid that Eddie would come to a sticky end,' confessed Amy. 'I just had this feeling deep inside, and now it seems I was right all along,' and she burst into tears.

Leaving her father to comfort her, Kitty went to make some tea. If she could have got hold of her brother at that moment she would have killed him for causing her parents so much unde-served pain.

Chapter Twenty-Eight

The three men were held without bail and questioned, then they were taken before the court. Eddie Simmons was charged with the murder of the air-raid warden and the others as accessories. They were sent to trial, which would take place later in the year. It was the talk of Southampton.

Gladys Freeman cut out all the information from the papers and sent it to Brian, accompanied by a long letter, bemoaning that fact that he had married into such a family, and despite her husband's warning, she also told him that Kitty had been seeing an American officer but omitted to add that Kitty was pregnant. She was keeping that little bit of gossip to herself to use when she felt it would do the most damage. Licking the envelope she sealed it with a smile of satisfaction. 'Ordering me out of my own son's house!' she muttered angrily. 'Well, I'll fix that jumped-up little bitch.'

When Brian eventually received the letter, he read the cuttings with some disbelief. He had never liked Kitty's brother, Eddie, but never did he put him down as a violent man. The Simmons family must be beside themselves. He was very fond of his in-laws. Amy was a gentle soul and Jim was a man to be admired. He felt nothing but pity for them and for Kitty, who would be trying to bring them comfort and support through such a diffi-cult time. When at the end of the letter he read the bit about the American, he wondered if it was the man who spoke to Kitty at the dance, the one he had forbidden her to see – and he was furious.

Lisette found him reading the letter and, seeing the thunderous expression on his face, enquired, 'Is everything all right, *chéri?*'

'No,' he snapped. 'My wife is going out with a bloody Yank!'

She went crazy. 'So! It is all right for you to 'ave an affair, but not your wife . . . the woman you said you would ask for a divorce so we could be together! You are a bloody 'ipocrite. How dare you? If you don't love 'er any more, why should you care about it? Answer me that!'

He jumped to his feet. 'Now don't get a cob on, darling,' and he went to take her into his arms, but she pushed him away.

'*Non!* Don't touch me. You 'ave lied to me all along. All you want is to 'ave sex with me, nothing more. If you meant what you said, you wouldn't care about your wife 'aving the same. It is good enough for you, you bastard, but not for 'er.' She picked up a plate and hurled it at him.

Brian ducked just in time. 'Lisette, darling, I do love you and I meant every word I said. It was just a shock, that's all.'

'Not 'alf as much as a shock that *she* will 'ave when you ask for a divorce – *if* you ask.'

'Darling,' he cajoled, 'of course I will. I want to spend the rest of my life with you, you know that.'

'So you say, but I wonder. Especially as now I'm carrying your child!'

Brian was absolutely floored. 'You – you're pregnant?'

'Yes I am, but you don't 'ave to worry. Go back to your wife,' she declared, gesturing wildly. 'I don't care! I will 'ave my baby, we will get by without you. It will 'ave a mother anyway.'

'Lisette,' he said gently, 'please come here. I love you and I *will* be here to bring up our child.' His eyes shone. 'I am so very happy.'

She walked slowly towards him and let him hold her. 'You don't 'ave to say this because I'm pregnant,' she pouted.

He held her close and said softly, 'You have no idea just how much I want a family with you. That's why I never took any precautions.' He tilted her chin and kissed her. 'I love you so much and we will be together. When I go home I'll instigate divorce proceedings and then I'll come back to France whilst it is going though, to be with you. You have my word. When is the baby due?'

'Around October sometime.'

'Let's pray the war will be over then. We will have a good life together, Lisette. Maybe I can work on the railway with your father. But no matter – I'll find a job; support you and the baby.'

'If that is really what you want, *chéri*.'

'It is, more than anything.'

As they sat curled up together that evening in front of a log fire, Brian thought of Kitty. What would her reaction be to a divorce, he wondered. If she was serious about this American, then maybe, in a funny way, the war had solved both their problems, but of course, he had only his mother's word for it. Nevertheless, if it was true and Kitty had found true love, as he had, then everything would be fine. If it was a passing fling, well that was too bad, he wouldn't blame her – how could he? His masculine pride had been momentarily dented when first he read about it, but Lisette was right, he was being a hypocrite. But he wasn't going to let anything stop him being with her and his child. Glancing down at her stomach, he placed his hand on it and smiled lovingly at her.

Whilst Brian was settled with his girl, Jeff was miles away from Kitty and missing her like hell. He had been dealing with the troops and equipment heading for Dresden, which had been annihilated by heavy bombing. Dresden had been a transit centre for part of the Eastern Front, but the air raids were also intended to destroy German morale. As Jeff had driven through the complete devastation and charred remains of what had once been a beautiful city, he felt morally saddened.

What was to be gained by this mayhem, he wondered, this terrible destruction, this awful loss of life? And how much longer could it possibly go on before someone, somewhere, had to sense to put a stop to it? He couldn't wait for it to be finished, to be able to live a normal life, to be once again with Kitty. Her letters were the only things that kept him sane during this madness.

He had already written to his parents and told them about her and how he eventually planned to marry her after the war. He hadn't mentioned that she was already married; that would only worry them. As it was, his mother had written asking him if he was sure of what he was doing, that wartime made things seem so different. Begging him not to make any definite plans until he had at least returned home. Well, there was no fear of that. No definite plans could be made until Brian came home and Kitty had gained her freedom.

He had hoped that once the divorce was pending, he might persuade Kitty to come to Boston and stay with him until she was free, but first they had this goddamn war to finish.

Meanwhile, Kitty and her family were having to cope with the aftermath of Eddie's arrest. Old friends, of course, were very sorry for their trouble; others were only too quick to point the finger of blame. The customers at the grocery shop gossiped behind Kitty's back as she was acutely aware of the conversations that came to an abrupt end when she approached. She tried to ignore them all, but it wasn't easy.

Her friend Jean stood by her and urged her to ignore the others. 'You'd be surprised what went on behind some of their doors, I can tell you!' she said as she and Kitty walked home. 'Makes me bloody sick. I bet you not one of them has never bought black market goods.'

'Maybe,' said Kitty, 'but that's a bit different to killing some-one.'

'But that was your brother, not you, and you aren't responsible for that.'

'According to Gladys Freeman, my family is a bad lot,' said Kitty wryly.

'That interfering old bitch! I bet she wrote and told her precious son all about it.'

Kitty hid a smile. 'No doubt. I bet she couldn't put pen to paper quickly enough. I just wonder if she's told him I'm pregnant. But what does it matter? Brian is too far away to make any difference.'

To her surprise a couple of weeks later, Brian wrote to her telling her how sorry he was to hear the news of her brother's arrest and he hoped her parents were able to deal with it as it must be a nightmare for them all. There was no mention of her condition, which was both a relief and a surprise. It wasn't a long letter; Brian only ever managed a page and a half. In fact he didn't say much else at all, except that he would be glad when the war was over and that, after all, he didn't think he would sign on for a further spell in the army as he had planned to do, and Kitty wondered what had changed his mind, but concluded that he had enough with the war. He didn't say what his plans for the future were, just that he was fine and he hoped she was well.

Kitty was back now in her own home. Now she knew that Gerry Stubbs was safely locked up, there was no reason for her to stay away. She still worried that he may have thought that she was the one that had shopped him. Well, she would worry about that if he were set free after the trial. Opinion was that he would be sent down. Gossip had it that the police had been after him for a long time and there was no way he would go free if they could make a case against him.

It was the following day that Kitty had a chance meeting with Nancy Brannigan. She was shopping for groceries in Lipton's and just ahead of her was Nancy.

Walking up behind her, Kitty said, 'Hello. How are you?'

Nancy looked somewhat startled at first, then said, 'Fine. I'm

231

fine. Sorry to hear the news of your brother.'

'Thanks. I expect you are upset about Gerry being in prison too.'

'No. No, I'm not. He was good to me, but somehow after our conversation I thought I'd be wise to get out of our relationship. So I moved out.'

'Oh, I'm sorry. After all, he treated you all right you said.'

'Yes he did, but as you must know he was mixed up with a nasty crowd and I decided it wasn't really healthy to hang around. Have you been to see your brother?'

Kitty shook her head. 'No, and I don't want to. My mother is heartbroken and I can't forgive him for taking that man's life, so I don't go near him. Dad was really upset.'

'I know it must be difficult for you, Kitty, but at least you don't have the worry of Gerry calling on you again.' She noticed Kitty's burgeoning stomach. 'Congratulations. I had no idea you were expecting. You and your husband must be thrilled.'

'Yes, of course.'

'Well, best be on my way,' said Nancy, and left Kitty to do her shopping.

Nancy Brannigan was shaken by the encounter. She couldn't help a feeling of guilt as she talked to Kitty, but she hadn't regretted phoning the police. Eddie had not only raped her and beaten her up, but had committed murder, and Gerry wouldn't bother Kitty ever again. It seemed a good result to her and now Kitty had her baby to look forward to.

Gerry Stubbs had been moved to Winchester Prison to await trial. He had no idea where the others were and he didn't really care. He had been picking his brains as to how the police had gained enough evidence to charge them. Someone had to have talked – but who?

Ernie hadn't given anything away when he was questioned as far as he'd heard, and no one else knew, except Kitty Freeman. He couldn't believe it was her. After all, she would have been sending her own brother down. He couldn't see her doing that, especially after he'd threatened her. It was a mystery, but when he did discover the culprit he would see they were punished, by God he would!

Eddie Simmons was in Wandsworth Prison. Before he had been moved there, he'd had a very upsetting visit from his father, a man he'd respected even during his troublesome teenage years. They sat opposite one another and Eddie was filled with guilt when he saw the drawn lines of worry on the face of his father.

'I'm sorry, Dad,' he said.

'How could you bring yourself to do this dreadful thing?' asked Jim, staring hard across the table at his son. 'I knew you were wild and reckless, but *never* did I think you were capable of murder.'

'It was an accident,' Eddie tried to explain. 'He came out of nowhere and I panicked. Before I knew it, I'd hit him and he went down. I didn't mean to kill him, honestly.'

'You have destroyed the man's family. He had a wife and teenage children; now they have no father. And you have broken your mother's heart and for that I can *never* forgive you.'

'How is Mum?'

Anger flashed in Jim's eyes. 'How do you think she is? Her world has been turned upside down!' Glaring at Eddie he asked, 'Why the hell did you go to the furrier's anyway?'

'I wanted the money to take myself off to London. Leave Southampton behind until the war was over and then I'd have taken a ship abroad and you wouldn't have been troubled by me any more. But I was picked up by the Military Police.'

'Running away again! How I could ever have a son like you I'll never know. Your mother and I tried to bring you and Kitty up with a sense of pride and responsibility, with principles. Yet you deserted your post in the army.' He shook his head and said, 'I can't believe you would do such a thing.'

'It's all very well for you!' snapped Eddie. 'You didn't see what I did.'

233

'I saw plenty in the First World War and it was much worse. There were men who knew that the next time they climbed out of the trenches and went over the top, they were almost certain to die, but they didn't run away! And had I been younger and not had a perforated ear drum, I would have been proud to serve my country again.'

'More fool them. At least I'm alive!'

'And facing a murder charge! A lot of good it did you!'

'If that's all you have to say to me, Dad, you might as well leave.'

Jim didn't stir. 'I was hoping to hear some sign of repentance on your part, but I've not heard it and that makes all this so much worse.'

'Of course I'm sorry. If that stupid bastard hadn't been there, I wouldn't be here now.'

Jim rose from his seat. 'I won't be seeing you any more until the trial. Your mother is more deserving of my time, and that breaks my heart to have to say that. Your future is now in the lap of the Almighty and you will have to pay the price for your misdemeanour. There is no one to save you this time.' And he walked to the door where the prison warder let him out.

Eddie was stunned at the coldness of his father. He had expected support and sympathy for his position and now he was aware that he was completely alone. His mother certainly wouldn't come and neither would Kitty, he was sure of that. He was sorry that his mother, who had always made excuses for him and had shown him constant love and patience, was upset. That was something he really regretted. She didn't deserve that and now he wondered if indeed he had any future. He could face the death penalty, and that was a sobering thought, but would it be any worse than a life spent behind bars? He was filled with self-pity.

Chapter Twenty-Nine

Jeff Ryder was travelling with the 157th and 22nd Infantry regiments when they liberated Dachau Concentration Camp. The sight of mountains of dead bodies chilled every single man to the bone, as did the skeletal people who still retained a vestige of life. Jeff knew that these terrible scenes would stay with him for ever. So enraged were the GIs there that they killed an SS officer who crossed their path and many of those who had surrendered, until a colonel intervened and calmed the volatile situation. Earlier that month, British troops had found the same horrors at Belsen. When the pictures hit the national papers in Britain, the public could not believe such atrocities could happen in a so-called civilised world. And when in late April, Hitler and his mistress, Eva Braun, committed suicide, many thought it was too good an end to such a monster. But surely now the war would soon be over?

Kitty's baby was on its way. When her waters broke she sent a message via the milkman, to her mother, who came rushing over, after alerting the midwife. They both arrived at Kitty's home at the same time.

After an examination of the expectant mother, the midwife left, saying it would be several hours before she was needed and she would call back later. Amy made a pot of tea and gave her daughter much-needed support. But between contractions, Kitty was tormented by her thoughts. What if, when she saw her baby, she hated it, this unknown quantity that had been growing inside her for the past nine months? She'd felt it move, felt it kick, it was part of her, but it had been conceived in violence. What if, after making the decision to have the baby, she couldn't love it?

As the hours passed and the contractions became more frequent, the midwife appeared as if summoned by a stopwatch.

'Come along, young lady,' she said firmly, 'let's get you to bed. By this evening you will be holding your baby if you follow my instructions to the letter.'

Gripped by pain, Kitty managed to say, 'I'll do anything you say to stop this!'

Laughing, the woman replied, 'When you hold your child, you'll forget all this, I promise.'

Kitty wasn't too sure, but eventually, when the time passed and the baby boy was safely delivered, she looked down at the small bundle and smiled. 'Perhaps you're right,' she conceded. 'The pain wasn't that bad after all.'

Amy leaned over and studied the child. 'He really is a handsome little fellow,' she said.

Kitty looked at the sleeping baby and studied his delicate features. Watched the way his mouth moved, his tiny fingers twitch, and was so overcome by maternal feelings that her doubts disappeared. It wasn't his fault that he was conceived in such a manner. During her pregnancy, Kitty had even considered having the child adopted, but now as she gazed lovingly at him, she knew she would never be able to part with him, come what may.

On 7 May 1945, Germany surrendered unconditionally. The church bells rang out all over Europe, bringing the joyous news. Brian rushed from the station to the house and, picking up Lisette in his arms, he kissed her and said, 'Thank God! Our child will be born in peacetime.'

Monsieur Pallier opened a bottle of champagne he had been saving and they all drank a toast to the future.

'Wouldn't it be wonderful if I was still here when the baby is born?' Brian said, with a happy smile.

Lisette, overflowing with happiness, smothered him with kisses and said, 'I love you. Do you think that's possible? Won't they sent you 'ome to England?'

'Eventually, of course, but there is too much to do before then. Equipment has to be moved, and you can't liberate a country and then leave. No, I reckon I'll be here for a while.' Holding her close he said, 'That's suits me just fine,' and he kissed her upturned nose.

Her father looked on with a bemused smile as he quaffed the wine. Holding his glass high he cried, '*Vive Churchill, vive de Gaulle . . . et Uncle Sam!*'

8 May was declared VE Day and in every English city, town, village and hamlet, people were dancing in the streets – and the pubs were full. There was much laughter, and many tears shed by those families who had lost someone in the war, but there was an overwhelming feeling of relief. Churchill made a stirring speech and was fêted wherever he went, cigar stuck in his mouth, his fingers giving the V-for-victory sign. A day to live in the memories, for ever, of all who were alive.

Kitty, now recovered from her confinement, rushed around to her family with the baby, as soon as she could, to share in the celebrations. Street parties were planned, precious rations pooled to allow for festive fare to be prepared to mark the event. Pub pianos were pushed out into the street and played. People danced, strangers embraced. It was a marvellous time, and after, families waited for the return of their kin. But the cost of victory was emphasised when the rations were cut again as supplies had to be shared with a liberated Europe, which had been starved by the Germans.

It would be a hard time for families of those who would be sent home early, the wounded and distressed. For others it was now a waiting game. Kitty waited to hear from her husband and her lover, wondering just how she was going to cope when Brian did come home.

Jeff had written to her, telling her that when the time finally came, he would be sent straight home to the States from France for his demobilisation –

which means, my darling, I won't be seeing you as soon as I would have liked. There is no likelihood of a quick trip back to Southampton, sadly, but rest assured as soon as I am able, I will return to England to see you and make plans for our future together. I can't tell you how happy that makes me. I love you and can't wait for us to be together again.

Kitty read the letter over and over, trying to picture his dear face. But the only face that was foremost in her mind was that of her husband.

Gladys and her husband celebrated that night in the local pub. She got absolutely plastered and Frank had to take her home. Whilst he made a cup of tea in an effort to sober her, she talked continuously.

'When my boy does come home he'll sort that bitch of a wife out, you'll see. I can't wait to see what she has to say about that Yank she's been having it away with!'

'He doesn't know anything about it,' said Frank, 'and in any case you don't know that they were anything other than friends.'

'Course she was sleeping with him! Didn't I see her going off with him carrying a suitcase? And,' she added with great relish, 'when I last saw her she was pregnant!'

'What's wrong with that?'

'It's not our Brian's baby, that's what's wrong with it!'

'You don't know that.'

'I do. I worked it out. From what I guessed he couldn't possibly have been the father, he'd been away too long.'

'You can't be sure and you're not to tell him. Let them sort their lives out themselves.'

She shot him a look of triumph. 'He knows already. Not that

she's pregnant, but about the Yank.'

Frank put down the teapot and asked, 'How can he know?'

'Because I wrote and told him when I sent the cuttings out of the paper about *her* brother being charged with murder.'

'You did what?'

She grinned smugly at him.

'You are a wicked and interfering old bitch!'

'Frank!'

'I don't know how I've put up with you all these years. You have a vicious streak in you a mile wide. I don't think I've ever heard you say a good word about anyone. Gossip is life's blood to you. You disgust me.'

She was unrepentant. 'It's a mother's duty to protect her children!'

'Children? Brian is a grown man, for God's sake, and you had no right to spread gossip like that. Christ, Gladys, war is bad enough. It changes people. It takes time to re-establish a relationship, a marriage, and you have set out to destroy theirs.'

She started to argue, but Frank would have none of it. 'Shut up, woman! I'll get you to bed. I don't want to hear another word.'

He helped her up the stairs into their bedroom and removed his two pillows. As he reached the door, Gladys asked, 'Where are you going with those?'

'To the spare room. I no longer wish to share a bed with you.' He slammed the door shut.

Even in her inebriated state, Gladys was shocked. In all the years they had been married, they had never spent a night apart. She tried to get off the bed to follow him, but the room spun around her and she collapsed backwards. Within minutes she was asleep.

Frank stood at the window of the spare room, curtains drawn back. He could put the lights on all over the house if he wanted to, he mused. No more blackout when there was an air raid, because hostilities had ended. He wasn't quite sure how he felt at this moment. A sense of relief, of course – no more wasted lives on the field of battle. His son was alive and he thanked God for that, but he was concerned for Brian's marriage. Gladys might be right about Kitty and the American and the baby. He didn't blame Kitty. He knew that Brian was a bit dour, lacking any sense of fun, and Kitty was young and lonely. But what would happen when eventually he did come home, armed with the gossip his mother had fed him? If there were problems, he couldn't interfere unless his son asked his advice. But he would control Gladys. She had done enough damage and he'd see to it she wouldn't do any more. It was time he asserted himself. In any case, it would be some time before any of the boys would be demobbed. By then things could have settled down.

Brian was in no hurry to be demobbed. There was plenty of work for him at the railway station. Troops, equipment and stores were still being sent to and fro, and he was able to see his child growing within the increasing girth of his woman. In bed at night he could feel the unborn child kicking. He found it a profound experience. He and Lisette would lie planning their future together.

During his time in France, Brian had picked up a lot of the language, and with Lisette's insistence, sometimes they would converse in French. 'The baby will grow to be multilingual,' she explained, 'but you must be also.'

He grinned broadly. 'No one at home will believe I can speak another language! I can swear at my mother and she won't understand.'

Lisette was horrified. 'Swear at your mother! That is terrible! You should treat your parents with respect, *chéri*.'

'You don't know my mother. She would try a saint.'

'And your papa, 'ow is 'e?'

'Oh, Dad is great. He works hard as a carpenter. He just needs to put his foot down more with Mum.'

'Put 'is foot down? I don't understand.'

'Be more masterful. Boss in his own house.'

★ ★ ★

The following weeks seemed to drag by to Kitty. She returned to her part-time job in the grocery store, leaving her son whom she had named Mathew, to the loving care of her mother. She missed the baby badly, but found the extra money useful in buying necessary things for her offspring. Amy was only too delighted to take the reins for a short time to give Kitty a break.

Kitty confided in her friend Jean, 'I need to keep busy; I am going slowly round the twist, waiting for my future to be sorted out. I don't know if I'm coming or going.'

'What do you mean exactly?' asked Jean.

'Well, neither of them knows about the baby yet, and Jeff writes all the time, beautiful letters, saying how he can't wait for us to be together, and as for Brian, he seems quite content to stay where he is. He loves France, loves the people, and now he tells me he's able to speak a lot of the language.'

'What, Brian? That doesn't sound like the man I knew.'

'Precisely! I can't make him out at all. When he left he wanted to stay in the army, then he wrote and said he'd changed his mind, but now it sounds to me as if he likes France so much, he may want to live there. The strangest thing is that before he went away, he couldn't stand foreigners or their food. But now . . .'

'It's the war, duck, it does things to people. Nobody is ever quite the same. I'm waiting to see if my Harry has changed when he does eventually return. Anyway, I'm surprised the old dragon hasn't told her son about the baby,' Jean commented.

'So am I. I can't imagine why old Gladys hasn't informed him. It's not like her at all. Well, I just want everything done and dusted, then I'll know where I'm heading.' But Kitty had to wait a considerable time.

The months passed by without either man being returned to his country. Some demobilisation had begun in June, but there were still thousands who waited, as they served as occupation forces. In July there was a general election and Clement Attlee was elected Prime Minister. Many thought that Churchill had been betrayed, but others were adamant that he was good for war but not for peace. And when the atomic bomb was dropped on Hiroshima and then on Nagasaki, it brought to an end the war in Japan, and there were more street parties.

Kitty didn't get involved. She was happy that the war had finished, but Brian and Jeff were still in France, so for her it didn't seem to make much difference.

Brian was in his element. Lisette was well, and as the day of the birth drew nearer, he was torn between the delights of being a father and concern that all would be well with her.

Monsieur Pallier tried to calm his nerves. 'It is all right, giving birth is normal. Women are born for this. Lisette, she is a 'ealthy girl. Her dear mother 'ad no problem; Lisette will 'ave no problem, you will see.' And he patted him on the arm.

His words came true in late September when Lisette presented Brian with a bonny girl.

The midwife had come to the house when Lisette went into labour. Both men walked up and down the small living room for what seemed an age, but the cry of the newborn baby sent them into hugs of delight.

'Monsieur,' said the nurse to Brian, 'you 'ave a daughter. You may go and see the mother, but don't stay long. She is very tired and needs her rest. You men are fortunate. You 'ave the pleasure, the poor woman 'as the pain!'

Brian walked softly into the bedroom and over to Lisette, who, apart from being exhausted, looked beautiful, her hair loose, spread over the pillow, and Brian was almost too choked for words. 'Darling, are you all right?'

'*Oui*. You want to see our baby?' And she pulled back the shawl from the face of the small bundle curled up in her arms.

Brian looked astonished. 'Did we do that?' He took the small hand in his and looked at each perfect finger. 'She is wonderful, so tiny, so delicate.' He glanced at Lisette and said, 'I'll never ever let anyone harm her. I will take care of her always, and you, my darling.'

Monsieur Pallier crept into the room and let out a spiel of French so fast that Brian was at a loss to know what he said, but by the look on his face it was obvious that he was delighted.

They were ushered from the room. Downstairs the two men drank to the baby's health. 'To *ma petite fille*,' said the Frenchman.

'To my daughter,' said Brian, his chest puffed out with pride.

Jeff was now stationed in Paris at American Headquarters, organising those troops who were to stay and those being sent home. The injured were first to go, of course, but there were many who remained for several months before being returned to their homeland.

It was Brian who was the first of the two men to be released. When he received his demob papers telling him to report, he was in total despair at leaving Lisette and Natalie, the baby. She was now five months old and the centre of his world. He spent every spare moment with her until Lisette would tease him, 'I 'ave lost you to another woman!'

He would always answer, 'Never. You gave me this child, and that makes you very special, but I have enough love for both of you.' They had decided not to chance Lisette becoming pregnant again until Brian had applied for his divorce and moved back to France. Then they would try for a brother or sister for Natalie.

On the day of his departure, there were many tears. He held Lisette and the baby tightly in his arms, kissing them. Lisette's tears mingled with his, and Claude Pallier wiped his eyes hastily so no one would notice.

Brian came over to the Frenchman, shook his hand and said, 'I will be back when I can. Please take care of them. Lisette has my address in England if you should need me.'

The older man clasped Brian in his arms, kissed both his cheeks and promised to do as he asked. 'You will return?'

'You have my word,' said Brian.

Three days later, he was back in Southampton. As he disembarked from the ship, he walked down the gangway with a heavy heart. His life was no longer here, he knew that, but now he would have to face Kitty and tell her he was in love with another woman, and a father to boot! He was not looking forward to it. But first he had to make his way to Colchester barracks to sign his papers and collect his demob suit. He would very soon be a civilian.

Chapter Thirty

Brian went to Colchester barracks, where he was issued his demob suit, shirt, tie and raincoat. As he handed in his uniform and changed into civvies, he felt very different, as if a stranger had emerged from the barracks. On his way to the station, it felt as if he was outside himself, watching this man. There were others on the train in the same position as him, homeward bound. They all chatted together, comparing experiences, but he didn't join in very much. He wanted to be left alone, to gather his thoughts. Already he missed Lisette and his child – the freedom of spirit being with them had given him. He felt as if he was shrinking back into his old persona, and that wouldn't do at all. He was no longer the Brian Freeman who left to fight for France. He didn't like him. Lisette had taught him how to let go, how to shake off that austere exterior. With her he was now able to put his feelings into words, to know that it was all right for a man to show emotion, that it didn't make him any kind of weakling, it made him human, and he liked the freedom it had given him.

Lisette . . . he sat back and smiled to himself. What a wonderful girl she was. She showed every emotion, be it anger, sadness or happiness. He hoped that little Natalie would take after her, and mused that Frenchwomen were certainly different from the English. He let out a deep sigh: now he would have to face Kitty. He couldn't march into the house and say, 'I want a divorce!' That would be cruel. He would have to play it by ear.

When he eventually arrived in Southampton, he went into the

nearest pub for a pint of mild and bitter, but although he enjoyed it, after such a long time, he realised that his taste buds had changed. He had grown to like the fruit of the grape and wondered if he would buy a bottle of wine on the way home, but decided against it. He smothered a wry smile. Kitty would be quite shocked if he arrived with one. After all, didn't he used to decry it as foreign muck? He sat back in his seat and wondered how he was going to play his return. He might have to share his marital bed with his wife before he told her of his plans, but he wasn't going to make love to her. That might be awkward, but he could make excuses. He was madly in love with Lisette and she had demanded that he be true to her.

'When you go 'ome, you don't have sex with your wife or I cut off your balls!'

He had laughed at her declaration, and had pulled her into his arms. 'Why would I want to when you are here waiting for me?'

'You 'ave to give me your word. You 'ave to promise me.'

'I promise. The only woman I'll make love to is you. On the baby's life I promise.' And that had satisfied her.

It was almost seven o'clock in the evening when eventually Brian stood outside his front door, key in hand. Through the glass panel he could see there was a light on in the kitchen and he could just hear the sound of a wireless playing. Taking a deep breath, he put the key in the door and opened it.

Kitty was mashing some potatoes when she heard the sound of the front door opening. She was startled and went to the kitchen door, a wooden rolling pin clutched in her hand.

Seeing this, Brian said, 'What are you going to do, clobber me?'

'Brian!' And she stood like a statue, pale and set, not moving, hardly breathing. As he walked towards her she said, 'I had no idea you were back in England.'

'I have been back a couple of days, but had to go to Colchester to be demobbed. You look well.' And he kissed her on the cheek.

The polite greeting was hardly the same as when he had come

246

home before, almost dragging her off to the bedroom, and it took her completely by surprise. 'Come in, let me make you a cup of tea.'

He took off his raincoat, hung it up and sat at the table in the living room. Looking around he saw that very little had changed. It was spotless, of course, as it always had been. There were the same curtains and cushions, the rug in front of the fire.

Whilst he was doing this, Kitty was in a state in the kitchen. She had been dreading his return, yet longed for it, as she needed to sort out her life and plan a future. She carried a tray with the tea into the other room.

'You look different,' she remarked.

'Really? How?'

'I don't quite know. Just different, and I don't mean in your civvies.'

'We have all changed, Kitty, in some way,' he said. 'I'm sure you agree with me. A war changes everything.'

'Does your mother know you are home?' she asked anxiously.

He burst out laughing. 'No, Kitty. She won't come charging round here, if that's what you're worried about.'

'Thank goodness for that!' she said without thinking, then realising, immediately apologised.

'It's all right. I know what you mean and I intend to have a couple of days of peace and quiet before I tell her.'

This was indeed a different Brian, Kitty thought. 'What are you going to do now you're home?'

'I haven't given it a thought. After all, I've only just arrived.'

'Yes of course. But in one of your letters you said you had changed your mind about the army.'

'Yes, I have. I have other plans, but let's just leave that until tomorrow, shall we? I really don't feel like a serious conversation tonight. I'm tired. The train was packed, and it was also very noisy. It's nice to sit quietly. Tell me, what have you been doing with yourself?'

Had he not heard the gossip about her and Jeff from his

247

mother after all, she wondered. But she couldn't tell him about Jeff tonight; the poor chap had only just got home. Yet there was no way she could hide the fact that she had a baby. Mathew was sleeping in his cot upstairs in their bedroom. How on earth could she begin?

She told him of her change of job. 'I work part time now in the local grocery store,' she said. 'Actually I enjoy it.' She told him of families who had lost sons, brothers and husbands, some of whom he knew. Described the street parties on VE Day and VJ Day. 'You should have seen the flags flying, the trestle tables in the middle of the road. It was quite a sight to behold.' She paused and looked at him. 'I'm so happy that you came through unscathed,' she said quietly. And she meant it. After all, she was married to this man and he had been a good husband, in his own way.

'It was pretty exciting in France too,' he said, smiling. 'The bells were all ringing. A few bottles of wine were drunk that day, I can tell you.'

'I can't believe that you are a wine drinker,' she laughed.

'I know, especially after all the things that I said about it.'

'Did you see a lot of fighting, Brian?'

'Yes, I did in the beginning. Landing in France wasn't a barrel of laughs, and I lost some good mates, but when I got sent to Dieppe, to the railway station, it was better. There were raids from German bombers, of course, trying to damage the tracks, but it settled down after a bit as the Germans were getting beaten back. I was luckier than some.'

'Despite all you have been through, you sound very contented, Brian.'

'Yes, I suppose I am. A war makes you think differently. I realise that you only get one chance in life and that life can be taken from you when you least expect it, so you must make the best of the time you have.'

'Are you hungry?' Kitty asked. 'I can make you a sandwich.'

'No, thank you, love. I had a meal at the station, but I am very tired. If you don't mind, I'd like to get my head down.'

Her heart sank. There was no longer an escape. 'I do have something important to tell you,' she ventured.

Brian, thinking she was about to confess her affair with the American, stopped her. 'Not now, Kitty. Leave it until the morning.'

'I'm sorry, but this can't wait. You'd better come with me,' she said, and walked towards the stairs.

He followed her, wondering what on earth she meant. He entered their bedroom behind her and saw in the soft glow of a night-light, a child's cot in the corner of the room. Kitty walked over to it and waited.

Brian stood for a moment trying to make sense of the scene before him, yet finding it difficult to comprehend. He made his way over slowly and peered at the baby asleep before him. The child was on its back, one arm above its head. It reminded him of Natalie and he smiled. Then looking up at Kitty he asked, 'Well?'

'This is Mathew.'

'How old is he?'

'Nine months.'

Brian gave his wife a strange look. 'He certainly isn't mine!'

'No, he isn't,' she replied quietly. 'I think we should go down-stairs. I don't want to disturb him.'

Gazing at the sleeping child, Brian tried to picture the American, but couldn't recall his features. 'Yes, I can see this can't wait until the morning.'

In the living room, he lit a cigarette and, looking at Kitty, asked, 'Is it the American's child?'

'So your mother did tell you about Jeff then?'

'Yes, I've known for quite some time.'

'But you never mentioned it in your letters.'

He ignored her and repeated his question. 'I assume this is the Yank's baby?'

Taking a deep breath she answered him. 'No, it isn't.'

He was shocked. This was Kitty, his wife, sitting before him.

He had come home to find her with a baby and it seemed not only had she been unfaithful to him with one man, she had slept with someone else as well. He was outraged.

'How can you sit there so calm and collected when you have been behaving behind my back with who knows how many men?'

'It wasn't like that at all!' Kitty's cheeks flushed red with anger. 'I'm not some cheap tart.'

'Well, forgive me if I don't see it that way. I've been away fighting a war, facing death, then learning that you were having an affair with an American and now, I come home to find you with yet another man's child. A great homecoming this is!'

'I was raped!'

He was speechless.

'I was raped,' repeated Kitty quietly, 'and this beautiful child is the result of that attack.'

Brian was completely lost for words for a moment. He didn't know what to say next. 'Did you know your attacker?'

'Yes. It was Gerry Stubbs.'

This was like a red rag to a bull to Brian. He'd always hated Stubbs, knowing that Kitty used to go out with the man and that he always felt that Gerry still had a soft spot for her.

'How very convenient,' he said with heavy sarcasm.

Tears welled in her eyes. 'That's not how I would describe it,' she said angrily. 'He pushed his way in here in a raging temper. He was furious that Eddie had put him on the spot, murdering the air-raid warden. He took his anger and frustration out on me! I was terrified. I thought he was going to kill me!' She burst into tears.

Seeing the obvious distress before him, Brian realised the truth of the matter. Passing his handkerchief he said, 'I'm sorry, Kitty, it was just such a shock.'

Eventually she pulled herself together. 'It wasn't my doing, I can assure you. I wanted nothing to do with the bastard.'

'Why didn't you have an abortion?' he asked suddenly.

Wiping her eyes she said, 'Don't think I didn't consider it. I actually went to this awful place to have one but when the woman produced some long metal knitting needles on this *filthy* kitchen table . . . I ran away.'

Brian's blood turned cold at the thought of what Kitty might have endured and his anger rose to boiling point. 'Right, tomorrow I'll pay the bastard a visit and teach him a lesson he won't forget!'

'He's in prison, awaiting trial.'

'Oh yes, Mother sent me the cuttings about the raid. It hasn't been settled yet then?'

Shaking her head, Kitty said, 'No. I just want to put it all behind me and get on with my life.'

'I'm sorry you've been through so much, but what now?'

'I am keeping my son,' she said defiantly.

'That's your choice,' he said quietly. 'We all have to make choices in our lives. I am no different. I have had to make an important one myself.'

Intrigued by his tone, she asked, 'And what might that be?'

'When I was in France, I met someone else.'

Kitty was taken completely by surprise. She had it in her mind that Brian wanted to live in France, but had no idea why. 'What do you mean, you've met somebody?'

'Another woman. Lisette, the daughter of the stationmaster I worked with. I'm in love with her.'

Kitty felt as if she had been kicked in the solar plexus. All the time she had been overcome with guilt because she was having an affair, breaking her marriage vows, fighting with her conscience – and then the baby, Brian had been having an affair with a Frenchwoman!

'You bastard! And here I was, worried to death about you, wondering if you were alive or dead!'

'I'm sorry, Kitty, but I truly love her.'

'What are you saying, you didn't love me?'

'No, of course I'm not, but you have to admit our marriage wasn't quite what you dreamed about.'

251

'That's not the point.'

'Quite right. The point is I want to marry Lisette and live in France.'

'You want a divorce?'

'Yes, I do. You see, we have a baby girl.'

Kitty was completely floored. 'A child – you and her?'

'Yes, her name is Natalie.'

'Well, I must say, Brian, you are full of surprises!'

'Well, you had a few for me. What happened to the Yank?'

'He's in France,' she said. She decided to tell Brian the truth. 'I'm in love with him and we want to get married.'

Brian was confused and angry. 'So why are you blowing a gasket about me and Lisette, for Christ's sake?'

'I'll tell you why – I have felt dreadful, thinking I was letting you down, worried about you going off to the war, knowing about us.'

He looked puzzled. 'I don't know what you mean.' Then as her words dawned on him, he said, 'Are you telling me this was going on before I went to France?'

Looking somewhat abashed she said, 'Yes, I'm afraid it was.'

'That bloke you met at the dance, the officer?'

'Yes.'

'You were having it off with him *and* sleeping with me when I was home on leave?'

She didn't know what to say.

'Well, did you or didn't you?'

'Yes I did! What else could I do? I didn't want to send you off to war knowing about us. You might have got yourself killed.'

He got up from the table and stomped around the room. 'That is the most disgusting thing I've ever heard!'

'Did you think I enjoyed doing it?' Kitty was now as angry as he was.

He turned on her. 'With me – or him?'

'That's not what I meant at all, and you know it.'

'You behaved no better than a whore.' He glared at her. 'I

would rather have known than have you having sex with me out of pity!'

'It wasn't like that.'

'Oh, please! Of course it bloody well was. So where is your lover now?'

'In Paris. He'll have to go home to Boston to be demobbed, then he's coming back here to see me.'

'Does he know about the baby?'

Shaking her head she said, 'No, I haven't told him yet, but I'm hoping he will accept the child when he knows the circumstances.'

'You take the cake, you really do. If I hadn't met Lisette, I could have been looking forward to coming home to a loving wife, only to be told she had a child and was leaving me for a bloody Yank.'

There was a sudden steeliness to Kitty's voice. 'That works both ways, Brian. Fortunately that isn't the case. We have both fallen in love with other people, so why are we quarrelling?'

He slumped down in the chair and said, 'I don't know. But it just seems so very messy.'

'No it isn't. You love Lisette, and you have a child. I love Jeff and will be going to live with him in Boston. It's very simple really. We just need to go to a solicitor and apply for a divorce, that's all.'

'You seem very sure that this man will accept the baby . . . what if he won't? What will you do then?'

With a shrug she said, 'I don't know.'

'Have you thought of adoption?'

'Would you ask your Frenchwoman to put your child up for adoption?'

'Of course not.'

'Then why suggest it?' she said angrily. 'I carried my baby for nine months. I gave him life – do you honestly think that, now, I could give him away?'

'No, but I was only thinking it might settle your problem with your American. It is a lot to expect from him to bring up another man's child as his own.'

'If it was you who had to decide,' she asked warily, 'would you accept Mathew?'

Without hesitation he said, 'No.'

'Whyever not?'

'Because every time I looked at the child it would remind me of how he was conceived.'

'But it wasn't with my consent.'

'I know that and the fact that you were violated makes it so much worse. I'm sorry, but that's just how I feel.' He added quietly, 'Don't you think it's sad that our marriage was a sham?'

'What do you mean, a sham? That's not how I see it at all.'

'Oh, come now, Kitty, it must have been if both of us found real love with other people.'

Looking across at him she said, 'Don't feel that way, please. You were a good husband, a bit dictatorial in your way, but you looked after me and I tried to be a good wife.'

'What do you mean, dictatorial?'

'Think about it.'

He grimaced. 'Yes, I suppose I was, but you know I've changed a lot.'

'Yes,' she said smiling, 'and for the better.' She frowned and asked, 'Were you unhappy being married to me, Brian?'

'No, of course I wasn't – you mustn't think that. I was different then and so were you; we led a different existence before I went away. My life seemed to open up once I joined the army. Then, during the fighting, you pray to survive. It changes a man. Then, of course, when I met Lisette, she changed me even more. French people are such an emotional race, and I suppose I learned to let go of my inhibitions. She told me I was stuffy!'

Kitty burst into peals of laughter. 'You were! Tell me about Lisette and the baby.' As she listened and watched him, it was a different man she saw before her. His eyes sparkled, he laughed at himself, explaining how Lisette had changed him and she could see just how happy he was – and was pleased for him.

'I'm happy for you, Brian. I really am.'

'And your American?' he said.

'Jeff is a lovely man, a lawyer in civilian life.'

'Will you mind leaving your parents to live in Boston?'

'To be honest, I don't know. It does sometimes worry me, but I want to be with him, so I have no choice.'

'What if he feels the way that I do about the baby?'

'It is something I will have to face. I can't be parted from my son.'

'Does Stubbs know he's a father?'

Kitty paled. 'No! And he never will.'

'Mother sent me the newspaper clippings about your brother, Eddie, as you know. I was sorry. Your parents must have been really upset.'

'They were – certainly Mum was. I can't believe Eddie was capable of murder. He didn't mean to kill that man. It wasn't premeditated. He just lost his head.'

'Well, I never did like that Gerry Stubbs. I always thought he lusted after you!'

'He did, for years. Because I kept him at arm's length, I suppose.'

'Well, I'm happy to hear that.'

'A lot of good it did me!'

'But that wasn't your fault. Why didn't you report the rape to the police?'

'He threatened to kill me if I did.'

'Poor Kitty. You must have been terrified. I am sorry you went through so much. Look, I suggest we make an appointment to see a solicitor tomorrow,' he suggested, 'and get things under way. As soon as it is possible, I want to go back to France to be with Lisette and the baby.'

With a wicked grin she said, 'I wonder what your mother will have to say about all this.'

Brian raised his eyes to the heavens. 'God only knows. I'm dreading it.'

'Oh, don't worry, she'll blame me for everything.'

He laughed. 'Yes, I'm sure she will.' He took her hands in his and said, 'Kitty, you were a good wife to me. I don't want you ever to think otherwise.'

She kissed his cheek. 'Thank you. It would be nice if we could remain friends.'

'Of course we will, I'd like that.'

'I think it would be better if you slept in the spare room from now on, don't you?'

Grinning he asked, 'Are you worried I might be tempted?'

Smiling back at him she said, 'I just think it would be better. Jeff and Lisette would agree, I'm sure.'

Thinking of the dire threats Lisette made to him before he left he said, 'Yes, I'm sure you're right. Come on, I'm tired and need to build my strength to face my mother!'

Chapter Thirty-One

Gerry Stubbs was not a happy man. He paced up and down the small cell, which he shared with another prisoner. They had already had words about Gerry's restlessness.

'For Christ's sake, will you be still! You are driving me round the bend and making me dizzy. I can't bloody well think with you constantly on the move.'

'Shup your face or I'll shut it for you!' was Gerry's response. It was really bugging him as to who could have grassed on him, and he wouldn't be satisfied until he found out. As far as he knew, only his two men and Eddie Simmons knew about the robbery. His man in prison had kept quiet and he had promised to see him all right for his silence. Jack, the other man, had been arrested with him, and had been totally dismayed by it, as he had been. There was only Eddie left. Now no way would he put himself in the frame for murder. It had to be Kitty. She must have been so disgusted and appalled that she had shopped them. It would have been a way to get back at him too for raping her. It was very stupid of her. A very dangerous thing to do and one he wouldn't let her get away with. He'd send a man round to see her. Find out once and for all and if it was her, then she'd pay.

The next visiting day, one of his heavies came to the prison and in low tones so as not to be overheard, Gerry whispered his instructions to the man.

'Right, boss, I'll see to it,' he said.

257

Brian had been home three days now. He and Kitty had visited a solicitor together. As the divorce was pretty straightforward, he didn't foresee a problem.

'Which one of you is going to cite the other for misconduct?'

They both looked dismayed.

'One of you must cite the other for adultery,' he said. 'You must decide who. Go home and discuss it and get back to me, then we can get things under way.'

Back in Harborough Road the discussion became heated.

'Well, you were sleeping with your Yank before I went to France,' Brian declared. It still rankled with him that Kitty had been sleeping with him at the same time.

'His name is Jeff!' snapped Kitty. 'You will be leaving England before me, so it had better be you. The neighbours will accept that a man has been unfaithful easier than a woman.'

'You didn't worry about the neighbours then, did you, so why worry about a bit of gossip now? I'm sure there has been more than enough already so a bit more won't matter!'

'Now you're being selfish,' she retorted.

'Me, being selfish? That's a bit rich, I must say! You were the first one to break your marriage vows.'

And so the argument raged until, in frustration, Brian said, 'I'm off to the pub for some peace.'

'That's right, run away just because things aren't going as you want. Nothing will get settled if you go, so let's get it sorted one way or another now!'

He pushed past her and said, 'I'll see you later, when you are in a more reasonable frame of mind.'

Kitty was as frustrated as her husband, and as the front door slammed she kicked out at a wooden chair, hurting her foot in the process. Cursing quietly, she limped around and sat in an easy chair by the fireside. This was hopeless! She had hoped that after seeing the solicitor she would be able to write to Jeff and tell him how Brian hadn't caused a rumpus after all, that he too wanted his freedom, that all would be well. She didn't want to see his name in the papers named as the co-respondent. After all, Lisette had a baby, sired by *her* husband. Surely that was worse. It seemed a childish argument, but now Kitty was feeling resentful.

She was about to get up and put the kettle on when there was a knock on her back door. That was all she needed – and if it was her mother-in-law, she'd send her off with a flea in her ear. But when she opened it, a burly man pushed her backwards, and closed the door behind him.

'Hello, Mrs Freeman,' he said with a sneer. 'You and me had better have words.'

He was a rough-looking individual with his heavy jacket like those worn by the stevedores who worked in the docks. He was unshaven and his breath smelled of stale beer and tobacco.

'Who are you? What do you want?' she asked, her voice trembling.

'Gerry Stubbs sent me,' he said.

'He's in prison.'

'I know, I saw him yesterday, he asked me to call.'

Now Kitty was really worried. Gerry Stubbs meant trouble. Ever since Eddie and the others had been arrested she'd been worried that Gerry would think she'd informed on him. 'Why? Why should he want anything to do with me?' She was trying not to show her fear. She went to turn away but the man grabbed hold of her arm.

'My guvnor wonders if you have been talking to the Old Bill.'

'The police? Whatever would I want to talk to them about?'

'A little case of murder?'

'Murder? I don't know what you mean.' The grip tightened, making her wince.

'Someone grassed on him and that rotten brother of yours. What happened, lady? Get a case of conscience, did you? Decide to be an honest citizen, pay back a few old scores?'

'No! No I didn't, I swear.'

He grasped her round the throat. 'I am not at all convinced that

259

you are telling me the truth, girl.' And he squeezed once more.

'I wouldn't send my own brother to the hangman,' she cried out. 'I couldn't ever do that.'

'Many a relative that I know would do so without batting an eyelid,' he said.

'Well, I wouldn't.' She was having trouble breathing. 'Gerry threatened to kill me if I ever said anything to anyone. Do you think I would defy him under the circumstances? I didn't say anything, I give you my word.'

'Tell me the truth,' he insisted.

She tried in vain to loosen his hold. Her senses were swimming as the breath was being squeezed out of her. 'I didn't do it,' she managed to gasp as she slumped to the floor, her attacker going with her, without releasing his hold.

'You are lying. You went to the police, didn't you?' he demanded.

With hardly any voice left she murmured, 'No, I didn't do anything.' His face blurred before her. I'm going to die, she thought. 'My baby . . .' she rasped, and then she blacked out.

Kitty came round with Brian bending over her, slapping her hands and sprinkling water from the tap over her face.

'Kitty! For God's sake, wake up. Please wake up!'

She slowly came to and put her hand up to her sore throat. 'Brian! Where am I?'

He helped her to sit up. 'For God's sake, Kitty. What's going on? I came home to find some man in the kitchen with his hands around your throat.'

She could hardly speak. 'Give me some water to drink, will you?'

He poured some into a cup and, stooping beside her on the floor, helped her to drink the soothing liquid as her hands were shaking. Then helping her to her feet he took her into the living room and sat her in a chair. 'Do you need a doctor?' he asked anxiously.

Shaking her head she said, 'No, I'll be all right in a minute. Just give me time to pull myself together.'

'Who was that man? Did you know him?'

'He's one of Gerry Stubbs' men.'

'Why the hell was he here?'

She held up her hand to quieten him. She was too shaken from her ordeal to be able to answer questions at this moment.

'We should call the police. Tell them everything.'

'No, Brian, please. I couldn't bear to have to go to court and tell them every detail. It was a dreadful experience as it was; I couldn't stand up in public and tell the whole sorry story. It would destroy me and then people would know that he was the father of my child.'

'Where is Mathew?'

'Upstairs, taking a nap. Please go and see if he's all right.'

He returned quickly. 'The baby's asleep,' he said. He put his arms around her. 'My God, Kitty, I had no idea things were so dangerous with Stubbs. If I could get my hands on that bastard I'd teach him a lesson.'

'What happened to the man in the kitchen?'

'He soon scarpered, but he should have quite a shiner in the morning.'

'You hit him?'

'Bloody right I did. He looked as if he was choking you to death. What did you expect me to do?'

'Oh, Brian, I never figured you for a knight in shining armour,' she said with a faint smile, yet the tears trickled down her cheeks.

'A nice strong cup of tea with sugar is what you need, love. It's good for shock. Now that bastard knows I'm home I doubt he'll be back.'

It was a very comforting thought, and Kitty was grateful for his presence. Had she been alone she felt she would have been unable to handle the shock. Having Brian there made her feel safe. He gave her a couple of aspirins and was most solicitous, making sure she was as comfortable as she could be. She was bruised around her throat where the thug had held her. It wasn't comfortable to talk and Brian insisted she go upstairs and lie down and try to sleep.

'I'll be here,' he said, 'so don't you worry.'

'I don't want to be alone,' she said.

'I'll make you up a bed here on the sofa and I'll sit by the fire. Don't worry about Mathew; I'll look after him. After all, I'm used to babies,' he added.

After she was settled, knowing Brian was nearby, Kitty was indeed able to sleep, for a while.

When it was reported to Gerry that Brian Freeman was back, he dismissed him as that boring sod, but his man said, 'His fist wasn't boring, guv. He's got a powerful right hand.'

Looking at the black eye, which hadn't entirely faded, Gerry grimaced. 'The army probably made a real man of him. Well? Do you think it was Kitty Freeman who grassed?'

The man shook his head. 'No, I don't. I believe her. She would have confessed. Besides, she's a decent sort, from what I could tell. She wouldn't sell her brother down the line and she hadn't forgotten your threat. She would have been too scared by that anyway.'

'Then who the hell was it? I won't rest until I find out.'

Nancy Brannigan wasn't worried about Gerry. He had absolutely no idea that she had overheard his conversation in the pub, so there was no way at all that she was a suspect. Her call to the police was anonymous and she had no regrets. Eddie had raped and attacked her – if he got away with murder too there would be no justice in the world. As for Gerry, for him to rape Kitty put him in the same league, in her book. Rapists could have no idea just how mentally destructive such an action was to the victim. She could scarcely bear to let a man get close to her. Gerry had been different; she was used to him. After the event he had been gentle and understanding, but now she had dismissed him from her life. Naturally she watched the papers to see what was happening, but she was starting to build a decent life for herself. She still went out and about, but no longer was she the girl without morals. She was learning to live differently and she liked it.

So concerned about Kitty was he, that Brian told her he was quite prepared to be the one cited in their divorce case.

Kitty looked at him with surprise. 'Really? What changed your mind?'

'You have been through enough, one way or another, so why make things difficult?'

'That's good of you,' she said. 'We'd best get back to the solicitor then.'

Two days later, Kitty was able to write to Jeff and tell him the good news. She omitted to tell him about the baby. That she would do later, before he went back to Boston.

> My Darling, [she wrote]
> I have some wonderful news. Brian is home and has agreed to a divorce. It seems that he has fallen in love with a French girl, and would you believe, they have a child! He is as anxious as I am to have his freedom. Divorce proceedings are under way as I write, but of course they will take some time. Brian wants to return to France to see his girlfriend and his daughter, meantime. I can't tell you how happy I am.
> I miss and love you,
> Kitty xx

As she mailed the letter she gave a sigh of happiness. Wasn't life strange? Who would have thought that things could change so much and, more so, that it had turned out so well between her and Brian.

Gladys Freeman wasn't so thrilled when she was told the news. It didn't make her happy at all! She had been delighted when her boy walked through her back door.

'Brian, love! How marvellous to see you.'

They sat and had a cup of tea together. It was in the afternoon so Frank was still at work.

'Now tell me all about it,' she said. 'I want to know what happened when they sent you to France.'

There was no way that Brian was going to relate the horrors of war to his mother, but he did tell her about his time spent in Dieppe, at the railway depot.

'It was great, Ma,' he said. 'It was almost like being at my old job, and the stationmaster and I got on very well together. I lodged with him.'

'Did his wife look after you?' she asked.

'His wife died a few years ago, but his daughter, Lisette, fed me. I was lucky to be there. I had it cushy compared with others.'

'You got my letter about Kitty?' she asked sharply.

'Yes I did – not that I thought it kind of you, especially during war time when I was helpless to do anything about it!'

She took his rebuke badly. 'It was my duty as your mother,' she retorted.

'No, it was your duty to mind your own business,' he snapped, and as she started to argue, he said, 'Anyway, it's all in the past now.'

'You've forgiven her?'

'We are getting a divorce,' he said.

There was an expression of triumph and satisfaction on the face of Gladys Freeman as she said, 'Quite right too! Such carryings-on.'

'No, you don't understand. I'm in love with Lisette and eventually I'm going to marry her.'

'You what?'

'We have a baby daughter, Natalie. We're going to be living in France.'

'You have a bastard child?'

Brian was furious. 'We have a much-loved child and we will make her legitimate when we marry.'

'Well, I never did!'

'No, you probably didn't,' Brian muttered beneath his breath. 'And Kitty is going to marry her American officer and go and live in Boston with him, once the divorce is through.'

Gladys was having an attack of the vapours, fanning her puce face with a newspaper. 'I have never heard anything so dreadful in all my life!' she protested. 'You getting a divorce is bad enough but marrying one of those Froggies is just too much!'

Brian strove to control his temper as he rose to his feet. 'Don't worry about it,' he said coldly. 'You'll never meet her, so you can keep your opinions for your neighbours, for no doubt they will certainly hear all about it from you.' And he walked out of the house.

He had definitely decided that he would never ever inflict his mother on Lisette, but he smiled to himself as he thought it might be fun to do so just once. Lisette would certainly give as good as she got. But no, he just wanted to be back in France with his two girls and intended to make the arrangements as soon as possible. He would write to Lisette tonight and tell her.

Chapter Thirty-Two

Jeff Ryder was thrilled to receive Kitty's letter with the good news of her divorce. He had wondered if Brian would be difficult about it and wouldn't have blamed him if he had been, but it seemed that everything had worked out well for them. He had tried to pull a few strings to get himself a quick trip back to Southampton, without success. He had no idea how much longer he would be required to stay in Paris. Although the war was over, it seemed he was as busy as ever, with finding housing for those troops who were staying on to help the French authorities put the country back together again, repatriating others. But he had managed to cable her some flowers; at least that was something. But he was totally frustrated. He wanted now to get back to civilian life and build his career and a home for his future bride.

When the bouquet arrived at Kitty's, it was Brian who took delivery of it as Kitty was at work. It must have cost a pretty penny, he thought as he stood the stems of the beautiful spring selection in water in the kitchen sink, awaiting Kitty's return.

She was delighted when she saw them and, taking the small envelope, she read the card inside. 'Great news, darling. I love you. Jeff.' Turning to Brian, eyes shining with happiness, Kitty said excitedly, 'They're from Jeff.'

Much to his surprise, Brian felt a pang of jealousy. It just didn't seem proper for his wife to be in receipt of such things from another man.

Seeing his sour expression, Kitty put the card away and pointedly asked, 'When are you planning to return to France, to the baby and Lisette?'

It was a stark reminder of his position. He hesitated and said, 'I'm going to see if I can get a booking on some sort of ship to take me to Calais or some other port, just as soon as I can.'

'Good,' she said. 'I'm sure she will be pleased to see you.'

'Will you be all right left alone? I don't want to go away and leave you to the mercy of one of Stubbs' men calling round again.'

'Why would he want to come back?' she bravely asked. 'I'm sure he was convinced that I was innocent. Had I been guilty I would have said, under the circumstances. He was choking me to death, after all. I'll keep the doors locked all the time anyway, and won't open them until I know who's there. Your mother isn't likely to call, is she?'

'No!' he said shortly.

'You've been to see her then?'

'Yes, and I stormed out of the house. She called Natalie my bastard child.'

'Oh, Brian, I am sorry.'

Dismissively he said, 'No matter. It's none of her business anyway. I'm going to find a job when I get to France, hopefully back on the railways. I'll send you what money I can.'

'Thanks.' She didn't tell him about the money Jeff had left in a bank account for her; she thought it would offend his masculine pride.

A week later Brian was fortunately able to get a place on a ship calling at Dieppe. As he landed in France, he breathed in deeply. How different the air felt here. On this side of the Channel he was a different person. He quickly made his way to the station.

When he arrived he went straight to the office of Monsieur Pallier. '*Bonjour, monsieur,*' he said as he saw his future father-in-law.

The Frenchman looked up and, with great delight, hugged him, kissing him on both cheeks, French pouring forth at a great rate. 'You 'ave returned!'

'Where are Lisette and the baby?' asked Brian.

'In the 'ouse. Go, go. She will be so 'appy to see you.' He hugged Brian again.

Lisette was bending over the kitchen sink washing clothes when he opened the door. 'Hello, my darling.'

'Brian! *Chéri!*' She flung herself at him, smothering him with kisses and soapsuds. 'You 'ave come back!'

Lifting her off her feet and holding her close, he kissed her and said, 'You doubted that I would?'

Giving him a piercing look she said, 'I 'oped you would, but I wondered once you got 'ome and saw your wife – I was worried.'

'I promised, didn't I?'

'*Oui*, but things can change. Did you sleep with your wife? I'll kill you if you did!'

He started laughing and spun her round in his arms. 'Oh, my darling Lisette, never change.' Putting her down he asked, 'Where is Natalie?'

'In the other room. She's sleeping.' Taking him by the hand, she led him through the doorway.

As Brian looked down at the fruit of his loins, he was overcome with emotion. 'My, but how she's gown!' He wanted to pick her up and hold her, but Lisette said, 'Don't disturb 'er, *chéri*. Let 'er sleep. There will be time to renew your acquaintance later.'

They sat chatting over a glass of wine. 'You wouldn't believe how much I missed this,' he said, holding up his glass against the light from the window, enjoying the red glints as he swirled the contents slowly and lovingly around the glass. 'When I first got home I went to the pub and had a pint of beer. Do you know, I prefer wine!'

Lisette clapped her hands with glee. '*Parfait!* I will make a Frenchman out of you yet.' Sipping her wine she asked, ''Ow was your wife?'

Brian told her everything. When he got to the rape and the baby, Lisette was very sympathetic. 'Poor woman. My 'eart aches for 'er. We 'ad enough of that sort of thing at the beginning of the war, when the bloody Boche invaded. They were carried away with being the conquerors. The "Master Race" – pigs they were! No woman was safe on the streets. I loathed them. I wanted them all dead!'

With a look of horror Brian asked, 'What are you saying? Are you telling me that *you* were raped?'

Glaring at him she said, 'Why? Would it make any difference?'

He was in turmoil and didn't answer.

With eyes flashing angrily, Lisette said, 'Do you love me, or not?'

'You know I do.'

'Do you love Natalie?'

'Don't be ridiculous. I adore you both, you *know* I do.'

'But if I told you that I was raped, that men stood in a line to take their turn as I was 'eld down by others – would you love me less? Would I be a different woman in your eyes? Would you leave us and go 'ome?'

Tears streamed down his cheeks as he said, 'No I wouldn't. I love you too much, but please tell me this didn't happen to you.'

'It 'appened!' she snapped. 'It's war.'

'I don't know what to say,' Brian said, his voice trembling with emotion.

Lisette sat silently staring at her hands, wringing them stressfully. 'I 'ad a bad time. The men were brutal. They laughed as they raped me, as if I was nothing – and to them I *was* nothing.'

'Oh, my darling,' Brian murmured as he caught hold of her hands in an effort to stop her distress.

'Fortunately I 'ad a good doctor. He repaired my body, but I 'ad to manage my mind myself.' She looked up at him. 'You never forget such a thing.'

'Stop! Don't tell me any more,' he pleaded.

'You men, you make me sick! You think you are the only

people to 'ave a 'ard time. Yes, you face gunfire and bullets and you die or you survive.' She got to her feet and stormed over to the door opening on to the garden. Turning back she paused. 'Well, I didn't die – I survived!' and she stomped outside.

'Lisette!' Brian rose quickly and followed her. Catching her by her shoulders, he said, 'Please, forgive me. I had no idea.' He turned her to face him and saw the tears brimming in her eyes and watched as they trickled down her face. She angrily brushed them aside.

'I am so sorry for being so stupid.' He gently pulled her closer and kissed the top of her head. He felt her slowly lose the rigidity that anger had given her and he cursed himself for causing her pain in reliving such memories. Inside him, anger raged against the soldiers who had brutalised the woman he held in his arms, but he kept these murderous thoughts to himself. They would only add to Lisette's anguish. At the same time, he regretted his remarks to Kitty about not being able to accept baby Mathew, if he was the one who had to choose. Now, through Lisette, he saw things differently. He hoped that her American was more compassionate than he had been.

'The American, your wife's lover, will 'e understand?'

'I don't know. I do hope so, for Kitty's sake. She really loves him.'

'Then it will be a test of 'is love for 'er, *non*?'

'Yes, I'm afraid so.'

Now Brian had left for France and the divorce was progressing, Kitty felt the time was right to tell Jeff about the baby. A letter was the last way she would have chosen, but she had no choice and she wanted him to know the facts before he went home to his family. It was very difficult to find the right words. It took her several days and several rewrites.

Jean had been on hand to try to help. 'You need to emphasise how dreadful it was for you to be raped.'

'Jeff is an intelligent man, he'll know.'

'No, love, he won't. He's a man. Men think of sex quite differently from how women do. For most women, sex and love mean the same. For men it's a need. They can have sex with a woman to fulfil that need without having any tender feelings towards her at all. They can have a gay old time, with as many women as they want, but . . . if they fall in love, then it's a different kettle of fish. You are theirs and God help another man who tries to lay a finger on you.' She laughed and said, 'It goes back to cavemen, dear. Men are ever the hunters. Look at another caveman and you're in trouble. Carry his seed and you're dead!'

Kitty laughed with Jean but thought there was quite a bit of common sense behind the comment and so as she wrote, she tried to explain to Jeff her true emotions, and how, after all the anguish and feeling of degradation, she adored little Mathew, who had no say in his conception. At the same time she assured Jeff that the only other thing she wanted in life was to share the rest of her days with him.

I know, darling, that this will come as a dreadful shock to you and I apologise for that. I know also that it is a lot to ask of you that you take my baby as well, but I'm afraid there is no way I will part with him. If you can't find it in your heart to do so, I will understand. I will always love you, whatever you decide.

Kitty xx

She addressed the envelope and kissed the back of it, but her heart was heavy. She thought of Brian's reaction to the situation. Jeff might well feel the same. Well, now it was out in the open. Jeff would have time to make a decision and there was nothing she could do about it.

After posting the letter, Kitty pushed the pram round to her mother's house where she took Mathew and let him play on the floor among the toys that Amy kept for him.

'He has grown so,' Amy beamed as she watched him.

'I wrote to Jeff today, Mum, and told him about Mathew.'

'Well, it was time he knew, wasn't it? It's only fair. But the waiting will be difficult for you.' She gazed at her daughter and added, 'Don't be surprised if you don't hear for a while.'

'What do you mean?'

'The news that you have a child will certainly shake him and when he knows how you became pregnant, he'll need time to get his head round it all. Be patient, is all I can say.'

When Jeff received Kitty's mail and saw the writing on the envelope he smiled and put the letter in his pocket to read later in the privacy of his room. He had some news to tell Kitty himself. He was being drafted back to the USA in a month's time. He hoped to persuade her to move over to Boston before her divorce was through, as he wanted her to help him choose the home that they would share when they were married.

A little later he sat on his bed, poured himself a drink and opened the letter . . . He frowned as he read one page after another and when he got to the end, he put it down beside him, stunned by the contents. Kitty raped, and now with a child of the rapist! He first thought of the dreadful experience she had been through and wondered how she could bring herself to keep the baby, the result of the painful episode. But knowing her as he did, he should have realised she would have seen past that and thought only of the innocent child. But how did he feel about it? In his mind he had planned their future, of having a family of their own. He couldn't think straight; he needed time to sort out his thoughts. Putting on his jacket, he walked the war-torn streets of Paris until the early hours of the morning.

The next day he went to see his commanding officer and asked for compassionate leave. Having been granted this, he rang a few contacts and was able to get a seat on an American military aircraft taking equipment back to England. Once there, he caught a train to Southampton.

Chapter Thirty-Three

When Kitty opened the door and saw Jeff standing on the doorstep, she felt the blood drain from her body. She stared at him for what seemed a lifetime, then she flung herself into his arms.

'Oh Jeff, darling, I am so happy to see you.'

He held her close, feeling her tremble with emotion. It felt so good to him to run his fingers through her hair, to inhale the scent of her. Lifting her, he carried her over the threshold and into the hallway, kicking the front door shut with his foot, where he kissed her longingly.

'Kitty, Kitty darling, I've missed you so much. Let me look at you.' He gazed into her eyes and softly caressed her sweet face. 'You look just as beautiful as I remember.' And he kissed her again.

'I am so relieved to see you are safe and sound,' she said. 'I was in constant torment in case anything happened to you. I don't know what I would have done had you been killed in action.'

'I told you I would come back.'

'I know you did.' Then she asked anxiously, 'Did you receive my last letter?'

'That's why I'm here. They're sending me home in a month's time and I had to see you before then to find out exactly what has been going on. Your letter was quite a shock, I can tell you.'

'You'd better come and sit down. Let me make you a cup of coffee first and then we'll talk.' Kitty felt she needed that short time in the kitchen to choose her words because she knew that this meeting could make or break her dreams of a future with this man.

'Where is the baby?' he asked.

'In the living room in his playpen. His name is Mathew.'

Jeff followed her and saw the child sitting playing with his toys. He looked up as they walked into the room and gave them a toothy grin. Kitty left them together.

Jeff gazed at Mathew, unable to comprehend the situation fully. As he did so, he wondered who was the man who had raped Kitty. What sort of a character was he and just how many of the father's genes were in this innocent-looking child?

Kitty carried the tray of coffee to the table and they sat together. Kitty said, 'I don't know where to begin.'

'At the very beginning, and tell me absolutely everything.'

It took some time. She told him of her history with Gerry Stubbs, how she gave him up as a young woman and later married Brian; the fact that Gerry was often in the background of her life; about Eddie . . . until the whole story unfolded.

Jeff sat there listening intently, but not only was he Kitty's lover, he was also a lawyer. 'I don't understand why you didn't go to the police when this Stubbs told you your brother had killed that man. This was vital information.'

'Because he threatened my life if I told anyone,' she protested.

'But they would have given you protection,' he insisted. 'Had you done so, he would never have been free to come along later and rape you.'

'So, you're saying it was all my fault?'

'No, Kitty darling, I'm not saying that at all. And why didn't you tell *me* about this? It happened before I went to France.'

'Because I knew what you would say! You would insist I went to the police. How could I be the one to send my brother to the gallows?'

'And when you were supposed to be helping out a sick friend?'

274

'It was just after I had been raped. I was covered in bruises. How could I let you see me like that?'

'Kitty, a relationship without trust is no relationship at all. Now, of course, I can understand why you were reluctant for me to make love to you.'

'I'm sorry, Jeff darling, but I just couldn't tell you.'

'Didn't you think I would understand?' he asked with a note of anger in his voice.

'I didn't know what to think. I was too scared to think straight.'

'I assume that Stubbs doesn't know you had his child?'

'No, I will never tell him,' she said firmly, picking Mathew up and feeding him from a bottle. 'Hopefully he'll be shut away for some time. No one but my parents, Brian and you know who Mathew's father is. Oh, and my friend, Jean. She would never tell a soul.'

'You told Brian?'

'I had no choice. He came home on leave and the baby was here. What could I do?'

'Yet you kept this information from me, of all people, Kitty. Why?'

Putting her hand to her head she said, 'I suppose I was frightened I'd lose you.'

'It had to come out at some time, yet you waited until recently.'

She became angry. 'I wasn't being devious, if that's what you think. Christ, Jeff! I had to tell my husband about us – and the baby, tell him I wanted divorce and my brother is on trial for murder. I couldn't face another problem.'

'I see.'

But Kitty wondered if he did. 'Does this change things between us?' she asked bravely.

He watched her with the baby nestled in her arms. The motherly love she felt for Mathew was very evident. He had pictured such a scene, but with Kitty holding his child, not some stranger's.

'I really don't know,' he answered slowly. 'You see, I had our future all planned; I was looking forward to it so much. Introducing you to my friends and family, having our own home, children, and all this has somewhat clouded the issue. I do love you, Kitty, please don't doubt that. I'll always love you, but I need time to think. There is so much to consider.'

Kitty looked downcast. 'When do you have to return to France?' she asked, putting the child down.

'Later tonight. This really is a flying visit, but I had to see you. I have to be at the military airport this evening, so I must get a train fairly soon.'

Her heart sank. Nothing had been decided, and deep down she felt as if all her dreams were turning into a nightmare.

'I'm so sorry, Jeff. I truly love you, but I love my son too. He didn't ask to be born. I need to be with him until he grows up and can take care of himself.'

Taking her hand Jeff said, 'I do understand that and I admire you for feeling this way. You are the child's mother and I wouldn't expect you to feel differently. If you did, you wouldn't be my Kitty. But I have to be sure that *I* can feel as strongly as you do. I have to truly believe I can care for Mathew too, and not resent him. If I can't, then it wouldn't be fair to either of you. This has all been so sudden, I just need time to decide.'

'I understand,' she said quietly.

'You say that Brian has met a Frenchwoman?'

'Yes, and they have a baby daughter. When the divorce is finalised, they plan to marry. He's going to stay in France.' She gave a half-smile. 'He's really changed, you know. This woman has done far more for him than I ever did.'

'Don't forget the war, Kitty. That changes us all in some way. With Brian, it widened his outlook and his horizons.'

'Like you widened mine,' Kitty said. 'You taught me so much. I want you to know that and I'll always be grateful.'

'When I was in France, I often used to imagine us walking together through the New Forest, you know,' said Jeff, his voice filled with nostalgia, 'sitting on the bench on top of our hillock. They were such happy times, weren't they?'

'I'll never forget them,' she murmured. 'Never.'

Looking at his watch, he rose from his chair. 'I would love to stay longer, you know that, but I have to go.' He took her hands, pulled her to her feet and gathered her into his arms. 'There is so much I want to say, and to discuss, but I was lucky to even get here. I have a lot to do before I leave France. When I am home in Boston I'll be able to see things clearly. I'll be in touch with you when I've reached a conclusion.' He kissed her gently. 'Take care, my darling. I do love you.'

But as she responded she couldn't help but ask herself whether he loved her enough to overcome the situation.

Closing the door behind him, Kitty picked up her son and walked upstairs to the bedroom. Holding Mathew over her shoulder, she wandered to the window, looking along the road. The road that Jeff had just taken, and she wept as she wondered if she would ever see him again.

Two months had passed and Kitty had not heard a word from America. Her mother had tried to comfort her by saying, 'Jeff will have so much to do when he first gets home, dear. You know, visiting family and sorting out any plans to start up his practice again. It takes time to settle back into civilian life. Just try not to worry. Be patient and give him time.'

Kitty had no choice as she hadn't a home address for him so wouldn't have been able to write if she so desired. Had she been able to do so, though, she would have resisted, as she felt that Jeff needed to be left alone to sort out his future, but she longed for the feel of his arms about her, dreamed of hearing him say all would be well, yet secretly dreaded his telling her that it was all over between them.

In any case, her thoughts were now elsewhere as Eddie and Gerry's case was coming to court and she wanted to be there to see for herself what transpired. She had advised her mother to stay at home as she thought it would be too upsetting for her. Amy had agreed, and so Kitty and her father made their way to the courthouse, leaving Amy to care for Mathew. At least he would take her mind off things, they hoped.

Jim and Kitty sat towards the back of the court and waited. It was full, and she could see the reporters gathered together on the front benches at the side of the room, chatting, notepads and pens at hand. There would be a great deal of publicity and she was thankful that she had kept her silence over the rape and Mathew's parenthood. The shame of it spread all over the local newspaper would have been too much to bear.

The three prisoners were brought up from the cells and into the dock. As Kitty gazed at Gerry Stubbs, standing so arrogantly, a feeling of loathing swept over her. It was so all-encompassing that it momentarily took her breath away. Her brother, Eddie, was looking more than anxious, which wasn't surprising as he was the one charged with murder.

Two rows behind Kitty sat Nancy Brannigan. She was here to see Eddie Simmons get his comeuppance! As he turned, casting a glance around the court, their gaze met. There was such a look of hatred in the girl's eyes that Eddie was quite shaken and he looked away, but not before he saw his father and sister. He hadn't seen his mother and prayed she wasn't there. He looked sideways at Gerry Stubbs and Jack Baker, wondering who had split on them. Gerry looked back at him with a thunderous expression and muttered something under his breath, but Eddie ignored him. He had more than enough to worry about to be concerned about Gerry Stubbs.

The day was spent with the opening statements from the counsels for the defence and prosecution, then the judge adjourned until the following day.

Kitty and her father walked home together in silence, neither speaking of their feelings, which for both of them were too painful to share, knowing that the serious business would begin on the morrow.

Gerry Stubbs returned to his cell feeling quite confident. The jury would never be able to convict them. There had been no witnesses. No, it was all a bluff. Soon he'd be free and able to get on with his life.

This was his counsel's defence the following day. In his opinion the case should never have come to court. However, when the prosecution called their first witness, it changed the case completely.

'Call Ernie Byers!'

Gerry felt sick in the pit of his stomach. Ernie had been the third member of the gang who, as far as Gerry was aware, had kept quiet during questioning whilst he served his short sentence for burglary. What the hell was he doing appearing for the prosecution?

It all became clear in a short space of time. 'The bastard's rolled over!' Gerry spat the words out. Both Eddie and Jack heard him and their shoulders slumped. Before, there had been hope; now they knew they were lost and would do time. For Gerry Stubbs and Jack Baker it would mean they would eventually get out of prison, but if Eddie Simmons was found guilty of murder, it could mean the death penalty.

The court case went on for three weeks. The police were called as witnesses, as were pathologists, who explained the cause of death, and the furrier whose stock they had stolen, as well as others who had information to add. Three weeks where the nerves of the Simmons family were stretched to breaking point. The only thing that held them all together was little Mathew. A baby needs attention, which was a godsend to them all, but eventually the day came for the summing-up. The day that the jury would be sent out of the room to make their decision.

The counsel for the defence tried to denigrate the character of the main witness, Ernie Byers. 'This man is a small-time crook, a thief, a burglar. By making up this story, he hoped to get time reduced on his sentence, that's all.'

279

But the counsel for the prosecution was a brilliant orator. He railed on about the loss of life of the air-raid warden – '. . . a man who was working for his country, an innocent man whose family are now without a father. Struck down so coldly by a man who was a deserter from the army. A man who ran away from his responsibilities. A coward, without any moral standing. And as for the others? Small-time racketeers, steeped in the black market, a scourge to their fellow countrymen. Out to make easy money . . .'

He went on and on until, glancing at Gerry Stubbs, Nancy could see he was gripping the handrail of the dock so tightly that his knuckles showed white. He wouldn't like to be described in such terms, she thought. It would really take the wind out of his arrogant sails. Her gaze moved along to Eddie, who was sitting white-faced and drawn, eyes cast down. Yes, you bastard, she thought, you'll get yours!

The jury was sent away to consider their verdict after listening to the summing-up from the judge. As it was getting late in the day, the court was adjourned until the following day. There was a sudden chattering among those who filed out of the doors. One of the reporters was heard to remark, 'They won't see the light of day for a long while.'

Kitty saw the tightening of her father's jaw and her heart went out to him. 'Come on, Dad; let's take a walk through the park.' She tucked her arm through his.

'To think a son of mine could be capable of such a crime,' he said, raw anguish in his voice.

'Don't go blaming yourself, Dad. You and Mum brought us up to know the difference between right and wrong. Eddie was always weak. He would have ended up in some trouble or other, no matter what.'

'But this is murder!'

'Well, maybe not,' she said. 'When the judge summed up, he said that if the jury thought that Eddie hit the man on the spur of the moment and it was not premeditated, they could consider manslaughter, which brings a serious, but lighter sentence. Not the death penalty.'

'No matter, Kitty. The poor man died.'

'Yes, we can't get away from the fact. Best get home to Mum. She'll be really anxious.'

Kitty was concerned that if Eddie was proven guilty of murder and received the ultimate penalty, her mother would really go to pieces.

Chapter Thirty-Four

Whilst all the courtroom drama was taking place in his hometown of Southampton, life was running smoothly for Brian and his little family in Dieppe. Monsieur Pallier had spoken for him and now Brian was doing the same work at the railway station as when he was there during the war. They all lived in the one house, where Lisette cooked for them and cared for little Natalie, who seemed to be growing daily, giving all of them hours of entertainment. But like her mother, she had a fiery temper.

'What a life I will have when she's a teenager,' Brian teased. 'I'll have two women throwing things at me!'

Lisette entwined him with her arms and, nibbling his ear, she said, 'But, *chéri*, you 'ave to admit that making up after a quarrel is so much fun.'

Chuckling, he said, 'Oh yes, but sometimes I do believe you go off at the deep end just so that later we will make love.'

'*Zut alors!* You think I need an excuse?'

Pulling her on to his knee he laughed and said, 'Never let it be said. I have never known a woman who was so ready for a tumble.'

She feigned anger. 'And, 'ow many women 'ave you known? 'Owever many, they didn't teach you much! You are much better as a lover now!'

'You are such a good teacher, my darling. You are all I ever wanted in a woman, but never expected to find.'

'And don't you forget it.' As she caressed him she said plaintively,

'I want another child soon, before Natalie gets too old. When do you think the divorce will be through?'

'I don't know. I've not heard anything from Kitty lately, but in her last letter she said her brother's case was soon due in court. I expect that is why.'

'What about 'er American? Do you know if she 'as 'eard from 'im?'

Shaking his head he said, 'She hasn't mentioned it and I don't know if that is a bad sign or a good one. Maybe I'll drop her a line tonight.'

Jeff Ryder hadn't yet written to Kitty. Since his return to Boston, he'd been on a constant round of visits to relatives, but at last he had time to himself. He had not mentioned Kitty to his family and they, being fearful that a wartime romance wouldn't last, were wise enough not to question him. Not that he had forgotten about her for a moment. There wasn't a day that passed when she wasn't constantly in his thoughts, but as yet he was unable to come to terms with the situation. He would walk through Faneuil marketplace, with its many fruit and vegetable stores, and imagine how much Kitty would love it. He rode on the Boston El, the tramway built above the city, and thought how much pleasure he would get from being the guide to his city and a different way of life. Introducing her to the shopping malls, the supermarkets, which were big and where she could buy almost anything without rationing.

He also started searching for premises to open his own practice, but as the same time he found himself viewing houses. Walking round them, visualising he and Kitty living there together – but Mathew was never quite in the picture.

It was early one evening when Hugo, his father, had invited him for a stroll around the block that Jeff admitted his dilemma. They were walking, admiring the open gardens that fronted the big and spacious houses, when Hugo broached the subject.

'Ever since you've been home, son, I've watched you battling with a problem and, from what I've observed, you haven't been able to solve it. I don't want to pry into your private life, but if I can be of help . . .'

It was almost a relief to Jeff. His father was a man he admired and respected, one he could trust to give an honest opinion and who would keep his confidence. 'I have a decision to make, Dad, which I'm having difficulty with.'

'I imagine it's to do with your young lady in England? Don't look so surprised. It wouldn't take a genius to work that out.'

'What do you mean?'

'You wrote to us in glowing terms about the English girl you were going to marry, but you haven't mentioned her since your return.'

Rubbing his chin thoughtfully, Jeff said, 'I know, and yes, it is about Kitty.'

'Do you love her?'

'Oh yes.'

'Then?'

They had arrived back at their house where they sat on the porch together. 'It's a long and complicated story, Dad.'

Filling his pipe, which was beside him on a low table, Hugo Ryder said, 'I'm not going anywhere, and your mother is out visiting.'

Jeff began from the first day that he and Kitty met, missing out nothing, their growing love, the trips to the New Forest, the major decision about the divorce. How Brian was now settled and had put no difficulties in their way. And about Gerry Stubbs. Then he told of Eddie's desertion from the army and about Gerry taking Eddie off Kitty's hands – until she paid the price. And how her brother was now being charged with murder. Then he told Hugo about Mathew.

'She sounds a brave girl, your Kitty.'

'Yes she is, but why did you say so?'

Puffing on his pipe Hugo said, 'She's been through a great deal already, and it takes a lot of courage to divorce your husband

and then to leave behind everything that is familiar – family ties, friends – to cross the Atlantic to a new country, a new environment – strangers.'

'I know, and we have discussed such a thing at length. Kitty knew that I would always care for her.'

'But you aren't, are you? This girl has been through hell and back, yet it seems to me she is made of sterner stuff than you. She is committed to the care of this child, when it would be so easy for her to hate it.'

'You don't know Kitty.'

'True, but the more you tell me, the more I'd like to. What is the real problem, Jeff?'

'I have to be sure that I can find it in my heart to want to take care of her child. If it were Brian's son, it wouldn't be a problem – but the son of the man who raped her? I find that hard to accept and I can't pretend about that, because if I did, it would eventually come between us, and I love Kitty too much for that to happen.'

'If you are uncertain, then you are right to take the time to decide. Unfortunately only you can make the decision, but I think you'll find the answer.'

Left alone, Jeff thought of his future without Kitty, and he was desolate. His father had been right: Kitty had survived after so many traumas. She was prepared to give up so much because she loved him, and he hated himself for his doubts, but he knew they had to be faced, if they were to have a future together. And still he didn't have an answer.

It was a further two days before the Southampton jury reached a verdict about the robbery and murder of the air-raid warden. Two days when nerves were stretched to breaking point for all those involved. And when the jury filed into the courtroom and took their seats, there was a charged air in court.

'All rise!' instructed the clerk of the court as the judge made his entrance. Kitty felt sick in the pit of her stomach and she didn't

285

dare cast a glance in the direction of her father.

The men standing in the dock were pale-faced and anxious. Stubbs and Baker had been charged with burglary and being accessories to the death of the warden.

The clerk of the court addressed the foreman of the jury. 'Have you reached a verdict on these men?'

'Yes.'

'How do you find in the case of Jack William Baker?'

'Guilty!'

'And in the case of Gerald Kenneth Stubbs?'

'Guilty!'

There was an audible intake of breath from many as the next question was asked. 'How do you find in the case for Edward Arthur Simmons?'

'Guilty of manslaughter!'

Kitty immediately looked at Eddie. He had put his hands to his head on hearing the verdict. She then looked at Gerry Stubbs. He was like a ghost, he was so pale. He stood shaking his head in disbelief. Baker was expressionless.

The judge looked grave as he stared at the prisoners. 'Justice has been served today in this courtroom,' he declared. 'You three men set out to line your pockets with ill-gotten gains, without respect for law and order. In so doing, the life was taken of a brave man. A man who was doing his duty for King and country. Who leaves behind a wife and children, robbed of his presence by three worthless people, and I intend to see that you pay for your crime. Jack William Baker you will serve *seven* years. Perhaps at the end of your time in prison, you will have learned that breaking the law is untenable.' He stared at Stubbs and coldly declared, 'You, Gerald Kenneth Stubbs, instigated the whole thing. You have lived beyond the law long enough. You will serve *ten* years. And you, Edward Arthur Simmons, a man who deserted his army post and, through blind panic, took the life of another without a second thought, will serve *fifteen* years. Consider yourself fortunate that you were not facing the death penalty for murder.'

The wardens either side of Eddie had to grab him to keep him on his feet as he almost collapsed on hearing the sentence.

'Take them down!' said the judge.

Kitty caught hold of her father's hand and held it tightly, as they sat in stunned silence. When eventually they left the court, reporters, taking pictures and firing questions at them, surrounded them outside.

'What have you to say about your son's sentence?'

'Will you be visiting your son in prison?'

'What was your brother like as a child?'

Kitty just held tightly to her father's arm and, blinded by flashbulbs from the cameras, kept her head down as she fought her way through what seemed like a mob, until they left them behind and were mercifully alone. They paused for breath.

'How on earth am I going to break the news to your mother?' Jim said. 'This will break her heart.'

'I think you'll find she's ready for bad news, Dad. During the time the case has taken to get to court, she has come to terms with the inevitable. The fact that he hasn't been given the death sentence will be a relief. Had that happened it may have been different.'

'I hope you're right. We had better get home as I'm sure she will have been on tenterhooks all morning.'

Nancy Brannigan left the court with a smile of satisfaction. Eddie Simmons had got what he deserved! She had not an ounce of pity for him. But there was one more thing she needed to do. Making her way to the entrance of the police station, she asked to be allowed to see the prisoner before he left, saying she was a friend. 'I'll be going away soon, so will be unable to visit him,' she said. 'I just want to say goodbye.' She was taken to an interview room and told to wait.

When Eddie was informed that he had a visitor, he was certain it was his father, so when he entered the room he was very surprised to see Nancy sitting waiting.

'You have just fifteen minutes,' said the police officer, who walked over to the door and waited.

'You are the last person I expected to see,' said Eddie.

'This is not a social call,' she said coldly. 'I remember that you raped me and beat me badly enough that I had to go to hospital. Even then, you threatened me. I remembered everything!'

He gave a startled look towards the police officer, but Nancy kept her voice low. 'Don't get your knees in a knot; I'm not making any charges. I don't need to now!' She sat back and grinned at him.

'What do you mean?'

'You are going down for a very long time – and I put you there!'

'What on earth are you on about?'

'I overheard Gerry and Jack discussing the raid in the pub and about you popping the old man, so I made a call to the police.'

'You what!'

She rose from her chair and said, 'It was through me that you got what you deserved, so that makes us quits! Enjoy yourself!' She walked towards the door and waited for the policeman to open it. Once outside, she walked along the road, laughing heartily.

Eddie was seething, as he was being led back to his cell. That rotten little bitch! He should have finished the job when he had the chance – then she wouldn't have been able to squeal on him! Now through her, he was going to be shut away for bloody years. He shook off the hand of the police officer. 'Let go of me!'

'That attitude won't wash where you're going, laddie. If you want to survive inside, you need to change.'

'Fuck off!'

When Kitty and her father entered the house, Amy was playing with Mathew. As soon as she saw them she stopped and, putting the child down, she asked, 'Well?'

'He was found guilty of manslaughter,' he said.

288

'Thank God! What was the sentence?'

'Fifteen years!'

Kitty noticed the trembling of her mother's hands as she said, 'That's better than the hangman's noose. I think we all need a strong cup of tea. I'll go and fill the kettle.' She took it and went into the kitchen. Jim made to follow his wife, but Kitty stopped him, shaking her head.

'Leave her, Dad. She needs a few minutes alone.'

'Perhaps you're right,' he said.

When they eventually sat at the table, Amy said, 'Well, now that is over I suggest we get on with our lives. Eddie made his choices, and we must make ours.' Looking at Kitty she said, 'You have your life ahead of you, what are you going to do?'

Taking a leaf from her mother she said, 'Well, I've not heard from Jeff, so I must assume that it's all over between us. Brian sends me money each month now that he's working, but I would like to get a full-time job. I would like to take a typing course in the evenings, but it's Mathew. I will have to wait until he's old enough for school.'

'Nonsense!' said Amy. 'I'll be happy to look after him during the day and your father and I will have him on the evenings you have to study.'

'But I can't expect that of you, Mum. You already have him whilst I'm working part time.'

'I would love it. We can go for walks when I shop and Mathew is a good child. It will give me something to do, Kitty. I need it,' she said, staring meaningfully at her daughter.

'Then that's what we'll do,' said Kitty, rising and hugging one parent, then the other. 'I do love you both and I honestly don't know what I would have done without you.'

And it was true. All the time she had waited to hear from Jeff, her mother had supported her with sympathy, compassion and good advice. Although Kitty was heartbroken at not hearing anything, and disappointed in Jeff for not writing, she knew she had to get on with her life.

As her friend Jean had said, 'You can't spend the rest of your life moping away. You have a child to bring up!'

As for her brother, Eddie, he had no such high expectations as the Black Maria carried him into the grounds of Wandsworth Prison. The sound of the heavy gates shutting behind him felt like a life sentence.

Chapter Thirty-Five

Gerry Stubbs had been in Winchester Prison for two months when he had a letter from Nancy Brannigan, saying she wanted to see him. This came as some surprise as he hadn't seen her from the day she moved out of his place. He was secretly pleased. He liked the fiery Irish girl and they had had many a good time together. She would be a delightful distraction from the daily grinding existence of prison life. He wrote saying he'd be happy to see her. Come visiting day he was restless, striding up and down the prison corridor outside his cell, waiting until the hour approached for the visitors to be admitted.

Nancy joined the queue outside the prison and waited with an assortment of people, each of whom wore an air of sadness and dejection. There was not a smile to be seen, but she supposed behind each one was a tale of despair.

One inside, one scrawny woman nursing a child told her, 'My old man's in for GBH. Stupid bugger! He came out of prison long enough to make me pregnant, then went down for five years. I don't know why I bother.'

They were eventually led through to a large hall where the tables were set out in a U shape – the visitors sitting on one side, and the prisoners on the inside, under careful watch of the warders.

Gerry walked in with his usual swagger and, smiling, said, 'Hello, love. This is a nice surprise.' He leaned forward to kiss Nancy, who proffered a cheek.

'You look well,' she said. 'How are they treating you?'

With an arrogant smirk he replied, 'All right. I've got it sussed in here; it's all wheeling and dealing, like always. How are you?' He helped himself to a cigarette out of a packet that Nancy had placed on the table. 'Didn't bring any of these for me, by any chance, did you?'

'Yes, I left them at the office.'

'Good, I can exchange them if I want to for other things. You do look well, Nancy. When I remember you in that hospital – there were times I thought you was a goner.'

'You weren't the only one. But I'm fine now.'

'Why did you walk out on me, girl?'

Tossing her hair, she said, 'I was fed up being used. You were good to me when I was sick, I'll never forget that, but in the end you only wanted me for sex and cleaning. I was fed up with being a dogsbody!'

He started to laugh. 'Well, you don't change. I missed our little spats.' He puffed thoughtfully on his cigarette. 'The one thing I do regret was you not remembering who gave you that beating. I wanted him sorted.'

'Oh, I know who did it, Gerry. I remember everything.'

He looked astonished. 'You do? The doctor thought you'd shut the memory out. Locked it away.'

'Oh, no. I always knew . . . it was Eddie Simmons.'

Gerry let out a mouthful of expletives. 'That bastard! I always suspected him, but I had no proof.' He shook his head and with a sympathetic glance in her direction said, 'I am sorry. If only I had known, I'd have made him pay.'

'He raped me in your office first, before he beat me up outside.'

He was enraged. 'He *raped* you?'

'Yes, because I was with you. I had a little dalliance with him when you were away to keep me from getting bored.' As Gerry started to protest she said, 'Now don't come it. You know I went with the GIs sometimes – you never minded that. What difference does it make?'

292

'He worked for me, that's the difference! I was his boss – he was out of order!'

Nancy just laughed at his outrage.

'But if I had known that he raped you, I'd have cut his balls off.'

'Nobody cut yours off when you raped Kitty Freeman,' she said coldly.

For a moment he was speechless. 'How do you know about that?'

'She told me.'

He began to bluster. 'Well, I was in a filthy temper. That bloody brother of hers had put us all in the shit, knocking off that warden. I lost a load of money selling those furs for a song, and look where I ended up because of him! Because of his stupidity I'm shut up here in this godforsaken place. She paid for her brother's lack of foresight!'

'Have you any idea what it does to a woman when she's been raped?'

He just glared at her.

'Of course not! Yet you were furious to know that Eddie had raped me. If you had known, you would have half killed him. But *you* did exactly the same!'

'That was different,' he said dismissively.

'No it wasn't.' Glaring at him she said, 'In my book that makes you as bad as Eddie.'

Ignoring her barbed remark, he said, 'I still don't know who put the boot in. There were no witnesses that night; I know that for a fact. The police must have got some information to go to Ernie Byers. They must have convinced him or he would never have rolled over!'

'You should be a little more careful where you exchange secrets with your mates,' she said softly.

'What are you on about?'

'I was in the pub just after I left you when you and Jack were talking about the robbery and Eddie knocking off the warden.'

'I never saw you.'

'No. I was just about to come out of the ladies' and I heard your voice, so I stood behind the door. I heard everything.'

He stared at her whilst his mind tried to understand what she was telling him. Then with an expression of incredulity he asked, 'Was it you who grassed me up?'

'I wanted Eddie Simmons to pay for what he'd put me through, so I made an anonymous call to the police.'

'You stupid bitch! By doing that you put me away too!'

'That settled the score for Kitty Freeman.'

He was quiet and threatening. 'You realise that you have just signed your own death warrant?'

She smiled slowly and with a look of triumph she rose to her feet and said, 'I'm leaving on the *Queen Mary* tomorrow with a load of GI brides. I'm going to New York to live with my uncle and aunt. I'm starting a new life and I'll be well out of your reach. Goodbye, Gerry!' And she walked away; ignoring the oaths he called after her.

He sat stunned by her news. Nancy, of all people! He still found it hard to accept. Never in a million years would he have put her in the frame. She had paid back Simmons in spades – that he could understand – but all because he took his revenge on Kitty, she had fixed him too. Bloody women! Between them they had all destroyed him and there was nothing he could do about it.

When she arrived back from Winchester, Nancy made her way to Harborough Road and knocked on Kitty's front door. When it opened she said to Kitty, 'Can I come in for just a moment?'

Once in the living room she said, 'I'm leaving for America in the morning and I wanted to say goodbye.'

'Whereabouts are you going?' Kitty asked.

'New York, to stay with relatives. I'm leaving Southampton for good. I just wanted to see you were all right.'

'That's good of you,' said Kitty. The sound of a child crying interrupted them. 'Excuse me,' said Kitty. 'I'll just get Mathew. He's been having a nap.'

Nancy hadn't seen Kitty since the child was born and as she carried him into the room Nancy stared at him and then at Kitty. 'He's Gerry's child, isn't he?'

Kitty wasn't able to deny it. The likeness was remarkable. 'Yes.'

'From when he raped you?'

Kitty nodded. 'Please don't ever tell him, will you?'

'I would rather die first. Anyway, I'll probably never see him again. How's things with you, Kitty?'

She gave a wry smile. 'A bit mixed up, really. My husband and I are getting a divorce. He met someone in France and is going to marry her and live there permanently. I was hoping to go to America too, but it's all fallen through.'

Nancy didn't question her further. 'I'd best be off. I haven't finished my packing. I just wanted to say goodbye.' She kissed Kitty on the cheek. 'Take care. I hope everything works out for you.'

'Good luck in New York!'

'I can't go wrong there. There are more of the Irish in the city than in Ireland!'

After Nancy had gone, as Kitty settled Mathew and changed his nappy she said, 'Well, good luck to her, I say. I just wish we were going with her, that's all.'

The following day, when she went to collect Mathew on her way home after work, Kitty passed on Nancy's news to her mother.

'She is a girl with a lot of potential, given the chance,' said Amy. 'Now she's away from that awful family of hers, maybe she'll make something of herself.' Glancing at her daughter, she said, 'I expect it made you a bit sad to know someone who is actually going to America?'

'Yes, I have to admit it gave me a bad moment or two.'

Amy frowned. 'I still can't understand why you have never heard from Jeff. He struck me as a man of his word.'

Kitty cuddled her son and said, 'Mathew is the only man in my life now . . . aren't you, you lovely thing?' And she kissed him.

Amy watched the scene before her and was saddened when she thought of what might have been. She and Jim had really liked Jeff Ryder. In her opinion he was the right man for Kitty and she often wondered what had happened when he went home. She supposed like many other men during the war, once back among familiar surroundings, things looked different. War destroyed so many lives one way or another.

Chapter Thirty-Six

Kitty's divorce was at last finalised and she was a free woman. As she read the decree absolute, she gave a wan smile. Free to what – to live alone with Mathew – to forever long for Jeff and what might have been? The thought of starting a married life with anyone else was unthinkable, but at least she was preparing herself for a career. Once she'd finished her typing course she would get a secretarial post in some office, work her way up the ladder, and be able to give her son a good start in life.

'You take care,' warned Jean, her constant friend. 'You'll end up a bloody old maid.'

'With a son? I don't think *maid*, is the correct term, do you?'

'Now don't you start getting bitter!' warned Jean. 'So it didn't work out – you're still young and attractive. I don't see you ending your days alone.'

'I'm sure Jeff won't,' she murmured.

Jean had no more words of comfort, knowing how her friend was pining for the handsome American officer.

'At least I know that Brian is happy, and that is a great relief,' Kitty confided. 'He and Lisette are getting married in November.'

'Are you invited?'

'You are joking! I'm sure the last thing the bride would want is the first wife there, watching! But she did write me a lovely letter, although sometimes it was difficult to understand,' Kitty mused. 'That was really nice of her. I answered it, of course,

297

and told her I wished them well.'

'How very civilised.'

'Yes it is,' Kitty retorted, 'and I meant it.'

'The thing that worries me,' said Jean, carefully choosing her words, 'is what happens when Gerry Stubbs gets out of prison? What if he realises then that Mathew is his son?'

'Mathew will be nearly twelve, and how will Gerry ever know? Who's going to tell him?'

'But Mathew is so like him.'

'I'll meet that when the time comes, if it ever happens.'

'Have you thought what you will say to the boy when he asks who his father is?'

'Yes, it has crossed my mind, and to tell you the truth, I don't know. But he's only eighteen months old, so I've plenty of time to think about it.' It certainly had occurred to Kitty, but she had pushed the thought aside. She'd learned that to live life day by day was the best way forward. But every day she wondered what Jeff was doing. Was he thinking of her or had she become a distant memory? She hoped that it was a good one and that he would still think kindly of her.

Jeff Ryder hadn't forgotten his Kitty at all. He had set up his own practice in the more fashionable part of Boston and was trying to settle down to a normal existence, but he was plagued by dreams of setting up a home, of being a family, of being happy, able to get on with his life. Instead of which, he was restless and miserable.

Knowing this, Hugo, his father, had suggested, one day in the autumn, that the two of them go fishing over the forthcoming weekend, as they used to do before the war, and before the lake froze over. It had been a welcome suggestion.

They drove to the lake and stopped in front of the small log cabin that belonged to them, and unpacked the car, carrying their fishing rods inside. They set about lighting a log fire and unloading the food bought from the supermarket, then lost no time in making their way to the lakeside, casting their lines, sitting on the small fishing chairs they had taken with them, well wrapped up against the cold.

'This is the life,' said Hugo, puffing on his pipe.

'Indeed it is,' agreed Jeff, feeling himself relax for the first time since his return.

It was not the time for conversation but for contemplation, and both men sat quietly, until one of them got a bite on the end of the line. 'Strike it, my boy!' called Hugo. 'We can have it for supper . . .' and then he too reeled in a catch. The men returned to the cabin well pleased with themselves. They stood at the sink together, gutting the fish and cooking them before settling in front of the fire, looking at one another with satisfied smiles.

'You should bring Kitty here one day,' said Hugo.

Jeff stopped eating, fork poised. 'Yes, perhaps I will,' he said.

'You know you want the woman,' stated Hugo, 'but what I can't understand is why you have waited so damned long!'

Jeff looked startled.

'I've watched you, my son, and never have I seen such a sad case in years! Moping around the place like a lovesick boy. So you didn't father the child, so what? It is a small human being that will thrive on love. It doesn't matter how the little one was conceived, Kitty is the mother.' Throwing another log on to the fire he asked, 'Can you see yourself living your life without her? Answer me that.'

Shaking his head, Jeff said, 'No. I'm still as deeply in love with her today as I was when I first fell for her.'

'Then for heaven's sake . . .'

Jeff started to laugh.

'That's the first time I've seen you look happy since you came home!'

'You are a wily old bird, Dad. You know that, don't you? You brought me here to give me a kick up the butt, didn't you?'

'Well, someone had to! Get on with your food.'

'Yes, sir.'

★ ★ ★

Three weeks later, Amy Simmons answered a knock on her door. When she opened it she received the surprise of her life.

'Jeff! How lovely to see you!' And she embraced him warmly. 'Come in, come in.'

As he stepped into the hallway he said, 'Thank you for the friendly greeting, Mrs Simmons. I did wonder what sort of a reception I'd receive.'

'Of course I'm pleased to see you, although I had expected you to arrive sooner,' she said pointedly, taking his overcoat from him.

'Yes, I know what you mean. I have been away far too long. But tell me,' he looked anxiously at her, 'how is Kitty? I called at her house but there was no answer, so I came here. Will she be happy to see me too?'

'Well, Jeff, it all depends,' she said sharply. 'Are you here to break her heart again, because if you are, I would rather you left now!'

He grinned broadly. 'I can see where Kitty gets her spirit from, and no, I'm not about to break her heart, although she may break mine.' He looked round as Mathew toddled into the room. 'Goodness, how he's grown!'

Mathew made his way over to him and held up his arms.

'He's going through the stage of wanting to be carried everywhere,' explained Amy.

Reaching down, Jeff picked up the child. 'My goodness, young man, you weigh a ton!' He sat in a chair, the child on his knee. 'Why is he here with you?'

'I look after him whilst Kitty works, and some evenings when she goes to night classes. She's taking a typing course.'

'What time will she be home?'

Looking at the clock on the mantelpiece, she said, 'Fairly soon. Here, give Mathew this rusk. He's teething and he likes to chew on it.'

'How is Kitty? Does she hate me for not being in touch?'

'I think you best ask her that, my dear,' she said and, deftly changing the subject, asked, 'How's your family?'

'They are all fine,' he said.

'How did you get here?'

'I docked late this morning on the *Queen Elizabeth*.'

'Really! What was she like?'

'Great! She's recently been renovated. After carrying so many troops, I imagine that there was extensive work to be done, but she's beautiful now.'

The back door opened and they both looked up as Kitty entered the living room. The first thing she saw was Jeff, sitting with Mathew on his knee. She couldn't move but stayed in the doorway, eyes wide with surprise, her face pale from the shock of seeing him.

'Hello, Kitty,' said Jeff quietly.

Amy took the child from him and said, 'I'm off to bath this one,' and diplomatically left the room.

Kitty, her heart pounding, said, 'Hello, Jeff. You're the last person I ever expected to see again. How are you? You look well.' She didn't move.

He gazed at her and said, 'And you look wonderful. Please, come here and sit down – or yell at me if you want to – but don't just stand and stare at me.'

She took off her hat and coat and hung them up, then, walking over to the table, sat beside him. Having regained a little of her composure, she said, 'I don't know what you expect of me, Jeff. You go back to Boston and tell me you'll be in touch and that's the last I hear from you, and now here you are, months later. What am I expected to do?'

'Give me a chance to talk to you, explain why it has taken me so long to come to my senses – and to apologise.' As he saw the pain registered in her gaze, he knew that he had a great deal to make up for. 'There has never been a day that has passed when I've not thought about you, Kitty,' he said softly.

Her days of longing, of waiting – and the hurt she suffered

through his silence – poured forth. 'You could have written,' she accused. 'You could have put that down on paper. You could have done something! Given me some idea of what was happening.'

'I could, but I didn't know what to say to you, except that I have never stopped loving you.' He saw the tears brim in her eyes. He stretched out his hand and covered hers. 'Please don't cry. I know that I must have hurt you deeply, but I'll make it up to you for the rest of my life, if you'll let me.'

These were the words she had been waiting to hear from the day that he left, but the pain of losing him had been so awful that she got to her feet and, storming up and down the room, raged at him. 'What right have you to come swanning in here now – when I've just got used to being without you – as if everything is fine, and then expect me to fall into your arms?'

'I have no right at all,' he said quietly.

'No you haven't! Have you any idea how I felt as the time passed and there was not a word from you? Have you?'

'No, Kitty, I haven't. I only know that I was miserable without you.'

'Well, it took you a bloody long time to do anything about it!'

'You are absolutely right, but there was a lot to consider, a lot to plan. I had to think of Mathew's future too. It had to be right for us all.'

At that moment there was a polite knock at the door and Amy came into the room with Mathew, all clean, scrubbed and rosy, dressed in his pyjamas.

'Kitty,' said her mother, 'I'll put Mathew to bed here for the night. Why don't you and Jeff go back to your place where you will have some privacy and continue your discussion there?'

Jeff looked at Kitty and said, 'Please, let's do that. We have a great deal to sort out.'

'Very well,' she conceded. Bending down she kissed her son good night. 'Mummy will see you tomorrow, darling. Be a good boy for Nanny.'

Ruffling the child's hair, Jeff said, 'Good night, Mathew. Sleep well.'

Kitty put on her coat and handed Jeff's to him. They walked in silence towards Harborough Road. Kitty didn't shake off his hold as he held her arm, but thought what a strange day this had turned out to be. How she had longed for Jeff to walk through the door and say he loved her, but now she was furious that he had done so. She was utterly confused.

When they arrived, she put the key in the door, walked into the kitchen, filled the kettle and put it on the stove.

'Take off your coat,' she said. 'I need to wash my face and hands.' She ran the tap and cupped her hands together, splashing her face, hoping that the chill of the water would help to clear her head. Then after wiping herself dry she returned to the living room with a tray of tea.

'How long are you staying in Southampton?' she asked.

'As long as it takes,' he said grimly. 'Until I can convince you to come back to the States with me, because I'm not leaving without you!'

'What about your practice? I assume you have opened one?'

'I have, but Dad is looking after it. After all, he's a damned fine lawyer.'

She let out a deep sigh. 'And what about Mathew?'

'Mathew is your son, he's a part of you; it doesn't matter who his father is.'

'It mattered when you went away!' she snapped.

He didn't deny it. 'It did then. It was just the shock of seeing him, I suppose, but I've had a long time to think, and now it doesn't.'

'And just supposing we were married and had children of our own, what then? You would be bound to feel differently towards them.'

Jeff ached to take her into his arms, to try to reassure her that he wanted both of them. He understood her anger and wished with all his heart he could turn back the clock and have been more compassionate to her needs when they last met.

'I would like to adopt Mathew, if you had no objections,' he said. 'Then he would have a father and I would have a son. Any children we had would be his brothers and sisters.'

'Those are brave words, Jeff, but I have to be sure of your feelings. I have to protect my son. He has been my life since you went away.'

'And I want him to be part of mine . . . ours. If you agree.'

'It's all too much. You can't expect me just to make up my mind in five minutes. Like you, I had a life planned when I thought you would never return and now you expect me to put it all aside. Just like that.'

'Do you still love me, Kitty?'

She gazed at him for a while, taking in every contour, every line of his face, and her tone changed. 'Oh yes, I never stopped. I will always love you, no matter what happens now.'

'I have an open ticket with Cunard,' he said. 'I was hoping that we could return to America as man and wife.'

She closed her eyes. Was she imagining all this? Was it some dream? She opened them and saw the anxious expression on the face of the man she loved. But she was still hurt.

'How could you treat me like that, Jeff? We had made such plans; I was prepared to give up everything for you – my family, my country. I would have followed you to the ends of the earth if you'd asked. Was it too much to ask that you find room for a child who came into the world as he did? Mathew is innocent in all this – and so was I! If you had returned from the war, maimed in some way, I would have still wanted to be with you because I loved you so much.'

'My father was right, you are made of stern stuff, and I feel that I failed you miserably. A man's ego often gets in the way, whereas the heart of a woman is all-encompassing. It makes women so much stronger than we men. I may be late, but tell me, Kitty – am I too late? Will you marry me, Kitty darling, and put us both out of our misery?'

She hesitated.

'Have you met someone else?' Jeff asked sharply.

Shaking her head, she said, 'No. The only man in my life is eighteen months old.'

'I can give you both a good life, Kitty. I can't bear to be without you any longer. Please say you'll come back to Boston with me.' But she was still uncertain until he stood up and drew her into his arms. 'Come here, darling.' He lowered his mouth to hers and kissed her longingly. 'I can't go on without you,' he whispered as he kissed her again. 'Please say you'll honour me and become my wife?'

How could she say no? 'I don't think I could survive another goodbye,' she said, her voice choked with emotion. 'But we have to talk about this in greater detail before I decide to go with you to Boston.'

'Anything you say,' he said, picking her up and twisting her round. 'Oh, Kitty darling, I love you so much.'

And talk they did – until well into the night, until they were both so tired making plans for the future, that they fell into bed completely exhausted, but not so exhausted that they didn't hold one another and love one another as they had done so many months before.

The next three weeks were frantic for the Simmons family. Being a divorcee, Kitty was unable to be married in church, but Jeff got a special licence and the wedding was to take place in Southampton's registry office, with Jean acting as maid of honour, and Jim and Amy as witnesses. Harry, Jean's husband, had returned safely and he couldn't take his eyes off his pretty wife.

Amy went shopping for a hat for the occasion, and just as she was coming out of Sands, the hat shop, who should she meet but Gladys Freeman.

Never one to miss an opportunity, Amy said, 'Hello, Gladys. I've just bought a hat for Kitty's wedding. She's marrying an American lawyer, you know!' Gladys just glared at her, but Amy went blithely on. 'I believe that Brian is getting married in November. Are you making the trip to France?' she asked, knowing full well that Brian hadn't invited her. He had written to Kitty telling her all his news and he'd not forgotten his mother's cruel remarks about his beloved girls, so she was not welcome at his wedding.

With a red face Gladys blustered, 'No, we won't make the trip. Frank gets seasick,' and she made her hurried excuses and walked away, leaving Amy chuckling to herself.

'Wicked old bitch!' she said as she carried on shopping.

The wedding day arrived and Kitty, standing beside Jeff, repeating her wedding vows, was deliriously happy and proud of this handsome man. It was a small gathering, with close family and friends, with the reception held at the Polygon Hotel, where Jim, as the father of the bride, stood to make his speech.

'Today was a very special day,' he began. 'I know now that my Kitty has married the man she truly loves and one that I'm delighted to call my son-in-law. A pity his law practice is so far away as it may have been helpful in the future, but never mind, we can't have everything! I'm not one for speeches so I'll ask you to raise your glasses to the bride and groom.'

Afterwards, Jeff rose to his feet. 'Thank you, Jim and Amy, for entrusting me with your daughter. Today is the happiest day of my life and I'm not at all sure I deserve to be here with this wonderful woman, who consented to spend her life with me, so far away from her family and friends. I am doubly fortunate, because not only have I gained a bride, but now I also have a son. I promise to cherish them both.'

There were a few tears in the eyes of the guests at his words. Kitty stood up and, putting her arms around her husband, she said, 'Thank you.'

Jean came over to Kitty afterwards and hugged her. 'I can't tell you how delighted I am for you, love, but I'm going to miss you like hell, so you'd better write to me often and tell me about your life over there in Boston.'

'I will, I promise,' said Kitty. 'I'm not sure I could have coped without you, Jean, and I'll never forget that.'

Whilst she was talking, Jeff had taken Jim aside. 'I know that Boston seems the other end of the earth,' he said, 'but it isn't that far away. When we are settled I intend to send you tickets to come and visit us, every year. I'll give you plenty of notice so you can arrange it with your work place. But I want you and Amy to be a part of our lives, despite the distance.'

Jim Simmons was overcome. 'Thank you, son. That will be great, especially for Amy. You know how it is with mothers and daughters.'

'It isn't that different for the father either,' said Jeff knowingly. 'You forget I have a sister, whom my father absolutely adores.'

Too full for words, Jim could only nod.

The following day, after a night at the Polygon Hotel, Kitty, Jeff and Mathew with Kitty's parents and Jean and her husband as guests, went to board the *Queen Elizabeth*. Champagne and canapés were served in the cabin on Main deck, as they all celebrated.

Looking around the state room, Jean sidled over to her friend and said, 'I could get used to this, you know.'

'It all seems like a dream,' said Kitty. 'I can't believe I'm here, sailing across the Atlantic. It's all a bit scary, Jean.'

'Hey, you're a GI bride! Only the others don't have their husbands sailing with them. Not having second thoughts, are you?'

'No. I love Jeff, you know I do, but it will all be so different, it'll take time to get used to it.'

'Listen, girl, that man is besotted with you. Look at him now.'

Kitty turned to see Jeff holding Mathew, showing him the scene outside the porthole. 'He'll be with you so what's the worry?'

Shaking her head, Kitty said, 'Imagine, who would have thought of this when the war began and I first met Jeff? Now Brian is living in France and I'm going to Boston. How our worlds have widened.'

'And yours will get even bigger,' her friend predicted. Then she laughed. 'I'll write and remind you of the small one here!'

There was the sound of a gong being struck and a voice calling, 'All visitors ashore.'

Amy came over to Kitty and, holding her close, said, 'Be happy, darling. I'll see you later in the year.'

'You will?'

'Yes, I will.' She beamed. 'Jeff is sending us tickets every year to come and visit you.'

'I didn't know that. How marvellous!' When her father came over to say goodbye, Kitty said, 'I've only just heard about the tickets for you to come over to Boston, isn't it brilliant?'

'You've got a good man there, Kitty. Look after him,' he said as he hugged and kissed her.

As she stood on the deck of the *Queen Elizabeth*, with Jeff holding Mathew in one arm, his other around her, Kitty waved to her family and friends standing on the dockside. She glanced at her husband. At least this goodbye was really only *au revoir*, as she would see her parents again in Boston when they came to visit. But it was goodbye to the life she knew and was familiar with, which felt a little sad. Once again Jeff was widening her horizons and she had a whole new life ahead of her. A new country, Jeff's family and colleagues to meet – a new set of in-laws. Jeff had assured her that her new mother-in-law was a very sweet woman! But whatever lay ahead, she was with the man she loved and she was in no doubt that she and Mathew would never regret leaving England.

As the ship sailed further, leaving the Southampton dockside in the distance, Jeff squeezed her hand. 'Happy, Mrs Ryder?'

'Deliriously!'

'Come along then, let's book our table in the dining room and then explore the ship. This is the start of our voyage of discovery . . . together.' They each took Mathew by the hand and walked along the deck, leaving the old life behind, filled with happy expectations of the new one before them.